THE GIRL
WHO NEVER READ
NOAM CHOMSKY

———— ❧ ————

THE GIRL
WHO NEVER READ
NOAM CHOMSKY

Jana Casale

Alfred A. Knopf
New York | 2018

THIS IS A BORZOI BOOK
PUBLISHED BY ALFRED A. KNOPF

www.aaknopf.com

Library of Congress Cataloging-in-Publication Data
Names: Casale, Jana, author.
Title: The girl who never read Noam Chomsky : a novel / Jana Casale.
Description: First edition. | New York : Alfred A. Knopf, 2018.
Identifiers: LCCN 2017028589 | ISBN 9781524731991 (hardcover :
acid-free paper) | ISBN 9781524732004 (ebook)
Subjects: LCSH: Self-actualization (Psychology) in women—Fiction. |
Self-realization in women—Fiction.
Classification: LCC PS3603.A826 G57 2018 | DDC 813/.6—dc23
LC record available at https://lccn.loc.gov/2017028589

Jacket design by Janet Hansen

Manufactured in the United States of America
First Edition

This book is dedicated to my mom

PART 1

CHAPTER 1

Deciding to Read Noam Chomsky

"I'D LIKE TO READ NOAM CHOMSKY," LEDA SAID. AT THIS POINT IN HER life she had a stack of books she kept by the bed and a splinter in her right hand. She should have thought more closely about cleaning out her microwave. She had class on Mondays, Wednesdays, and Thursdays. Each week she'd sit in the window seat at the back of her school's library and study. On this day she had cried listening to "All You Need Is Love" as she took the subway to school. She didn't want people to know she was crying, so she took great care to blink away as many tears as she could, but she did so hope that *there was nothing you could do that couldn't be done.* She ate a partially crushed scone as she studied that afternoon. Later she'd have another scone before bed. This was the only time in her life she consumed multiple scones in one day. As she ate she thought about the boy who lived in the apartment across the street and the word *Umbria.* The scone was blueberry, and after she finished it she folded up the wax paper and put it in her left coat pocket.

The only reasons she'd remember for wanting to read Chomsky were all the varied intellectual ones that took precedence in her mind: an article she'd read, a speech she'd heard, a professor's suggestion. She didn't think of that day or that boy in the coffee shop, but the influence was no less significant, as faint and feckless as it was, a startling, disintegrating moment between herself and this stranger bursting and scattering like any and all moments of her life. She gave little more attention to it at the time than to the scone or to herself crying over a song she loved.

The coffee shop itself was near her apartment and one she frequented often. "This café is so small, but its aesthetic is exceptional," was the way it had been described by a middle-aged woman in trendy clothes who once stood next to her in line. The woman bought a large coffee and some type of vegan muffin. Leda thought the muffin looked tasty and bought the same one and then took a bite and realized it was vegan. From then on when she thought of the café she thought of it as *so small with an exceptional aesthetic and terrible vegan muffins.* Not long after, they'd started selling vegan donuts that were considerably better, but Leda would never find herself trying them. If she had, it's unlikely she would have amended her perception of the place. It was already burned into her by the ephemeral moment beside that woman in line.

That day, though, she ordered a hot chocolate and sat at a table in the corner. What she loved most about sitting at the coffee shop was not the coffee or the shop but the brief, listless feeling it gave her of having her life together. She could sit beside the richness and warmth and see herself as something so divinely competent. *This is what it is to be an independent person,* and she'd take a sip. *This is what it is to be a cosmopolitan person,* and she'd take a sip. So easily could she lose herself in the sense. It was haunting and complicated and undeniably silly. Outside she watched as a woman picked up dog poop in a plastic bag. *At least I know that I don't really have my life together. At least I know that I don't know,* she thought. She sat for a while longer before noticing the boy to her right. He was smartly dressed, with flood pants and thick-rimmed glasses. His hands were large, and he was reading *American Power and the New Mandarins.* She leaned forward in her seat and ran her fingers through her hair. Most days she held a very strong belief that her hair looked terrible except right after she'd run her fingers through it. She fixed her shirt and adjusted her boobs, which had been lost in her bra to some degree. The boy looked like he was about twenty-four and possibly went to Boston University or was applying to a funded graduate program. She hoped he'd come over and say something charming or witty, as she imagined a man with such nice glasses might. She cleared her throat to get his attention, but he didn't look up from his book.

She got her phone out of her bag as noisily as possible and then sighed loudly, but nothing. After waiting a bit longer, she got up and walked past his table, headed for the napkins. She took three. He didn't notice her. She reached her hand down to the fourth napkin; for a second she had a sense that he might be watching her, but when she turned around she saw he hadn't looked up. She stood there for what was an inappropriate amount of time to get napkins, but she couldn't help it. *Why can't I just go talk to him?* she thought. He had such a dumb sweater on and his face was sour. She considered that maybe he wasn't even reading but pretending to read, seeking that same sense of solace she felt sitting with her hot chocolate. *Who is he in this coffee shop? No one, just like me. Can't we be no one together?* In an unprecedented strike of confidence, she decided to walk up to him. It was impulsive and decisive. If you'd asked her then, she may have said her hair always looked nice and that she didn't need to run her fingers through it at all.

"What are you reading?" she asked him.

"What?"

"That book."

"What?"

"What are you reading?"

"Oh . . . It's by Noam Chomsky."

"Oh."

The silence between them felt stale and all-consuming. She searched for the right segue into marriage and children, but there was nothing.

"I just needed a napkin," she said, waving the napkins.

"What?"

"Oh, nothing . . . Can I have this chair?" she said, pointing to an empty chair that didn't belong to his table at all but to the empty table beside him.

". . . I guess so?"

She dragged the chair noisily in the direction of where she had been sitting. When she sat back down her hot chocolate was cold. She pretended she got a phone call and left.

That was her last encounter with the future BU graduate.

A few weeks later she bought *Problems of Knowledge and Freedom* in a small bookstore specializing in rare and overpriced books. Walking through the aisles, she ran her fingers down the spines of books and smelled the softness of paper over her, under her. She didn't think of the boy or the napkins, but she did think of Noam Chomsky as the book cover grew sweaty in her palm. She relaxed her hand, wiped the sweat on her skirt, opened the book to page 53, closed it, and took a deep breath.

———∽———

CHAPTER 2

The First Innate Truth

NEARING HER EARLY TWENTIES, LEDA HAD BECOME OBSESSED WITH being linear. Latitude and longitude had formerly been ascribed to maps and a vague notion of Christopher Columbus she stored on the dwindling shelf of third-grade history in the back of her mind. To be linear was to be lines of thinness from her head to her feet. Lines and thinness. Thinness like her legs lifted over her head as she lay on the beach watching her legs, stinging sand in her eyes, blue everywhere. Lying down she could get away with it, but standing it was undeniable to her that she was not nearly linear enough. "Latitude Is Attitude," she saw on a T-shirt once and never understood. Even as she was now so concerned with linearity and the latitude of herself, that T-shirt was still a confused lake in her mind. The girl who wore it had large breasts. And that was all she really remembered. *I do not want to live in the horizontal of my stomach. I do not want to be my thighs. I want to be linear.* This compulsion to be linear began at age twelve and would persist until her death. It was very important, VERY IMPORTANT not to be fat. This was the first innate truth of her womanhood.

CHAPTER 3

——◇——

New Year's

ON HER WALK HOME SHE THOUGHT ABOUT A PRESENTATION SHE GAVE in class. She considered that maybe she talked for too long. The desperate face of the pretty girl in the front row plagued her. *Why did that girl look so desperate? Was the presentation too long? Boring, maybe?* She thought of herself standing and talking away like an idiot. She tapped her thigh as she walked and turned the music up in her earphones, then turned it down a bit. The song was about a girl getting a New Year's kiss. *New Yearsssss,* she thought.

One New Year's she got kissed by a boy she knew from childhood. His name was Sol, and he talked slowly. As children they had played at each other's house here and there, until one fateful afternoon when Sol invited her into his parents' room to sit on their waterbed.

"This . . . is . . . my parents' . . . room."

The room was small, smothered by the oversized waterbed. The purple sheets worsened the skewed bed-to-room ratio. Sol sat down first and bounced lightly.

"It's a . . . waterbed."

She sat down next to him and felt the wave of the bed below; to her right was a framed picture of a cat on the nightstand, and to her left was Sol, smiling. She liked the waterbed and wondered what it must be like to sleep on. Then Sol's father came in and said: "This is very inappropriate."

That was the last time Sol and she ever spent any real time together, save for the New Year's encounter, which could be described as brief at best. A girl she had only just become friends with her freshman year of college invited her to the party. "Come to my party!" the girl said as she wore a beige peacoat.

There wasn't any dancing, and Leda spent the night standing around, awkwardly attempting to make conversation with strangers. A cognitive neuroscience major from Harvard talked to her for a while.

"What is it you study?" he said.

"Writing."

"And what are your plans with that?" He was drinking soda but was taking small enough sips that it seemed like alcohol.

"I don't know . . . I mean, I want to write, but I'll probably teach. I'd like to write, you know, but I'll have to teach."

"Oh, well, it sounds like you've got it all worked out," he said.

She wondered why this Harvard student was judging her. He had neglected to untuck a pant leg from his sock and his hair looked as if it hadn't been washed in a considerable amount of time. She folded her arms and regretted wearing such a low-cut shirt. The neuroscientist (or whatever he was) eventually walked away and she thought, *Don't go.* Being alone was decidedly worse than reevaluating her life choices. Then she saw Sol.

He looked the same as he did when he was ten, only maybe a little fatter. He was wearing what appeared to be a vintage shirt with the 7UP logo on it. *What would ever possess him to wear that? Does he think it's irony or something?* she wondered, but didn't fully want to consider because she was so grateful for the potential company.

"Sol!"

He turned to look at her and blinked hard.

"Oh . . . wow . . . I can't believe . . . it's you." He blinked hard again.

"Yeah, it is. How are you? Where are you these days?"

"Oh . . . you know . . . around." He blinked hard again. By now she realized he'd developed a tic. *Maybe he's been through trauma. Maybe he's lived a life I couldn't understand beyond waterbeds and 7UP.* She felt suddenly compelled to fix whatever it was in him that was causing all the blinking. She reached out, gently touching his arm.

As their conversation muddled on, she realized that he was as bored and desperate as she was fumbling through this New Year's night, and such a realization led to the immediate bond of: we are both bored, lonely, and miserable. Had Sol more social understanding, he might have attempted to talk to someone else. Since he didn't, she didn't feel the need to pretend she'd rather talk to anyone else either, so they stood together for the two hours leading up to midnight, mutually accepting each other's forced but dearly appreciated company.

"I wish there was dancing," she said.

"Like . . . *Dance . . . Dance . . . Revolution?*"

"No. I mean, like, real dancing."

"Oh . . . I can't . . . really dance."

"I'm sure you're good at it." She looked at his pants. They were a little stained.

"Not . . . really . . . but I'd . . . dance with you . . . if you wanted."

She thought that was sweet.

At 11:59:50 everyone started counting down to midnight. The sudden collective loudness was startling. She thought, *Here we are all alone pretending to have time together.* Then it was midnight.

There wasn't a moment for her to think about kissing Sol. Before the party, she got dressed in the foaming need to have a New Year's kiss. She watched her naked reflection in the mirror, and although she wished to be more linear, she traced the outline of her hip bone and thought of a boy holding her, kissing her. But standing there with clumsy, slow, ticking Sol, she didn't think of kissing him. When midnight hit, she watched the crowd in unison undulation, and right in between "Happy" and "New Year" he kissed her as her head was turned. Just the corner of her lips. Slowly, clumsy, gentle. She felt a swell of warmth in her checks, his 7UP pudgy irony pressed against her. It was over by the time it began, and she didn't know how to act afterward, but it would be remembered in her life as the single most erotic New Year's kiss she would ever receive.

When leaving the party, she and Sol exchanged phone numbers in the ritual of feigned interest in further communication. They said their goodbyes for too long, and she stumbled a little as she walked away. She put on her red winter coat and thought about the waterbed. The rolling motion, and sleep, a dream about a boat, blue, and a feathered mask she bought and hung in her room as a child. Before leaving she held the doorknob for a moment, feeling the winter cold draft through the bottom of the doorway and her palm pressed against the cool steel of the knob. *This is the New Year.* As she went to push open the door, Sol called out to her.

"Leda."

She looked back at him filling an empty space in the unwinding party. She wanted to call out to him, but she just waved.

CHAPTER 4

—◦∽◦—

Hollandaise Sauce

LEDA WATCHED A WOMAN IN THE SUBWAY SEAT ACROSS FROM HER with a grocery bag. The woman was older and held a container of hollandaise sauce on her lap. She moved her hands over the lid, opening and closing it as she chewed indiscriminately. The smell of the hollandaise sauce filled the subway car, and Leda turned away a bit to avoid the stale odor of food on public transportation. The woman's clothes were dirty and the grocery bag looked as if it had been used many times to carry many things. Her face was gray and her eyelids were sunken. Leda noticed a small brooch attached to a faded ribbon in her hair. It didn't make the woman's appearance any better, any less gray, any less unkempt, but it was there. *I guess you always have to do something with your hair,* she thought, and touched her own hair, silky and young. Somewhere, she imagined, this woman had done many things. Soft things and hard things and was beautiful with a brooch. There was a countertop she held on to and a man who stood beside her telling her fancy possibilities that made her laugh lightly and feel probable. The woman got off at the next stop. Her coat brushed Leda as she pushed past and the smell of hollandaise lingered behind.

For the rest of the ride Leda spent her time folded into herself. She listened to music and watched the people moving then still. Somewhere in her knowledge of cosmopolitan life she was aware that attempting to meet the gazes of strangers was dangerous. Her mom said, "You are moving to the city now. You will no longer be able to look at anyone." Leda looked at anyone. She would look at men and catch their stares floating in the underground current. *Yes, I will sleep with you,* her stare would say, *but not really, because I am only looking at you, and I wouldn't sleep with you anyway.* Sometimes men would meet her stare; sometimes they wouldn't. Her fragility and feelings of linearity hung in the balance so thinly that her sense of self could inflate or deflate in the precious few seconds of a stranger's glance. It was a troubling and weightless system of moment-by-moment worthiness or worthlessness. It was exhausting and oftentimes depressing. Sometimes so much so that she wouldn't bother with it at all and would look at her phone instead.

The train was mostly empty. There was a man in a suit to her right. He wasn't looking at her. She leaned her head back against the seat. The subway was warm, and she was almost too hot in her coat. For a moment she thought about taking it off but decided against it after remembering what she was wearing. She'd recently ordered a shirt from an online store called Amour Vert. All the clothes were made of tree pulp or vegan silk. If you spent more than two hundred dollars they'd plant a tree. She'd wanted the blouse in a print of delicate yellow flowers, "wildflower" they'd called it, but it was sold out in her size so she went with the green stripes instead. Now that it was hers she thought she liked the green stripes more. It flattered her complexion, she thought, and it made her look linear, she thought. By a happenstance of so little she would never be the girl who wore yellow flowers and because of it she'd be convinced she liked green stripes. Either way the blouse was too sheer to be worn comfortably on the subway, even if just in front of the guy in the suit who wouldn't look at her.

She lifted her head back up and pulled off her gloves. First she tucked them into each other and placed them on her lap, then in her bag, then she thought better of it and put them in her coat pocket. This was how it was in the wintertime as she made her way from train to school and home again; the panic and the subsequent relief that she hadn't lost her gloves were a triumph realized multiple times a week. The lost gloves of her life would be left in the places as follows: two subways, a park bench, a bagel shop, a boat. The boat was a rowboat, and the glove was her father's. It was a big leather glove borrowed from him as they went fishing the single time in her life she would ever go fishing. He told her a story about a radiator, and she felt sick from the tide. The long, narrow blue horizon grayed as the weather turned to rain. He rowed them back to shore, and she watched her father struggle with the oars. She felt younger than she was until she saw him struggle. At that moment she realized she was an adult now, and her father struggled with rowing. She didn't remember the glove until he asked for it later, and then she knew she'd lost it. It was the left glove.

The subway rolled beneath her, pulling through the only stop that was aboveground. Suddenly, the car filled with natural light and the people became instantly softer. Outside she could see the city unfolding rapidly. The buildings, a park, the people were too small to see from the train. Then as quickly as everything was before her it sunk away back into the underground of artificial light.

The next stop was hers. As she got up she saw a small child holding a piece of colored chalk. The little girl looked around dazedly and tried to draw on the subway door. Her mother pulled her back, and the child dropped the chalk. Leda watched her look for it but instantly forget it as her mother handed her a little plastic flower. The girl spun the flower in her hand and smiled. Leda couldn't see the chalk, but she worried about it rolling around loose behind them. She wished she could say, "Your chalk. You forgot about your chalk." She watched the little girl walk off ahead of her, holding her mother's hand and spinning the flower. She stepped off the train and checked for her gloves. They were still in her pocket. She looked back for the chalk, not that she would have picked it up, but to see if it was there. It wasn't, but she thought she'd heard it rolling as the train roared away.

CHAPTER 5

Writing

LEDA GOT HOME AND THREW OFF HER JEANS. IT WAS LATE AFTERnoon, and the sunshine was still brilliant and warming, filtering in through the half-drawn blinds left neglected from morning. She played an Édith Piaf record, and then a song by a band she couldn't remember the name of. It was something like "Leelong," but it wasn't Leelong. She changed into a white tank top and her bad underwear, turned the heat down, stretched out on the floor, and flipped through a magazine. Her bare feet were pressed up against the wall, and she kicked in beat with the music. The magazine article was about fifty ways to please a man in bed. *How stupid,* she thought. *Most of them don't even know one way to please a woman.*

"Try dressing up as a naughty nurse and use a stethoscope to hear your man's heartbeat pound away!" it read.

Leda imagined that there were many sad women reading this article and doing tentative Google searches for stethoscopes, and perhaps even a few went through with the whole charade. *Somewhere in the world right now a woman is holding a stethoscope and a penis at the same time,* she thought. She flipped through the rest of the magazine, smelled a perfume sample, and took a quiz entitled: "What Kind of Sexual Warrior Are You?" which yielded the result: "You are fierce and relentless. No man can get out from under you, and that isn't a bad thing!" Leda wondered who wrote the quiz and how they came up with the criteria for the descriptions. *What a depressing job,* she thought, but she still appreciated it. It was nice to be a sexual warrior. She could agree that she was fierce and relentless, so much better than "coy and demure," as another description read. After a while everything was boring in the way it always was, her apartment, sitting around, the magazine, the music, her bare feet pressed up against the wall. She thought back to the train, and the walk home, and the smell of her neighbor's cooking, something peppery and bright. The day had reminded her of a story she'd thought of writing about cherries. She got out her computer and started typing.

The summer I went from a C cup to a D cup was the best summer of my life. I'd started work at a cherry stand and the long days of sitting, as well as the incremental sugary snacks, had caused me to gain a little over ten pounds. All of July I was in denial but by August I'd started to note the difference, so I'd skip breakfast or walk to work. I never attempted to lose the weight in any significant way, and, in retrospect, there must have been some kind of subconscious attempt on my part to preserve it because as soon as I could no longer wear my smallest clothes I found a certain solace, a liberation in no longer caring. Before that I'd spent so much time and concern over my weight, but the day I switched bras marked a march toward the heaviest and ultimately the freest I would ever be.

Leda sat up and reread what she wrote and thought it was okay but lacked a certain polish. She braided a braid in her hair and looked at her knees. One of them she'd missed when shaving. She'd spend much of her life with unshaven, or nearly unshaven, legs. There would only be two occasions that she'd actually shave in the way she had intended. One was a Wednesday at the age of thirty-seven and one was a Sunday at the age of fourteen. She'd never consider leg hair removal to be a failure of her life, but really it was.

That night she finished her story, ate pizza, and masturbated before bed. She thought of a man tying her up and having sex with her from behind. The man was no one in particular because it wasn't about him. When she slept she dreamt of fifty ways to cherry, and when she woke up she rewrote the ending to her story twice.

CHAPTER 6

Workshop

"I REALLY DON'T GET THE ENDING," THE GIRL ACROSS FROM HER SAID. "Are we supposed to feel sorry for the main character? Because I really don't. And it's boring. Why do I care?"

"I don't really have a problem with the ending, but I feel that the cherry thing is too heavy-handed. It's clearly an allusion to virginity," the boy two seats down said.

Leda dreaded her Thursday class all week. It was a fiction workshop given by the editor in chief of her university's prestigious literary journal. She'd registered for the class seconds after registration had opened under the influence of friends who'd said things to the effect of: "You have to take a class with Patricia Rainer!" "Patricia is the best!" "It will change your life!" The very first day Patricia Rainer came to class in a coat with a fox hair collar and Leda thought, *I'm not going to get along with this person.*

The class itself was populated by hipsters who name-dropped Jack Kerouac and small-batch coffee roasters. They were edgy. They were clean. They held crippling insecurities managed by entitlement and a distaste for popular music. It was not uncommon for many of them to rip into a story with the kind of zeal that could only be attributed to a lingering despondency related to their parents' divorce or some such problem. This was what Leda held on to as the skinny girl across from her with the bralette and pinched face tore her story apart. Leda would think, *Maybe you should take up ice-skating and then you would have more confidence and wouldn't feel the need to tell everyone they are terrible. You are only sad because you are terrible, but ice-skating may help you feel better about yourself.*

"I also think it's heavy-handed, but I think it only comes across that way because nothing happens. It's a story about nothing," Pinched Bralette said.

"I don't have a problem with that, though. Just 'cause it's about nothing doesn't mean nothing happens," the boy beside her said.

His name was Nick and Leda had been in two classes with him in the past, including a poetry workshop. She remembered this one poem he wrote about being in the woods with his father. He used the word *evergreen* and she thought that was nice. They never spoke much outside of class, but they did have one conversation standing in line for the elevator. He'd asked her what she was taking next semester and told her about a place nearby that gave out free sand-wiches on Fridays. As he spoke she thought he seemed like someone who had never touched breasts before, a sense she derived from an almost indiscernible nervousness in the way he breathed, a sound that could be described as an almost whistle at each inhale. Upon noticing it she felt taller and more luminous. For the most part she lived her life thinking of herself as a person, Leda. But then all of a sudden, out of nowhere, out of the cold harsh common dregs of patriarchy, some man would jump up and remind her she was in fact not a person at all but a woman. Usually it was derogatory, but on rare occurrences, as it was with Nick, it would remind her of the blissful and unequivocal truth: they were afraid of her. All of them. It made her feel limitless and powerful. No longer human at all, something more, something greater, a superhero flying through the sky and sinking away the breaths of all mortal men.

She was happy that Nick had found it in himself to defend her work against Pinched Bralette. Pinched Bralette, who was otherwise known as Abby, doodled on a notepad as he spoke.

"I thought the perspective was really nice," he said. Pinched Bralette looked up for a second, squinted her eyes, and went back to drawing. *Go ahead and draw, asshole,* Leda thought.

She waited patiently as the conversation turned from whether

her piece was boring or not to whether Cleo was a good choice of a name for her main character. One girl said: "I like Cleo, but I think she seems more like a blond than a brunette, but maybe that's just me." Leda underlined "Cleo" in her notes, writing, "blond?" in the margin.

Leda was not permitted to speak until the end of the workshop, but if she could have spoken she would have said, "But what about the polish of it? Does it lack a certain polish that keeps it from being any good?" But she couldn't, so she just sat there and nodded, silently unanswered.

As the critique came to an end, Patricia, who had formally said little more than the occasional "Ummhmm," began to stir as if she were planning on speaking. Throughout the workshop, Leda kept looking at her for at least some kind of facial reaction, but the professor looked as dull and unassuming as the gray-blue turtleneck she wore. Finally, after Pinched Bralette said, "You know, you should really read *Big Sur* by Jack Kerouac," Patricia spoke.

"That's an excellent suggestion, Abby. Jack Kerouac is one of my absolute favorites." She nodded thoughtfully at Abby, and then turned to face Leda and took a big breath in her very calm and particular manner.

"I think there are a lot of things working with this piece. I very much appreciate the use of the cherry stand. It gives the story a sort of rural quality that I quite like. I don't think it's a story about nothing, but I have to say, I think, Leda, you need to really consider what it is you're saying here. In this case your heroine is a sort of superwoman. She has risen above any personal insecurities or vulnerabilities. She's almost a poster child of this feminist ideal. And as much as I appreciate the idea that you are getting at with that, I think you may have more to offer us than this."

The room was quiet and maliciously still. Patricia had such control over the way she spoke that it seemed to forbid the possibility of any interruption. Leda didn't notice any of it though; she didn't even really consider the way Patricia spoke or the soft way she turned the paper in her hand. She just heard what she said and sat there feeling smaller and smaller. Her story and its cherry stand melting away into an oblivion witnessed by twelve hipsters and herself in mortifying silence.

When she got home she heated up some soup, but she hadn't done it right because it exploded all over the microwave. She ate a sandwich instead, but the cheese was old and dried out. She called her mom as she ate.

"I hate workshops. I always leave and think, 'I'll never look at that story again,'" she said.

"I understand that, but you can't get so down on yourself. You know you're a great writer," her mom said.

"Do I know I'm a great writer? I feel like a failure."

"Stop it! You're not a failure."

Leda always called her mom to complain about everything terrible in her life. Most conversations ended with her saying something to the effect of "And I'm getting fat" and her mom telling her she was not getting fat. Her mom understood precisely what made her tick. What pulsing affirmation was needed to get her through from day to day and week to week and month to month and year to year. Leda called, and her mom answered, and they loved each other like one, two, three. Easy, fresh, perfect.

"I thought you said you didn't even like this professor," her mom said.

"I don't like her. Well, I don't know. It's not that I don't like her; it's just that I feel like, she basically said the whole story is a joke. That I don't know what I'm talking about. It just makes me think that maybe I just don't know anything. Maybe I'm just believing all this stuff about myself, and none of it's true."

"I think you're giving the whole thing too much thought right now. Go to bed. You'll feel better tomorrow."

"Okay, but I'm also getting fat."

"You're not fat, Leda! I love you. And you are a great writer. Don't forget that, ever."

Leda let herself eat an entire bag of Hershey's Kisses that night. She thought about Pinched Bralette and sexless Nick. She tried not to think about what Patricia said, but whenever she did she'd feel a burning in her chest and her ears would buzz a little. It was nervousness or sadness or the feeling of uncertainty that she'd become so accustomed to, a feeling that would be familiar all her life. The next morning she did feel better, but she never went back to the cherry stand story. Years later she'd find a copy of it and read the first paragraph. It did lack polish.

CHAPTER 7

—◦❧◦—

Showering

THE PROSPECT OF A HOT SHOWER WAS SOMETIMES THE ONLY REASON to walk, to move, to let the day pass by like a reflection. There was so much misery and boredom in day-to-day life but showering was a momentary respite from it all, the steam, the warmth, the limitless possibility that filtered through the sound of the water pounding her back. *Anything is possible, and I am naked,* she would think, insulated by the shelter of the shower curtain.

On a rare occasion she would take a bath instead. Taking a bath was a promise that she'd make, usually in simultaneous acceptance of misery. *I missed the train and will be late, and they will be mad at me, but later I will take a bath so I can float on their anger.*

During her final exams she made such a promise to herself when she had accepted the reality that the next three weeks she would be stuck in her apartment studying. The tub filled as she undressed. Standing in front of the mirror, she ran her hand over the curve of her rib cage, then her waist. She thought she looked very linear and that her breasts looked lovely also. The mirror fogged, softening her poses. She leaned over the bath, the water so clear it was almost not clear at all. She dropped her hand in and let it sink into the stark heat and thought to add bubbles. Deftly she pulled her arm out of the water and held it, letting the water drip as she reached for the bottle at the corner of the tub. It was empty. She placed it back in its spot to continue its reign as the-empty-bottle-in-the-corner-of-the-tub. The bottle sat there for two more months until a Saturday at four o'clock when she was arrested by a whim to do an intensive cleaning of the apartment. The sun was going down as she scrubbed away an ingrained Cheerio on the kitchen floor and thought of what her future children would look like. She threw out everything that had been inexplicably saved in a fluttered moment of grasping the transient nature of life. Reorganizing the bookshelf, she put the Noam Chomsky on a higher shelf between Willa Cather and Proust. The Willa Cather she had read, the Proust she had read half of. She stopped cleaning when she realized she couldn't wash the window by her bed. It was muddied from the outside, and given the building height there'd be virtually no way to clean it by herself. She thought of ladders and spent the rest of the evening watching TV. Her intentions of organizing her closet went unfulfilled.

She put her hair up to avoid getting it wet and to admire herself in the mirror as she pulled it into a bun. *I look best with my arms raised,* she thought, *but there are so few situations in which to raise them.* She sunk into the bath. The sound of the water enveloping her parted the silence of the room. There was her, and her body in the water, and stillness, and her neck against the back of the tub. She looked up at the skylight above the shower. It was remarkably clear despite the steam. The sky looked like early afternoon sky, but she figured it must be around three by now. She lifted her hands out of the water. They looked small and childlike. In so many years they'd hardly changed. She remembered herself at ten in a vain attempt at taking violin lessons. Her fingertips would get raw as she pressed down the strings to make F, F-sharp, and G, or something like that. The instructor told her she had soft hands and said that if she practiced more she would build up calluses on her fingers and the strings wouldn't hurt her as much. That night she lay in bed, her bird lantern spinning inverse silhouettes of robins and blue jays over her bureau, then closet, then toy chest. She thought of her fingers growing raw as she vigorously mastered "Twinkle, Twinkle, Little Star." She pinched her hands to her palms and fell asleep. Two months later she quit violin.

Soon after, her violin made its way casually from the corner of her bedroom, to the closet, to the attic. She didn't think of it much, but her mother mentioned it from time to time during conversations about "things Leda had been great at."

Her first year of college she decided to move from the dorms to a studio apartment that was "so cute" and "so full of light." The place needed bookshelves, so she made the decision to sell her violin. She did not hesitate on the decision, not even as she climbed the small, ill-proportioned stairs leading to the attic in her childhood home, not even as she moved her old dollhouse it sat behind, not even as she carried it to the pawnshop.

The pawnshop smelled like eggs and the man who worked there spoke with a burly voice and didn't have soft hands. Her violin was in his hard hands that already had calluses but not from violin.

Walking back from the shop, she imagined her little violin, the relic of her fourth-grade musical ambitions, displayed beside other relics of past lives. Her arms felt unburdened as she walked caselessly to the train station. *Violin cases are heavy and they knock your knees,* she thought. She had gloves on so she didn't think of how soft her hands were, but she may have thought it if she didn't have gloves on. She wouldn't have had gloves if it hadn't been so cold and hadn't been winter. She may have thought many things if it had been spring. As she reached the train station, she motioned the few notes she could remember on her wrist. She was deliberate in her spacing, mimicking the ambitious fingering she categorized in her mind as professional violin playing F-sharp C-flat, F-sharp C-flat, F-sharp C-flat. As she boarded the train she thought, *This is the last time of this in my life and this is never going to be this way again because this is over.* The bookshelves she bought were auburn.

Leda lifted her knees out of the bath. She held them as still as possible until they looked like they were floating. *My violin is out somewhere with someone, and it is not mine,* she thought. She imagined it sitting there with the pawnshop man, getting dusty as he spoke in his burly voice and wrote receipts with his calluses. She got out of the bath. Her hands were pruned and she was clean. It felt good even though she was dizzy from the steam.

CHAPTER 8

—❦—

Lunch with Elle

LEDA SAT CASUALLY SO THAT ONCE HER FRIEND ELLE GOT THERE she would think, look-at-Leda-my-casual-friend-who-sits-so-casually. This was not something she knew or understood; rather it was embedded in the posturing she associated with waiting for someone. She wanted to look impossibly relaxed so she kept fixing her hair and taking small sips of water. It was the only way to be sure that she looked prettiest and was hydrated. *When Elle gets here I will tell her about that guy who talks to me at the bagel place and offered me a parfait. Elle will laugh,* she thought, and fixed her hair again.

Elle was the kind of girl who looked like a paper doll. This was mostly due to her adept mannerisms, and the clothes she wore, which emphasized how unimaginably small her frame was. People would say things to Elle like: "Look how skinny your thighs are! Your thighs are like my arms." Elle would disregard these comments by saying: "I love cheeseburgers!" As Elle walked into the restaurant Leda thought, *I wish I was more linear like Elle, but I'm glad my breasts are bigger than hers.*

"I am so sorry that I'm late. Have you ordered? Cute purse, by the way." The girls embraced before Elle sat down.

"Oh, thank you! And seriously, don't even worry about it, I just got here. You look great."

"Do I? I feel like I haven't slept in days."

"You really do." She did, exceptionally put-together, as if someone had simply folded the perfect outfit over her.

"So before we get into anything else. I have some news," Elle said.

"What?" Leda imagined that the news was in connection to a pair of shoes Elle had sent her six pictures of over the last week and a half.

"I got an internship with a publishing house!"

"Oh my god. Are you serious? That's fantastic!"

"I know. I'm so excited."

"What publishing house?"

"It's called Besting Publishing. They publish neuroscience textbooks that are marketed to universities in Honduras."

"That sounds great!"

"I know, that doesn't sound that interesting, right? But it's a good start, and I mean, it's hard to get any of these types of internships because so many people apply, and there are usually only like three spots." Elle took a drink of water and looked around the restaurant nervously.

She thinks I don't think this is a big deal. She's worried it's not important, Leda thought. "This is a really big deal. It'll be really important."

Elle smiled. "Thanks. I think publishing is the place for me. I mean, it has to do with what I love, books, and on top of that there are a lot of good-paying jobs if you can work your way in. You have to network is the thing. The thing is to network. Have you ever had the Cobb salad here? It's so good."

Leda looked down at the silverware she had prematurely unwrapped from her napkin before Elle arrived. She had attempted to put the fork and knife back into the napkin, but it looked too messy so she just separated them.

"I haven't."

"We'll have to order it . . . unless you were thinking something else?"

Leda was planning on ordering the grilled cheese and tomato with French fries. Salad for lunch was a distant notion she associated with mortgages and weddings. Elle ate salad now. Last week they'd had lunch, and she ordered some kind of steak dish with cheese melted on it.

"No, I'd love to try it!" Leda said. She was not about to eat fried food in front of paper Elle.

The waitress came over and Elle ordered with fast control. Her voice clicking on words like *iced tea* and *dressing on the side.* Leda thought of how best to order. It was a thin thought sequestered between futile motions of public consciousness. She came to the conclusion to use the word *just* a lot and to flutter her hands.

"I'll just have the Cobb salad too. And just water is fine," she said, fluttering her hands.

The waitress nodded. *Just* had been successful.

"So what's new with you, Led? Any news?"

Leda thought about the boy and the parfait, but she figured she should wait with that anecdote now that Elle had such big news.

"Nothing, really . . . You remember that story I sent to that literary journal? I got a letter from the editor, and she said even though this story isn't right for them, she really liked my writing and would love it if I sent something else."

"That's awesome!"

"Thanks, yeah. I was excited about it. Are you taking Pam's class next semester?"

"No." Elle sat up very straight. Her torso looked like a washboard. "I think I'm going to focus more on publishing from now on."

"I hope you keep writing, though. I always really liked your stories." She thought back to a story Elle had written about a woman who sold combs.

"Yeah, I mean, I will. It's just, as far as things go professionally, it's time for the fantasy to end, you know? I mean, it's all well and good to keep writing, but I also want to set realistic goals." Elle smiled.

"Yeah, I get that." Leda recognized the familiar wave of cruelty and cattiness that lingered in the comment, a rich but common display of the unabashed hatred and simultaneous press for superiority any woman could feel for another woman at any given moment.

"I guess I've always figured the fantasy is supposed to last at least through college," she said. She knew her response was bitchy, but that bitchiness was survival in a friendship like this one.

Elle did a sort of sideways nod and looked out the window. "I guess I don't really know what I want," she said.

She seemed sad, and that sadness surprised Leda, in at least as much as here it was right in front of her. She felt like for a moment she could see it all: small, paper Elle in her oversized clothes waiting for Cobb salad. It wasn't fair to let the vulnerability of her friend stay open like that.

"There's this boy who keeps talking to me at a bagel place, and he gave me a free parfait."

"Are you serious?" Elle lit up at the endless potential of talk of an anonymous boy. The girls theorized as they picked at their salads over what the best way was to approach the situation so that she and parfait-bagel-guy would marry. They came to the conclusion that the next time Leda came in for a bagel she should say, "That parfait you gave me was delicious." The plan was seamless through the glow of easy lunchtime conversation.

On the way out of the restaurant they decided to go for coffee at the same café Leda often frequented. As they sat down, she felt a calm fall over her through the familiarity of the place. The smell was warm and sharp. It was loud in the usual way. Elle ordered a complicated coffee. She got tea.

"The thing is, I'd like to cut my hair shorter," Elle said.

"How short?"

"Like a bob or something," she said, touching her hair.

"I think that would be pretty."

The girls walked out together talking about Elle's internship. She appeared very sure of herself, as was evidenced in the way she carried her shopping bags and how she clicked on words like *opportunity* and *branding*.

"I can't wait to be working," she said.

"Oh, is it paid?"

Elle shifted the shopping bags. "No, but it's like a job."

Leda nodded, figuring "like a job" meant something for a twenty-year-old or at least for Elle. *I hope I never have to have "like a job,"* she thought. She looked down at her purse. *Here is my purse, which is a purse, and here is Elle, who is like an adult. She is almost an adult but less so than my purse is a purse.*

Leda noticed Elle limped a little as they stepped off the curb to cross the street. "You're limping. Did you hurt yourself?"

"I rolled my ankle while pretending to be a ballerina in my room," Elle said.

The girls said their goodbyes on the corner. Elle walked off limping a little, with handfuls of shopping bags around her emphasizing the smallness of her frame. Leda imagined Elle in her bedroom holding on to *internship* as she danced to Cobb salad and bobbed hair. *She looks so linear,* thought Leda, *like she could just blow away.*

CHAPTER 9

—— ⚬❧⚬ ——

Joining a Gym

FOR BREAKFAST SHE'D MEANT TO HAVE A YOGURT BUT DECIDED SHE didn't feel like a yogurt, *and why would I ever want to eat a yogurt anyway when I can have a jelly donut?* she thought as she passed the donut shop on her way to school. It was so lovely: the silent indulgence, the sweet jelly, the gleeful $2.57 with tax.

The day felt as if it had started off right. In class she offered to read out loud, and when someone asked who Derrida was she had the answer at the ready. Afterward she walked down the hall and smiled at a boy she'd once talked to. He didn't notice her, but she didn't care. In that moment she even thought maybe she'd have another jelly donut on her way home. *Maybe I'll get two.* As she turned the corner it all fell away—the donuts, the linearity, the boy and his faultlessness; she caught a glimpse of her jumbled reflection in the window by the elevator, and it was awful. She was disgusting. She was fat. She was shaped like a teardrop, a hunched teardrop walking around and smiling at people and living her life like she deserved a place on this earth. *Who in the hell do I think I am?* she thought, and she fixed her shirt and sucked in her stomach and walked past that reflection as fast as she could, as fast as any teardrop could have managed.

That night she sat down and looked up gyms online for nearly two hours. She found one by her apartment that was rated highly on Yelp, apart from one girl who complained that "the bathroom is filthy" and included a picture of a crumpled-up piece of toilet paper beside the sink. Despite the toilet paper, Leda decided to e-mail and ask what their rates were. A guy named J.C. got back in touch with her nearly immediately and tried to pressure her into signing up for a personal trainer. "Do you have any idea about the potential of your body?" he wrote. "No," she responded, "but I'm just looking to do the elliptical for right now." He scheduled an appointment with her, and two days later she was walking herself past the donut shop to the gym.

J.C. turned out to be gay, and it may have been for this reason that she signed up. Maybe if he had been a straight guy, the judgmental straight guy in her mind who'd kick her out of bed and make her feel bad about her hip bones, she may not have wanted to pay $49.95 a month. J.C. was kind, and he talked about his boyfriend. He didn't care about her hip bones and that was refreshing.

Her first day at the gym she felt vaguely motivated and completely out of place. She walked in wearing the new workout clothes that she'd frantically shopped for all weekend. She tried to seem as together as possible. *Am I meant to take a towel along with me? What are all these little towels for, anyway?* She made her way from the locker room through the weight machines, all of which were being used by men. She walked past machine upon machine, each with an angry-looking man of varying size, lifting and squeezing and bending and pulling. *Where are all the women?* she wondered, and then she saw them. They were all together in a group at the back wall of the gym using the cardio equipment, running, stepping, pedaling away to a more linear reality. She climbed onto one of the few empty stationary bikes and started to pedal slowly. The girl to her right was wearing earphones and was watching a *Real Housewives* episode as she pedaled at a calm, rhythmic pace. The woman to her left wasn't watching *The Real Housewives,* or anything, for that matter. She was pedaling as hard as she could. The display on her machine said she'd already burned 467 calories. She was drenched with sweat and looked tired and unapologetic. *Which one am I?* Leda thought as she pedaled harder than the rhythmic girl but less hard than the unapologetic woman.

As she did this she thought about school and about the summer ahead. What she wanted and where she'd be. On occasion she caught a whiff of cigarette smoke from the open window. On occasion she felt melancholy about the potential of having to come back to the gym tomorrow. After about fifteen minutes of rhythmic, fast pedaling, she felt tired and less worried about being a teardrop than she had the day she'd eaten the jelly donut. She got off the bike and felt the pull in her hamstring with each step, a physical reminder of her desperation. As she walked past all the men and their weights, she looked back at the women running and biking and stepping. *Keep running, ladies,* she thought. *You'll never get away.*

In the locker room an older-middle-aged woman was crouched down naked.

"I dropped a little gold key," she said, looking under a bench, "if you happen to see it."

"Like a diary key?" Leda asked her.

"Wow, that's a great reference," the woman said. "A little bigger than a diary key."

She helped the woman for a few minutes, looking under the sink and by the showers. The woman's body was linear enough, but it was still lumped in places. Leda figured there might be something wrong with her for not being more ashamed of how lumped she was, but in the moment she didn't pay much attention to it. Finding the key felt pressing and more important. She helped her look for a little while longer, but in the end they both gave up.

"I'm sure someone will find it," the woman said, but Leda didn't think it was likely. She couldn't imagine what this little gold key looked like, and she couldn't imagine that anyone else would be able to either.

That night she canceled her gym membership and ate a piece of cake. Two days later she'd think about rejoining as she tried on a pair of jeans. In her was a yearning greater than hunger and greater than thirst. It was an unyielding trauma and torment that plugged away in rhythmic consistency. It was sanity and insanity and cellulite that would never go away.

CHAPTER 10

Loneliness

SHE COULD HEAR IT IN THE SOUND OF A COIN DROPPING AND IN LEAN-
ing down to grab it, the rush of blood as she stood back up. In the
touch of a gum wrapper in her pocket and in the redness of her coat,
the space between each button. On the nape of her neck and in the
sound of cereal pouring. She was lonely.

At night she would wrap her arms around herself and run her
hand over her back with her fingertips. *My back no one is touching,*
she would think. The daytime was mostly taken up, but the quiet
moments that were not taken up were wrought with emptiness. On
her lunch break at school she was surrounded by couples walking
through their springtimes together. She'd sit in a corner with a sad
sandwich pretending to read on her phone as she listened to them
sputter inanity at each other. *Won't I get to talk about light fixtures?*
Doesn't someone care what type of light fixtures I like? she thought.

There were many things she could not do alone. Many places that
would emphasize her pain and all the beautiful things she violently
hoped for. She once heard a girl at a party talk about the Saturday
night she went to a nice restaurant by herself.

"You wouldn't believe it, but I went to Il Capitano alone last Saturday," the girl said.

"You could have called me, I would have gone with you," another
girl said, touching her shoulder in condolence.

"No, I decided just because I'm single does not mean that I can't
go to a nice restaurant on a Saturday night. I mean, really, do I have
to have a boyfriend to have dinner? It's insane."

The wide-eyed stares of all the other girls listening to the story of the lonely meal circled the girl. Leda looked at her and thought, *You are lonely and kind of fat like me. You are fatter, though, and probably more lonely.*

The girl took a nervous bite of a crostini and then said, "And it's a great way to meet guys."

Leda would get together with her friends for girls' nights and they would go out to eat or to a bar to have wine and appetizers. She'd dress up and wear extra eye makeup. It was nice to feel like she had somewhere to be. Her friends would laugh and talk about men. They would say things like, "I *so* needed this girls' night," or "I wish he would text me." The night was always an array of happiness and absence, but really, at least it was a way to not feel like you were as glaringly single, alone, without. There were so many times when to just stand without a man seemed like the most painful way to stand, and girls' nights provided a parenthetical escape from this burden. Most weekends, though, she just stayed home.

One Sunday afternoon Leda braved a Klimt exhibit at the MFA alone. Her friend Sonja canceled last-minute because the guy she was seeing wanted to get lunch.

"He was really hungry, and we stopped at this great taco place," she said.

Leda envisioned them eating tacos as they laughed and talked about all the great sex they were having and what light fixtures they liked.

She walked alongside the Klimt paintings, focusing on what she must look like to all the other museumgoers. She stood up as straight as possible and came up close to each painting and then moved far away, as if she had some deep understanding of perspective. She took out a small pocket notepad from time to time. In the notepad she wrote: "dreamlike" and "colorful." That was the last time she ever used the notepad. Years later she would find it in a box marked "mismatch" and would wonder what "dreamlike" and "colorful" meant.

Upon noticing a girl laughing an embarrassed laugh at her boyfriend's whispers in front of *Adam and Eve*, Leda decided it was time to go. *I wish I was* The Kiss, she thought, and neglected to visit the gift shop.

On the train ride home she smiled at a boy, but he looked away.

That night she microwaved soup and watched four hours of a game show she didn't know the name of. She dreamt about the boy on the train whispering to her about melted candy neatly spun and then rehardened.

The loneliness was manageable enough with girls' nights and busying oneself, but the ever-present need for sex was not. It was like a phantom limb that she'd reach for. Every day she was reminded that there was no arm. Sexless by a trauma that didn't exist. *People aren't meant to live like this,* she'd think when she'd smell sweat or eat a lemon ice. Sometimes she'd be alone in an elevator with a man and be reminded of just how much she burned for touch. She would get dizzy just from sensing his body beside her. It took all her willpower not to jump on him and try to have sex between floor stops. She never acted on the impulse, of course, although there were several occasions when she almost attempted conversation. Once a man in a suit who smelled like rhubarb asked her what time it was. She answered, "Yes," and before she had time to explain that she was so lonely, and that she did love rhubarb, he was gone, out of her life forever on floor seven. The rest of the day she walked around thinking up everything she should have said instead of "Yes" that could have led to their subsequent love affair. "It's four thirty" seemed most plausible.

Leda had never actively been conditioned to believe that she needed to be with a man to be happy. Her mother certainly was not the type to instill values of happily-ever-after or any fairy tales of the sort. Since she was three years old her mom had been saying, "Dreams first, boys second." Leda had a vague memory of herself in a sandbox allowing a little boy to steal a shovel away from her and her mother taking it back, saying, "Dreams first, boys second." From then on she wanted to believe shovels were a part of her dreams, and that no boy would steal a shovel away from her again.

By middle school there were no more sandboxes, just glitter eye shadow and flavored lip gloss. It became clear that the girls who were worshipped, the girls who mattered, were the girls who were "going out" with boys. There was Sandy Lourrie, who was dating Kyle Fielding, and wasn't she pretty, and it's no wonder Kyle would want to date her. Isn't Kyle so hot? She's so lucky, but really it's no wonder 'cause she's so pretty. Maybe Sandy will invite us to her birthday party, and we'll get to hear all the great things about Kyle.

When she was sixteen her cousin dated a doctor. At the family Christmas party all the women gathered around, saying, "A doctor, did you hear? A doctor. She's dating a doctor. Did you hear that she is really dating a doctor?" The rest of the night her cousin floated around on her doctor and ate potato salad with swift overachieving mouthfuls.

Leda wasn't in any way conscious of why or how being with a man made you superior, but it was an inescapable fact that was muddy and absolute. Once a girl had a boyfriend she had solidified her desirability through the commitment of a man. She was linear enough to be loved. She had won.

Leda remembered a woman at her mother's work who had been promoted to vice president of the company. There was a party for her that Leda attended with her mom. The cake said "Congratulations Susan!" Everyone talked about Susan and how she really deserved this, and did you know she went to Yale? Isn't that amazing? After they gave a toast, Susan made a speech. She thanked everyone who had helped her, and talked about gardening because she was alone and all she had was her azaleas. Everyone smiled politely as Susan went on and on about her garden. Leda thought, *This woman is talking about her garden to show us she is happy, but she is talking so much we can see that she is sad.*

Leda did not want to be Susan. Somewhere beyond her shovel dreams it was clear that for her life to really mean anything she would need to be with a man. It was plain and yearning, powerful and stifling. And above all else, she wouldn't be lonely.

CHAPTER 11

Stars

LIKE SO MANY TIMES BEFORE, LEDA ONLY *THOUGHT* SHE WANTED TO go to the party. All her young adult life she clung on to the idea of *party* as a representation of social perfection. In her mind there were streams of colors and dancing and pithy conversation between bright cocktails and four-inch heels. If she were ever to stop and consider what *party* actually was, not solely as the conceptual fantasy she envisioned but in its naked and fluorescent reality, she would have been aware that what it meant was the physical realization of how alienating social interaction could truly be, and she would not have gone. Instead she put on lipstick and a short dress.

When she walked in, Sonic Youth's cover of the Carpenters' "Superstar" was playing in the background. *It's such a sad affair,* she thought along with the lyric. The party unfolded in the living room before her eyes. People standing around, talking, holding drinks. Someone somewhere laughed, but she wasn't sure where.

In the kitchen was Kate, the girl who invited her. Kate wore crop tops in winter and was blonder than necessary. Leda didn't particularly like or dislike Kate. For her, Kate fell into one of those in-between categories of friendship. They met in their Comparative Zoology class, where their tentative interactions developed through confusion over exoskeletons and homeostasis. After the semester ended there was the standard moment of will-this-friendship-continue-now-that-we-don't-have-to-try-to-understand-homeostasis? For a while it did. Kate asked Leda to coffee, and Leda texted Kate on occasion. If they bumped into each other they would always embrace. She even thought: *I like Kate. She's my friend,* after they chatted about pesto for a few minutes waiting in line at a sandwich shop.

A few weeks later she asked Kate if she wanted to grab lunch. Kate said yes and motioned excitedly. The Friday they were supposed to meet up Leda didn't hear anything from her, so she texted, "Hey, girly, are we on for lunch??" She never heard back. The rest of the day she envisioned all the reasons Kate hadn't responded. *Maybe she had a death in the family or her phone broke. Maybe she doesn't like me,* she thought. That night on her way home she went for a slice of pizza. Kate was there with some friends, sitting in a booth, laughing and motioning excitedly, just like she had the day they agreed to have lunch. *She's so fake,* Leda thought, and walked all the way around the restaurant to avoid bumping into her. As she fell asleep that night she relived the moment Kate mispronounced "horticulture" in class.

Three months later she got the mass e-mail invite to the party. It said: "Come to Kate's Super Fun Unbelievably Cool Over-the-Top Amazingly Excellent Party!" Underneath there was a picture of a sloth with a party hat. Leda thought the invitation was obnoxious and pretentious, and she was also still very hurt about the lunch, but it didn't stop her from wanting to go. She knew that fickleness was the exchange for loneliness and was hoping that at least she'd meet someone.

"Leda! I'm so excited you came!" Kate enveloped her in a flurry of blondness.

"Yeah, thanks so much for having me!"

"Your hair looks so cute."

"Thanks. I love the apartment."

"Oh, yeah, it's great, right? Good for parties, anyway."

"Yeah, it's so big."

"Well, help yourself to a drink. We have beer on the porch."

That was the last time Kate and she ever spoke. Kate had six more parties, but Leda didn't attend. Years later she would hear Kate married a guy named Gage and worked at a bank.

Leda waited near the door for her friends to arrive. She had invited Anne, a friend her mom once described as having a slutty face. While she waited she pretended to admire Kate's book collection, which consisted of the Twilight series, three diet books, and Chaucer. *Fat: The Enemy* and *The Canterbury Tales*. It was a lot of looking busy to do, but she didn't feel like forcing conversation with strangers. Once Anne was there she figured things would be easier.

Despite her slutty face, Anne was a good friend. She and Leda had become close over the last few years and would sometimes spend hours on the phone chatting about boys and being bloated. Anne was one of the few people on earth who rarely judged the emotional impulses of others, and because of this, Leda confided in her long secrets of quiet desperation with little worry. Anne invited her boyfriend, Luke, to the party. She was never single and Luke was her newest boyfriend.

"He's nice but emotionally unavailable," she would say. Leda had never met him before.

"Leda!" Anne walked in just as Leda was about to pull out a book on the dangers of processed foods. The girls gave each other a big hug.

"This is Luke."

"Hey, I'm Luke."

Leda shook his hand. She could see what Anne meant about him being emotionally unavailable.

They got drinks and started to talk about school in an empty, distant way. Had Luke not been there they would have been talking about him, but since he was, they danced around their familiar conversation topics while Anne worked to occasionally include him.

"Luke plays softball. Don't you, Luke?"

"Yeah."

"Oh, really? That's cool," Leda said, and took a small sip of her beer. She hated beer, but it was preferable to standing there with a soda having to explain why she wasn't drinking. She'd grown accustomed to drinking intolerable drinks at parties by holding her breath and taking small sips. Once a doctor asked her if she drank.

"Socially," Leda said.

"What does 'socially' mean? I always wonder," the doctor asked.

"It means that you drink enough so that no one asks you why you aren't drinking."

She often looked back on that conversation as one of the most profound and true things she would ever say. It was the cornerstone to her doctrine of personal drinking habits.

"Leda, are you here?"

"What?"

"Do you know any guys here?" Anne said.

"Oh, I thought you said, 'Leda, are you here?'"

"No."

"Oh . . . No, not really."

"Babe, do you want another beer?" Luke said, wrapping his arm around Anne. He tucked his hand in her back pocket. Leda tried not to show her disdain, but she hated couples who couldn't stop touching each other in public. She remembered a couple at the train stop sharing an ice cream. They were giggling and passing the cone back and forth between kisses. She seriously considered pushing them onto the tracks. It wouldn't be until years later that she realized all the anger was just loneliness.

"Thanks, babe," Anne said as she kissed Luke before he walked off.

"Luke seems nice," Leda said.

"Yeah, he is."

"And he's cute!" She didn't really think he was cute, but this was courtesy.

"Thanks, yeah, he is. We got in a huge fight today, though."

"Why?"

"He didn't want to come to the party 'cause he wanted to play video games. Yes, that's a true story, and this is my life."

This was a common fight between the two of them. Leda spent many Saturdays texting with Anne as she sat in Luke's apartment watching him play video games. Sometimes he'd take her out for Applebee's afterward, and her texts would dramatically switch from things like "I can't stand this" to "We're eating breadsticks!" Breadsticks appeared to be the difference between a good relationship and a bad relationship.

"That's insane. How did you get him to come?"

"I promised him he could play video games all day on Saturday and Sunday next weekend."

"That seems worse than not coming to the party."

"Seriously, I know."

"He seems sweet, though."

"Yeah." Anne smiled. "He is." She looked warmer and more relaxed than she had seconds before, as if she'd thought of something wonderful and bright. It was the same kind of look a person gives when they get good news or are nearing the start of a vacation. Leda felt an intense pang of jealousy.

The rest of the evening Luke didn't leave Anne's side. He kept touching her elbow or wrapping his arm around her or kissing her cheek. Leda tried to look away for the most part, but it was impossible not to acknowledge. "Aww," she said when he kissed her hand. Anne pretty much ignored the situation or playfully fought him off. She'd whisper apologies to Leda from time to time about him being all over her, but clearly she loved it on some untouchable level that their friendship fell beneath. *In the tiers of Anne's life I fall below neck kisses,* Leda thought. It wasn't anything to feel bad about, really; what there was to feel bad about was the lack of kisses on her own neck. *If only,* she thought, taking a breathless sip of beer.

The night alienated her more and more from the solid notion she had of herself. Anne got a bit tipsy, and she and Luke spent the remainder of the evening kissing on the couch. Leda walked around and tried talking to some people, but she kept bumping into couples. She talked to a red-haired drunk girl who kept chattering on and on about some guy named Max Sass.

"And he's so funny," she said.

"Yeah, but what kind of a name is Max Sass?" Leda remarked.

"But he's so funny," the drunk girl said.

"Yeah," Leda said.

Even she has someone, she thought. *If I were more linear I wouldn't be alone. Maybe they can sense how sad I am. Maybe they know I'm sad and so they stay away from me. I am sad and not linear enough, and that is everything.*

If she had not invited Anne, and if Luke had not come along and been so nice but emotionally distant, if the redhead didn't have her Sass, or if she had taken Anatomy of the Mind instead of Comparative Zoology, her night would not have been the night that it became. There would not have been the desperate burn of low party lights and couples folded into each other. There would not have been the culmination of so many little things solidifying. But that was the night. It was that.

"I'm Alex."

"Hi, I'm Leda."

Alex was in his early twenties and skinny. His face was long, and he moved a lot when he spoke. For a second she thought there might be something wrong with him, but then she realized he was just trying to be charming.

"There used to be this guy that I'd see at school all the time and I thought his name was Frank, so I'd be like, 'Hey, Frank, does it stank?' I thought he and I had this, like, great thing between us." Alex waved his hands with each syllable. "But it turned out his name wasn't Frank at all," he said. "He just never corrected me."

She laughed harder than the joke warranted, but it felt good.

"I think you're really pretty," he said.

"Thank you." She fixed her hair, hoping to prove it might be true.

"I've never heard the name Leda before, except in that poem."

" 'Leda and the Swan.' My mom loves that poem. She named me after it."

"But isn't that poem, like, about rape?"

"Well, it's more complicated than that, I think."

"Are you, like, good at reading or something?"

"I guess . . . I am." She didn't know what "good at reading" meant, but she was willing to ignore the possibility that what he said was as stupid as it sounded.

"I like you, Leda-the-swan."

"I like you too." She smiled.

"I live in the apartment next door. Do you want to, like, come over? I mean just to hang out."

"Umm . . ." She didn't know what she wanted, but she answered him from an impulse of wanting what it was that she did not know. "Okay, just for a little while."

Leda had never gone to a boy's apartment after a party. Her sexual past was short and based on ideals of love and monogamy. She'd only slept with her ex-boyfriend. They dated six months and she waited until he committed to her before she'd even consider sleeping with him. *We'll just make out,* she thought, consoling herself with limitation.

The apartment wasn't exactly next door. It was behind Kate's place through a little park. They walked together and said common things about school and movies. When they got to the center of the park Alex ran up and jumped on top of an abstractly shaped climbing structure.

"Look at me!"

She did look at him: tall, thin, anonymous boy on conceptual playground equipment. *The structure is shaped like me walking through a park with this boy at a party,* she thought.

"You're up high," she said, not knowing what the proper response was to "Look at me."

"Come up here. It's kind of cool. You can see the little clock tower over there."

Leda walked over and Alex helped her up. She could feel his warmth beside her. It was nice.

"See." Alex pointed off.

"Oh, yeah." She couldn't see anything, but it was so warm standing there that she thought it was best to pretend.

As they walked up the steps to Alex's place he held her hand, and she remembered what sex was. Years later she would remember the squeeze of his hand, the grind of his dry palm, and stairs six and seven.

Inside, his roommate was still up in the living room watching TV. She was a heavier girl with a sallow complexion and sulky face. Leda greeted her with the hi-I'm-not-a-slut-please-don't-judge-me hello. The girl smiled slightly. Leda knew the greeting had been a failure.

"I have to go clean up my room. You can hang here with Mel for a minute," Alex said.

Oh Jesus Christ, Leda thought. She sat down on a stained easy chair. Her thigh pressed up against a hot-water bottle that she could feel had grown tepid. The coffee table was littered with discarded boxes of candy and several remotes, as well as a cat toy. She thought for a minute on what to say. *If only I could tell her everything. Tell her about the party and when I was six and skinned my knee racing with the little boy who lived next door and had just moved in from India and only knew the word "constipation." But I can't tell her that, because I have to pretend that I don't care about anything in the world but right now.*

"You have a cat?" Leda said.

"No."

"Oh, I saw the cat toy . . ." She pointed to the fish-shaped cat toy on the table.

"No, I made that for my nephew."

"Oh, sorry. I thought it was a cat toy."

"No."

"Oh, okay, sorry."

She decided that was enough talking. The girls sat silently until Alex came back. Leda attempted to wave goodbye a little as she headed to his room, but Mel didn't respond.

"Here it is."

The room was small with three big piles of clothing on the floor and a bed. On the walls were a few band posters. She recognized the bands and wasn't impressed. Alex's musical aesthetic slipped him into the category of guys with pedestrian tastes that she tried to avoid. It was disappointing.

"I like your room," she said.

"Yeah, it's kind of messy."

Alex stood by the door and started to point out different things in the room. She began to wonder when they'd actually sit down. It was late, and she was tired. His nervous tour of his hideous bedroom was making the night more and more depressing. She thought back to Anne and Luke. *They're probably having sex right now,* she thought.

Anne once said Luke was good in bed, and the comment plagued her. She'd never had good sex and wasn't sure if it existed, at least for a woman. But maybe Anne was doing something she wasn't, and that was the problem. She sat down on the bed quickly to distract herself from the thought.

Alex sat down next to her and for a while they talked about bike riding and jawbreakers. She felt bored and alienated by the conversation. *What's wrong with me?* she thought. *I'm not having fun with this cute guy. He's kind of cute, isn't he? I should be happy.*

"Can I kiss you?" he asked.

"Sure," she said.

Alex kissed her. There were preemptive tongue thrusts and the taste of beer. He held her face, then let go, then held it again. She appreciated the effort despite the awkwardness. He stopped kissing her suddenly.

"Do you want to have sex?" he said.

She felt a wave of heat through her body.

"It's just, you're so pretty . . . and, I don't know," he said.

"I'm really not good with . . . I just get really emotional," she said.

"It's fine, don't worry. We don't have to."

"I'm sorry—"

"It's really totally fine. We can just kiss."

They lay on his bed together, and soon he touched her breasts. The sheets were striped and soft. She could feel the breeze from under the cracked window. It made her a little cold. Then he lay on top of her and then the flood of everything drowned out everything that for so long had made her feel so subhuman. It wasn't so much that here she was, wildly turned on by this boy, but rather that here she was, turned on by herself *with* a boy.

"Do you have a condom?" she asked him.

"Yeah."

She watched him move effortlessly through the room toward the closet. She hadn't before seen him in such fluid motion. It was startling. *This fluid man is going to be inside me soon,* she thought. *I am on this bed, and it is like a raft. I am on this bed, and that man is on an island getting a condom.* Alex opened the closet, revealing a poster of a woman in underwear whoring an unattainable standard of beauty. After rummaging through his closet he came back and sat beside her. "So should we do it now?" he said.

"Um, okay."

She took off her own dress and underwear and lay down, sucking in her stomach. DO I LOOK PRETTY NAKED? was the universal question of female sex, and this moment was no confirmation of the fact. He didn't say anything about the way she looked, although had he said something she wouldn't have believed him. It was the catch-22 propagated by the whore in his closet.

Alex took off his clothes. He was considerably thinner than he looked dressed, which was disappointing since even in clothes she could tell he was much skinnier than she was. *Great,* she thought, *fattest by default,* and she sucked in her stomach even more.

He pulled off his boxers, and then suddenly there was a naked penis in the room, jarring and unfamiliar. *The worst part about having sex with a strange boy is his strange penis,* she'd later reflect.

They kissed a little longer, but he was eager to get going, and she wasn't about to stop him, or do anything expressive, for that matter. It was important to maintain some type of calm, controlled, and happy appearance of woman-during-sex, although she certainly wasn't sure why this was.

He had a hard time getting it in, and she had to help him, to which he said "Thank you." It was slightly painful as he moved back and forth. He tried holding her breasts, but the position was too awkward so he just gave up. Every so often he'd ask her if she was okay. She wondered what he was worrying about not being okay. *Doesn't he know if I weren't okay I wouldn't say anything? Maybe I don't look like I'm enjoying this enough,* she thought, and wrapped her legs around him. Above her was the ceiling, painfully still, and below her was the raft bed floating in space.

"The condom feels funny," he said.

"Really? Maybe you should change it."

He took it off and put on another one. She had to help him put it in the second time. She was hoping he'd finish soon.

"Is this good?" he asked.

"Yeah, is it good for you?"

"Yeah. And you're okay?"

"Yeah, I'm fine."

"Okay."

The motion over her got more stilted and fast. *Okay, it's almost over,* she thought, *and where am I going to sleep? Here in this striped raft?* The motion stopped.

Alex lay beside her. She looked at him. Now he was someone else. Someone she'd slept with. He was stranger and closer to her than he'd ever been. She noticed his hair had a cowlick and had probably just been cut. Now she wanted to tell him everything about her night and about the smell of a wardrobe she used to hide in as a child and why she slept with him, but instead she just said:

"Did you like it?"

"Yeah, did you?"

"Yeah."

He kissed her, and she thought, *Now our kisses are different because there is nothing more we can do. We had sex and that is it.*

They each put their underwear back on and Alex gave her an oversized T-shirt and pajama pants to sleep in. They smelled strongly of him, although she couldn't have known it because she didn't know his smell. She tried to remember the exact feeling of what it was to be in her own pajamas, but she wasn't able to think of it. Alex lay down and she lay beside him. They were silent for a while.

"Are you tired?" he asked.

"Yeah, I am." She wasn't tired.

Alex leaned over her and shut off the light. They sat in the darkness. *So this is what it's like to not be sleeping alone but to still be lonely,* she thought. She ran her hands over her thighs and touched the elastic on her underwear. It was the same as it was so many times in the morning after a shower when she pulled them on.

Alex turned over a few times beside her and then sat up.

"Do you mind if I put on my star lantern? I usually can't sleep so well without it." He didn't wait for her answer. He leaned to the side of the bed and turned on a small lantern. The room lit up with stars. Leda was familiar with these stars, not because she had seen them before, but because she knew she'd never slept without them either. Alex was soon asleep. She lay there staring at the ceiling and the fantasied constellations. In the closet was a naked girl and under the blanket was herself lying in the universe of this boy she met at a party. She fell asleep.

——— ❦ ———

CHAPTER 12

The Day After

THE NEXT MORNING SHE WOKE UP THIRTY-SIX MINUTES BEFORE ALEX. She spent the time having to pee very badly and worrying about the proximity of the bathroom to Mel. *Where is the bathroom? Will Mel be in the bathroom or yell at me for using the bathroom?* For lack of any other option, she decided to brave the situation. It turned out her fears were unfounded. The bathroom was just across the hall, and Mel was nowhere to be seen.

She sat on the toilet. Early daylight filtered through the scalloped glass pane of the small window, and for a moment she felt comfortable in the familiarity of morning and the privacy of the bathroom. There was little motivation to go back to Alex.

As she washed her hands she looked at her reflection in the mirror. She still had most of her makeup on from last night, although her eyeliner had smudged. Her hair was messy but manageable. She rinsed her mouth out in the sink and tried her best not to think too hard about the night before.

Alex was still asleep when she got back to the room. She climbed into bed beside him and tried to stay as still as possible. Fourteen minutes later he woke up.

"Hey," he said, blinking and looking skinny. "Have you been awake for a long time?"

"No, I was asleep," she lied.

"You weren't asleep. You should have just woken me up."

"I did."

"What?"

"Nothing. I'm just kidding."

"Oh."

For whatever reason Leda had felt the need to pretend she was sleeping. There was something about sleep that perpetuated her as comfortable with sex, and with him, a submission that she felt she needed to concede to. It was a complicated dance so intrinsic to the situation that she didn't even give it any consideration before performing the charade. She lied about it for fear of looking weak, but she would have never dared to wake him up. She didn't understand why this was. Not even a little. Not even years later looking back on herself in that room, young, sleepless, and weak.

They got dressed in near silence. She became very deliberate with buttoning the front of her dress, her fingers pressing the cool of the plastic through the small threaded hole, her hands moving delicately in the silent, clumsy moment.

"Are you hungry?" he asked her.

"Yeah, sure."

"Mel's having company over so we really can't be in the kitchen. I don't really have any food in there that's mine right now anyway."

"What do you usually do for breakfast?" Leda asked.

"I usually steal one of Mel's bagels, but she's in there now so we can't," he said.

"Oh."

"I don't have any money so we probably can't go out to eat."

"Oh, that's okay," she said.

Alex grabbed for his coat on the floor and, reaching into the pocket, pulled out a can. "Do you want this energy drink? It's warm, but it's still good."

"No, that's all right."

They sat on the bed a little longer and talked about basketball. Leda wondered how she managed to say as much as she did. After a long silence followed by one more basketball comment, she suggested it was time to go. Alex walked her to the door.

As they stood together in the doorway facing the delegation of future physical and emotional contact, she wanted so much. She wanted him to ask for her number, wanted him to say something about liking her and thinking she was pretty. She had an urge to jump into his arms, to run with him to conceptual playground equipment forever and ever. She held her breath; inside her ears was her heartbeat. Alex looked at her, smiled, moved in close, and put up his hand for a high five. With seemingly few other options, she high-fived him.

"Thanks so much," he said to her.

She walked off reliving the high five over and over again in her mind. By the time she'd gotten to the end of the block, she realized how sore she was from the sex and started to cry. Her breathing was stilted and her tears were soft and few. They did little more than sting her eyes, and when she blinked she felt as if she could see a blurred reality as painful and real as it was undeniably her own. A little girl passed who looked at her and clapped in the air.

"Summer," she said as she clapped.

To Leda everything was unearthed in that "summer": her day, her night, the party, and the strange penis. She wanted to scoop the little girl up. Feel solace in her weight. She imagined herself and this summer girl walking through the city. Getting ice cream and just laughing the day into infinite pieces. She'd give summer a bath before bed and tell her a story as light and airy as that clap. She stopped crying by the time she'd reached the corner and decided to text Anne.

She texted as she walked: "I had sex with that guy last night . . ."

Anne responded nearly immediately: "WHAT??? That guy with the short hair?? What happened?? You better give me the details!!!"

Leda's hands were shaking as she typed. She didn't want Anne to think she was happy. Anne had had sex with strangers before. She'd always act like it was some funny thing. She'd say things like, "I totally had sex last night." And, "Remember that hot guy I mentioned? I totally had sex with him." Leda would go along with it, but she knew Anne well enough to know it wasn't so funny. It wasn't so *totally*. On one occasion Anne started crying and confessed that she bled all over the bed midway through.

"I don't know," she said through sobs, "he must have just ripped my skin or something. It was just awful, and he hasn't called."

Leda talked to her for three hours that night, reassuring her that he'd call, that she was skinny and looked good naked. The next day when Leda texted her asking how she was, Anne acted happy. She acted as if everything was okay, and she never mentioned the bloody sex ever again.

Leda didn't want to text about the sex she had with Alex. She wanted to call Anne and explain it all to her. To explain the high five, as if somehow that would make her feel better. She knew that it would. She texted back:

"Can I call you?"

Anne: "Can I call you in an hour? I'm still with Luke and we're going to get bagels."

Anne: "Actually maybe two hours?"

Leda stared at the flat message on her phone. She wanted to ignore it or to write something like: "No! I'm not a whore like you, Anne! Call me now!" But she just said: "Sure! No worries!"

She walked the rest of the way home checking her phone, hoping that Alex would message her on Facebook or something. It was completely irrational, but she didn't care.

When she got home, the apartment seemed emptier and more lonely than ever before. The auburn bookshelves were still there as always. Her disheveled bedsheets looked accusatory in their two-day-old misshape. She watered the plant as if that was something she did daily. For some unknown reason she felt bad going straight to her computer. It was as if her room and all her things would judge her, see her for her pathetic self, or maybe it was her need to hold on to the momentary hope that he had left her a message when she knew that it was really just her and the plant all along.

She sat down and checked her Facebook page. No messages. No friend request. Nothing. She tracked him down immediately even though she didn't know his last name. He was friends with Kate. His page was private so she couldn't see anything but his profile picture. It was of him standing on a surfboard with his arms in the air in what must have been a surf shop or something to that effect. His face was nearly indistinguishable, as he had sunglasses on and the picture was a little bit out of focus. For whatever reason it infuriated her. There he was, distant and smudged, just laughing it up in some surf shop.

She Googled him. There was a soccer team he'd been a part of in middle school and a bike race he did in college. There wasn't much else. She clicked through his Instagram account, but he'd only posted a few pictures of a vacation to Montana. A cliff. Some mountains. A rusted bicycle. She scrolled through the pictures again. With little else left to do, she did a Google image search. A lot of "Alexes" appeared. Some were the famous "Alexes" you'd expect, and some were regular-people "Alexes" and some were naked porn "Alexes." She clicked on one of the naked ones. His face was fat and meaty and his body was muscular in the expected way. He was holding his grotesquely large penis. She thought back to the sex, her Alex, and the way he was stilted and having to change condoms. She thought of her belly fat and cellulite. An image of herself in an unfortunate pair of khaki shorts flashed through her mind. It seemed plausible that her current angst could be understood by the width of her thighs. *Maybe I really am gross*, she thought, and then Anne called her.

"Hey," she said.

"Hey," Anne said. "So what happened?"

"Well, I talked to him for a long time, and he was like really funny. I don't know, then he just invited me over to have sex, and then we just did, but now I'm, like, freaking out, and I don't even know why."

"Why are you freaking out?"

"I don't know! I just want to hear from him and I don't know why." Her voice started to crack over the phone.

"Did you give him your number?"

"No, I wanted him to ask. I did find him on Facebook." She didn't feel it necessary to elaborate on the rest of her search. "His page is really private. I don't want to friend him first though. I just want him to initiate things."

"You could go to his house and pretend you forgot something, and then give him your number."

"I'll look crazy if I do that."

"Well, I went to a guy's house once and pretended I left something. It was this guy I knew from, like, mutual friends. He was, like, kind of nerdy, but, like, sweet and funny and we went on this really cute date where we got fondue, and I had just broken up with Adam so I was really on the rebound, and so we ended up having sex. And the thing was that all night long he was all, 'Oh my god you're so pretty. I really want to see you again. We should totally hang out.' And so I really thought I'd hear from him. And then three days passed, and I didn't get a text. I didn't get a 'Did you get home safe?' Nothing. And then, like, randomly he friended me on Facebook so I sent him a message, which he ignored, so then I sent him another message and said I left something at his house and wanted to come get it, and so then I went to his house and knocked on the door, and I know he was home 'cause his car was there, but he didn't answer. So then I got home and there was this *long* Facebook message that was him saying all this stuff about how he usually doesn't have random hookups, and that he felt really weird about it, especially 'cause we didn't use a condom. But it's like, who writes that? He made me feel, like, totally slutty, like I'm just having all these random hookups and not using condoms or whatever. So then I wrote him this nasty message back saying he was bad in bed, which was kind of mean, but I really felt like he deserved it 'cause I cried for, like, two days over that. And I mean why did I deserve to cry? And why did he say all that stuff about wanting to see me when he really didn't mean any of it? I mean *why*? I also told him he'd better find my bra."

"But you didn't really lose your bra."

"No, but I didn't want to seem like I was lying."

"I just hate myself for this. I hate myself for caring about any of this. I have a paper that I should be working on, and instead I'm worrying about this idiot."

"Yeah, but don't beat yourself up, Led. It's not your fault."

Leda looked out her bedroom window. It was still bright out, but it was getting later. She could swear she smelled the cedar windowpane and the dust from behind the computer.

"It isn't my fault, but I know I can't stop it, and that's what I hate."

The girls talked for a little while longer. Anne mentioned a fight she had with Luke regarding his reluctance to make their relationship Facebook-official.

"He says, 'Why does it matter?' but he clearly just doesn't want people to know," she said.

She told Leda that she'd leave Luke if he wouldn't really commit to her, but Leda knew better. She'd heard Anne on so many occasions suffer through such atrocities, and it never really changed. Sometimes she'd be with a guy who treated her better; other times she'd be with a guy who'd treated her worse. The selfishness of the men never wavered, and she was always caught at the mercy of someone else's whim.

Leda heard Anne say: "Luke is just a very sensitive person," and promised herself, *I will never be like Anne. I will never do something this destructive to myself again.*

After she got off the phone, she checked Facebook for the seventh time. She refreshed the page three times after that just to be sure, and between each refresh she went back to his profile. Then she decided to run a bath to take her mind off of it. She played Miles Davis's "Blue in Green" on repeat and stayed in the water until she became dizzy from the steam. After that she ate a cheese and avocado sandwich. The bread was pretty stale, so she heated it in the microwave beforehand.

As the light in her apartment darkened into the familiar evening sable, she sat illuminated by her computer screen in the same haze that could not be amended by a bath or a sandwich or Miles Davis. She clicked between Facebook and her e-mail, as it was the only contact information she had listed on her profile. As she clicked between the two, in her lap was Balzac's *Old Goriot. You shall sound the depths of feminine corruption, and measure the immensity of the miserable vanity of men,* she read, then refreshed the page. *But if you have any real feeling, hide it like a treasure; never let it be suspected or you will be lost. You would no longer be the executioner then but the victim. If you ever fall in love, guard your secret well!* And she refreshed the page.

It was late, and she didn't receive many new e-mails, but she still hoped. At around eleven she got one from an animal rights group with the subject line: "Skinned Alive." Against her better judgment she clicked the accompanying video. It was about the fur trade. In the video she watched as they ripped the skins off live raccoons. One image would haunt her forever and ever, even as the skin on her own hands became callused and loose with age, even as she was too old to remember most things, she'd think of it. The raccoon was tied to a board or a tree by its tail. There was a lady standing beside it pulling and pulling the skin off of its body inch by inch, as if it weren't a living being. The animal struggled and fought a futile fight. It did not know that there was no hope. Leda watched that raccoon fighting against its own death. And after that she could not sleep. When she blinked she saw it every time, and there were so many blinks that night. So many little deaths in her eyes. She thought of Alex too. And in between it all she was alone in her apartment.

—◦✑◦—

CHAPTER 13

Remembering

"I JUST THINK THAT SHE COMES ACROSS AS SUPER NEEDY AND OBSES-sive, and I just think that it's, like, well, why did she sleep with him? I mean, she couldn't have really thought that a hookup with some random guy was really going to turn into anything real," Pinched Bralette said.

"I have to agree with that. I think most people who have random hookups don't really think it will last," a short, self-indulgent boy named Hunter said.

She didn't have it in her to listen to the group today. She took notes as best she could, unsure of anything that she felt, or what time it was, or whether there really was anything beyond her breathing in that moment. The voices of the people around her were clear and distinguishably their own. She wrote "Everyone has a voice that is their own" on her paper and underlined it twice as they complained about the first line of the story.

She thought of a ballet class she'd taken as a child. The instructor, Madeline, had lined the class of six-year-old girls up in a tight little row. Leda had a vivid memory of herself looking down at her leotard and her little ballet shoes. She'd tap the toe of her ballet slipper against the linoleum because she loved the sound of it. After lining them up Madeline handed out a different animal hand puppet to each girl. The girls were meant to dance with the puppets on their hands. Leda wanted the horse or the cat puppet; she'd have settled happily for the dog or peacock; the only one she didn't want was the dinosaur. *Just not the dinosaur. Please, anything but the dinosaur.* She got the dinosaur. When Madeline handed it to her, pulling it taut over her little hand, she didn't complain. She'd learned the dance instructor had little affection for children or things they desired. She'd once sent home a little girl who cried over not getting the pink streamer.

After the puppets were in place, each child was instructed to take a leap over a small beanbag marker on the floor. Leda liked the little beanbag. She wanted to hold it in her palm and feel its weight, but she couldn't, so she just stood there with her dinosaur, tapping occasionally against the floor. She waited in line to take her leap. The girl in front of her, a dark-haired girl with bony shoulders and a white leotard, skimmed the edge of the beanbag with her foot as she landed, and Leda thought that she could do it better, that she could leap over it and not touch it at all. She got as far a running start as she could and leapt with all her childhood might, believing in her beanbag-leaping abilities, believing that she and this dinosaur were really dancing. Her mom took a picture of her in her midair euphoria and hung it up in a pink frame on her bedroom wall across from her bed. Every time she'd look at it she'd think of the dinosaur, and that it wasn't what she really wanted. She was leaping over the beanbag, though, and so really it was a good day, and this she would remember too.

"I don't like the whole thing about her hands being like the ocean or the water or whatever it is. I mean, what does that mean?" Hunter said.

No one ever questions songs, she thought. *No one ever questions what songs mean, you just listen to it, and you love it. Fuck you all.* She sang her favorite line of "Oblivion" over and over in her head. *It's my point of view. It's my point of view.*

Her phone vibrated in her bag. She looked down at it quickly; a girl she used to know from middle school had messaged her on Facebook. *What could she be messaging me about? What is it that is keeping me from screaming right now?*

The class continued in the way that it did. There was apparently so much wrong with her story, so much wrong with her. She thought of herself then, going to law school. Becoming a real estate agent. Something far away and tangible. She thought of herself in a gray pencil skirt saying, "Objection!" or "There's one and a half baths." *I'd look good in a pencil skirt,* she thought. Years later she'd order one from Nordstrom, but when she tried it on she'd think it made her look hippy. It didn't, not at all. She looked long and lean in it, and when she pulled her hair back, standing sideways, looking at her reflection in the mirror, she looked maybe the most beautiful she had ever looked. Despite her intention of sending it right back, she'd neglect to return it and would find it months later buried in a hall closet, creased in a plastic bag. She'd donate it to charity. "It's brand-new. Somebody should get some use out of it," she'd say as she handed it over. *As if "brand-new" could mean something in this context,* she'd think.

As the class began to wind down, she checked the clock and promised herself ice cream at home. *In a half hour you'll have ice cream.* Patricia pulled herself forward in the way she always did when she was about to speak, slow and level like a great ship. *Here we go,* Leda thought. *Now she is going to tell me why I suck. I know I suck. Let's go home and have ice cream and be a lawyer.*

"Thank you, class, I appreciate everyone's comments on this very interesting piece that Leda has turned in. I'd like to start off first by saying that I don't, for the most part, really agree with anyone's comments. I think this is what I would describe as an honest piece. This retelling of a bad one-night stand is vulnerable and painful, and, quite frankly, brave. And while I appreciate Abby's point that the heroine comes across as needy, or obsessive, or dependent on a man, I'd say that that is what is sort of genius about this. Now it is debatable whether or not the character succeeds here, but I'd hesitate to call her a failure. And the story itself is far from a failure." Patricia leaned toward Leda, handing off her notes. "And if I had a crystal ball, I'd say this story will be published."

Suddenly it was as if air had been pumped back into her lungs. She felt like her body was rising, as if she were leaping far above the class and their comments, not touching them even along the edges. It was the absolute most fearless she could ever feel.

She wanted to thank Patricia as she left the class, but she didn't know what to say so instead she just smiled. Patricia smiled back and started walking out with her.

"I do really think that story is quite an accomplishment, and you need to send it out to publications. Have you been sending any of your work out?" she said.

"No, I mean, I really haven't. I've always felt that my stuff lacks a certain polish."

Patricia shook her head, steady as a ship. "It's easy to always question and to never feel quite ready, but you are ready, and you should be sending your stuff out."

Leda tried to keep pace with Patricia's step. Her walk was heavy and long. Something about her that could have been deduced from the way she spoke, and the thinness of her lips.

"It's so encouraging to hear you say that. It's just so easy to get discouraged."

"Don't be." Patricia turned toward the elevator. "Are you going this way?" she asked.

"No, I have another class on this floor."

"Well, if you ever want to stop by my office for a chat, please feel free."

"Thank you. I'll definitely do that sometime," Leda said.

"Great. Well, you have a good night."

"Bye."

As Leda walked away she regretted not saying "Thanks, you too," after Patricia had said "have a good night," but the thought was little disruption to what she would consider to be one of the best conversations of her life. She'd relive it years down the line, remembering it as Patricia having told her she was a great writer. She'd forget the long, heavy walk and feeling sorry about saying "Bye" instead of "Thanks, you too." She would remember the way Patricia said: "Don't be." And she'd remember how when she got home she immediately sent off a story to *The New Yorker* even though she knew it wouldn't get published.

"It's more symbolic than anything," she'd have said if someone asked her why she submitted it, but of course no one ever did. She was alone as she sent it, she was alone in her "Bye," she was alone eating the bowl of cookie dough ice cream and how sweet it was.

CHAPTER 14

❧

Success

THE NEXT SIX MONTHS AND TWO WEEKS OF LEDA'S LIFE WERE UNREC-
ognizably calm. She found a certain focus within herself that would
only be revisited the summer after her granddaughter was born. Her
class schedule was fairly light, and on weekends she spent more time
with her family. Her mom would tell her that she "looked healthy,"
and that she "seemed happy," and although Leda wouldn't take
much notice of her mother saying these things, they were true. She
read a lot of Flannery O'Connor and on Wednesdays got soup at an
organic soup place. She went to three shows with Anne at a little
music club downtown. At one of the shows she got hit on by a cute
boy named Caleb. He was tall and baby faced, and he told her that
his band played at the club Monday nights.

"I have a band and we play Monday nights," he said.

"Do you?" she said.

She didn't believe him about the band, but it felt good to flirt.
And when she left that night, she could feel herself float. Anne said:
"Why didn't you get his number? Why didn't you want him to buy
you a drink?" And Leda said: "After what happened with Alex I do
not want to go out with anybody right now." And Anne said: "What
about marriage?" And Leda said: "I don't know." And she really
didn't know.

Most of her focus was on her writing, and she wrote some of her
favorite pieces during this time. It was then that she first considered
writing a novel. It was then that she saw herself as put-together and
capable. When she blinked visions of how she considered herself, it

was herself in a Chanel suit and heels clicking down the sidewalk. It was her linear by the way she stood, linear by posture.

On the last day of this six-month-and-two-week stretch of clarity, she opened a window in her apartment that she had formerly believed to be warped shut. The landlord had pointed it out when she moved in.

"That window won't open, but all the others do," he said. "It's warped."

She was lying around in pajamas and watching bad TV all day. It had been very cold, and so she'd decided to spend her Sunday inside. She'd made pasta and called her mom and wrote a poem about pumpkin carving. On an impulse she tried to open the window. She had never tried to do it before. The window stuck a bit, but as she bore her weight pushing up against the pane, it loosed and drew open with a long, heavy slide. The cold air hit her in a crisp, nice way. Outside was her city block and the darkness. She could hear distant traffic, but she didn't really listen for it. The stars were fairly visible despite the brightness of the streetlamps. And when she breathed she could feel a coldness in her lungs that felt as young and fresh as she did then. Clicking heels in her mind, linear as an impulse.

When she went to bed, she shut the window but left it open a crack. She always slept better in the cold. And when she woke up she didn't remember any of her dreams from the night, but it was morning so she felt the strange kind of promise of a new day.

PART 2

—◦❧◦—

CHAPTER 15

Meeting

SHE MET HIM IN AN ART APPRECIATION CLASS. SHE'D SWITCHED TO IT only moments before registration closed because she had a strange feeling that she should. Originally, she'd signed up for an art history class, but on a brisk and pulsing whim she switched. How fateful that decision would be. How blissfully ignorant she was, believing herself the arbiter of her own life. No more predictable than the cinnamon she'd sprinkle on the foam of her latte, each flaking granule falling as evenly and imprecisely as she met John.

He was tall and blond, and when he spoke he seemed quiet, something she immediately liked. She first noticed him about a month into class. That morning she twisted her ankle so she took a cab to school. It was colder than it had been, and she treated herself to a hot chocolate. She held it in her hands; the heat through her gloves was mesmerizingly warm against the winter morning, so much so that she mistakenly thought the person in front of her was holding the door open for her. She walked right into the closing door, spilling the hot chocolate all over her gloves. Her hands went from hot and burning to unbearably freezing as the liquid quickly cooled the drenched wool. She pulled her gloves off and didn't know what to do with them. They were cheap and soaked, so she threw them in a trashcan on the street corner. It was really the only practical thing she could do. When she finally made it to class, she could feel her ankle sore from the stairs (the elevators were broken), and her hands were still cold. *This day is already hell,* she thought.

The art appreciation class had been a disappointment. The professor was in her mid-thirties. She was a mousy woman with a bad pixie haircut who wanted so desperately to be hipper than she was. She'd name-drop indie bands that she assumed the students were listening to, and most days she'd blast Pandora through her iPhone as they shuffled into the room. Occasionally she'd mouth along to lyrics of songs by The Cure and Leda would think, *Why are you trying to be so hip? Don't you realize you aren't hip? You are just as not-hip as the rest of us, only you are older, and it is time to let it go.* Her name was Cheryll with two *l*'s, a fact she explained the first day of class.

"My mom named me Chantel, which I hated, so I changed it to Cheryll. Why the extra *l*? Honestly, I couldn't tell you," she said. Leda believed that Cheryll didn't know why she spelled her name like that. She believed that there were probably many things that she did and didn't know why. Cheryll taught the class by showing slides of different art pieces and asking whether the students liked them or not. Whatever the students said or thought, Cheryll would listen and nod and always agree.

It was slow and grating and Leda found herself for the most part chronically disengaged. Occasionally Cheryll would say something interesting about a piece or an artist, but generally it was just some student rattling off their issues with Ellsworth Kelly.

"Now, I'm very curious as to what you all think of this piece," Cheryll said as she clicked to a slide of Vermeer's painting *Girl Reading a Letter at an Open Window.*

No one raised their hand, a common reaction from the bemused class.

"Come on, guys, one of you must think something about this gnarly painting." Still no one responded.

"Well, how about we hear from someone we haven't yet," Cheryll said, reaching for something, anything at all.

"Laura, what do you think of the piece?"

Laura was a girl Leda'd had several classes with in the past. She rarely spoke and had a nervous laugh. The one meaningful encounter Leda had with her was being paired up with her in her modernist literature class. The two of them were meant to give a presentation on a section of "The Waste Land." Before they began Laura said,

"I'm not really good with poetry." And that was about all Laura said. Leda was left to navigate through the presentation alone. At the end of it Laura turned to her and said, "Thanks. I'm sorry." After that Leda made a point of never sitting next to her for fear of ever having to work with her again.

Laura looked up at the painting. She'd been drawing or writing on her notebook. Her skin was olive and shined in the overhead projector light. She looked terrified.

"I think it's ummmmmmmm. I like it?"

"Why do you like it?" Cheryll asked.

"I don't know."

"Come on, there's no wrong answers. What is it you like about the painting?"

"I think ummmm. It's ummm. I don't really know, actually. I guess I just like it. I'm not really sure why or anything."

"You don't know at all?"

"No, not really, ummmm sorry."

"Not even a little?"

"Umm, ummm."

Cheryll, who usually by this point would concede and move on to harassing a better-prepared student, stood stock-still; her body posture was stiff and her expression resolved. Her usual demeanor was small and yearning, peppy and desperate, but it was as if a calm had come over her. As if she'd all at once been made aware of what a fool she was for wanting to be hip so badly in a group of college students who were supposed to respect her. It was as if she'd suddenly realized her life was as futile as her haircut.

"Well, you must have *some* idea why you like it. I mean, you're saying that you like it. What do you like about it? I don't think it's a really hard question to answer."

"Hahahahaha," Laura nervously laughed much too loudly. "I don't know."

"The colors? The light? The subject matter? What? I mean, this is Vermeer. I wouldn't call his work exactly inaccessible. I could easily tell you a thousand things I like about this painting and you can't tell me *one*?"

A palpable tension fell over the class. Leda looked around quickly. Everyone seemed to be as terrified of the ensuing awkwardness as she was. She looked at Laura, who had turned purple in the impressionist glow.

"I, I, I'm, well, I'm, I, I'm—the colors?"

"What is it that you like about the colors?" Cheryll snapped back.

"They are ummm. Well, I don't know exactly—"

"You don't know what it is you like about the colors? You like the painting because of the 'colors'"—Cheryll air-quoted "colors"—"but you don't know what it is you like about the 'colors'?" She air-quoted again.

"No, I—I like the way that they're vibrant, I think."

Good girl, Leda thought. *Don't let her rip you to shreds.*

"What do you mean exactly?"

"I, I don't know—"

"Again you 'don't know'? I'm not asking you to split the atom here. I'm expecting you to know why you like something. I mean, for god's sake, if you don't know why you like anything how can you live your life? How can you wake up and pick out what clothes you'll wear? Or what cereal you want to eat for breakfast? Or who you want to fuck?"

The word *fuck* hung in the air. Leda had heard plenty of professors use the word, and Cheryll of course used it every chance she got. But this was the only time in her life she would hear it used in this way. It was penetrative and violating, stripping and vulgar. She could imagine Laura then as a child sitting at a large table dwarfed by everything around her or naked under the weight of some hideous man. Her fat rolls exposed and jiggling as the man ferociously *fucked* her.

And then John raised his hand. He did it in such a way that even if she wanted to, Cheryll couldn't have ignored it, the bend in his elbow or his expression, strong and still. Leda would remember how blue his eyes seemed, how even as he was sitting she could notice his height.

"John," Cheryll said.

"Could you tell me about that Tom Hunter painting that was inspired by this? I saw it in an exhibit once, and it was really incredible," he said.

"That is one of my absolute favorite paintings of all time." Cheryll's face softened. The tension in the room instantly defused and Laura was spared. Cheryll continued on about the painting; she smiled and gestured as she spoke, enlivened by the question. Leda watched John nod in response, his face kind.

He seems like someone who would be a good boyfriend, she thought.

That night she texted Anne: "I think I have a crush on someone in class."

She'd save that text, and years later she'd reread it to remember a feeling that was as fleeting as that girl with her letter by the window and the all-surrounding *fuck.*

CHAPTER 16

———⌒⌒———

The First Date

JOHN AND SHE HAD BEEN HANGING OUT AFTER EVERY CLASS SINCE two weeks after "the Laura incident," as they had started to refer to it. He would walk her to her next class, and they'd talk and flirt right up until she had to go in. She liked the way he never rushed her. The patient way he seemed as happy as she was just to be there. Until then she had firmly believed that most guys would spend only as little time as was needed to get a girl to stay around. "You always want to be there more than they do," Anne would say. And it was true. Leda's ex-boyfriend was a myriad of attention deficit–like behavior. Sometimes she'd see him, sometimes she wouldn't. Sometimes he'd call, sometimes he wouldn't. She would, though; she would always want to be there or want to talk. Before meeting John, she assumed that it was just the difference between men and women, that women were somehow kinder and more patient. With John she became reassured in the possibility that humanity wasn't singularly female.

By the end of the semester a tension had emerged between them. Leda would stand in the hall with John, talking about cats and the potential of homemade mayonnaise, and all the while she'd be thinking: *Ask me out. Ask me out. Ask me out.* The waiting grew tiresome, and she started to worry that maybe she was misjudging the whole thing. *Maybe there's something wrong with me. I really hate my arms. I wish I had thinner arms.* Anne would ask every day about the progress of the flirtation, and at a certain point Leda began responding with things like, "Yeah, I don't know. I'm kind of over the whole thing." Then one day she walked past the school's café window and John tapped the glass to get her attention. He motioned for her to come in, and right then she knew that she was wrong about all of it, and that he hadn't noticed her arms.

She came in and sat beside him at the counter. They chatted about school and their upcoming finals. She could smell his coffee when he'd lift his cup, an aroma that with all its bitterness suddenly smelled sweet to her.

"Are you free this Saturday?" he asked.

"Yes," she said.

They talked awhile longer and exchanged phone numbers. Leda waved at him through the window as she left. She felt truly happy and light; the prospect of a date with John calmed the frantic energy of being single. In a few days she'd be on a date with someone. Life seemed in control. Life seemed brilliant. On the train ride home she watched a girl in a bad skirt silently sing along to music. She tried to guess what she was singing. She texted Anne in the places where she had service.

"We're going out!" she texted.

"Ahh!! So exciting!! It sure took him long enough ☺"

She didn't respond to Anne's text for a while. *Whatever, Anne. Just be happy for me.* The light from outside filled the train momentarily. Leda got a text from her mom.

"Look at this picture I found. Three years old," it said over a picture of herself in a hot pink bathing suit with a Ninja Turtle hat. There was a Band-Aid on each knee. *You skin your knees like that so much when you're little and you can never imagine a life with unskinned knees, but then suddenly you stop skinning your knees and everything is different.*

"I love it ♥," she responded.

She laid her head back against the window. She was tired, still elated though, still light, still in a glow. *I'll wear my red shirt that makes my boobs look huge,* she thought. The window felt cool on her temple. She knew she'd wear her good underwear even though they wouldn't have sex. *Something to look forward to,* she thought. *And is there really anything better than something to look forward to? Am I doing anything but trying to feel good?*

The night before the date she could hardly sleep. She kept living hypothetical conversations over and over in her head as she lay there.

I'll say: You look handsome.

And he'll say: You look gorgeous.

And I'll say: Thanks.

And then maybe I'll wink or shrug my shoulders, kind of.

And then at dinner he'll say: What do you like to write?

And I'll say: I like writing about women. I write for women.

And he'll say: You only write for women?

And I'll say: Yes, I'm fine with that. Aren't you?

And he'll say: Yes.

And he'll smile in the way he does. He'll get what I mean. He'll see me as I am.

And then when he leaves he'll try to kiss me, and I will kiss him back, but I won't open my mouth really. I mean, I will but only like this and only a little bit, like this. And she kissed her arm. *I should really try and go to sleep.*

As she got ready for her date she let herself fully indulge in all of it. She played OutKast's "So Fresh, So Clean" as she danced naked and got dressed. She looked at herself in the mirror. *I am kind of linear,* she thought, *even though I ate a lot of chocolate through finals. I look like sex.* She wore her darkest lipstick and her best push-up bra. When she left her apartment, she looked at her reflection in the mirror and winked at herself. It was the only winking she'd do on the date. She'd explain it all to John two summers later.

"It's like the date is with myself. Seeing you is always nice, but getting prettied up and feeling beautiful, that's all it's really about."

"So relationships are about you feeling pretty?" he asked.

"Not totally, but basically," she said. "But when you think about it, isn't everything in life about feeling pretty?"

They had planned to meet up in front of a coffee shop in Harvard Square. She looked for him outside, scouring over the little court-yard, anticipating his tallness. She checked her phone. No text. He was late. After a while, standing around outside made her feel self-conscious so she decided to wait for him inside. She sat in a chair by the window, a seat away from a gangly-looking boy with a laptop. The boy was young and attractive in a sort of brooding way. Leda noticed he was staring at her, and so she smiled at him. *Maybe this brooding boy likes me.* She tapped her phone against the bar and sighed. The boy continued to look up at her here and there, smiling, catching her gaze, and acting as if he were about to speak. He may have thought many things about what to say or what to do to attract her. He may have had her if he'd thought of something to say. She would think of it in her early forties, one afternoon as she cleaned out the attic. The dust settled around her as she pulled out a box of unused frames. She'd lift a flap of the box, the smell of cardboard, the light filtered in thin lines of the attic window; she would think: *If that boy had talked to me who might I have become?*

Moments later John appeared in the courtyard. He stood with his hands in his pockets and looked clumsy and nervous. It was endearing. She got up, paying a light glance to the brooding boy who was watching her leave.

She ran up to him. "John," she said. And he turned around. "You're so late," she said.

"I'm sorry. Did you think I wasn't coming?" he said.

"I wasn't really worried."

"I was going to text you, but my phone died on the way here."

"Likely story." She smiled. *Does he know that I am flirting? Because I am trying to flirt. Maybe I don't know what flirting is. Maybe I never have flirted and I should be at home eating leftover spaghetti.*

"Should we go eat?" she asked.

"Let's do it."

The sun was low in the sky and over the river the light had dissolved from blue to copper as it touched down on the current. The air smelled like springtime, the brisk freshness of it something she would later associate with the early days of dating. A tall, thin girl in a romper walked her bike past, looking first at Leda and then at John and then back to her. Leda felt a rewarding sense of superiority. She shot a glance at the girl and smiled. *I'm the prettiest,* she thought, but it wasn't even a thought at all. It was more a rising up in her, a boiling that would rise and fall her whole life through, a barometer of self-worth.

They chose the Mediterranean place on the corner. She had only ever been there once before, on a particularly terrible blind date with a pudgy British guy who wore a bowler hat and informed her that "rape accusations ruin the reputation of many fine men."

"If they don't want to be accused of rape, maybe they shouldn't rape," she'd said.

She thought about telling John about the date, but considering he'd suggested the restaurant, she worried he'd take it the wrong way.

They ordered a hummus and falafel vegetable platter. Leda had been conscious not to order meat, as about a month before John mentioned he was a vegetarian. When he asked what she wanted to order, she hardly let him finish the question, saying in a quick over-panicked voice, "Vegetable platter."

"I don't mind if you order meat, you know," he said.

She took a deep breath and calmed herself, figuring there was only room for one nervous, vegetable-related outburst. "No, I really do want the vegetable platter."

"You're sure?"

"Yes, definitely."

As she ate dinner she worried over having something on her face or in her teeth. She unconsciously covered her mouth with her hand as she chewed. She didn't want to eat the last falafel even though she was still hungry. *I'll eat the leftover spaghetti at home,* she thought. He paid for dinner, which was something she wasn't used to but always hoped for. Her mom had told her, "The man should always pay for dinner." She'd considered this piece of advice an outdated relic of a bygone dating era.

"Mom, things are different now," she had said.

"Things will never be different. Women will always give more of themselves to men; at the very least let them pay for dinner."

With her ex-boyfriend she'd split the bill or paid for both of them pretty much every time. He treated her about four times in the six-month relationship, and when they broke up because he wanted to move to North Carolina to join an energy-efficient farm, she came to realize how foolish it had all been. She'd tell friends, "I looked back and thought: All that money I spent and for what?"

After dinner she and John got tea and sat on a bench in the court-yard in front of the coffee shop where they had met up at the beginning of the date. It was cool out now that the sun had gone down completely. She shivered slightly at first, but drinking the tea kept her warm. John talked in the quiet way she had begun to adore. He asked her about living in Cambridge and what she liked to write about and if she'd ever been published.

"I like to write about women," she said. "But I haven't really been published. Well, actually, I was published in this school journal, but I don't think it really counts."

"That most certainly counts. What was the story about?" he asked.

"It was about a girl whose friend wants to be in *Playboy,* and she's all against it, and then she ends up with the opportunity to be in it, and so she considers it even though she's this feminist and she thinks it's horrible and all that. For a minute she's flattered."

"Wow."

"Yeah, well, I feel like we all like to believe we're above wanting to feel pretty."

"Are you?"

"I don't think so."

Soon after, it was time to go home. It was getting late and her tea had grown completely cold. They walked together to the subway and had to part ways, as their trains ran in opposite directions. *Will he kiss me?* she thought, but at the same time didn't want it to happen. She wasn't sure why; it was anticipation and fear and tiredness from the night. She decided to hug him quick and to not give him the chance. "Goodbye, John. Text me," she said.

Their first kiss would take place on their second date, and it would be at the train station in a moment similar to this one. John would hold her shoulders and the kiss would be simple and short.

She sat on the train and watched John walking off from their first date. Her heart felt fluttered, as if someone had run their hands over it. An older woman who sat beside her started chatting with her about a play she had just seen. Leda nodded and asked all kinds of questions about how it was and where it was and who was in it. She was very interested in the play, as if she and this woman shared some experience that night that was exactly the same, a blazing exuberance between them that was intimate and destined to be brief. As the subway came to the woman's stop, they nodded to each other in a silent agreement about which neither of them knew.

When Leda got off the train she checked her phone, and then checked it again right after she got in the door of her apartment. He hadn't texted. *It's not reasonable for me to expect him to text tonight, but god I hope he does,* she thought. She ate cold leftover spaghetti standing at her counter. And as she put on her pajamas, she heard her phone buzz. It was one of the best sounds she would ever hear in her entire life. She wouldn't consider why or how it was possible to feel so different from the day before, to feel so much because a man sat beside her on a bench and listened to her talk and bought her a tea. She wouldn't ever believe how it could send her afloat and light her up and be everything to her.

"I like you," the text said.

CHAPTER 17

The Phone

AND SO BEGAN THE OBSESSION WITH HER PHONE, EVERY BUZZ, EVERY
vibration, every moment, needing it by her side, checking it nearly
constantly. The feeling of hope when she'd hear it or feel it at the
bottom of her bag and that utter, and merciless, joy at seeing his
name.

John

it would say and then she would open the text or answer the call, her
heart rising inside her throat, and she would always stop breathing
for a second and then swallow. The day she stopped the pattern of
heart rising, stop breathing, swallow was the day that the relationship actually became serious. It was a Tuesday and John had texted,
"What park? I'm on the corner now." They wouldn't commemorate
the moment, although they did happen to have cake later that night
by coincidence. The cake was red velvet and she had two pieces.

In those early days together, the pulse of her existence was beating almost entirely by when she'd hear from him. She'd check her
phone first thing when she woke up, before she could even fully
focus her eyes, when she still felt tired and weak from sleep. If he did
text her, the morning would seem more lucid; she'd be energized for
the day ahead, ready and excited for the next texts. At night they'd
always talk before bed. He often went to bed later than she did and
so she'd stay up and wait for him, sometimes so late that she'd have
to sit up to keep from falling asleep, but then she'd hear her phone go

off, and she'd feel rejuvenated, her heart rising, her breath stopping, her swallow. "Hi," she'd say.

She and John could easily talk for hours. They could maintain conversations about the most useless topics.

"I don't understand why people like string cheese."

"I like string cheese," he said.

"I'm not surprised you like string cheese. You like all sorts of disgusting food."

"But string cheese isn't disgusting. String cheese is like a phenomenon of cheese."

"You would think that, wouldn't you, because you love disgusting food," she said.

Anne was jealous of it. It became a wedge in their friendship, one that would take years to fully play out and was mostly handled with catty remarks and the occasional backhanded compliment.

"How is it possible to talk on the phone for five hours with someone?" Anne said as they ate pizza.

"I don't know. We just talk about everything."

Anne shifted in her seat. "I just think that's, like, a really long time. I mean . . . five hours just seems crazy."

"You know—but we don't realize it's five hours." Leda felt compelled to defend herself, her pizza growing cold in the attempt. *I can't really explain the boat conversation, but maybe she'll understand if she realizes how funny the boat conversation was.*

"We had this conversation about boats where . . . you know how boats can sometimes have, like . . . I don't know what they're called. They're, like, those big things. It was just, like, about the *Titanic* basically, but my point is it was really funny and so we just ended up talking about boats."

"Boats?"

"Yeah." She took a bite of crust. It was cold.

"You guys are weird. Five-hour phone conversations are weird," Anne said.

"Don't you and Jory talk on the phone?" Jory was the guy Anne was currently dating.

"No. We text, of course, but you know how I don't like to talk on the phone. It's just different. It's more about passion with us."

And that's when Leda realized Anne was jealous.

"Passion is everything, isn't it?" she said.

Anne texted less frequently after that, but Leda didn't mind. She had John now, and anyone else's texts just seemed like a letdown anyway. She'd feel her phone go off and then reach for it with so much hope and anticipation, only to be dashed by friends and family. *I don't care about your damn haircut, Katrina!*

All of this was a certain kind of wonderful suffering, a pain she put herself through. She'd send a text, and if John didn't text back fairly soon, she'd wonder, and she'd worry, and she'd let her day be so wielded by his word. "How are you?" and that was happiness. She'd be over the moon and flying through her life, looking down on everything else so shrinking below her.

She remembered an old friend who was dating a terrible guy. His name was Omar, and he was always showing up or not showing up or talking to her or not talking to her on whatever whim he felt. The girl's name was Allison. She was tall and blond and really, really pretty. Leda remembered envying the way she could effortlessly wear such low-rise jeans. They took a photography class together and Allison would often talk about Omar and all of their problems. Leda would listen but think her own thoughts as Allison would tell horrible story after horrible story, all the while saying things to the effect of, "But he does care about me—I know he cares about me— he does care about me." She remembered Allison telling her about how Omar had invited her out for dinner, one of the rare occasions that he actually did, and then halfway through started rushing her out so he could go hang out with his friends.

"We were only there a half hour," Allison said.

"What did he say to make you leave, though?" Leda said.

"He didn't really say anything. He kept being like, 'Are you done? Are you done?' I just knew all of a sudden that he had plans so I stopped eating." She stood on her tiptoes to pin her print to the clothesline to dry. It was of a flower with raindrops on it. Only part of it was out of focus. "I had my hair cut that day and everything 'cause I was so excited that we were actually going to go out for dinner."

"But that sounds so crazy. Why would you stop eating?"

Allison kept moving as she spoke. She looked even more brilliant in the red of the darkroom light. "I just know how he acts when he has plans."

"But what I mean is, why would you do that just because he had plans? Why not eat really slowly? Why not tell him it's not okay to act like a dick?"

"I know. But he did text me like an hour later . . . See." She smiled and held out her phone. The text said, "Hey."

Leda never met Omar, but she did see him across the quad once. She and Allison were on a break midway through class. It was a warm spring day and they sat opposite each other at a picnic table. Allison smiled and laughed and looked so blond and so pretty. All of a sudden her face changed, and she jumped up and swung over beside Leda.

"Oh my god, he's over there," she said.

"Where?"

"Over there. Do you want to meet him?"

"Yeah, where though?"

Allison pointed to a very short, fat man standing with a group of guys. He was laughing and talking, and he looked so small and fat.

"That's Omar?!" Leda couldn't believe that this was the man who had brought so much misery to Allison's life. *He looks like you could just flick him,* she thought. *And there he is just laughing like that. As stupid as hell.*

"I don't know if I should introduce you," Allison said. "He looks busy."

"You've slept with this person, right?"

"Yes."

"Well, then, who cares! Just go up and talk to him."

"It's . . . I . . . ummm. I'll introduce you another time."

The last time she saw Allison was the day of their final. Allison said something at the beginning of class about a fight or some disagreement that she and Omar had. She said she'd cried all weekend and hadn't eaten. But she didn't seem that sad, she seemed so used to it all and ready to move on, and so they talked about other things, about the summer ahead and Allison wanting to go to Europe next year to study abroad. All the plans seemed good, as if she were letting go of it all, and it seemed then as if she were happy. And then in the middle of talking about Paris and Milan and boating at her parents' lake house she said, "He hasn't texted me." Leda could only see her back as she spoke, her thin back and her arm reaching out, supporting herself on the photo enlarger beside her, the curve of the muscle, her elbow, her wrist. And that's when she noticed that Allison's arm was shaking.

She hadn't really thought much about Allison until meeting John, and then she only thought of her once. It was a Thursday, and she decided she needed bronzer. She took a shower and lay on her bed naked, flipping through a Victoria's Secret catalog. There was this picture of a model wearing a pink floral corset. "Spring into Spring," it said. Leda didn't care for the corset, but the girl's contoured face and languid expression made her think, *Maybe I should get bronzer.*

She ate an apple as she walked to the train and texted John about getting dinner later. She hadn't seen him that Saturday because he said he was busy. He hadn't said why, and although she didn't really think anything of it, it still bothered her that he hadn't given an excuse. They'd talked that night, and he hadn't mentioned anything in particular that he did, which made it even worse. Anne said, "So he just didn't even give an excuse?" Leda said back, "No, but I'm not worried." And then she ate nearly an entire package of Oreos.

As she got to her stop she checked her phone. He hadn't texted back. She walked the six blocks to the mall and checked it again, nothing.

In the makeup store she immediately felt overwhelmed. Apparently there were many, many bronzers, and she certainly had no sense of which one to choose. She checked her phone again. A salesgirl with green mascara asked her, "Do you need help?" Against her better judgment, Leda responded, "Yes, I'm looking for bronzer."

"What kind of bronzer are you looking for?" the girl asked.

"I don't know, actually . . ."

"Well, what does your skin look like in your most sun-kissed state?"

It was then that Leda regretted ever saying that she needed help. The girl took a test compact from the shelf.

"This is my absolute favorite. It's from this company called Irrational Discord. It has a very smooth, bold look."

She took a cotton makeup pad and wiped the sample bronzer.

"You always want to wipe the samples first," she cautioned.

Leda wondered whether she was speaking from experience. The girl wiped the top layer of powder off and then, taking a second pad, acquired a generous amount of bronzer.

"Just along your cheeks," she said, swiping the makeup across her face.

"Take a look."

Leda looked at herself in a nearby mirror. She didn't look more contoured at all. She did look her most sun-kissed, though. She looked as though the sun had kissed her many, many times.

"Do you love it?" the girl asked.

She knew that if she protested in any way, she'd be in for more time with the green mascara girl. She certainly didn't want to try on any more bronzers with her, nor did she imagine that the two of them would come to a consensus on what makeup aesthetic could be considered successful, but more than anything she wanted to check her phone and see if John had texted.

"I love it!" she said.

She checked her phone. John still hadn't texted. *It's been almost an hour, and I haven't heard from him all day,* she thought. She wiped her face almost immediately after the salesgirl walked off, but she held on to the Irrational Discord bronzer for some time before stealthily discarding it behind the liquid foundation. Leda had a sense that Green Mascara would be offended if she saw this, so she took great care that she did it while her back was turned.

After that she walked around and looked for an alternative bronzer. She tried one that was lighter. *Does it look like anything?* she thought, and she put it back and checked her phone. She tried two more that were still light. And then one that was redder. And then another one that was sort of dark and shimmery. She checked her phone three times in between trying them on and looking in the mirror, her expression increasingly more worried and forlorn, as it was reflected back to her. *Where is he? Maybe there's something wrong. Maybe he's dating someone else. Why am I not contoured?* She wiped her skin clean with alcohol for the sixth time and noticed that it had become red from all the wear. *Maybe I'll just get a lipstick instead,* she thought. She tried a red lipstick. A bold red lip was something she had always envisioned was possible somewhere in her life. In her mind she was the kind of girl who threw on bright red lipstick and laughed with her hands up, looking impossibly chic. But there in that mirror it was just her and her worn cheeks and residual sun-kiss and bright red lips staring back at her, worried and tired, and it was then that she thought of Allison and her shaking arm. *I'm not better than her and her shaking.* She wiped off the lipstick and left the store.

She checked her phone only once the rest of that night. When she thought of not hearing from John it made her ill; she felt a nausea that was specific and markedly foolish. She made a point to try not to think about it. She ate pizza and read Margaret Atwood's *Cat's Eye. I don't collect many marbles because I'm not a very good shot,* it said. Without meaning to, she fell asleep and had a very specific dream about having sex with the boy from the bagel shop. He had a very large penis in the dream, so large that he couldn't fit it in her, but she wasn't worried; she just kept laughing with her hands up in the air. "It's such discord," she said to him.

In the middle of the night she woke up to pee and found that John had tried calling five times. He'd sent seven texts as well, explaining that he'd lost his phone and that he was so sorry and that he would have loved to go out for dinner. It made her happier and more gratified in that moment than any of the morning texts, or the five-hour conversations, or anything else John had ever said or done before. It was nice to know that at least he was shaking too. She didn't text back until the next day.

CHAPTER 18

The First Time Having Sex with John

AFTER HER EXPERIENCE WITH ALEX, LEDA DECIDED THAT SHE WANTED to wait before she had sex with anyone else. She'd express this idea to John at an Indian restaurant on their fifth date.

"I think it's better if we wait to have sex." She didn't look away from her piece of naan as she spoke.

"I think that's a good idea," he said.

"I knew you would," she said. "I just really wanted to be clear about everything before it gets too serious."

"Are you worried about things getting too serious?" he asked.

"No, I'm not worried."

John smiled. She watched him scoop saag aloo onto his rice and take a bite. She admired how thoughtless he seemed in the motion. He ate in a way that was abandoned of all self-consciousness. She always found herself eating meticulously when in front of friends or dates, taking small bites, covering her face with her hand as she chewed, obsessively wiping the corners of her mouth with her napkin. Later she'd notice John maintained the same type of disregard about his bathroom habits. Her whole life she struggled with the fear that people would take notice of how long she was missing after excusing herself. *They'll think I'm pooping,* she'd think as she tried to poop as quickly as possible. John, on the other hand, never seemed to worry. Sometimes he'd be in the bathroom for a short time and then other times he'd be gone for longer. She'd ask him about this soon after their six-month anniversary. She had a meeting with a professor in the morning. John waited with her outside of the professor's office.

"I really have to go to the bathroom," she said.

"Then go."

"No, I don't want to be in there for too long. It'll be weird."

"Who cares?"

"But she'll be waiting for me."

"Then she'll wait."

"No! That's crazy."

"You're the one being crazy. If you have to go to the bathroom, go to the bathroom," John said.

"Don't you care if people are waiting for you when you're in the bathroom?"

"No, why would I care?"

"Because then they'll judge you that you've been in there for a long time."

John shrugged his shoulders. "It seems insane. It's not like they don't go to the bathroom too."

Leda considered then that maybe neurosis over bodily functions was a purely female trait.

"I won't be able to go anyway," she said.

All the fear went away eventually. Soon she ate wildly and ravenously in front of him. No longer concerned that he'd judge if she ate too much, no longer needing to eat a second dinner at home after the date, the silent leftover spaghetti and its guiltless indulgence as she'd stand by the fridge still dressed up from going out. The bathroom habits would also break down after living together, and eventually she wouldn't even worry about pooping with the door open. No longer afraid to be human or unfemale. Real intimacy estimated by audible farts.

It wasn't easy to abstain from sex with John. Of all the men she'd made out with (there had only been five), she never felt like she did when she was with him. With most of them she needed to convince herself that this was good, that their tongues and all that saliva were somehow what it was meant to be. *This is kissing. This is just what it's like,* she'd think.

One of the boys told her she was a good kisser. His name was Neal. He had red hair and a swollen-type face. She knew she should return the compliment, but all the while, as he kissed her, and touched her face with his roundish, feminine hands, and put his tongue delicately this way and that, as if he had written out a plan for kissing her years before they had ever met, she had been thinking that she never, ever wanted to have sex with this person. She imagined his roundish, feminine penis and him delicately thrusting it in her this way and that. So she said, "Thanks, you're something too."

The other boys were similar to Neal in the sense that they always seemed to be thinking of ways to impress her. They seemed to kiss with so much thought, so much pressure on themselves to get it right, as if she would pull away from them and say, "Wow, you really are as amazing as you wish you were in your head!" Leda wondered if sex was something that burdened men in the same way bathroom habits had burdened her.

John was different. John was rough. He was uninhibited, unthinking. He held her and dove for the things he wanted. It was as if his body were responding to her body without any conscious effort or control, an abandonment so rich and unyielding that she felt almost shocked by it. Never had she considered that this is what she could want from a man. There was in her a person who would emerge in these times that was so different from the person she had thought herself to be. She could hear her own voice, pale and fragile like a squeak or a listless cry. *How frightening to love being so small,* she thought.

Leda decided to have sex with John soon after she realized she was in love with him. It was raining and they had been in the Public Garden. They walked along the center pond and saw ducklings. It was warm but not hot, and John held her hand. How good she felt with her hand in his. If she had drawn a picture of her hand in John's it would have looked as if her hand was so enveloped that it hardly existed. But if she could have expressed the feeling of it, she would have drawn her own hand large and raised up, bigger than the pond, bigger than anything else; she may not have even drawn him at all.

They sat on a bench for a while and watched the day pass. John told her about having never been on the Swan Boats, and she thought they should take a boat ride together sometime.

"Let's ride the Swan Boats next weekend," she said.

"That would be great," he said.

The rain picked up, and they ran for cover in a nearby Starbucks. John grabbed her arm.

"We have to outrun the rain," he said, weaving her through trees unnecessarily. *I wish I could outrun the rain forever,* she thought.

He ordered an espresso and she ordered a tea. They stood together and waited for their drinks. He made fun of a man wearing a fedora with a feather.

"Look at that asshole," he whispered, nudging her to the direction of the man.

Her tea was made first, and John handed it to her.

She walked over to the milk and sugar in a viscerally hurried manner. The tea clouded with milk as she poured it. She couldn't find a stirrer, but she didn't care. She was thinking of something he'd said earlier in the day.

As she headed back to the counter she saw a couple standing beside him. She couldn't hear what they were saying through the noise of the café, but she knew they wanted directions because of John's gestures and pointing and then leaning in with his phone to show them a map. As she walked closer his voice became audible only by pitch and she heard him say, "Boylston Street." The moment was so small, so unimportant. It could have passed by like so many others. It was like blowing the seeds off a dandelion or waking up in the morning, so much of it was nothing, and then Leda thought, *I'm in love with him,* and suddenly it wasn't nothing at all.

That weekend they went out for a fancy dinner at a restaurant that had live jazz. She wore her pinchiest high heels and sexiest red dress. It was so low-cut and fit her so perfectly that she didn't even need to worry about being linear in it. Men all stared at her, and John said that it was like walking around with porn. She took offense until he explained:

"What I mean is I feel like every man in this room wants you."

She pretended to still be annoyed, but she loved hearing him say it. Feeling like that was some kind of burden and some kind of freedom and little could she distinguish which was which, so she ordered a sundae for dessert, and she ate the cherry languidly, but when she saw a group of men at the table next to them watching her, she slouched forward, put the stem down, and chewed it up fast.

She and John had sex for the first time that night. It was the best first-time sex she'd ever had. It was a little painful, and she certainly did not orgasm, but she was relaxed, she was herself, and she loved him. They did it twice that night and once in the morning after she stood up out of the covers and John said, "You're the most beautiful girl I've ever seen."

Afterward they went and got brunch. She had to wear her dress to breakfast, and as she buttered a scone, she sensed that the lady at the next table was saying something bad about her.

". . . pregnant . . ." was all she could hear.

"That woman is talking about me. She thinks I'm a whore," she whispered to John as he ate eggs.

"Aren't you?" he said.

Leda smacked him across his forearm.

"I hate you," she said, but it wasn't true. Not even a little. Not even at all.

CHAPTER 19

—◦◦—

Really Good Sex

LEDA HAD BECOME USED TO THE IDEA THAT SEX WAS SLIGHTLY PAIN-
ful and that that was just what it was. She'd still feel an urgent need
to do it, but very often when she'd stop and think about it she'd
wonder why exactly. The concept of feeling actual pleasure from sex
seemed ambitious. No one she knew had orgasms during sex. Her
friend Katrina admitted it to her at the library. The two of them were
discussing the large penis of a guy she had just started seeing.

"It's like this." Katrina first motioned the length and then the
girth. "No, wait, more like this." She widened her hands. "Honestly,
when I was blowing him I could hardly get my mouth around it. If
it hurt my mouth, can you imagine what it would be like to have *sex*
with him?"

Leda shook her head. "I would never. Are you sure this is
worth it?"

"Well, yeah. I mean, I want to have sex with him . . . I mean,
shouldn't I be able to have sex with him even if he has a really big
penis?"

"I wouldn't want it near me."

Katrina pulled a book off the shelf absentmindedly. She leaned in
close to Leda. "Can I tell you something?"

"Yes."

"I've never had an orgasm during sex." She spoke as quietly as
possible, as if Leda would somehow be appalled by the ineptitude
of her vagina.

"I haven't either," Leda said.

"Really?"

"Yeah, never."

"But doesn't that make us weird? Are we weird?"

"I don't think so."

"That's a huge relief. I thought I was some kind of freak."

"I kind of think orgasming during sex is a myth," Leda said.

"Do you think so?"

"Kind of . . . Yeah."

"Why doesn't anyone talk about it?"

"I don't know. No one wants to be the only one."

A few weeks later she and John went for a walk in the woods. The day was no different from any other day. She wore a green shirt and they got bagels after spending the night together. They drove outside the city and went for a walk through a state park. It was hot and she could smell the greenery thickly settled in the air. John told her a funny story about his brother buying a shimmery scarf, and they were lulled between each other as they walked holding hands. Somewhere, although it couldn't be said where, they came to consider that they should have sex in the woods. The suggestion had been mutual really, but Leda would remember it as her own idea. They saw a clearing off the path and through the trees.

"We're going to break our necks," John said as they walked over roots and broken branches. Leda could hear each of their steps on the pine needles.

"Break our necks?"

"I meant our legs."

She stepped carefully and thought about her flats and that she shouldn't have really worn flats to have sex in the woods, but really none of her other shoes were appropriate either.

"Where are we going to do it?" she asked him.

"There." He pointed to a large tree with bushes all around.

"In the bushes?"

"Against the tree."

They walked over, and she could feel her heart speed up. There was a dull buzzing and somewhere far off in the quiet she thought she could hear traffic.

"Is this a good idea?" she asked him.

John looked boyish standing there. He had on a plaid shirt and jeans that had badly frayed on the cuffs.

"I don't know. Do you not want to do it?"

"Do you think someone will see us?"

"I don't think so," he said, although he looked unsure. "We should hurry up, though. The sun is going down."

He walked up beside her and kissed her neck.

She leaned against the tree. It smelled like waking up early and felt almost heated below her palms in the humid August air. She pulled her jeans down and helped guide his penis in. In that moment she anticipated the obligatory pain that she'd grown so accustomed to. Something that she imagined she'd have the burden to bear the rest of her life like some kind of sex goddess warrior battling penises and yeast infections. But it didn't hurt. John came quickly and pulled out.

"It didn't hurt at all," she said.

They weren't sure what to do with the used condom. It wasn't feasible to carry it back to the car, so they dug a hole and buried it and decided that pinecone babies would grow out of it. They promised each other that they'd come back and visit those pinecone babies one day.

"Will we remember these woods? Would we recognize our pinecone babies?" she asked.

They walked back in dusk and got ice cream.

It wouldn't be until well into their relationship that she would have her first orgasm during sex. Soon after, she'd orgasm regularly. She'd tell Katrina about it, but Katrina was single and still sleeping with strangers.

"I don't think I'll ever have one," she'd say.

"You will when you meet someone you love and are comfortable enough with." But even Leda knew as she said it that she was lucky and that some women would be battling their whole lives. *And then you must really feel like the only one,* she thought.

They never did go back to the woods.

CHAPTER 20

─── ❧ ───

Being in Love

IT WAS SUMMER. SHE SPENT SO MUCH TIME IN THE SUN. IF SHE HEARD love songs she sat with them. She'd blink them if she could. Sometimes she'd tear up at long lines like "At laaaastt." If she were in front of people she'd hold back the tears. Swallow them away because she knew that you couldn't tell someone how good it felt to sit with those songs. You couldn't say, "I'm blinking each one of these songs."

She and John got ice cream and walked by the river. She and John slept in on Sundays and ate bagels. She and John said "I love you" as they'd part and hang up the phone and sometimes while kissing and sometimes while cooking. She and John held each other's elbows and took silly baths. She and John ate pizza and went to shows and once they went dancing and spun. She and John frequented fairs and the inside of each other's body outline as they'd sleep pushed up against each other. She and John walked home and got dressed up and did so much listening to each other speak.

On Saturday they went to a parade and Leda got cotton candy. John took a picture of her eating it, and she thought she looked pretty holding it and taking a bite. It was so pink and her face looked bright. She posted it on Facebook later and got fifteen likes.

They stopped at a bookstore, and she bought *The Possibility of an Island*. It ended up horizontal in her bookshelf over the Noam Chomsky, but she did read it.

They walked back to his apartment, and she skipped a little. There was the sound of passing cars on the busy road silencing into the quiet of his road as they turned the familiar corner. There was a fence post they passed, the white of the paint chipped and blurring as they walked. He lifted her over a puddle. She laughed and looked back at everything behind them growing farther and farther away as she tried to balance herself over his shoulder.

They had sleepy sex when they got home, and the room was hot and dusty. Afterward she held her legs up in the air.

"I hate my legs," she said.

"I don't," he said.

She went to turn on his fan. The floor, the pine boards so emblematic of the room and the blue of the walls. Her hand pressed up on the windowsill and the cool air of the window fan as she turned it on.

She lay down back beside him with her face on his chest.

"I just wish it could be like this forever," she said.

"I think it can be," he said.

"You think it can be this good forever?"

"Yes," he said.

"But how?"

And John said something back, but she couldn't hear him over the fan.

CHAPTER 21

Christmas

"WHEN I WAS A LITTLE GIRL I WAS OBSESSED WITH HOW JIM HENSON died. My mom told me he died of pneumonia and it always scared me because she'd say that he died 'cause he didn't take care of himself. She told me that that's why you should always take care of yourself and it scared me 'cause . . . I don't know. Maybe then I realized you could die from something without even knowing that you could. Like if you didn't watch out you could just die just like that without even knowing," Leda said. She took a deep breath into the phone and could hear her own breath for a second, sounding distantly not her own.

"I thought he died of strep throat," John said. "My mom told me the same thing, but she said that it was strep throat. I was terrified too. Every time I'd get sick I'd think of it."

"Really? I always thought it was pneumonia. How weird that we both had the same random experience. What are the odds of that?"

"It really is strange."

"I have this memory of myself sitting on the washing machine in the basement and listening to my mom tell me about it."

"I don't remember when they told me, but I remember my dad saying that sometimes artists live in their own heads and are so preoccupied with their work that they don't take care of themselves enough," he said.

Leda was quiet for a moment. She was lying in her old bed at her parents' house. Her feet were balanced on the head of her childhood bear, who sat proudly pressed up against her bed frame. "Do you remember the song 'It's Not Easy Being Green'?"

"I do."

"I loved it. Even as a kid I think I had some sort of connection to it." She rolled to her side and looked up at the window. It was gray out in the bleak way winter always seemed to be. "There was this episode of *Sesame Street* where this lady came on, and she sang it. Do you remember that?"

"I only remember the Kermit version."

"This was some famous singer. She made it so much sadder." Leda thought about that woman and her face, but she could only remember her red lipstick and her hair. "I should try to find a video of it. I bet there's something online."

"Yeah, probably."

"Do you think we love each other 'cause we're both afraid of the way Jim Henson died?" Leda asked him.

"I think it's possible. Then again, maybe everyone has heard some version about Jim Henson dying, and we're all scared."

Leda considered this for a moment. She kicked the bear up into her reach and held it. Its black eye was worn at the center. She touched the coarseness of the scratched plastic and tried to remember how it got like that.

"No, I think it's just us . . . I should go to bed. It's really late. Merry Christmas, John."

"Merry Christmas, Leda."

❧

JOHN GRADUATED THAT SPRING. HIS PARENTS INVITED HER TO A CELebratory dinner at a fancy restaurant. She wore a dress that was more see-through than she realized. It wasn't until she got there and went to the bathroom that it became apparent that her bright purple underwear and gold lace bra were showing through. She could even make out her belly button, which looked squished in the fluorescent light of the restaurant bathroom. *I look like a crazy lunatic. And my belly button is disgusting,* she thought, and felt extremely self-conscious for the rest of the night. His mother was a thin, unforgiving woman and Leda knew it would be unlikely she wouldn't notice. At dinner she said something like, "It's no wonder that John likes you so much," which Leda couldn't help but assume was in direct reference to her dress and squished belly button.

That summer John got an internship in web development at an ad agency that wasn't far from her apartment. Leda would meet him on his lunch break. They'd walk together to a small sandwich shop or to the pizza place and then sometimes to the café afterward for coffee. One Thursday they found a journal on the side of the road. From reading the first few pages they decided that the person was female, went to college, and worked as a barista at Starbucks. Many of the entries were devoted to her crush on a fellow barista named Chazz. From what Leda could tell Chazz was aloof and unresponsive to many of the girl's flirtations, which included spilling straws in front of him so they'd have to pick them up together and asking if he could see her bra strap through her shirt, to which he responded, "No."

A few pages of the journal were devoted to future wedding plans. The girl was a decent artist and drew beautifully detailed pictures of floral arrangements. Leda especially liked one centerpiece of sunflowers and snapdragons.

The last entry was dated on Thanksgiving. Leda read it out loud to John as they walked back to his internship.

"Listen to this: 'I've met someone. His name is Ori and he's super cute! He has red hair and dimples. I never thought I'd really want to date a guy with red hair, but here I am dating Ori. We went on our first date last Friday, and I've heard from him every day since. It's so weird to hear from a guy every day like this. With Ronnie I'd only hear from him like the hour before the date. This is so much better! I have to say though—and this is the part that bothers me— I was really bored on the date. It's not so much that Ori is boring or anything. In fact he's really funny, but it's just that I always get bored with every guy. I got bored with Ted, and Ronnie, and now Ori. I'm starting to think there's something wrong with me. I like him a lot, but I just found myself daydreaming and kind of wishing I was home. It's like I know I'd be having more fun on the couch in my pajamas watching *Desperate Housewives*. I want to be with him, and I can't wait to see him again, but I just feel like I know I'll be bored and feel alone. Is this my life? To die alone, is that my destiny?' And that's the last entry."

"Wow, she has problems."

"I don't know—" Leda flipped back to the sunflower and snapdragon page. "I think she's just thinking too hard."

ॐ

THAT FALL LEDA DECIDED TO APPLY TO MFA PROGRAMS FOR CREATIVE writing. When she told John he said: "I think that'll be perfect for you."

She only applied to schools in Boston so that she could stay close to him, and she filed her last application wearing a bathrobe. She and John had sex that Saturday morning and that Sunday she bought a pair of boots that she'd later return because the toe box pinched her toes. The lady at the store asked:

"So why are you returning these?"

And Leda said: "They're too tight on my toes."

The lady at the store said: "Show me where."

Leda pointed to the spot where they were tight on her toes.

"That's just the toe box. I can fix that," the lady said, and took the boots to the back of the store. She came back seconds later and said, "Try them now."

Leda tried them, but they were still too tight.

"Well, have you tried wearing them around the house to stretch them?" the lady said.

"Yes," Leda said.

"Here, let me try it one more time." And the lady disappeared to the back of the store again. Eventually, after two more attempts at taking them to the back of the store, the lady gave up and Leda returned the boots, but the return didn't go through and she had to have a lengthy battle of calling the store and then the credit card company and eventually she got it straightened out over three months' time. The week after she finally was refunded for the boots she got an acceptance letter to the program she wanted to get into most, and she cried out of utter elation.

❧

"Leda, i have to tell you something."

John called her early that morning. She'd been woken up by her phone going off over and over again on her nightstand. At first she thought that he was talking about this fight he'd had with his mother the day before.

"What happened?" she said.

"Google wants to hire me."

"What? What are you talking about?" Suddenly the vision of his mother and the fight all fell away. It became starkly morning, dusty and bright.

"I applied to this job like two months ago, and I thought there was no way in hell I'd hear anything back, but then this morning I got this e-mail from their recruiter saying they want me to do a phone interview."

"Are you serious? That's incredible!" she said.

"The only thing is, the job is in California."

"California?" She could hear her voice on the word, but the sound was like a spark, her life sizzling away at the ignition. She could see John then in her arms little and pocket-sized with blond hair. Disappearing into the *C,* rolling away at the *i* and the *a.* "Are you gonna go to California?" she asked.

"I can't go without you," he said. "Would you go with me?"

"Like, live with you in California?"

"Yes."

"What about grad school? And my mom?"

"I don't want you to give up grad school, but this is such a huge opportunity for us. I mean, if I got this job, my career would be set. We wouldn't have to stay long, just a year, maybe less than a year, and then move back here. Just to get it on my résumé. Could you defer your acceptance?"

"No, they don't allow it." Leda sat up in bed. It didn't seem right to be lying down for this conversation anymore. "What would I do out there?"

"You can write. I'll be making enough money to support us."

She imagined herself sitting at a desk and typing away as John walked around with a briefcase and maybe a pipe.

"Well, when is the interview?"

"It's tomorrow. If it goes well, they'll fly me out for an in-person. Look, we don't have to decide anything right now. I just found out and was excited and wanted to tell you. There's still a really good chance that I won't get it."

"I want you to get it, John."

"Yes, but I'm not going without you. I just want you to know that."

Leda leaned back in her bed. She could feel the bed frame pressed against her. It hurt her shoulder blades, but she was too distracted to really care. *He wants me to move in with him. And it feels like dying,* she thought. "Where in California?"

"San Francisco," he said.

The next day Leda went to a coffee shop at the same time as John had his phone interview. She sat by the door and watched different people shuffle in and out as she drank a flavored latte that she had mistakenly ordered. She'd meant to just order a regular latte, but the girl at the counter had misheard her. A cute guy came in holding a newspaper. His hair was black and curly and he had just enough facial hair to be attractive. She watched him in the sort of bemused, distant way she often did when she saw attractive guys now that she was with John.

"I can't believe you're even considering not going. Your boyfriend wants you to move in with him. He wants to take you to California. CALIFORNIA!!!!!" Anne texted.

Leda looked at the text for a while. She tried to think of what to say back, but it was hard. She started typing "What about my mom?" and then "What about grad school?"

The boy with the facial hair and newspaper was staring at her. She smiled, sort of, to be polite, but then looked back at her phone. She checked her e-mail: "Neiman Marcus Style Guide" and "Save the

Whales" and then "The Republicans Are Trying to Ban Abortions."
She tapped the abortion e-mail.

> Leda,
> Republican lawmakers are trying to ban abortion
> after 20 weeks—

"Is this seat taken?"

She looked up from her abortion e-mail. *The newspaper-facial-hair-guy,* she thought, but it wasn't the newspaper-facial-hair-guy. It was a frumpy-looking man with disheveled hair. He had on a sweat suit and was holding a briefcase that was held closed with a bungee cord.

"Umm, I was just leaving, so actually you can have the whole table." Leda felt sorry to dash the man's hopes like that, but she'd learned over the years that being polite toward the disgusting men, who probably would have never begun to consider hitting on someone who was as disgusting as they were, wasn't some duty she was required to perform. For very long she'd tried to be polite whenever one of them would approach her. She'd assumed that they were lonely or sad, and that she could at the very least converse with them for a second, but over time she realized there was something universal in the pursuits of all men. That whether it be a handsome, misogynistic jock who thought he was a smooth talker, or a smelly man with a bungee briefcase, they all just wanted from her.

"But wait—" the bungee man said. "I want to tell you something."

Leda stood up and started to head for the door. Suddenly the man reached out and grabbed her arm.

"I just want to tell you something," he said.

A fear swelled up in her like a burning. She could feel it in her ears. A ping. His hand was tight on her elbow. It was dirty and his fingernails were black with grime.

"I just want to tell you something," he said again.

Leda yanked back hard and managed to pull her arm loose without much trouble. He reached for her again, but she stepped back. She wanted to scream at him. She wanted to say: "Fuck you! Don't fucking touch me, ever!" But instead she didn't make eye contact and leapt for the door.

When she got home she entered her building through the basement so she could throw her coat in the wash, and as she leaned over the machine to turn the dial to the hottest cycle she whispered, "Don't ever touch me," quiet enough so no one could hear.

⌒

JOHN FLEW OUT TO CALIFORNIA THAT MONDAY FOR THE IN-PERSON interview. He called in the morning when he got there, and his voice sounded shaky and nervous.

"This is crazy, isn't it?" he asked her.

"No," she said, "this is a great opportunity," but her voice broke on "tunity," and so she figured she was probably little comfort to him.

After she got off the phone, she ate a bowl of cereal but didn't realize until she'd nearly finished that the milk had started to clump. She dumped the rest down the sink before discovering that her disposal had broken so she had to scoop up the bits of cereal and milk chunks with a paper towel. The rest of the day she waited to hear from John. Her afternoon class had been canceled, and she didn't feel like going out. She watched a terrible Lifetime movie about a woman who had been beaten and raped and then got pregnant by her rapist. It was called *What She Does.* After that, she tried to read Proust, but she only managed a few pages. She ate chocolate. She burned reheated mac and cheese. At three John called and told her the interview had gone really well and that he'd hear back in the next couple of days.

"That's fantastic!" she said, and even though she meant it, she felt so dizzy as she said it. She took a bath but was too restless to relax. *I can't do this,* she thought. The next hour and a half she spent cleaning out her refrigerator, and as the sun started to set, her apartment dimming in the way it had so many evenings before, she suddenly had a whim to listen to the version of "It's Not Easy Being Green" she remembered from childhood. She looked for it for nearly an hour, but no matter what she Googled and how she worded it, she couldn't find the version she was thinking of. She'd close her eyes and see that woman singing with such sadness and red lipstick, but she could never find it. Eventually she found a cover by Andrew Bird that she settled on, and she listened to it on repeat a dozen times. *And I think it's beautiful, and besides, that's all I want to be.* After the twelfth time she heard it, she stood on her bed and sang it out loud, certainly loud enough for her neighbors to hear, although she didn't worry that they might be bothered. She said, "green." She said, "green." She said, "green." "Important like a river," she said. "Why wonder?" she said. That was the last time she'd ever listen to the song. Later in life she'd hear it from the kitchen, muffled by the sound of the microwave, but that would be it. She wouldn't remember the moment either, standing on her bed, or how loud she was. She'd never say those words again. She'd never wonder why. At 8:37 she texted John: "I'll go to California with you."

PART 3

CHAPTER 22

San Francisco

LEDA GRADUATED ON A TUESDAY, AND THE THURSDAY AFTER, SHE WAS deciding which underwear to take with her to California. It wasn't until then that she realized just how many unattractive pairs of underwear she had. Most of them she wouldn't have dreamed of wearing in front of John, but now that she was moving in with him, it dawned on her that he would be seeing *all* of her underwear, the big ones, the torn ones, the period-stained ones. It also became obvious that she really didn't own that many pairs of sexy underwear. Sure, she had her date-night lace ones that were overpriced and caused yeast infections, and her cute girly cotton ones with little floral designs or sassy taglines written across the butt like "Foxy" or "Night In" and her favorite, which said "Genius."

"Don't you think that's patronizing?" John had asked her when she wore them in front of him.

"No, how is it patronizing?" she said.

"Well, do you think they really mean it that you're a genius or do you think it's supposed to be ironic?"

"I think they mean it for me."

She had never considered what the implication of having so much ugly underwear could possibly be, but now, as she sorted through her drawer, so many truths of her inner being seemed physically manifested in her choice of undergarments. *I value comfort,* she thought. *I value affordability,* she thought. *I value cotton,* she thought. She decided to make piles of which to take and which not to take, marking three Post-it notes with "Yes," "Maybe," and "No fucking way." By the time she sorted through all of it, the "No fucking way" pile dwarfed the other two. She texted Elle and asked her if she had a similar problem when she moved in with Shane. Elle texted back: "I only wear thongs." *Shut the fuck up, Elle,* Leda thought, and pushed the "Maybe" pile in with the yeses.

☙

THE DIFFICULTY OF LEAVING RIGHT AFTER GRADUATION WAS THAT the lease on her apartment wasn't up until September. Luckily the landlord agreed that as long as she could find someone to take it for the summer, he'd give her back her deposit and make no issue of her breaking the lease. She put up a Craigslist ad under the subject line: "Cute and Cozy Studio Available." She got six e-mails within the first twenty minutes. Four were from guys, one was from a girl, and the last was from a frantic-sounding couple hoping to live there together. She wrote back to the couple first and explained that her landlord would only allow one person to live there and that the place was way too small for two people anyway, to which she got an immediate response of "Would you talk to your landlord and just check maybe? We can pay an extra 25 dollars a month and my boyfriend can do yard work." *Jesus, this poor girl.* Leda imagined her desperately e-mailing from studio to studio, trying to make this living-with-her-boyfriend fantasy come to life, even if it meant sleeping in the kitchen while her boyfriend raked leaves. *I wonder if she's gone through her underwear yet,* she thought.

She e-mailed the single girl to see if she wanted to come look at the place that afternoon. She figured it would be safer to have the girl come than the guys, given the fact that she'd be alone. She didn't even have to consider it really; she knew she'd never put herself in a situation that had so much potential to end in rape. So much of her life was devoted to the avoidance of getting raped. It was like a ticking in her mind, a gauge of safety that was always active. *I shouldn't walk down that street,* it would say. *Is there anyone walking behind me?* it would say. *I can't go out that late,* it would say. *It's not safe to meet guys from the Internet alone.* And so she e-mailed the girl. To be extra cautious she searched her on Facebook before offering to meet. Her name was Marilyn Larmont, and in her picture she was strawberry blond and pretty and smiling with sunglasses, holding a lollipop. "Very Lolita," someone wrote in the comments. She felt safer seeing the girl in her lollipop glory, but even so, she asked to meet at the café around the corner. The girl happily agreed. "I was going to suggest the same thing," she wrote. She clearly didn't want to be raped either.

Marilyn was less pretty in real life, but she still had the kind of strawberry-blond lollipop look from the photo. After greeting each other and seeing that neither of them was secretly a rapist, they walked back to the apartment.

"I'm in the middle of packing everything up," Leda said as she unlocked the door, "so don't judge too harshly."

Once they were inside Leda couldn't help but be critical of her little home. She imagined what Marilyn must be thinking seeing the old fridge and tiny oven, seeing her bed next to the mini sofa. Everything seemed so painfully her own in that moment. Her bathroom door and her slippers pushed to the side. *Here I am,* she thought. *I'm small and I'm pressed together just like my slippers.* It was then that she first felt a sense of relief at the thought of moving in with John.

"Oh my gosh, I love it!" Marilyn said.

"Really?" Leda said. She looked at her kitchen floor, which had coffee stains and a crack running down the middle of the linoleum.

"Yeah, it's exactly what I want." Marilyn walked around the small space with a light, sort of whimsical confidence. She was the type of person that Leda usually couldn't stand, someone who laid claim to a place just by being so impossibly hip. She just stood there in her loose-fitting beanie with her fingernails that were manicured with green nail polish only on the ring finger, and everything was hers. Marilyn touched the bureau and opened the closet. Leda looked at her thin legs sticking straight out of her miniskirt. She was wearing Mary Janes and knee socks, and her thigh-to-calf ratio was nearly equal. *She is so linear,* Leda thought.

"Yeah, I've looked at, like, three places, but two of them were in a basement and the third was basically just a room in this old lady's house. This is exactly what I've wanted," Marilyn said.

"Well, I've loved it here so I totally understand that. Are you going to school in the city?"

"Yup."

"Oh, nice."

"Why are you leaving again? Did you say?"

"I'm moving to California with my boyfriend."

"Oh, that's cool. What are you doing out there?"

Leda didn't know how to phrase her answer. *I don't want her to think I'm doing nothing. I don't want her to think I'm a loser. I don't want her to know I'm scared.* "I'll be working on my novel. My boyfriend got a job at Google so that's why we're going."

Marilyn looked her up and down quickly. She seemed more scattered and less whimsical.

"That, oh, that sounds really nice." She folded her arms and pulled off her beanie. "You're really lucky."

There was a nearly imperceptible shift in the dynamic between the girls. Leda felt a wave of self-assuredness that surpassed the potential of Marilyn's thin legs. She no longer worried about the apartment being so small or her own, or that she would never have dared to wear knee-highs. She was moving with her boyfriend to California, and that meant something, at least to Marilyn, who was feeling foolish in her beanie. Who was to say why someone else's life or legs meant anything to either of them, but in this room that was a kitchen and a bedroom and a living room, there was so much suffering in the silence. Marilyn agreed to take the apartment.

"Good luck in Cali!" she said as she left. And Leda watched her put her beanie back on as she rounded the corner of the block, disappearing, thin and whimsical if not still scattered.

⌘

TWO DAYS BEFORE LEDA LEFT, HER MOM CAME OVER TO HELP PACK UP the rest of the apartment.

"You have so many candles," she said as she emptied out a drawer by the stove.

"I get them as gifts. I don't even like candles, but it seems like that's what everyone always gives me at the family Christmas parties."

"Why don't you like candles?" her mom said. She pulled another candle from the drawer and held it at a distance so she could read the label without her glasses. "'Pumpkin Autumn.'" She smelled it. "It smells like nutmeg. Everyone thinks pumpkin smells like nutmeg."

"I can't light them."

"What do you mean you can't light them?"

"I'm afraid of lighting matches."

"That's ridiculous. You can't be afraid of lighting matches."

"People get burned."

"No one gets burned."

"I've gotten burned."

"What, when you were eight? Leda, you've got to know how to light a match. What are you going to do your whole life?"

"John can help me or I'll buy one of those lighter sticks."

"Do you have matches?"

"Yes."

"Come over here. You're learning how to light a match."

Leda walked over and grabbed the matches from their designated spot in the window above the sink.

"Okay, you just hold it like this and you strike it fast with some pressure. See? It's easy. I'll show you again."

Leda watched her mom then. She was the kind of woman who was so effortlessly elegant at all times. She had a certain feminine ease about her. A consistent togetherness and softness that never wavered despite how tough of a person she actually was. She was the type of woman who had grace. She was the type of woman who lit matches.

"You try it now."

Her mom handed her the matchbook. She tore off a match and struck it fast with some pressure. Her hands shook as it lit up strong and bright.

"Good, now light the candle," her mom said.

She leaned over the counter cautiously and lit the Pumpkin Autumn candle and blew out the match.

"There," her mom said. "Now you're ready to go to California."

A few minutes later the apartment smelled like nutmeg.

∾

IN THE END IT TOOK HER NEARLY THREE DAYS TO PACK UP THE ENTIRE apartment and decide what she was and wasn't bringing to California. Much of her stuff was going into storage, a sort of insurance policy on coming home in "less than a year," as she and John kept saying to each other. It was easily discernible what she would and would not need in "less than a year," except when it came to packing up her books. She waited until the very last moment to put them in boxes. Her whole apartment stripped apart from her bookshelf, and the piles of books beside her bookshelf, and on top of her bookshelf, and beside her bed, and in her kitchen book drawer under the sink. She made a rule that she would only take the books she hadn't read yet, but it was torture packing all the others away. *Please don't ever leave me,* House of Mirth. She organized the boxes in order of what she thought she'd like to read most, with the least likely on the bottom (*Gravity's Rainbow*) and the most likely on top (the only Tom Perrotta book she hadn't read yet). When she came across the Noam Chomsky, she flipped through the pages; they were still so crisp and free of fingerprints or stains. The book felt weighted and smooth in her hand. She smelled it again for the second time since she bought it, and tucked it about halfway down the pile. She figured she'd get to it before John and she would be back in New England. She imagined herself sitting in a fancy window seat of an old Victorian looking out on the bay, reading Chomsky and sipping some kind of lemonade or piña colada. She sealed up the box with red duct tape and wrote "Books" with a thick black Sharpie across the side. She took a step back and looked at her books all taped up like that in their box, and then she drew a heart around it. "Books," it said in a heart.

∾

THEY TOOK A LATE FLIGHT BECAUSE IT WAS THE CHEAPEST, BUT IT became apparent pretty quickly that there was very little chance that she'd be able to sleep. Her seat was broken and wouldn't lean back all the way; despite this the man behind her still managed to poke her in the back with his knees at least every fifteen minutes. John offered to switch with her, but she still preferred to be by the window. She was hoping to see the bridge as they landed. Every time she nearly fell asleep she'd get restless and think of all the stresses in her life. She'd feel the vibration of the plane lifting her away from her old self, her little apartment, her parents, Christmases with snow, and then she couldn't sleep. *I'll be home for Christmas,* she'd think and try to find a more comfortable position. *I'll see my parents and the snow.* John fell asleep almost immediately, which was disheartening. Occasionally she'd wake him by accidently bumping his elbow or jostling his seat. He'd wake up slightly and in a half-sleep stupor he'd say things like: "What time is it?" or "Aren't you tired?" Leda would answer just to have something to do even though she knew he wasn't really listening. Four hours into the flight she was becoming a bit delirious from exhaustion, restlessness, and lack of recline. She intentionally bumped John's shoulder and jostled his seat. "Talk to me," she said. But John just turned his head to the other side and said, "Almost there."

After that she tried to read but couldn't get into her book. There were no movies to watch so she decided to try to write a little bit. She wrote a poem. It went:

> *On the flight*
> *City at night*
> *No peanuts*
> *Going nuts*
> *No hope*
> *Rope a dope.*

She read it over and then titled it: "Seat Without Recline." The next time she flew she took the poem with her, and after that she deemed it her lucky flying poem. Five years later it would be lost in an unfortunate washing machine accident in her jean pocket.

She got up to use the bathroom about an hour before landing. There was a line, but she didn't mind waiting. It was nice to stand. The lady in front of her was a short, older-middle-aged woman with curly hair and bright lip liner. She had a shirt on that said "Florida" that was tucked into her khaki shorts. She turned and smiled at Leda.

"You'd think there'd be more bathrooms on this flight with all the people," she said.

"Yeah, it's true. I guess there's only this one and then the one for first class."

"They probably have two. There's no way they're waiting as much as we are. This is my third time up and every time I've had to wait."

"Yeah, it's pretty bad." She began tiring of the woman.

"Are you going to San Francisco or on to someplace else?" the woman asked.

"San Francisco."

"Oh, isn't that nice. It's a beautiful city, you know."

"That's what everyone keeps saying."

"Is this a vacation?"

"No, my boyfriend got a job at Google so we're moving out there together."

"That's incredible! What fun. You'll have to visit Fisherman's Wharf and the bridge, of course. Oh, you're just going to love all the cute little houses. It's been a while since I've been, but I remember just loving all the little houses."

"Yeah, it looks beautiful in all the pictures I've seen."

"It's the second most beautiful city in the world only to Fort Lauderdale, my hometown." The lady pointed to her shirt. "Fort Lauderdale has beaches you just wouldn't believe. The water is so blue."

Leda nodded. "I'll have to go sometime."

She got back to her seat and finally dozed off twenty minutes before the flight landed. She woke up to John shaking her arm.

"Look, the bridge," he said, pointing out the window.

But she couldn't see anything.

"Sorry, I thought I saw it for a second," he said.

❧

AFTER THEY GOT THEIR LUGGAGE AND RENTAL CAR, THEY HEADED OUT toward the city. Even though they were staying nearly an hour south, and it was almost 1:00 a.m., they couldn't resist it. Leda felt a sense of anticipation, cool and stark and wandering. She wanted to see the bright lights of the new place, all the buildings and beautiful little houses and the bridge. When she blinked she envisioned herself like Mary Tyler Moore, just tossing her hat into the air. Tossing and tossing.

On the drive in they passed rows and rows of palm trees. *I am no longer on the East Coast,* Leda thought, and she tried to take a picture of a tree as they stood at a stoplight, but it came out too dark and blurred. She deleted it.

They came upon the city skyline, but it didn't look particularly like anything special. John wasn't sure where the city center was, so they headed toward the tall buildings. They drove cautiously but without much direction, turning down any road of vague interest. Both of them kept an eye out for the Victorian houses they had seen in pictures, but there wasn't anything like that. There were a lot of older buildings, and the streets seemed empty except for the home-less people.

"Where is everyone?" Leda said.

"It's very late," John said.

"It's a city, though."

"I don't know . . . ," he said.

They drove up a steep San Francisco street. Her body fell back against the seat, but she pulled herself forward and held on to the dashboard. She looked out her window at the world growing more and more angular, no longer perpendicular to her perspective.

At 1:52 a.m. they gave up on their ambition with the city— whatever that had been. Between them in the silence and exhaustion little could be confirmed. As they headed south Leda looked back. She could see a bridge lit up in the night.

"Is that the Golden Gate?" she asked.

"I think it must be," John said.

She unrolled her window and leaned out, the wind blowing her hair in her eyes; she couldn't get a good view, but there was some satisfaction in the effort of trying to see.

"At least we saw something," she said.

But it was the Bay Bridge she was looking at, drifting farther and farther into the night. The Golden Gate was nowhere in view.

CHAPTER 23

Attempting to Swim

As part of john's relocation package, google put them up at a Residence Inn in Campbell, California, a small town emblemized by its historic water tower. The town center had a few restaurants and a cute vintage candy shop that Leda would be disappointed to later discover was actually part of a chain.

John woke up early for work. He kissed her in her sleep before he left, something she would only vaguely remember later when mentioned.

"You didn't say goodbye to me before you left," she'd say when he got home.

"Yes I did. I kissed you goodbye," he said.

She woke up at 9:28. It was dark despite the shades being drawn. The room was set up like a studio apartment, with a little kitchen and small living space. The bed, pushed to the far wall, overlooked the rest of the room. Leda switched on the bedside lamp. She walked over to the sliding glass door that acted as the room's only window and led to a "patio" that was a really only a slab of cement with a plastic lawn chair on it. She slid the door open a bit and looked up. The sky was bright and sunny, but the building's overhang kept the room dark. She leaned out and reached her hand until her fingertips touched the sunlight. *I wish there was no overhang. I wish it wasn't so dark. I think I'll go have eggs,* she thought, and quickly got dressed to make the hotel's breakfast buffet before it closed.

The inn was divided into little faux townhouses separated by concrete walkways that all led to the main building, which consisted of a lobby and dining room. Out front was a small pool. When she first heard that the inn had a pool, she pictured herself swimming and swimming and sitting by the pool and just swimming, but even in the dark of night when they arrived, she could see that the pool was not much bigger than a large bathtub. It was disappointing, to say the least.

As she rounded the corner of the last townhouse she nearly collided with a housekeeper pushing a cart of towels and toilet paper.

"Sorry," Leda said.

"That's okay."

The girl didn't look like she was much older than Leda was. Her hair was pulled back and she had a beautifully slender face. Her features looked so delicate, as if they could have almost been drawn on. Leda felt a strange feeling flush over her. It was almost like déjà vu, like she'd known the girl or seen her or bumped into her in this exact same way before.

"Sorry, I'm in your way," Leda said.

"No, sorry, my fault," the girl responded, redirecting her cart as Leda stepped aside.

The feeling persisted. She almost wanted to ask the girl, to say something like, "Do I know you? Is this real? Where do we go when we die?" But of course she let the moment, like so many others, just pass into the transient void of it all.

When she reached the dining hall they were starting to put the food away, but she had just enough time to grab what was left of the scrambled eggs and to make herself a waffle on the waffle iron. The hall was empty except for a young family who were finishing their breakfast. The father sat typing on his computer, taking intermittent bites of oatmeal. His wife was cutting up a sausage on one of her children's plates. Their two boys sat, staring at the TV propped against the wall. They looked almost identical, but one was slightly older.

"Eat your cereal, Aaron," the mom said. She had an accent that Leda figured must have been from Australia or New Zealand.

"Finn, don't kick your legs. You're shaking the table."

Each boy had platefuls of food and a side bowl of cereal. The little one dazedly chewed on a piece of waffle, but the older one didn't look like he'd eaten anything. Leda looked at the mother: she had a small container of yogurt in front of her that she hadn't opened yet. She leaned over to the older one and tried to coax him with the eggs. She wiped the face of the younger one. Her arms looked thin and neat and almost nonexistent as she moved around managing the children. Leda looked at the father: he finished his oatmeal and continued to type. *I will never be a mother with a closed yogurt. I will always open my yogurt and my husband will not finish his oatmeal before me.* Leda ate all of her breakfast, even the scrambled eggs, which were terrible, in silent protest to the woman's starvation.

As she walked back to her makeshift townhouse Leda decided she would go for a swim. It wasn't all that hot out, and even though the pool was so small she figured anything would be better than spending the day in the shade of the overhang waiting for John to get home. She got back to her room and jumped in the shower so she could shave all the requisite hair for public viewing. Now that she and John had been together awhile, she no longer worried about shaving her legs every time she saw him or making sure her bikini line was perfect; more often than not she was stubbled. On nights when she knew they were going out and would probably have sex, she'd be sure to shave her vagina into the neat little trim vagina shaving pattern she'd developed over the years. It was a hassle, but fairly early into her pubic hair years she learned that being natural was unacceptable. As far as she knew, all of her friends shaved. It was an unspoken understanding for the most part, although she did have the distinct memory of being thirteen and playing truth or dare at her friend Kristen's sleepover and someone asking Kristen if she shaved. The girl who asked was kind of heavy and had a mean-looking face. Her name was something like Arugula, but it wasn't Arugula. Kristen introduced her, saying, "This is my friend, Something Like Arugula, from camp." The girl didn't seem all that happy to be at the party. She kept yawning and every so often she'd interrupt the conversation by saying things like, "This party is lame," or "We should go buy some wine coolers." She was really into wine coolers. She told this story about how she and her friend Ryan (this boy she knew who she described as "so hot") would sneak her mom's wine coolers and get drunk on the back porch of her grandmother's house.

"Is Ryan your boyfriend?" A sporty, petite girl named Kayla asked.

"No . . ." Something Like Arugula hesitated. "Well, one time he almost kissed me, but we were really drunk."

It was Kristen's idea to play truth or dare. She told Leda about it almost two weeks before, during gym.

"We're going to play truth or dare," Kristen said with a kind of nervous resolve.

"That should be fun," Leda said.

"Yeah, I'm really good at it," Kristen said.

Leda wondered how exactly you could be good at truth or dare.

At the party she could tell right before Kristen was going to bring it up, because the same nervous resolve came over her as it had the day in the gym.

"Okay, guys," Kristen said, clapping her hands. "It's time to play *truth* or *dare*."

Without giving it even a moment to settle in on everyone's mind, Something Like Arugula jumped on it.

"All right, since it's your party I'll ask you first. Truth or dare?" Kristen looked a little shocked. She clearly had anticipated the crowd of sleepover girls would react with the same nervous resolve she had over the idea.

". . . Okay," Kristen said. "Truth."

"Do you shave?" Something Like Arugula asked.

"Of course I shave. Who doesn't shave their legs?"

"Not your legs, jeez." Something Like Arugula rolled her eyes. She took a triumphant pause. "You know . . . down there."

Kristen looked a little startled, but she didn't miss a beat.

"Well, of course I do. Who doesn't do that?" she said. She really was good at truth or dare.

"Good, 'cause girls who don't are nasty. Ryan said it smells bad and it gives people crabs."

All the other girls nodded in agreement.

"Yeah, it's true," Kayla said. "It's really nasty."

Leda couldn't help but feel a sense of shame over the whole

exchange. She thought of her own vagina tucked away in her striped PJs and floral underwear starting to grow its own mass of nasty, crabby hair. She imagined hot Ryan telling her how smelly she was as he sat on a porch drinking wine coolers. It was the first time she'd ever really thought about her body hair in that way. Something Like Arugula had sparked in her a kind of unforeseen disgust, like there was already something wrong with her for something she had absolutely no control over. A week after the sleepover she started shaving her legs.

The impression made that night was her introduction to the doctrine that WOMEN HAD TO SHAVE THEIR VAGINAS. From that moment on she'd be reminded of just how crucial it was fairly consistently throughout her life from media, and friends, and guys on rare occasions. By the time she was having sex it wasn't even a question if she would shave or not, although she really didn't like shaving. Pretty much every time she did it she'd nick herself and have to wait until she stopped bleeding to put her underwear on. Even if she somehow managed to avoid nicking herself, shaving irritated her skin and she thought the bikini bumps were ugly.

Nearly two years into the relationship she'd mention it to John. "I don't really get why guys like the way it looks shaved. The bikini bumps are so ugly."

"I don't like it," John said.

"You don't like bikini bumps?"

"No, I don't like girls shaving."

"How can you not like girls shaving? Don't all guys like girls to shave?"

"I don't really know what all guys like, but I think it's stupid. And I think it looks sexier unshaven."

Leda didn't really believe John at first. It seemed impossible that any man could love a woman with pubic hair. But even when she finally did believe him (the day she tried a new cream designed to minimize the irritation from shaving and broke out in a rash from it and John said, "I don't understand why you're doing this. I really like girls not shaved, and it's making you miserable"), she kept doing it. It didn't matter that he didn't like it or that she didn't like it, she just felt like she had to do it. It was a compulsion so inexplicable and intimate. It ran in her mind like little clicks of things she had to do. Eat. Drink. Shave your vagina. It wouldn't be until one Sunday nearly eight months later that she would finally consider the absurdity of the compulsion. She'd had the stomach flu all week and was finally well enough to take a proper shower. As she got out of the bath, she felt dizzy from the steam so she lay down in bed and, without meaning to, ended up falling asleep. She woke up feeling disoriented from the unintentional nap, and as she got up to grab the wet towel off the bed, she saw a pattern of little dark stains neatly dotted on the sheet. It was blood from shaving. She looked at herself and saw the smears of red dried on her skin. It looked as if she'd cut herself all over. There were all these little pathways in between bikini bumps where the blood had run. *This is ridiculous,* she thought. She felt a kind of wave come over her. It was as if one of those clicks that had compelled her so readily to mutilate her body hair on a near day-to-day basis had snapped into a louder click. A click that said: *You are being an idiot.* A click that said: *Stop being an idiot.* A click that said: *You are not an idiot.* After that she stopped shaving, and it was one of the few best things she would ever do in her life.

Leda found her bikini squished beneath the socks in her big suitcase. The advantage of trying it on in the near darkness of the hotel room was that when she looked at herself in the full-length mirror she looked as best as she possibly could in a bikini. *In near darkness I am almost like a bikini model,* she thought. Deciding what to wear over her bikini for the sixty-foot walk over to the pool wasn't easy. She'd forgotten to pack any of the cover-ups she owned or any dress that could appropriately be worn over a bathing suit. She also worried that there was only one lawn chair and there wouldn't be anywhere for her to put her clothes as she swam. She had a vision of herself taking up the lone lawn chair with her clothes and someone coming over, attempting to sit, and being dismayed by her clothes being there and then saying something like, "Whose clothes are these on the lone lawn chair? I need to sit on this lone lawn chair and I can't because someone has taken up the lone lawn chair with these clothes." She had a very specific propensity for worrying over situations where she would be of the greatest inconvenience and some inconvenienced stranger would be outraged by her utter lack of consideration.

"Why do girls always worry so much about being polite all the time? Stop being so crazy!" John would say.

But she couldn't stop. She once accidentally apologized to a plant for getting into the elevator first.

"But didn't you notice it was a plant?" John said.

"I thought it was an old lady," Leda said.

With the lawn chair situation so up in the air, she decided worst-case scenario she'd just fold clothes up and put them beside the pool. She put on a pair of jeans and one of John's loose-fitting concert T-shirts. She didn't have a beach towel, so she grabbed one of the bleached white bath towels that the hotel supplied. She looked at herself one last time before embarking on her swim. She had her jeans and her loose-fitting T-shirt over her bikini top and her hotel towel in hand. *I look like a crazy lunatic,* she thought, and then headed to the pool.

Unsurprisingly, no one was swimming. Leda was happy to see that there were in fact two lawn chairs, and so she didn't think it would be an issue if she left her clothes on one. The pool looked out onto the parking lot. A large man was loading the back of his truck with some luggage and what looked like fishing gear. Seeing him, Leda suddenly became very aware of herself. It seemed foolish to be in a bikini pretty much ever, but given the context of the pool, the absurdity of it all was palpable. She stood beside the lawn chair and used it to steady herself as she slipped off her jeans. She folded them neatly in a perfect little jean square that would wait for her primly as she swam. *Perfect,* she thought. In the midst of her fantasy fold she noticed something squished up on the ground by her feet. *What is that?* The thought sort of clamored in her mind, it was so quick, and then it rose from confusion to resolve in such a fast and hideous way: *My bathing suit!* She'd accidently untied the side string of her bikini bottom as she folded up her jeans—she was naked from the waist down in a Residence Inn parking lot pool. Her life was about to end. She quickly grabbed the bathing suit and jumped into the pool still wearing her oversized T-shirt. As soon as she was concealed by the water, she put her bottoms back on. Her hands shook as she tried to tie the bow. *Faster, tie it. Oh Jesus. Tie it, you idiot!*

Covering her genitals, and regaining her bearings, Leda looked around for any witnesses. The only person she could see was the man with the fishing gear, but he was leaning over the passenger seat of his truck. She and her nudity and soaking oversized T-shirt were alone. She thought it was best to act as if nothing happened, as if she were just a regular girl going for a swim in this parking lot pool of the Residence Inn, so she took off her soaked T-shirt and tried to lay it neatly enough by the pool. She smiled a lot, as if she were enjoying the sunshine, and swam forward a bit and then did the backstroke for a few strokes, paying very close attention to having her arms come out straight and then go back close up by her ears, just like she learned in the three swimming lessons she took the summer she was seven. The pool was so small that it only took about five strokes to go from one side to the other. She looked over at her jeans folded so neatly on one of the two lawn chairs, just mocking her in their order, her towel on the ground beside them, unapologetic evidence to the whole incident. *How long can I stay here pretending to be happy?* she thought. It turned out she could stay pretending to be happy for twenty-three minutes. She finally decided it was time to leave when the New Zealand or Australian family arrived. As they walked toward the pool, the older boy who hadn't eaten stopped suddenly and said, "I don't want to swim," and then threw up all over the side-walk. Leda took this as her cue to exit the pool. It turned out that it didn't matter how neatly her jeans were folded after all, since she doubted the couple noticed as they were cleaning up vomit. As she passed she heard the mother say, "It's okay, baby." And even though it obviously wasn't directed at her, Leda felt calmed by the sentiment.

When she got back to the room she showered and changed into PJs. She watched some bad scripted show on MTV and ate the micro-wave pizza. By three o'clock it was nearly pitch-black from the over-hang shadow, and she had to turn on all the lights. John got home at 5:30 and she told him about the breakfast and the pool as if so many things had happened to her that day.

"You didn't say goodbye to me before you left," she said.

"Yes I did. I kissed you goodbye," he said.

"I wasn't awake, though. Don't ever leave for work without waking me up first."

"But I figured you'd want to sleep."

"Yeah, but still, just always wake me up."

After that he always woke her up before leaving for work, and even though sometimes she couldn't fall back asleep, she still preferred it.

CHAPTER 24

A Room with a View

IT TOOK THEM THREE WEEKS TO FIND AN APARTMENT IN THE CITY. The search had been an exhaustive one, which consisted of scouring listings on Craigslist, making countless phone calls, and driving an hour to the city nearly every night to make open houses and showings. Formerly Leda had romanticized the idea of searching for an apartment with a man. It seemed so adult and chic. There would be white fences and granite countertops and her just spinning around living rooms with high ceilings. Her naïveté was unearthed after walking into the very first apartment. It smelled like cat pee and had a bedroom that was completely taken up by the fairly small bed.

"You just buy an armoire and put it right out here in the hall. It has a beautiful hall," the Realtor said. She had a desperate smile and an older-looking suit. "Do you have an armoire?" she asked.

"We don't . . . It doesn't have a closet?" Leda said.

"No, no closet, but you know . . . you just buy an armoire."

After that both she and John dramatically lowered their expectations.

"I thought we'd be in a Victorian. What's the point of living in San Francisco if you can't live in a Victorian?" she said.

"I'd settle for a bedroom that has a closet at this point," he said.

Their thirteenth viewing in, just as they'd really begun to lose hope, Leda came upon an ad for a townhouse "with views" in Noe Valley. That night they rushed to the open house, and as they walked through the door and saw the big glass windows and the everlasting view of the city running into the bay, they looked at each other and said almost simultaneously, "This is it." Two days later they moved in. John held her as they looked out onto the city, and said, "A writer needs a good view." And then she felt restoration in her high ceilings and all things as beautiful.

The first few days in the apartment she felt a sense of total possibility. The only furniture they had was a blow-up mattress and a folding chair. It was a bit strange to be in such an empty space, but the lack of clutter was invigorating. The rooms echoed and sometimes she'd call out the whistle from *The Hunger Games*. She spent her time writing a short story about a chef who made exceptional flan and eating leftover pizza while she read Joan Didion. They didn't have cable or Internet yet, so she put washcloths under her feet and skated around the bedroom. Anne texted her: "What are you up to?"

"I've put washcloths under my feet and am skating around the bedroom," she texted back.

"What?? You're losing your mind!"

"No, it's fun! What are you up to?"

"Watching Jason play *Mortal Kombat*."

It was a moment of respite from her former life of singleness. Knowing that John was coming home and they would get takeout and curl up on the blow-up mattress and watch movies was all she needed to navigate the isolation of those first few days. It didn't seem like what it really was: her alone in an apartment waiting for John.

Midweek the Comcast guy came. He was in his late thirties and thin and walked with an uppity, sexual kind of step. Leda had this sort of odd impulse to impress him.

"So you're new here, huh?" he said.

"Yeah, just moved in." She felt leaving out the pronoun made her seem more relaxed.

"What do you think about the city so far?"

"Seems really great."

"Yeah." He took a piece of cable and cut the end of it. His hands moved in a fast, knowing way. "Have you hit any of the clubs?"

"No, not yet. Any recommendations?" Leda had been to one real club in her entire life and spent most of her time throwing up in the bathroom from bad Chinese takeout.

"Let's see . . . Well, honestly, you really need to go to Oakland to go to anything decent."

"Oh, yeah?"

"Have you been yet?"

"No, not yet, but I've heard great things."

"Yeah, it's great there . . . Do you smoke at all?"

"Yes." She didn't smoke.

"Well, I know a lot of good places in the area if you want some names."

"I'd love that!" She smiled and nodded to seem like she was really interested.

"Great, I'll write them down for you on the way out."

Leda felt uncomfortable for the rest of the time he was in her house. As a result the Internet password she created when he set up the Wi-Fi was 3U988, a conglomeration of her not thinking and just typing something random into the keyboard as quickly as possible. He handed her his card on the way out with a list of places to buy weed and the names of a few clubs he liked in Oakland.

"Maybe I'll be seeing you in Oaktown," he said as he handed it to her.

When John got home she told him about the Comcast guy.

"Why was he asking you if you smoked weed?" John said.

"He was just being friendly more than anything, I think."

"Leda, that's seriously inappropriate. I mean, he was supposed to just come and put the cable in and instead he's like weirdly hitting on you and seeing if you want to smoke with him?"

"I don't think he was hitting on me really. I can't really explain it." She thought back on the guy and his knowing hands quickly cutting cable wires.

"I'm surprised you said that you smoked."

"What was I going to say?"

"How about, 'No, I don't.'"

"Yeah, but why do that? He would have thought I was judging him or something, and I just felt like I was never going to see this person again, so why am I making some kind of thing out of it?"

"You don't have to pretend to be someone you're not."

"I don't ever pretend anything."

The week wore on, and that weekend they went to Ikea and bought furniture and plates. For the most part it was everything she could have ever wanted in her life then: looking at furniture with a man, planning their little home together, the air of domesticity ripe with Swedish meatballs and fiberboard. But she would remember the time in Ikea less than the cable man in her apartment. Less about the moment they bought their green desk and more about how nervous she was writing 3U988. John would ask her: "Do you like this lamp?" And she'd say: "Yes, I do." And then that night, as she lay in her new bed looking off at her new view, she wondered why she lied to that man, how could she be so wanting from someone who had no real bearing, and why her life could be so misrepresented by no one but herself.

CHAPTER 25

An Average Day in the First Month
of Living in San Francisco

8:42 a.m.: LEDA WOKE UP AND STILL FELT TIRED EVEN THOUGH SHE'D had enough sleep. *Is it possible to wake up from things being too quiet?* she wondered. She leaned over to her nightstand and grabbed her phone. One text from Anne. One text from Elle. She didn't bother reading Anne's. It was long and about Jason. It was too early in the morning to hear her complain about Jason not texting, or Jason forgetting her birthday, or Jason wanting to try anal. These kinds of texts used to palpitate the day, but now it just seemed like she and Anne were living such painfully dissimilar lives. She felt older than Anne and maybe more exhausted. Anne was exhausted too, but her exhaustion was so childish, so rooted in the trivial anxieties of youth. It seemed pointless to go on and on about yet another bad relationship where the greatest concerns were things that would never matter in any relationship that was worth anything. On more than one occasion she wanted to tell Anne what she really thought. She wanted to say, "Anne, the guy is a total piece of shit. Find someone nice," but of course you couldn't say those kinds of things to a friend. Friendship was about tolerating someone else's constructed realities, letting them settle their own neuroses and not intervening. Who was she to tell Anne that Jason was shit? Who was she to tell her that if she found someone decent, she wouldn't be fighting about anal, she'd be having it?

Elle's text said: "Sorry! I meant to text back like forever ago. It's blue. How are you, girly??"

Leda had to reread her last text to Elle, which was from a month before. She'd asked her what color coat she got from this store they both liked. Elle taking a long time to respond was pretty customary in their friendship. Leda tolerated it for the most part without any type of pettiness or passive-aggressive retaliation, but again, now her life seemed so different. She was living in San Francisco with John. He was taking a good job so that they could have a future together. Dealing with paper Elle and her lame texts seemed foolishly juvenile. Why should she desperately write back when she hardly wanted to talk to her in the first place? *Fuck off, Elle,* she thought.

She grabbed her computer from under her nightstand and checked her e-mail and then Facebook. She read an article Mel posted about toxoplasmosis and how this scientist from Prague believes that toxoplasmosis is so prevalent that it explains why so many people are doing all these extreme sports and all this crazy stuff and aren't scared, just like how the mice aren't scared of cats when they become infected. *Maybe I have toxoplasmosis,* she thought.

10:14 a.m.: She got up to pee after no longer being able to hold it. After peeing she looked at herself in the bathroom mirror. She lifted her shirt and sucked in her stomach. She pushed down on the pocket of fat above her belly button. *If only I could lose this.* Her face looked tired and she thought maybe a little bit drawn. She smiled at herself. "It's not like that," she said to her reflection, a phrase that she'd remembered from a book and would say to solace herself on occasion.

She ate half a banana with peanut butter for breakfast. Then she turned on the TV and watched a marathon of *Say Yes to the Dress* for nearly three hours.

1:23 p.m.: She shut off *Say Yes to the Dress* just as the episode came on with the woman who was dying of some kind of rare kidney disorder. She'd seen it before, and it bothered her. It was sad and hard to watch, but more than anything it was just so atrociously voyeuristic. It was like emotional pornography. You too could be touched by this sick woman in her tenderest moment. In the end the girl did get a nice dress and she looked happy despite dying. *Even if you're dying* *you're happy to be marrying. No man is worse than death,* Leda thought, and shut off the TV.

The apartment was getting hot. She opened the sliding door to the porch to let the breeze in. Outside a man was cutting weeds in his garden. She watched the way he moved back and forth in the tall grass of the overgrown embankment. She didn't want him to notice her standing there in her pajamas with her messy hair, but she still stood there and watched for a while longer. *How rhythmically he cut those weeds. How neatly he placed them in a pile.* After that she made a grilled cheese for lunch and ate it as she flipped though the Oriental Trading Company catalog.

2:39 p.m.: Leda felt resolve in wanting to get started on her novel. She'd had this idea for the longest time about this woman who ends up getting cheated on and ruined by her friends who expose her at her job and her whole life sort of unravels and she loses any real sense of who she is. She'd told the idea to John and he thought it was fantastic. He said: "That sounds fantastic! What are you going to call it?" And she said: "I'm going to call it *Eleanor.*"

Leda sat down at her green desk. She'd never been successful at writing at a desk, but now in the new place with this new adult lifestyle, and all this new Ikea furniture, she felt motivated to become a desk user.

Her original plan with the novel was to make a complicated outline the way one of her professors had taught her.

"All writers use outlines," he said. "If they say that they don't, they're lying."

Leda worked on the outline for twenty-two minutes before coming to the conclusion that this advice was misguided at best. She ended up with a Word document that looked as follows:

Chapter 1: Introduce Main Character Eleanor

- Brunette (Possibly a redhead—make this point shown without describing her, looking at her own reflection—friends' reaction? Or maybe something her mother says—mother's name: Sheila)

· Smart (Goes to a prestigious school—has fantastic vocabulary)
· Complicated family (Get back to this later but something to do with Sheila)

Chapter 2: Conflict

· Relationship (Things falling apart, cheating)
· Work conflict (Her friends ruining things for her at work)

Chapter 3: Resolve

· Things resolve??

She texted Katrina about it, as the two had taken the class together.

"I just wrote the stupidest outline in the history of outlines. Prof. Brimbley doesn't know what he's talking about."

Katrina never responded.

Leda tried to write out a bit of the first chapter but gave up. She laid her head down next to the computer and closed and opened each eye one at a time in succession, so that the keyboard looked first here, then there, then here again. *Closer but really still farther,* she thought.

3:17 p.m.: After abandoning her attempt at writing for the day, she had a sort of vague ambition to organize the bookshelves. Just a few days before, she and John had haphazardly stacked their books onto the new shelves.

"Let's just get them out of the boxes, and then we can worry about them looking nice," he said. Leda had agreed at the time, but now seeing her Tolstoy squished between his book on film theory and his book on postmodernist theory she felt a compulsion to fix it. She sat beside the first shelf, a small white bookcase made from fiberboard and epoxy, and started ripping the books off. The fast motion of it and the sound they made hitting the floor gave her a certain satisfaction. She moved faster and faster and allowed the books to fall and hit each other harder and harder as they landed in a pile on the floor. Once the shelf was empty she looked down at the pile of books. The Noam Chomsky was on top, and without thinking much, she picked it up and gave it the honor of being the first book on *her* shelf. The other bookshelf, which was metal and tall and modern-looking, she'd leave for John's theory books, but all her lovely books would be together, and when she'd look over at them, she'd know that the Tolstoy stood alone, and there was so much comfort in the thought.

4:42 p.m.: The fog rolled in. The room darkened and out the window she could only see the tops of trees through the rolling gray of haze. She slid her back against the bookshelf that she'd just filled and watched the air looking so opaque and closed in. No longer could she see the city; no longer could she see the bay. The limitation of it was a consolation, as if there wasn't anything else. As if her day couldn't have been anything more than it was.

6:35 p.m.: She spent the last few hours before John got home unapologetically watching TV. There wasn't anything on, but it didn't matter. When she heard John's key in the lock, a feeling of anxiety and anger waved over her. John came in smiling. He tossed his keys on the table.

"Hi, beautiful," he said, and at that moment she wanted to kill him. *You're happy 'cause you aren't here watching* Storage Wars. *Well, fuck you for that.* She didn't say hi back.

8:47 p.m.: They went out for dinner, and she felt a little bit better about the day after that. John told her about this guy at work who had sent this desperate Facebook message to this girl he went on a terrible date with.

"He said he loved her in it and that he thought they'd end up together one day."

"Are you serious?"

"Yeah, we were all telling him not to send it. What can you really say, though? You can't tell him he's crazy and that she's going to think he's crazy and will probably never speak to him again."

"I think he's just a virgin," Leda said.

"I'm not sure if he is."

"I am. I'm sure he's a virgin and just feels completely alone and wishes things were different so he's ready to do anything."

"Or maybe he just wants to love somebody," John said.

"That's probably what he thinks, but really he just wants to feel like someone wants him." She took a bite of her falafel. "I feel sorry for him."

10:46 p.m.: She and John had sex that night. They role-played that she was a cheerleader and he was the coach and that she'd have to blow every guy on the football team in order to get on the squad unless she just had sex with him. It was great. She came really quickly, and they cuddled for a long while afterward.

"Why did you separate all our books on the bookshelves?" he asked.

"I don't know," she said.

John fell asleep soon after. The fog had rolled back out and she could see the view of the city again. She thought about toxoplasmosis. *Maybe I have toxoplasmosis. Maybe that's why I'm not scared, even though I should be.*

11:59 p.m.: She fell asleep.

CHAPTER 26

———❦———

Rochelle

LEDA DECIDED TO JOIN A MEETUP IN AN EFFORT TO MEET NEW PEOPLE. She'd realized that being home alone all day was taking a toll on her. At first she'd considered getting a part-time job, but she struggled with the idea. It didn't seem right that she'd be working at a crappy job just to keep from being depressed and lonely when she was supposed to be writing. The whole condition of her leaving Boston and her grad program and her mom was that she'd be working on her novel for the year. It was her only real solace in moving across the country for a man. *I didn't give up grad school to make coffee for rich tech hipsters just 'cause I'm alone,* she'd think. *I can't give up my dreams just to feel like I'm not lonely.* She searched Meetups online and found one that met Wednesday afternoons at a local bowling alley/bar.

"Do you think I should do this?" she asked John.

"Why not? You want to meet new people in the city. It could be fun," John said.

"I worry it will just be a bunch of weirdos."

"You'll be there, and you're not weird."

"That's true," she said, and she sent an e-mail.

It wasn't easy picking out an outfit for the Meetup. It was like dating in that there was some sense of anticipation that you should look nice and try to impress, but it was not dating because you weren't trying to sleep with anyone. *How attractive am I trying to be for these strangers that I don't want to fuck?* she thought. In the end she wore a pair of jeans and a loose-fitting sweater. When she got to the bowling alley, she was happy she hadn't dressed up any more than she had, as all of the people there to meet "new friends" were men. She wanted nothing more than to turn and walk away, but the woman she spoke to on the phone spotted her almost immediately.

"Hi there, are you looking for the Meetup?" she asked. She was a tan girl with really muscular arms and white eyeliner.

"Umm, yeah."

"Welcome! Are you Le-da or Rochelle?"

The fact that there were only two options was further confirmation that there really were no women.

"I'm Leda."

"Hi, Le-da." The woman strongly emphasized the two syllables as if the name were split in two. "I'm Stephanie. You're right on time. We're all over at that table right there." She motioned to the lone group of people in the bowling alley at 12:30 on a Wednesday. "So grab yourself a seat, because we're just about to get started."

Leda walked over to the group of men. She smiled slightly and folded her arms. It was her best attempt at conveying the emotion: *I don't want to sleep with any of you. I'm with someone, and even if I weren't with someone, I wouldn't want to sleep with any of you. If I could leave right now I would, but Stephanie is holding me here against my will, so please just leave me alone.*

"Hi, I'm Jeremy," a tall, lanky man with long, thinning hair said. The crossed arms and slight smile had failed. He reached a hand out.

"Hi, I'm Leda." She shook his hand. It was her repulsion at having to touch him that would prompt her to so deeply consider the touch itself, its clamminess, its coarseness, its limpness. So few other times in her life would she give a handshake such thought; the best handshakes, she'd hardly notice.

"You're the first woman here." He pointed around at the other men, who all seemed as unfortunate as he did. "Lucky you," he said, leaning in. His glasses were fogged.

Leda laughed politely.

"Well, I guess Stephanie is here too," he said, nodding to himself solemnly. He was wearing a patterned shirt and was sweating a lot. Leda couldn't help but feel sorry for him. Being single was hard. *Poor Jeremy and your sad day here trying to bowl with strangers to meet a girl.*

"Stephanie seems nice."

"She's very nice," he said. "This is my third Meetup with her leading, and she's great."

"So have you gone to a lot of these?" she asked.

"I've been to eleven," he said.

Leda tried to think of a polite way to ask how many Meetups it usually took to actually meet someone you liked, but she couldn't think of a way to word the question, so it grew silent between them.

"Stephanie just knows how to handle herself," he added.

"Yeah," she said. It stayed silent for a minute more.

"So what do you do?" he asked.

She didn't know quite how to respond. For the last four years of her life she would have said, "I'm a student," and it would have been that easy. But now she couldn't define herself in three words. She didn't want to say she was a writer because it wasn't really true, and she couldn't say she was a wife or a mother or was working here or there. The strange purgatory of her existence was at least a five-sentence explanation.

"Okay, guys. Rochelle is here," Stephanie generously chimed in. A heavy girl with black hair and grayish eyes stood beside Stephanie. She too looked disappointed upon seeing the array of awkward men standing together in the bowling alley. Stephanie explained that usually what people do is chat for a few minutes with one person, and then make their rounds to everyone else so that they get a chance to meet everyone.

"There really are no rules, but my rule is that you should at least say 'hi' to everyone. Mmm-kay?" she said, looking around the group in the most patronizing way possible to look around a group of people. "Now just enjoy yourselves, bowl, and meet up! Woo!"

Before Leda had time to start to pretend to want to talk to Jeremy again, Rochelle walked up to her and handed her a piece of paper.

"Hey, I'm Rochelle. Here's my e-mail. I'm not sticking around with all these gross guys, but let's get coffee or something sometime."

"Yeah." Leda smiled back at her and took the paper. "That would be great. My name's Leda." She put out her hand. Rochelle shook it and Leda didn't even notice that her handshake was too strong.

A week later she was headed to meet Rochelle at the coffee shop. John dropped her off on the way to work. She felt nervous. Once again it felt almost like some kind of strange date she didn't care all that much about. *It's like the entire feeling of my life,* she thought, *like nothing is happening really, but I'm nervous anyway.*

Rochelle was already there when she got to the coffee shop. She looked a little more disheveled than Leda had remembered from the Meetup. She had headphones around her neck and her hair was pulled back loosely.

"Hey, Rochelle," Leda said, more as a question than a statement, as if she wasn't quite sure this was the gray-eyed girl she'd remembered meeting among the strange men.

"Hey!"

The girls embraced politely.

"I'm glad you found the place. No one ever seems to know where this coffee shop is when I tell them about it," Rochelle said.

"Well, we just used the GPS. I hadn't heard of it before or anything."

"Who's 'we'?" Rochelle asked, blinking in a sort of flurried manner. She looked off to the side a bit.

"Oh, sorry. My boyfriend, John, dropped me off on the way to work." Leda had an impulse to tell Rochelle about moving to California and about being alone in the apartment and trying to write a novel and how hard it was to feel so much like the way things were.

"Oh, so you have a boyfriend? That's really lucky," Rochelle said. "I've been chronically single."

"Oh, well, believe me, I was the queen of chronically single before I met John. Like, *so* single."

"Yeah, but what are you, like, twenty-two? I'm thirty-eight. It's not cute at my age anymore."

She couldn't believe Rochelle was thirty-eight. She looked so much younger, and yet, now as she said her age aloud, Leda noticed something in her face. It was just in the corners of her eyes, a sort of looseness and tiredness. It was simultaneous with this observation that she realized Rochelle was strange.

"Thirty-eight really isn't old," Leda said.

"My biological clock is ticking. I want a child." Rochelle paused and stared at her as if somehow she could solve her maternal dilemma right there. Leda felt inexplicably obliged. *Answer her, answer her,* she thought, and said quickly:

"I'm sure you'll have a child. Thirty-eight is still really young."

"Who really knows what will happen," Rochelle said. "No one can really help me. Do you want some tea? This place has the best tea."

"That would be great." Leda started for the counter.

"Oh, I meant I'll get it," Rochelle said.

"You really don't have to do that."

"No, please. You can get it next time. Passion fruit? That's honestly their best tea."

"Sure, passion fruit sounds amazing." Leda was so disoriented by the strange woman and her gray eyes buying her tea that she really would have said yes to anything in that moment. *"Dog turd tea. Sure, love it. It's my favorite."*

Leda sat down at the table and texted John.

"She's really weird."

"How is she weird?" he texted back.

"She just seems weird."

"Just get through it. You don't have to see her again after this."

"Here's your tea," Rochelle said, handing her the passion fruit tea.

"Oh my gosh, you really are too sweet." Leda took it from her gingerly. Rochelle had added cream without asking.

"No, you just owe me for next time," she said, winking. She sat back down and looked off to the side a bit. "So what does your boyfriend do?"

"He works for Google."

Rochelle shook her head. "Seems like everybody out here works in tech. My landlord works for Facebook."

"Oh, yeah? Well, I guess all the jobs are out here and everything," Leda said. She wasn't sure if Rochelle had reason to dislike the tech industry, but she decided to try to change the subject. "I've never been very tech savvy myself."

"Me neither." Rochelle seemed somewhat relieved. Although it was hard to tell what she was feeling, as she was still looking off to the side. "So what do you do, Leda?"

Leda wasn't nervous to answer this question with Rochelle. It was impossible to fear the judgment of a person with such poor eye contact.

"Well, it's not really an easy question to answer. I'm an aspiring writer, I guess would be the most accurate thing to say, but of course I would never want to say that I'm 'aspiring' because it sounds so pretentious and stupid. But I'm not making money writing, even though I'm trying to be a writer, so I guess that's really what I am." She held the tea up as if she were going to take a sip, but she knew it was still too hot to drink. "And you?"

"I'm a playwright and an actress myself."

"Wow, that's exciting!" Leda was skeptical of the claim.

"Yeah, I do mostly nonverbal plays that are in dance form. Sort of like interpretative dance. You could say I'm really a dancer more than anything, but I only like dancing in a way that tells a story. And usually that story is something I write. I did a performance at Berkeley a few years ago."

"Oh wow, that's really impressive!" It still sounded crazy, but Berkeley legitimized it to some degree.

"Yeah, I can send you a video of it sometime."

"I'd love that."

Leda tried to keep the rest of the conversation light and happy. She told a funny anecdote about how she and John went to buy a trashcan at Target, and when they went to pay it was two hundred dollars.

"I didn't even know two-hundred-dollar trashcans existed!" Leda said. "And I certainly didn't think if they did they'd be sold at Target. Who knew?"

"Haha, well, I guess I'll know where not to buy my trashcans!" Rochelle said.

Despite Rochelle being a bit strange and her poor eye contact, Leda was enjoying herself. She did like the passion fruit tea, and it was nice not to be spending the morning alone. John would be home later and they could cook dinner and watch a movie, and it would be a good day. She felt that what she was doing more than anything was building a decent day. Tea with a friend, writing in the afternoon, cook dinner with John, maybe get ice cream. It was sustainable. It was nice. *What else is life really than building each day one by one to something that you can tolerate? What is it but slowly shaping time through tea and ice cream?* she wondered.

An hour and a half later the conversation started to lull and it was time to go.

"I should get going," Leda said. "I need to try and get a little writing done."

"Oh, of course," Rochelle said. "We should do this again sometime soon."

"I would really like that." She wasn't quite sure whether she would really like it or not. "Let me just step out for a second and call a cab."

Outside it was bright and summery. The warmth was nice and in it she felt a sense of possibility. It was the same feeling she had felt that first week in the apartment. *Things will be okay,* she thought.

When she got back inside Rochelle had her headphones on. Leda walked over and Rochelle quickly pulled them off.

"Sorry for the headphones. I just can't stand listening to them." She motioned to a group of guys behind her.

"Oh, are they saying something really dumb?" Leda tried to imagine what they could be saying that would have offended her.

"I don't know what they're saying, but I just can't stand surfers."

Leda looked back over at them. She hadn't really noticed before, but they were all in wetsuits.

"You don't like surfers?"

"No, I had a bad experience once."

"Like on a date?"

"Nope. A group of them raped me."

Rochelle was looking off to the side as she said it, but Leda would remember her vivid gray eyes staring straight at her. From then on anytime she'd hear the word *rape* she'd see Rochelle and the brilliant stare that she never really met.

"Oh my god, I'm so sorry."

"Well, I used to always go for walks on Ocean Beach. I'd usually go early morning, like five a.m. or sometimes six. Just when it was getting light out. It's really pretty to watch the sunrise, and it's great exercise to walk in the sand. This one morning I went—it was still pretty dark out so it must have been a little earlier—there weren't a lot of surfers on the beach yet, just a handful, and I was walking and this group of them were standing together talking. And then one of them yelled, 'Hey, I want to suck the sand out of your pussy.' And I didn't even know what that meant, but I kept walking and didn't respond or anything. Then I had this really strange feeling like there were people behind me. And you know you get that feeling all the time. I get that feeling like fifty times a day, but usually you turn around and there's no one or there's maybe like a mom pushing a baby carriage or something, but I turned around and they were right there. It was five guys. I don't remember what they all looked like, except one was really short and one was really blond. He had white eyelashes. Then two of them grabbed my arms, and I started screaming and the third one covered my mouth and they dragged me behind a sand dune. There was seaweed and all sorts of sea debris everywhere. And then they held me, and they couldn't really take my clothes off. It took them a really long time, actually, 'cause I was wearing a romper, and they couldn't figure out how it worked. It was strange because I knew I couldn't get away 'cause four of them were holding me and covering my mouth, but I, like, wanted to help them undress me. Not because I wanted them to, but because they were getting so frustrated and the one guy kept going, 'Fuck, fucking bitch. Fuck.' And it's like your brain doesn't really recognize what to do with someone raping you, but your brain does know the circumstance of taking your clothes off, so it was this really weird feeling of knowing this thing about what should happen but not wanting it to happen. And then I just started crying and shaking. And then they all fingered me, which is something I hate, so in a way to me that was the worst part. Like, I never let guys do it to me so for them to do it . . . it was this horrible violation of everything about myself. I can't really explain it. And the one guy was the one who really raped me. The blond one who I think said that pussy sand thing, although I don't really know for sure because I didn't really look at him when he said it. Another one, the short one, kind of tried, but I think he was hesitant or something 'cause he only did it for like three humps and then he stopped. And all the others kept screaming all this stupid macho crap like 'Yeah, fuck yeah. Ride it,' but they had like their dumb surfer inflections so it was even more awful. Then one of the ones that had been holding me jerked off on me. I think he was trying to come on my face, but he missed kind of and came on my neck and I could feel it run into the sand. It was gross. And then they just said something to each other in these low, muffled voices. I couldn't really hear 'cause I was crying so loud, and then a few seconds later I just felt them all let go of me at once, and they ran off super fast. One of their wetsuits was still half off. And then I got dressed and had to walk back to my car like that. It was really scary too 'cause I was just afraid they would come back. There was no one around besides other surfers, and I wasn't going to ask any of them for help. I got to my car and I was okay. But now, you know, I just can't stand surfers."

Leda didn't know how to respond. The same feeling of unease overtook her that she'd felt watching the raccoons being skinned alive. "I'm so sorry. That's just so awful . . . Did you report it?"

"Yeah, they did a medical exam and took down the information. It was on the local news. They never found the perpetrators." Rochelle blinked in a flurry again.

"When was this?"

"Two years ago."

"I'm so sorry."

"Well, I'll tell you what, I will never go somewhere where there aren't any women ever again. It's a bunch of men on a beach. Women shouldn't go there."

"But it's not your fault you went for a walk on the beach, Rochelle." Leda's phone started buzzing. "Oh shoot, the cab's here. Do you want me to cancel it and call another?" She wasn't sure how to handle the situation, but leaving Rochelle right as she'd confessed her rape didn't seem right.

"Why?" Rochelle said. Her demeanor brightened. "We can do coffee again next week!"

That night Leda relayed the story to John.

"Do you think she's telling the truth? It seems so weird that someone you just met would suddenly tell you she was raped," John said.

"It seemed true. I mean, that whole thing with the headphones and everything. I mean, who would do that?"

"It would be really messed up."

"I feel really bad, but I don't really want to hang out with her anymore. I know that's awful, but there's clearly something wrong with her. I mean, who tells you about their rape when you hardly know them? It's so crazy, right? I have to go, though. I can't just not see her again after she told me all that."

They did a Google search of Rochelle and the incident. An article came up.

"San Francisco Woman Sexually Assaulted by a Group of Surfers on Ocean Beach," it read.

"That has to be it. I feel so bad." She read the article. It didn't say Rochelle's name, of course, or even really describe much about her other than saying she was a local playwright. The details were vague. It wasn't explicit enough to tell you how horrible any of it really was. It made it seem like something had just sort of happened on the beach. *If you'd just read it in the article you'd think it just manifested itself,* Leda thought. *As if no man's mind could be that evil. As if no man would try to suck the sand out of your pussy.*

"Maybe I'm wrong about her," she said as she finished reading. "Maybe she just needs a friend and doesn't have anyone to talk to. I should at least give her a chance."

The next week Leda met Rochelle for lunch at a diner that served organically raised and ethically sourced artisan burgers. Leda ordered the watercress aioli veggie burger and pomegranate lemonade. Rochelle got the coleslaw combo. She chewed with her mouth open and left her dirty napkin on the table in between wipes.

"The thing I hate most about 7-Eleven is that they only have two kinds of toothpaste, but you know, it's so much closer to my house than Walgreens," Rochelle said.

"Yeah, that's frustrating," Leda said, and tried not to look at the napkin.

"Isn't it? I wrote them about it, but I haven't heard anything back."

Leda tried to stay positive. *Do I really need to have friends that are interesting? Maybe she's a good person, and shouldn't that be enough? Who am I to not want someone in my life?*

At the end of lunch Rochelle asked her for her number.

"So that way I can bullshit you at home too," she said.

"Oh, yeah, sure. Here." Leda typed it into Rochelle's contacts.

"Great, I'll text you," she said, winking.

That night Rochelle texted forty-seven times. If Leda didn't respond right away she would send three or four more texts, usually in the vein of "Hey girl, where are you?" or "I'm watching *Big*. I love Tom Hanks's little brother." And then, "Oh wait I mean his best friend. I always thought that was his little brother. Weird!" Leda kept up with it as best she could. She tried to keep a balance between not seeming rude but not encouraging it either.

Over the next three weeks Rochelle didn't let up. She texted nonstop. Anytime Leda looked at her phone there was a notification from Rochelle. The whole thing was maddening, but every so often a text would reveal just how lonely she was and Leda would feel sorry for her again.

"Ate my last TV dinner. I wanted to go out for lunch, but it stinks to go out alone so much. The waitresses all know your orders," she texted.

"We'll go out next week together!" Leda responded. She couldn't help herself.

John thought the whole thing was insane.

"You should really stop talking to her. I know she's a sad person, but you can't be her charity friend. That's not right either."

"I know, but I feel terrible," Leda said. "She's so lonely and that whole thing with the rape. I just feel terrible to just leave her like that."

"You shouldn't. You can't do this forever. You tried and that's nice, but you can't possibly maintain this."

"I know, but I still feel so bad."

"But where will this go? What could this possibly ever be?"

She saw Rochelle two more times after that. Once for the lunch she'd promised and once again for coffee. There was no breaking point in the whole thing. No moment of the last straw or reason to stop talking to her other than all the reasons that had always been. It just was the way it was. That moment in their lives together, their fragile friendship formed around rape. Rochelle only ever mentioned the beach again once, and then it was a story of how her mom and she flew kites there when she was a child. All the while as she spoke Leda thought of the rape and those surfers, the sand and the seaweed, and the long walk to the car.

"I was always good at flying kites," Rochelle said.

When it was time to go the girls embraced one last time.

"Take care of yourself," Rochelle said. "I'll see you soon." She patted Leda's shoulder and winked before she turned to walk away.

Leda stopped responding to Rochelle's texts for the most part after that. She tried to think if there was some other way to end the whole thing, but there really wasn't. Occasionally she'd answer and just say she was busy with a new job. Rochelle seemed to understand. She stopped texting and Leda figured that was it. But six months later she received an e-mail. "Here's that video of my performance at Berkeley as promised. It took me a while to track down. Hope you are well," it said. In the video Rochelle was alone on a stage. There was one spotlight on her and this fierce drumbeat was playing. She was wearing a white dress and dancing viciously to the beat. Her hands were in the air, her black hair tossing to the rhythm. It was wild and raw and gutty. It was really quite good.

CHAPTER 27

The Beginning of the Descent

THE FIRST CHANGE LEDA BECAME CONSCIOUS OF WAS THAT WHEN she'd drop something she wouldn't bother to pick it up. She'd been doing it for a while and hadn't really noticed until she dropped grapes out of the fridge as she went to make herself lunch. They fell on the floor hard. The sound was sort of permeating, as if it made a ring or a boom or echoed in the apartment, but really it didn't make much of a noise at all. She looked at them on the kitchen floor. It was remarkably unremarkable the way they looked then. Green grapes in a plastic bag on linoleum. Like some kind of modern art piece extracted from its context and no longer art. What she didn't want more than anything was to pick them up, but that feeling was not an act of defiance or an act of anything more than just her inability to feel a sense of motivation to lean over and take them in her hand and put them back on the shelf in the refrigerator. *I don't even want to lean,* she thought.

The weekdays started to feel like an obstacle she had to navigate. On the weekends things were fine. She and John would take day trips all over the coast. They'd go see the redwoods or drive to Point Reyes. It was monumentally different from the feeling of looking at the grapes. It was youthful and sexy. They'd take pictures together, and she'd post them on Facebook, and all her friends would be jealous of her.

"I want your life," Anne once texted.

These were the best of times. It was as if the city and its landscapes were laid out only for the two of them. Their own little world wielded through snacks in the car and dinners in Carmel.

But on the weekdays everything once laid out was folded back up. The view of the city, alienating in its outstretch. The hills no longer a vantage point but a steep climb. She'd try to get out of the apartment, but having nowhere to go was depressing. She'd make small tasks for herself—grocery shopping, mailing a package, buying Pepto-Bismol—but she had to walk everywhere because John had the car. The bus was an option, but to get downtown she had to wait at stops in the worst parts of town. It wasn't like Boston, where there was the train that went everywhere and went quickly and you could stay underground. But really the deterrent was in knowing that every walk, every errand, every attempt to get out of the apartment was only in order to make existence bearable, tolerable, sustainably less depressing.

Her last attempt at preserving her sanity through forced excursions was on a Tuesday. John had left for work early and already texted that he was going to be home late. She hadn't written anything in four days. Really, she hadn't even tried. It was sunny and bright out, and so she thought, *Maybe I could write in the park.* She took her laptop and walked down to the little park near her house. It was half a dog park and half a children's playground; the play structures and sandboxes were quarantined away with a fence. Along the side of the dog part of the park were a few benches that were generally empty. Leda sat down on the one closest to the playground. In reality she didn't belong to either side of the park, but she thought maybe someone would mistake her for a nanny. *That's my hope now. That strangers will think I have a reason to be in a park,* she thought. She pulled out her computer and reread what she had been working on. The paragraph she'd written the week before wasn't as good as she remembered. It was already discouraging, and she hadn't even started writing yet. She looked out on the playground. A lone child sat on the seesaw. He weighed it down but seemed content despite it. The other few children played around him, climbing on structures or running around screaming, but he just sat there looking up, as if he were anticipating rain but wasn't bothered by the prospect of it.

The people in the dog section of the park would pass by her and shoot her sorry, accusatory looks. She couldn't really blame them, as she imagined that she did look odd sitting there with her laptop in a dog park/playground, even for a nanny. A black Lab walked over and sniffed the bench she was sitting on.

"Hi there, buddy," she said. He sniffed her hand, but as she reached to pat him he turned unapologetically and went on his way.

Twenty minutes passed. She tried to start a short story about a boy on a seesaw and his black Lab, but it just came out sounding silly. Just then an older lady holding a terrier walked over to her.

"You know there's a café with Wi-Fi just over there." She pointed across the street.

"Oh, I know. I'm not using the Internet. I'm just working on something," Leda said. The lady was dressed in a rich-lady bohemian style. Her gray hair was perfectly done up in a short, strict manner.

"Wouldn't you rather work in the café?" she said.

"Oh no, I'm writing and I can't usually write in public places."

"Isn't this a public place?"

"I mean noisy public places."

"Well, I just thought I'd let you know so you wouldn't be sitting here for no reason."

"Thanks."

The lady nodded, put her dog down on the grass, and walked away. Leda relived the conversation a couple of times in her head and then left the park.

The weeks that followed were long and empty. She hardly wrote. Cleaning the bathroom became a respite from the monotony of everything else. She tried painting once, but it went awry. She read a book about a man who rode his bicycle into oblivion. She hated it but finished it anyway. Mostly, though, she'd watch TV or go on Facebook.

"Oreos make everything better," Katrina posted, and she liked it.

On a Wednesday she thought, *All I do is sit around and think about my arms being fat,* and then she picked up a small Styrofoam ball she found inexplicably lying on the bookshelf and threw it against the wall, but it was too light and too soft to make any impact. It hardly hit the wall at all, really.

John tried to be considerate. At night he'd offer to take her to dinner or to go to the mall. He'd get home late from work usually, though, so most everything was closed. Sometimes they'd just drive around.

"Have you heard of Youth Lagoon?" John asked her on one of their nightly drives to keep her from going crazy. He'd always discover new bands and tell her about them. Early in their relationship it had been something they'd bonded over, but since moving to California things had changed. Most of the time when she would listen to new music it was in the car or walking somewhere, but now that she spent so much time in the house there were seldom any opportunities for her to discover anything. She lost touch with the latest and greatest, and what was worse was that even the bands she loved from before she no longer really kept track of. At first she didn't think much of it. John still knew everything and would share stuff with her when they'd drive at night or go on their little day trips on weekends, but slowly it started to get to her. Sometimes he'd play an album for her for the first time and would start singing along. He already knew all the words, and she didn't even know the band's name. He was living a life at work and in the car and with music that she could no longer share. His own life was lyrical and new, and she was just waiting around for him to share it.

"No, where would I have heard of Youth Lagoon? I don't leave the house. I don't talk to anyone."

"I don't know. I just thought maybe you'd read something about them," he said.

Leda opened the window. It was a typically cool night, but she didn't care. She wanted to feel like there was fresh air in the car.

"I think you'd really like them," John said. "There's this one track, I think it's, like, number ten or something."

"I don't want to listen to music," she said.

"Well, okay, but just listen to this one track."

"I don't want to. I'm sick of all your new bands."

"Let's just listen to this one track, and then we can listen to something old."

Leda rolled the window back up. It was too cold. "I don't want to listen to old music, John. I don't want to listen to any music. I'm sick of the music always being your music."

"How is it my music?"

"You're the one who knows everything new. I don't ever know any of these bands. I used to know everything. I didn't even know Jack White had a solo album. Do you get what I'm saying?"

"No."

"Look, I just . . . I can't . . ." She tried to think of a way to phrase it to him. "I used to listen to music all the time, and when I did it was this thing that was my own, and now whenever we listen to music it's together, and it's bands that you've found and know, and I don't know anything anymore."

"I'm not stopping you from listening to music. Why don't you listen to it in the house?"

"Because I don't like to listen to music in the house. I like to listen to music in the car or when I'm walking somewhere. Most of the time I'd listen on the train on my way to school."

"Okay, I get that, but why not just listen in the house now?" His face became illuminated under a stop light.

"Because that's not me. That's not real. That's me making a fake life so I can live out here for you and your life, John. I already am doing everything for *your* life."

"I don't think that's fair."

"It's not fair, maybe, but it's true."

"You have to find a life out here, Leda. I can't do that for you."

"Find a life out here? I'd like to see you move somewhere with no job and no school and not knowing anyone and just 'find a life.' You had a life already built here waiting for you, and I had nothing. I've been trying to keep from killing myself. That's my life out here. That's what I've found."

"If you really feel that way, then you should see a therapist."

"See a therapist?! I'm going to get professional help to live in San Francisco and support your career? What bullshit is that?"

"What do you want me to say, Leda? It's temporary. We'll move back to Boston, and things will be fine."

"Fine, but don't play me your stupid bands anymore. I don't want to hear them."

"Jesus, Leda."

"Jesus nothing!" she screamed. "All I want is my life back. I moved out here and did all this and I just want my life back! I look like a loser. I'm a loser." She started crying and covered her face. The sound in her hands of her own tears and her own crying was a sound that was real and loud and she could hear it.

After that John said nice things. He hugged her, and told her that he'd start looking for a job soon and that they'd move back to Boston and that everything would be great like it was. They drove to the ocean and parked by the barrier. It was dark, but they could still see the whites of the waves, the cyclical motion of the earth and the moon's pull silent in the car. On the way home they listened to Youth Lagoon.

CHAPTER 28

Fristmas

THEY GOT A SMALL CHRISTMAS TREE BECAUSE THEY DIDN'T HAVE enough ornaments to fill up a regular-sized one. Beyond that, it only seemed right, given that it was just the two of them in their little apartment. Leda had visions of getting a bigger and bigger tree each year so that by the time they'd have children they'd have a full-sized one and enough ornaments to fill it.

Apart from decorating the tree, it hadn't felt like Christmastime, really. It was sunny and in the mid-sixties most days. On Saturday they went downtown and there was skating in Union Square below palm trees. A band played Christmas carols on Caribbean steel drums.

"Who'd ever think you could miss feeling cold," she said to John over a tinny "Little Drummer Boy."

They decided to have their own little Christmas the week before they would be going home to visit their families. How oddly comforting it was to have this private little couple's Christmas. It put so much misery into perspective, as if tinsel and stockings were enough to compensate for all the lonely afternoons spent in the house.

She cleaned the entire apartment that Friday before "Fristmas" ("fake" + "Christmas"), as they called it. It was an ambitious endeavor; she even washed the cabinets. At first it felt cathartic in the way that cleaning often could, but as the day rolled on, and her back started hurting, and she pulled a piece of floss off the floor from behind the toilet, she started to think about how this was the life that so many women in history had lived, that all they did was clean like this all day, every day, and from them she could not really extract her own form. She saw herself as pale and tired, falling asleep at night from an exhaustion that was cruel and unrelenting and waking up the next day to nothing but the same. *And here I am cleaning things John would never think to clean because he's a man, and he's never thought about cabinets being dirty. No, he wouldn't find this floss behind the toilet. No, his back will never ache like this.*

Later on in the day she took a break and looked through a Victoria's Secret catalog. There was this one picture of a model in cotton underwear holding up a pillow shaped like lips over her breasts. The picture stood out because the model didn't look that skinny. She was, of course, as skinny as any of the other models, but the way she posed made her look kind of like she had a bit of a belly. Leda couldn't stop staring at it. It was as if they'd missed this one bad picture. That it had somehow snuck its way into the catalog among all the other glossy, perfectly formed shapes. She had an impulse to cut the page out and save it. As she got up to get the scissors she thought better of it and put the catalog in the recycle bin instead.

The next morning they woke up and exchanged gifts under the tree. She bought John a guitar that she'd been saving for. He bought her a locket from Tiffany's. It was an enormous surprise. Nearly six months before, they had gone in to take a look at the jewelry just for fun. She had seen the silver locket and really liked it.

"It's done in the style of the 1920s. It's from the *Great Gatsby* collection we've done after the film," the saleslady said. She leaned in over the counter. "Tiffany's did the jewelry for the movie, in case you didn't know." Neither of them had known.

Leda really loved the little flower pattern on the front and even though it was big and so intricate, it looked subtle and beautiful on her. John offered to buy it for her right then, but she refused because it was so expensive.

"It's stupid to buy Tiffany's," she said as they walked out of the store. "You just pay for the label."

Opening it on Fristmas morning, she had not anticipated that it could make her so happy. John had put a little picture of the two of them inside, which was really quite thoughtful.

"A locket, about a book, for a writer," he said as he fastened it around her neck. When she texted Anne about it she couldn't help herself and said, "John bought me a locket from Tiffany's!!"

And Anne wrote back, "Wow! I've always wanted something from Tiffany's!"

They baked Christmas cookies and watched *Home Alone.* At around three in the afternoon they had really good sex. *It is our first Christmas living together, and it isn't real in any way because Christmas is really next week,* she thought as she lay in bed beside him. The room felt stuffy and thick. She could faintly smell asphalt that had been freshly laid on the street.

That night they went out to dinner. She wore a dark blue dress and her only decent pair of heels. They laughed and talked, and it felt like dating from when they had first gone out. Before dessert came she went to the bathroom, and as she was washing her hands, looking down at them sudded and wet, she had a fleeting feeling of panic, like the feeling of anticipation when a doorbell rings or the moment you hear your name being called in a crowd. *My whole life is going by,* she thought. As quickly as the feeling came it was gone, and she dried her hands on a towel.

On the drive home they talked about the trip back to Boston and seeing their families and all the things they'd do when they were home. It was such a relief to think that she wouldn't be alone in the apartment for a whole week. *Tinsel and I'll be home for a week,* she thought.

"It really doesn't feel like Christmas out here, does it?" she said, and she rolled down the window and the air felt warm and there were palm trees and somewhere on the street someone laughed and said, "Hell yes."

Some minutes later they drove up the big hill that led to their apartment. Leda looked back at the view that revealed itself with the climb. The city lights were bright and speckled and tossed over the landscape like stars. "It looks like a spread-out Christmas tree," she said.

CHAPTER 29

The Reading

KAROLE KANER HAD BEEN ONE OF LEDA'S FAVORITE PROFESSORS. SHE was an aloof woman who wore indefinable writerly clothing (*Is that a vest or a robe or just a dress maybe?*). She wrote mostly flash fiction, and she said things like, "If you send your work out, you will get published." And, "Good writing is an end in itself." Every time she'd workshop a story she'd treat the work with the same respect you'd give to a published piece. She once told Leda that her story was "punchy and fun and as bold as anything I've ever read." When Leda found out that Professor Kaner would be giving a reading in San Francisco she couldn't wait to attend.

The day of the reading Leda put on a nice blouse and a pair of boots. It wasn't quite indefinable writerly garb, but she felt she looked nice. She was nervous and excited in a way she hadn't been in a very long time. Suddenly all the feelings of independence of the life that she'd known before welled up in her; she felt as if she were walking straighter then. *I walk straighter when I have somewhere to walk*, she thought.

The event was being held at a small bookstore in the more trendy part of the Mission district. When they got there it immediately became apparent that they should have gotten there earlier. The entire place was packed. People were pressed with their backs against the wall. Leda found an empty spot next to an aging hipster and his overdressed date. John stood behind her since there wasn't enough space to stand side by side. Such a large crowd was surprising. The majority of writers struggled to fill rooms, or so had been her experience in Boston, anyway. But the crowd in San Francisco was different. It was a room filled with techies and wealthy bohemians all clinging to their mid-thirties as if that were youth, reaching for anything that might make them seem with-it and intellectual. *As if it were cool, as if they were young, as if they gave a shit about books,* she thought.

Besides (and no doubt in connection to) the larger crowd, the room overwhelmingly stunk of farts. It was likely that the bookstore's ventilation system hadn't been designed to hold so many farts at one time, or maybe it was the wine and cheese offered for everyone to snack on; whatever the reason was, it was unbearable. She looked back at John and scrunched her nose.

"I know," he mouthed in response.

As they were being squished and smelling farts, an older woman was reading a short story. She looked messy and was wearing big, unflattering glasses. Her expression was one that said, *Don't doubt me because I look this ridiculous. I look this ridiculous on purpose.* Leda couldn't really follow what she was reading. They had missed the first part, and it was so boring and so pretentious that it was impossible to retain over the farts.

"Ellia had cruelly disinterested sisters. One for the stars. An expatriot to her husband's parasol," she read.

Someone in the crowd made a little "hmm" sound of approval after she read "ex-patriot of parasols," or whatever it was. "Hmm" was the only acceptable sound you could make during a reading. It was the intellectual form of cheering. Whenever a writer would reference *The Great Gatsby* or some other book that everyone on earth has heard of, you could be sure to hear a chorus of "hmms." What they really meant was, "I HEARD OF THAT! I KNOW THAT REFERENCE!! ME! I EXIST TOO! I'M LITERARY AND I EXIST!! I READ *THE GREAT GATSBY* IN HIGH SCHOOL. ME! ME!! ME!! I MATTER!! MEEEEEE!!!!!!" *Maybe if you actually were relevant you wouldn't need to confirm it so often,* she thought. *Or maybe you're saying "hmm" to cover up the sound of a giant fart. Frankly, I'd rather hear the fart. At least then we'd know you were relevant.*

The bookstore itself was a crisp, modern-looking place. It had a sort of minimalist/hipster aesthetic, with a table at the center that had little novelty gifts and trinkets that undoubtedly sold more than the books. Leda liked the watermelon erasers and the bookmark that said "Reading > everything." A girl near the table nudged her boyfriend and motioned to a duck-shaped stapler.

"How brave I was then. The earth looking iridescent from the open plain," the lady read. Leda tried to imagine what an iridescent earth would look like. On display on the top shelf just to the right of the podium was a coffee table book with a topless woman on the cover who had the largest breasts Leda had ever seen. *Tits,* it was called.

"The infamous people she'd always known. He lit his cigarette, cool," the woman continued, and Leda just looked at the nipples and areolas and round iridescent earth tits.

The story ended with some kind of thing about a divorce. It was a bit of a fallaway ending, as was customary for writers who took themselves so seriously. The final line ended on an image that was supposed to sort of emblematize everything that the story was about without actually fully making sense.

"And she stirred that pasta for a very long time. Thank you." The lady did a final slight nod and everyone clapped and a few people said "hmm."

"And now for someone who needs no introduction at all," she said, and cleared her throat.

That's probably not true. We probably have no idea who this person is, Leda thought.

"His stories have been published in the online journal *The Ocean Online Review* and *Semester,* as well as in *Retrovia* and *The Gunther Quarterly.*"

No one has any idea what any of those are. You could literally be making each of these up, and I would be just as impressed as I am right now.

"And he was recently short-listed for the very prestigious Catacomb Award."

That means nothing to anyone.

"He'll be reading a selection from his newest short story collection, entitled *Iceberg Ashes.* Please welcome Steven Ellington."

Steven Ellington was a gaunt, frail-looking man who wore decidedly nicer glasses than the lady before him. He was in a tweed jacket, as was expected of him by probably the majority of people in his life, and when he spoke he had the tendency to look off as if this were a considerably larger room than it actually was.

"Thank you, Christine. Wasn't that impressive?" he said. "Christine and I go way back to our graduate school days. Just kidding."

Everyone laughed politely.

"Was that a joke?" Leda whispered to John. John shrugged his shoulders and shook his head.

"No, but truly we have been friends for quite a while. This is a story I wrote after I lived in Hungary for six weeks. It's called 'Budapest, My Hidden Mesopotamia.'"

Oh Christ, Leda thought. The story was as terrible as its title. It was another typical trope of the literary community that drove her crazy: centering a story on a place so you didn't have to actually have anything to say. The whole thing reminded her of something her cousin Reid once said to her as he was showing her pictures of his trip to Paris. He was flipping through them quickly on his iPhone.

"The Eiffel Tower," he said, and showed her a picture of the Eiffel Tower he took. He paused for a second and looked at his photo. "I've often wondered what the point of taking pictures of something like the Eiffel Tower is. I mean, this certainly isn't the best picture of the Eiffel Tower, and everyone has already seen a picture of the Eiffel Tower, so really what's the point of taking it?"

"To show that you were there," she said.

"Yes, but I'm not even in the picture," he said. And to that she didn't really know what to say because it was true. And here was Steven Ellington in tweed reading his story about Budapest that certainly wasn't the best story about Budapest ever written, and it seemed like an exercise in futility, a picture to show you were there when you weren't even in the picture.

After Steven Ellington, there was a woman who read a story full of imagery and lists.

"There were two pinwheels, a flashlight, a pack of matches, six different pairs of shoes, and a double-breasted comb," one of them read, and everyone laughed because for this audience that passed as humor.

Then there was another man who read a story about going on a trip through the woods with his dying father or some such thing, and right as he read the line "I'd known love in those woods that I'd never know again," a crazy street person could be heard screaming from outside, "My face, my face!"

If this is what it means to be a writer then god help me, she thought. But then her professor came on. It was thrilling for her to see Karole standing there, this imposing woman in her writerly clothing who had said so many things that Leda told herself at night to make the future seem less uncertain.

"I hope you guys have been enjoying tonight as much as I have," Karole said. "I fear you'll feel nothing but pity when you hear my story, which pales in comparison to what everyone has been reading. But anyway, here we go, it's called 'Celery.'"

The story was different from anything that anyone else had read that night, that was true. It was funny, and it was about feeling alone. Her style was restrained and fluid. And as she read, Leda blinked visions from her childhood that she hadn't remembered until then. For brief moments she was no longer in the hip little bookstore with watermelon erasers and tits. As Karole read, "That evening there was a change," she felt like she was somewhere far and close all at once; a restoration of all the little implosions from the night came together. So much was made brilliantly vivid by the words.

There were two more readers after Karole, but by then Leda couldn't wait for the reading to end so she could go up and say hi and tell her professor how great the story was and how her class had been so inspiring and maybe ask her for advice on writing a novel.

The room became chaotic and loud as the reading came to a close. Everyone made a dash for the wine and cheese. A few skinny hipsters were fighting their way to Steven Ellington. The lady with the big glasses was laughing and nodding. Leda pushed her way through the crowd and John followed close behind. She could see Karole gathered around with the other writers. They hugged and congratulated each other on the reading. Karole was holding a wineglass. Her hair was curled nicely, and she was wearing an elaborately embroidered poncho or vest of some kind. Leda tapped the back of her shoulder. "Hi, Karole."

Karole turned and smiled at her. "Oh, hi . . ."

"I just wanted to come say hello and tell you how much I loved your story. It was just fantastic. Honestly, it was so, *so* good. I just loved it. It's always so inspiring to hear your work. It just makes me want to go home and write."

"Thank you!" Karole looked at Leda for a second. "I'm sorry, what's your name again? Were you in one of my classes? I'm just terrible with names. I'm sorry."

Leda was immediately embarrassed. *Of course she doesn't know who I am. I'm just some idiot without an elaborately embroidered vest.*

"No, it's fine. It's Leda. Yeah, I was in your class a year ago."

"Sorry, I'm just so bad with names."

"That's okay, I'm sure you have a ton of students."

"Well, you know how it is. Are you writing these days?" she said.

"Yeah, I'm working on a novel, or trying to, anyway. I just moved out here to San Francisco with my boyfriend, John." Leda motioned back to John.

John leaned in and offered his hand. "Hi, nice to meet you."

Karole shook it and nodded. "Well, you just keep writing. You know that's half the battle," she said.

Leda couldn't help but wonder what the other half was.

◦◦◦

"WELL, THAT WAS THE ABSOLUTE WORST," JOHN SAID AS THEY LEFT.

"Yeah," she said.

"Don't let that woman get to you, she's just some crazy old lady."

"Yeah," she said.

When they got outside the air felt fresh. It smelled so good.

"Wow, you forget the whole world doesn't smell like farts," John said.

Leda nodded. She too had gotten used to the smell.

———— ❧ ————

CHAPTER 30

Blackfish

As a child Leda had a fascination with orcas. It started soon after seeing *Free Willy,* a film that had made an indelible impression on her. For years everything she owned was orca related: orca stuffed toys, orca stickers, orca T-shirts, and a plastic orca family that she played with in a tub of water. She soon decided she wanted to be a marine biologist when she grew up, and in the third grade she wrote an extensive report on the difference between transient and resident pods. This childhood interest, like so many others, fell away as time went on. By the fifth grade she no longer drew so many orcas on her notebooks, and by the sixth grade she no longer wanted to be a marine biologist. She still found the animals to be beautiful and mystifying all the way into her adulthood, and when someone would mention *Free Willy* she would say, "I loved that movie as a kid."

When the trailer for *Blackfish* first came out John texted her from work. "There's a movie coming out about SeaWorld and the orca that killed that lady," he said. Then he sent her a link. Leda had forgotten all about that story. A few years before, there was a horrifying incident where an orca named Tilikum attacked and killed his trainer at SeaWorld. At the time, SeaWorld claimed that the attack was due to trainer error, saying that the whale had mistaken his trainer's ponytail for a fish and had accidentally drowned her. Leda hadn't given the tragedy much consideration. It was sad, but SeaWorld appeared to be handling it, and freak accidents around big animals were seemingly reasonable. It hadn't stirred up any emotion in her beyond the feeling any tragedy would. But things were very different for her watching the trailer to *Blackfish*. The minute she clicked the link and the story line revealed itself she was captivated. It was then that she first learned that Tilikum had killed two other people previously and that he had been taken from the wild at a young age. She'd formerly believed that all of the whales now in captivity had been born there; this story of his capture and subsequent psychosis was disturbingly mesmerizing.

The rest of the week she spent hours online reading about the orcas. She watched videos and listened to interviews.

"Did you know Flipper killed herself?" she said to John.

"Really?"

"Yeah, she held her breath until she died. Apparently, after the show ended the studio just left her to live basically in squalor, and she died like that right in front of her trainer."

"That's horrifying," he said.

"I know," she said. "And it's real."

She ordered a book called *Death at SeaWorld* and had it overnighted from Amazon. She read it in one sitting.

"You finished it already?" John said the next morning.

"Yeah, I couldn't put it down."

"Leda, I think you're obsessed."

"I'm not obsessed," she said, but when she thought about it she realized he was right. Hours of the day would just pass by, and she wouldn't even notice it. It was as if she were doing research for some kind of report or really important paper for an academic journal, only she wasn't writing anything for anyone. All the research she did was just to feed some kind of inexplicable thirst inside of her.

That Saturday they went to see the film. She hoped that seeing it would calm her and she wouldn't care as much afterward. She got gummy bears and a Diet Coke. *Once I see the movie then I'll be over it,* she thought, and ate a red gummy bear. The film was gripping and tragic. Tilikum's life was one filled with fear and abuse and so much sorrow that it was almost unfathomable. The attack too had been completely misrepresented. He hadn't accidently caught his trainer's ponytail in his mouth, mistaking it for a fish, but rather deliberately grabbed her and dragged her into the pool, viciously thrashing her body around so violently that he dismembered her and actually scalped part of her skull. They had to pry his jaws open to get her mangled body out of his mouth. As the credits rolled Leda was still holding tight to the full bag of gummy bears. Her palm was sweaty against the plastic. That night she went home and watched the trailer again. If she could have watched the film again she would have.

The weeks to follow, she kept up with all of her research. She knew everything there was to know about the case on Tilikum. If she'd been asked to testify in court on the whale's history she could have done so with great authority. She learned the lineages of all the whales and which pods the wild ones had been taken from. Occasionally, she'd remember things she'd learned in the report she'd written in the third grade. It was in those moments that she saw something in herself that was wild and untamable. It was as if deep inside she had buried this childhood obsession and all it took was something to reignite it for it to emerge just as strong as it ever was. That which she believed she'd outgrown was really just dormant and waiting. It scared her.

John began to worry.

"It's not healthy for you to be home like this all day just watching whale videos," he said.

"I don't *just* watch whale videos all day," she said.

"What I mean is, I just don't think this is leading anywhere."

"What leads anywhere?" she snapped. "What at all in life that you enjoy has any kind of real purpose?"

It was such an intense compulsion. What impression of herself could she have given off then? How could she explain giving up grad school and moving to San Francisco and what it meant to her to have John? Could she have painted an accurate picture of herself, lying in her bed watching YouTube videos of orcas? Was it any different from herself as a child with a plastic orca family? The father cruising this way, the mother leaping that way, the baby staying near. Could she have said anything of her life then besides *starvation*?

She decided that the only thing to do was to go on a trip to see the whales in person. John hadn't accrued a ton of vacation time at Google yet, but she figured they'd be able to manage a long weekend. San Juan Island in Puget Sound wasn't too far away from San Francisco, so it seemed perfect. She looked up what the best time of year to go was and where to stay. She found a small house for rent. That night she showed John a link to the whale watch she wanted to go on. John thought the trip would be fun.

"I think it would be good for both of us to get away," he said.

She e-mailed the people with the house for rent and found that it was booked for the next three months straight. By the time it would be empty, the whales would have already left for winter. She looked for somewhere else to stay, but everything affordable had already been booked. She Googled "best place to see orcas," and that's when she found Telegraph Cove in British Columbia. The area was almost completely desolate. There was fishing, and of course the orcas, but little else. She found a few houses for rent that were much more affordable than the places on San Juan. She decided to e-mail about one of the properties, a good-sized house on Cormorant Island in the village of Alert Bay. She e-mailed:

> Hi,
>
> I was looking to rent your house for the weekend of the 22nd. It would be for myself and my boyfriend. We're coming from San Francisco and are looking to stay for two nights. Let me know what your availability is like.
>
> Thanks so much,
>
> Leda

The next morning she woke up to this e-mail:

> Hi Leda give me a call 778-432-0092 —Pat

The e-mail was so short and curt. When she read it she was half asleep, and her first reaction was a mix of embarrassment and anger. She reread her own e-mail, which seemed so long-winded in comparison with Pat's. *Maybe this is what's wrong with me. That I say too many things and try too hard. Maybe I should be direct like Pat,* she thought. *Pat seems like a bitch.*

But when she called Pat, Pat wasn't a bitch at all.

"Hello," Pat said.

"Hi, umm, is this Pat?" Leda said.

"Yes." Her voice was warm sounding, like that of a woman who was good at baking or blow jobs. Even from the few words she'd spoken Leda could hear her thick Canadian accent.

"This is Leda, ummm. I e-mailed earlier about the house for rent?"

"Oh, yes, hi! I should have known when I saw the area code. So you're coming from San Francisco, eh?" she said.

"Yes, uh huh."

"So were you planning on flying into Port Hardy?"

"I hadn't really figured that out yet. I was thinking of just driving up from Seattle."

"Oh, that would be really hard to do, honestly."

"Really?"

"Yes, see, that's why I asked, because I saw that you were wanting just the two nights and the thing of it is that, and it's beautiful here so don't get me wrong, but it's just not easy to get to. You'd really need to fly in and even then you'd be cutting your time super short because, you know, the traveling just takes a long time out here. So, you know, I just wanted to be sure you'd know kind of what you're getting into with it."

"Yeah, I guess I haven't really looked into the whole thing enough." Leda could hear a level of disappointment in her own voice that she hadn't anticipated. It was then that she realized just how sad she was. How different her life had become, and not just the external of it. Her own voice held wavelengths that were too deep to ignore.

"Don't get me wrong," Pat said in her warm, capable-sounding tone. "It's just beautiful here. And driving up through British Columbia would just be a phenomenal trip. Just breathtaking, but you need more time with it."

"Yeah, see, originally we were going to go to San Juan Island, but it's pretty booked up at this point. See, I just really want to see the orcas. It's something I've wanted to do since I was a child." Leda searched for the right words to express what she was meaning, but all she could think of was, "It's just something I really want to do."

"Yeah," Pat said. "San Juan is really beautiful too. I think if you could find anywhere at all to stay there, that would be your best bet. I don't want to discourage you, but, you know, I just wanted to let you know about what a trek it is and all. I just want you to get your money's worth, you know. I don't want you to waste your time."

"No, I appreciate that." Leda listened to the way Pat had said "waste your time" and "discourage." She wished that what she'd really said was *I love whales too* or *You'll get to see the whales*.

After John got home they scoured tons of travel websites for places to stay on San Juan. John was adamant about them finding a place. Even as Leda gave up on the search, he kept looking. She thought that was really sweet. In the end they decided they'd just go next summer.

"Even if we're back in Boston," he said.

But she knew as he said it that they wouldn't be back in Boston at all.

That night Leda couldn't sleep. She stayed awake and wrote a short story about a woman who wanted to see whales so she drove up all the way through British Columbia with her boyfriend and then when she got there, right to Telegraph Cove, right to Johnstone Strait, she walked out of the car and into the water and just walked and walked until she disappeared into the water. Her boyfriend screamed and called for her, but all he could see was the piercing black backs of orcas coming up for air.

Two weeks later Leda got a job at a coffee shop.

CHAPTER 31

Routine

WORKING AT THE COFFEE SHOP, LIFE WAS THE COMPLETE OPPOSITE OF the way things had been. Almost every day she'd wake up and have somewhere to be. It was hard work, and she hated standing all day, but she found such comfort in the certainty of it. John was at work, and she was at work. It was easier to explain to herself. *If I meet someone and they say, "What do you do?" I can say, "I'm working at a café and working on a novel." Or I don't have to mention the novel at all.*

Originally John hadn't thought it was a good idea.

"What about being a writer?" he said.

"I'm hardly writing now, John."

"I just feel terrible that you're having to do this." He shook his head and looked so sorrowful. She touched his elbow.

"I bet I'll write more if I get out a bit," she said.

"Will you?" he asked.

"Yes," she said, but she wasn't sure it was true.

The coffee shop was only one stop away on the bus, so she didn't have to worry about walking through sketchy neighborhoods or too long of a commute. On the bus she'd listen to music, and life almost felt like it had when she was a student. *It's all like it used to be, just like that,* she thought, and she'd turn up the music in her headphones.

At work she'd smile a lot at customers and say, "How are you doing?" and "Have a great one." The interactions were small but precious in the wake of the vast isolation she'd been feeling. She did burn herself quite a few times and one burn scarred on her wrist. She'd used the emergency burn kit and everything, but it still scarred. She'd notice it while showering or putting on bracelets but rarely at any other time.

There was a boy named Allen who worked at the coffee shop. He had a tattoo of a cross on the back of his neck and he wore hipster glasses and had thick, dark hair. His fingernails were a bit too long, but this was really the only thing she found to be unattractive about him. He was very nice to her her first few weeks and on occasion she thought he was almost flirting.

"Cinnamon, yum," he'd said.

But when he learned that she had a boyfriend he stopped flirting, and this made her respect him even more. He was still nice, though, and they got along well. They were almost-friends in the superficial way you could be with someone of the opposite gender. They ate lunch together and Allen would do fake British accents throughout the day. John was jealous, but Leda didn't care.

"I don't think you should have a guy friend that you're, like, seeing all the time and everything," he said.

"Yeah well, I don't see him all the time. We never talk after work." And it was true. The starkness in contrast of her life at work to her life at home became palpable. On occasion she and John would be out at dinner or out for drinks, and she would be so caught up in thinking about what had happened at work that she would hardly talk. John's life was something that seemed different from her own, as if he lived in this grown-up world of stock options and 9:00 a.m. meetings. Very often she'd have to remind herself that she wasn't just working at a coffee shop like any twentysomething-year-old. Very often she'd have to remind herself that she and John were actually supposed to be living the same life.

Allen told her he'd been working at the coffee shop for the last three years. He'd explained to her that he'd moved to San Francisco on kind of a whim and that his real ambition was to work in tech but that he didn't have the skill set.

"Couldn't you take classes?" she'd asked him once when they were on break.

Allen nodded as he thoughtfully chewed an Oreo.

"That's what I'm planning, or actually, what's even better is my buddy has this really well-funded start-up and he said he could teach me some CSS, and I could work for him."

"Wow, that would be amazing."

"Yeah, I feel good about it."

"When do you think you'd be able to quit working here?"

"Probably over the next few months."

"That's too soon!"

"Sorry, but I have places to go," he said, and pretended to smoke a cigarette. "This is an electric cigarette, by the way, because I'm fancy."

She laughed and took one of his Oreos.

There were three other people she shared shifts with besides Allen. There was her manager, Tina, a large girl who wore bright lipstick and generally kept to herself. Leda didn't mind working for her, as she was fair and didn't expect too much from anyone. "I know this isn't your dream job," she'd say loudly anytime someone complained, "but as Tim Gunn says, 'Make it work.'" On a rare occasion she would even let the baristas go home an hour early with pay. Leda liked to imagine that Tina was someone who had a lot in her life besides the coffee shop, and that was why she always kept to herself, and that was why she was so nice to everyone. She liked to imagine that she was happy.

Besides Tina and Allen, there was a girl named Callie who was living in the city with her best friend and was taking summer classes at art school. Callie was super skinny with a very elegantly placed nose ring. She had sort of a long, aloof way of talking. Leda never did find out much about her. Whenever she asked her a question or tried to make small talk, Callie would take an enormous pause and then respond with a one- or two-word answer that made it virtually impossible for the conversation to continue. The best example of this is:

LEDA: Hey, Callie.

CALLIE: . . . Hey.

LEDA: How was your weekend?

CALLIE: . . . Good.

LEDA: Did you do anything fun?
CALLIE: . . . Yeah. I did.

The other person was a boy named Zeke. Zeke was from an island off the coast of Portugal. He was studying full-time at Berkeley and working his way through school. He had a cold, quiet demeanor. Leda didn't really talk to him much because Allen hated him.

"Zeke is an asshole," Allen said after she first met him. "Don't bother talking to him."

"Why?" she said.

"It's a long story, but basically I just really hate the kid," Allen said as he steamed milk. "He's an asshole."

A great many things happened in the time that Allen and she worked together at the café. She was hit on by a millionaire tech tycoon, an old woman accused her of being a "slobbery mess," and she and Allen made up a song called "Waffles and Espresso Will Get to You." But the defining moment between them would happen on a Friday when he missed his shift.

That morning as Leda got to work only Tina was there.

"Have you heard from Allen?" Tina asked.

"No," Leda said. "Did he call in sick?"

Tina shook her head in the kind of pensive way she often did. "I'll call Zeke and see if he can come in."

It turned out lucky that Zeke could come in because the day ended up being considerably busy. It was hot out and everyone wanted iced drinks. By the afternoon Tina gave them an extra break.

"Why don't you two go sit down and rest for a few," she said. "Things seem to be slowing out here finally."

Leda looked at Zeke, who met her stare with the same cold expression he always bore. They walked to the little back patio at the rear door by the Dumpster. Zeke took out a cigarette, and Leda sat on one of the three stools that were out there.

"You don't smoke, right?" he said as he went to put the pack back in his breast pocket.

"No," she said.

He nodded but then paused. "You don't mind if I do, though?"

She was taken aback by his courtesy. "No, I don't mind," she said.

The two were quiet for a minute. Leda hadn't ever really taken the time to look closely at Zeke. Most of the time she was too busy working or goofing off with Allen to notice much about him. He was actually more handsome than she'd thought of him. He had high cheekbones and big eyes.

"Don't you want to sit?" she asked him.

"No, if I sit I won't be able to get back up. I'm super tired."

"Late night?"

"Finals. That's why I'm super pissed I had to come in today."

"Yeah, that must suck. I'm surprised Allen didn't show up."

"Why?"

"'Cause he's usually always here," she said.

Zeke scoffed and tossed his cigarette. "I know he's your buddy or whatever, but you shouldn't trust Allen."

Leda didn't answer.

"I'm not trying to offend you or whatever, but Allen is the kind of person who isn't doing anything with his life. He's been here for eight years. Did he tell you that?"

She shook her head.

"Yeah, he dropped out of school and moved here when he was twenty. He's not like you."

"What do you mean?"

"Well, you're not gonna be here forever. You're not messed up like Allen. I mean, he has problems. You just shouldn't really trust him is all."

"I think he said his buddy has a start-up that he's gonna go work for in a few months."

Zeke smiled and waved his hand dismissively, "Nah, that's something he's said for years. It's not true. He lies a lot."

"Well, I don't know, maybe he's just going through a rough time. There's nothing wrong with working in a coffee shop, anyway. I mean, look at us, all of us, look at Tina." She said "Tina" but she was thinking of herself.

"There's nothing wrong with working in a coffee shop. My parents run a grocery mart. That's what they do for a living. I don't have a problem with it. But that's not the situation with Allen. He's not like the rest of us. He's just a messed-up person who isn't serious. I know he's funny and fun to be around or whatever, but you should just be careful."

"He's always been nice to me," Leda said. She didn't feel it was right not to defend him.

Zeke shrugged. "I'm not trying to convince you of anything. I just know how things are with him, and you should know about it so you don't waste your time."

She didn't know what to say in response.

"Come on," he said. "We should go back now. It's been a while."

The next time Leda saw Allen at work everything was the same. He was goofing off and telling jokes. He didn't mention not showing up the other day or being sick. But as the day wore on Leda couldn't get what Zeke said out of her mind. She felt guarded with Allen in a way she never had before. Everything he did or said she thought about with a certain level of scrutiny that was logically unwarranted.

"I think I might go to Yosemite this weekend," he said.

"Oh, that's cool," she said.

"Yeah, I like going alone and just getting lost somewhere. I always go off the main paths and try to get away from it all. It keeps you grounded and centered, you know?"

"Sure," she said. *You sound like a total fucking idiot. You'll probably get eaten by a mountain lion and the poor mountain lion will end up getting shot by the police because you're such a fucking idiot.*

In the weeks that followed, Zeke's warning persisted. She tried to forget about it. She missed the free and fun times. She missed singing "Waffles and Espresso Will Get to You." But it was impossible. Now she noticed so many inconsistencies in Allen's character that she had never seen before. He was late almost every shift. He missed shifts regularly and never called in. If he made someone the wrong drink and realized it, he'd still try to pass it off on them without them noticing. In an odd way she started to hate him for all these little things, and yet she couldn't bring herself to stop being his friend. Instead she just let things get slowly distant enough where she could maintain the lightheartedness without letting herself be invested.

She and Zeke became closer too. He had a car and often offered her a ride home. At first she hid her friendship with Zeke from Allen, but in time she didn't care and was open about it. Allen didn't seem as bothered by it as she would have thought. It was strange how things could mold and change and she was a part of it, and yet at the same time just a witness to it all. As if her life at work were some organically living thing that she huddled in the lungs of, rising and falling with its breath but unable to alter its rhythm. She'd explain it like this:

"In the end I really wasn't friends with either of them. Sure, Zeke and I got closer, and I respected him immensely, but we just weren't the type of people to really be friends. We didn't get along like that. Zeke was right about Allen, though. I found out soon after I'd quit that he'd been stealing money from the cash register. Tina fired him, but to her credit she kept the whole thing hush-hush, which probably saved him some considerable jail time. I'm not sure where he is now, but I know he left California. Anyway, it didn't really matter. I quit the job and that was that. I didn't really think about those people anymore. It almost feels like it never happened. I was grateful then, though. It got me out of the house and it kept me sane."

—⟳—

CHAPTER 32

Getting Engaged

LEDA HAD TO QUIT HER JOB AT THE COFFEE SHOP BECAUSE OF AN injury she sustained to her ankles. Three weeks prior she'd noticed that she started to feel a dull ache when she walked. She iced them a few times and tried to rest as much as possible, but the pain persisted. Her doctor suggested she see a podiatrist, who quickly assessed the situation, saying, "You have very flat feet. You need more arch support."

"Really?" Leda said. "I've never had this problem before."

"Yes," the podiatrist said. "That's how it works. You get to a certain age and you start having problems. I've seen it happen many times."

"What about the hills?" Leda asked. "I've noticed that it hurts worse when I walk up and down hills. I was thinking maybe I'd hurt myself 'cause I'm not used to walking on hills so much."

The podiatrist looked at her with a blank expression. "No, I think it's your low arches. Here—" She leaned over to a drawer and dug out a pack of inserts. "Start with these and see how you're feeling with them. If they don't help, you'll probably need customs."

Leda looked down at the inserts. "So I just put these in my shoes?"

"Well, that's the other thing," the podiatrist said. "I think you need a more supportive shoe. I'm going to write down the name of a few brands that I think will be good for you. There's a store downtown that specializes in arch support shoes. I think you need to invest in a pair."

The shoes the doctor recommended turned out to be stark white sneakers that had giant flat soles, not too different of a silhouette from a medical boot.

"I'm going to look like a crazy person," she said to John. "And I don't even think I need them. I swear it's the hills that did this to me."

The shoes did help her ankles initially, but after a few weeks she started to get worse again. The long days on her feet at the coffee shop were taking their toll, and the doctor told her to rest. The only realistic choice in the circumstance was to quit. It was sad to say goodbye to everyone but a relief to be getting a break from it. It had been so long since she'd been trapped in the house, bored all day, that she didn't really remember it. She looked forward to lying around and catching up on bad TV. She had plans to organize the hall closet, and of course in the back of her mind she was hoping she'd write more. There was an unwarranted sense of hope.

Leda and John had very often discussed marriage. In her mind she aligned the whole move to California with the intent of having a family. She envisioned herself telling her future children about it, saying, "Mommy loved you so much that she sacrificed for you before you were even born." It was a nice feeling, thinking that she was already doing something that wasn't just for herself, already mothering.

She realized too that having John in her life was a blessing. So many of her friends were still single and miserable. They were going on bad dates while she was just steps away from being married and starting a family. It wasn't always the case, but more often than not, it felt like the holy grail of womanhood.

A month after she quit working at the coffee shop she and John celebrated their fourth anniversary. John made reservations at one of the fancy restaurants they'd been wanting to try. He bought her an expensive bag, and it was warm enough that she could wear a dress to dinner. They ordered a bottle of Champagne to celebrate. Their conversation was, as it always had been, the exchange of best friends. It was perfect.

"When are we gonna get married and have babies?" she asked him.

John rolled his eyes playfully. "You and wanting a baby," he said. "Is that all you think about?"

"Sometimes." She thought back on a pair of baby booties she'd seen in the window display at a high-end baby boutique. They were shaped like bees. As she looked through the shop window that day, there seemed no greater aspiration than to make a baby's feet look like bees. "What about getting married?" she said.

"What about it?" he said, pretending the thought hadn't occurred to him.

"Stop, you know what I mean."

"No, you're right. We should really think about it."

"Are you serious?"

"Yes, I mean, it's been four years. We should really probably be getting engaged."

Leda felt dizzy with a kind of high that was inexplicable, like someone had snapped Pop Rocks inside of her. It was almost like being turned on, the same sense of urgency and desire, only rather than directed to a person it was directed at the conceptualization of *commitment* and *bridal*.

"Are you serious?" she said again.

"Well, don't you think?"

"Of course I do."

"Should we go look at rings together or do you want me to surprise you?"

"No, I don't like surprises. Let's go look together."

The next morning she called Anne to tell her the news.

"You actually said that to him?!" Anne said after Leda told her how the conversation had started.

"Yeah, I mean, we always talk about marriage and having kids."

"I'm, like, shocked. I could never say that to Eric." Eric was her current boyfriend; he was socially awkward and considerably unattractive. Leda didn't understand why they were together, really. She felt Anne could do much better.

"Well, John and I just talk about everything."

"But isn't it more romantic to wait until he asks you on his own? I mean, this is so planned. It's almost like you asked him in a way."

Leda knew that Anne was just being jealous and catty. She tried to be patient of it, since she knew Anne and Eric had been fighting a lot over the last few weeks.

"I don't think this is less romantic."

"Not less romantic necessarily, just . . . like, you just want the guy to come up with it all on his own. I don't know. If it were me I'd just want it that way."

"Why? Don't you want control over your own destiny? Why should getting married be some bullshit thing that the guy comes up with whenever it strikes his fancy? I understand tradition and wanting a man to propose to you and wanting a ring and the whole deal. I get it, and I want a lot of that myself, but at the same time why should I sit there and wait for him to decide everything about my life? Shouldn't I have just as much say as to when we get married as he does?"

Anne was quiet for a second and Leda worried that maybe she'd gotten too worked up.

"No, I hear you. I guess what I meant is, I wouldn't have it in me to say anything to a guy about what I want like that."

The next three weeks Leda spent hours online looking up information about rings. It was such an easy way to pass the time that she didn't even feel bored being stuck in the house. She and John visited nearly a dozen different jewelry shops looking for a place with the best stones for the best prices. Eventually they decided on a local shop that specialized in wholesale, custom rings. Leda found a band she loved that was simple and classic. The center stone was just over a carat. It was round and sparkling and had the most ideal cut, according to everything she'd read online. John loved it too.

"It looks so perfect on your hand," he said. "So delicate."

The salesperson wrote down all the information about the ring so that John would be able to come buy it on his own.

On the drive home Leda felt exhilarated. Everything in her life was coming together. She and John would be getting married soon. She'd have a beautiful ring. It felt like adult life, in the way she had envisioned it when she was very young.

"Do you think you'll go back and buy it tomorrow?" she asked him.

"I don't know," John said.

"But the lady said they can't hold on to the stone so you shouldn't wait too long."

"I just don't know."

"About the ring?"

"About getting engaged right now."

"What do you mean?"

"I just feel confused. This whole thing has made me really anxious."

"Anxious about getting married to me?" Leda couldn't focus on what he was saying. It felt like his words were floating out of him and into the air. Like they were just hanging there in the car, not really leaving and not really staying, just floating in the air beside her. *Why aren't you more upset right now? Why aren't you sobbing? Don't you hear what he's saying?* she kept asking herself.

"I'm not sure what I feel, but I know that when I start thinking about getting married I just feel panicked, like I can't breathe."

"But you're the one who wanted to do this."

"I do want to do this. I'm just saying I feel anxious about it, and whenever I think about it, I just feel like we shouldn't do it right now."

"When do you want to do it?"

"I don't know."

"But it's been four years. I moved out to California for you."

"I know you did."

She felt herself start to warm into a kind of anger that she hadn't known she was capable of. "So while we were ring shopping you were just planning to tell me this in the car the whole time?"

"No, I didn't plan this at all."

"So this was just some revelation you had all of a sudden?"

"No, I've thought about it before."

"And you decided to tell me about it in the car on the way from ring shopping?" The thought that they'd just minutes before been discussing diamond clarity seemed violently cruel.

"I didn't decide anything. I really hadn't planned on saying anything right now. Honestly, this wasn't premeditated at all or anything like that."

"You think that makes it better? That instead of planning out exactly what to say and knowing how you felt and sitting me down in a really thoughtful, caring, thought-out way, that just randomly saying it in the car like it's no big deal. Like in the same way you'd say 'Let's get coffee' or 'I need to stop at CVS for . . .'" She tried to think of something you'd stop at CVS for, but for the life of her she couldn't think of anything. "For some napkins." *Damn it,* she thought at her weak example. "You think it's better that you weren't planning on ripping my heart out, but really it only just makes you an asshole."

John was quiet. "I'm so sorry, Leda. I don't mean to hurt you in any way. I really don't."

"Well, how did you think I was going to react?"

"I didn't think of it."

"No, obviously you didn't, because if you had you wouldn't have had me going around to ring shops for three weeks like a complete delusional idiot." She looked at him. His sweet, boyish face and bright blue eyes. His lips were the same as they always were. She felt so distant from him then. "It must be convenient to never have to think of anything, and to just do whatever whim strikes you whenever, and to not have to constantly worry about everything. It must be great to be a man," she said.

"I'm sorry," he said quietly.

They were silent the rest of the ride home. When they pulled up to the apartment, she jumped out of the car before he even shut off the engine. She ran inside. It felt good to run up the stairs. Her knees pulling: straight then bent, straight then bent. Her feet hitting hard against each step. She raced to get her key out before she could even hear John coming up behind her. Usually they went inside together and John would always be the one to unlock the door. There wasn't any real reason that it happened this way; it was just a routine they had settled into as unconsciously as they'd ended up in California for nearly three years.

Once inside, she went straight to the bedroom and locked herself in. Living together didn't give her the kind of upper hand that dating did. When they were dating it was easy to use the distance to her advantage during a fight. It allowed for him to miss her in a way that living with him never could. Her mom once told her that she didn't think living with a man before marriage was a good idea.

"Men take you for granted easily. If you're just there supporting him and taking care of him, what is his motivation to marry you?" she'd said once.

At the time Leda thought the sentiment archaic. Sure, it may have had its place in a world where women were expected to stay at home and cook meatloaf all day, but not in a modern era where marriage could be just as much of a burden for a woman as it was for a man. Now sitting in the locked bedroom and listening to John open their apartment door, her heart racing in anger and a sad sort of anticipation, she wondered if maybe her mother had been right.

He walked down the hall to the bedroom, each step louder, creating a false sense of urgency. He knocked on the door. "Leda, please," he said.

She didn't answer.

He tried to open the door. "Leda, please open the door."

"I just need some time," she said. She thought it was the perfect thing to say and was hoping his reaction to her "needing some time" would be to freak out and continue to beg to see her. She wanted him to not be able to bear the thought that she needed some time.

"Okay, I understand that," he said. Infuriatingly, he had not known what the correct reaction to her needing time was. She waited a few more seconds, hoping that maybe once the time started he wouldn't be able to take it, but she could hear him walking away down the hall. *Idiot*, she thought.

Alone in the room, she wasn't sure what to do with herself. She went to text Anne but hesitated. She knew that Anne would be happy to hear about her troubles, that she'd take a sort of sick satisfaction in the way that only another girl could. The thought of it angered her, but beyond that she felt that telling Anne would admit to some kind of failure. She decided not to tell her until she was sure that it was definitely not happening, and even then she'd come up with some excuse about it being the money for the ring or something. As a girl, she couldn't admit to her best friend that she had failed at the fairy tale, especially not when her friend was so jealous. It was complicated, but it was just the way it was.

She opened her computer and went on Facebook, but she couldn't pay attention to anything she was looking at. "Beach Day #besties," a girl she vaguely knew from college, had posted a picture of herself and her friend standing arm-in-arm in bikinis. *Eat a sandwich, you cunts,* Leda thought. She shut the computer and lay back on the bed. *I should be crying. Why am I not crying? Cry. Cry!* She relived the conversation from the car over in her head. It was awful, but she still didn't feel like it was really happening. John had never been the kind of guy to be commitment-phobic. It was something that she loved about him. *Maybe he just needs to talk.* She got up from the bed and went downstairs.

"I'm sorry," he said as he saw her. "I don't know what I'm saying right now."

"Look, I shouldn't just get so upset." She sat down beside him on the couch. "We should just talk about this. What is it you're worrying about?"

"I don't know what I'm worrying about." He sighed a heavy sigh and ran his hand through his hair, a gesture he only ever made when they were fighting. "Sometimes I think about getting married and it seems like the best thing ever, and then other times I think about it and I just start panicking."

"What do you think about when you start panicking?"

"I don't know. It's nothing really. It's more a feeling than a thought."

"But this is the thing, John. You've never been the type of guy to be like this. I'm in total shock over the whole thing."

"I know. I feel the same way. I don't know what's going on with me."

"So what do we do?"

"I don't know."

"Come on, that's not helpful. I mean, you need to try a little harder than that."

"I guess what I keep thinking about is just that I had wanted to do all this stuff before I was supposed to get married that I didn't get to do yet."

"Like what?" Leda tried to imagine what he possibly could be talking about. Her mind immediately went to wanting to sleep with more women, even though she knew that wasn't the case. "Do you mean date other people?" she had to ask him anyway.

"No, of course not, jeez. I just mean, like . . ."

"What?!" She hadn't meant to yell, but she felt the anger building up again.

"Well, sometimes I just think I would have liked to travel more."

"That's it? We can travel. I'd love to travel."

"I don't mean travel exactly. I mean I'd always thought I'd live in different places. I always wanted to live in Colorado for a while."

"Colorado?"

"Yeah."

"But we moved to California."

"I know, but it's just something I've wanted to do."

"Colorado?" Leda tried to place the concept of Colorado in her mind. It was in the middle of the country, away from the ocean. There were cowboys and Republicans. What John wanted with it all of a sudden she couldn't understand. His secret ambition felt like a betrayal. It was as if he'd revealed that all along he'd been an anteater. *Colorado?* she thought. *Who are you?*

"It's not about Colorado," he said.

"Then why are you saying it?"

"Because you asked me to."

"Okay, but why Colorado? I mean, all along you've just been wanting to move to Colorado, and you haven't said anything for all this time? Why didn't we just go to Colorado instead of California if that's the case?"

"It's really not about Colorado. I'm sorry I said it. I was just using it as an example. I don't know what I'm feeling. I just feel like I'm not ready."

"But we've always talked about marriage. Do you think that I would have moved across the country with you if we weren't going to get married?"

"Of course not. I do want to marry you someday."

"So I'm expected just to wait until you're ready? Whenever that might be? We've been together for four years. We've been living together and building a life together. How would marriage be any different from what we're doing right now?"

"I don't know, but it just is." His face looked sad.

"But I love you," she said.

"I love you too."

She started to cry. *I can't, I can't.* She tried to catch her breath, but she kept crying harder and harder. All the realness was at once. He hugged her and she wanted to push him off, but she couldn't bring herself to do it.

"I don't know what to do," she said through the tears. "Do you want to break up?"

"Of course not!"

"But you don't want to marry me." And she cried even harder at hearing herself say the words out loud.

"I'm so sorry." He hugged her more. She kept thinking of what it all meant. *Things are no longer like they were. He can't really be my best friend anymore.*

"I need a tissue," she said. She got up from the couch and went to the bathroom. It was nice to get away from John for a few seconds, to be driven by something other than what he was saying, even if it was just her runny nose. They didn't have any tissues so she used toilet paper. It was the cheapest brand, so it was rough on her skin. *I'll never buy this cheap crap again,* she swore to herself, as if the ambition not to buy the cheap crap extended to anything and everything in her life.

She looked at herself in the mirror. Her eyes were swollen from crying so hard, and her makeup had smeared. It surprised her to see her own face that way; it had been a long time since she'd looked in the mirror after crying. The last time was at the age of fourteen after a girl at school called her bloated. She didn't look that different than she had then. It was as if she'd been kidding herself all along, thinking that she'd been aging.

She grabbed a wad of toilet paper and went back to face John. When she saw him, she had a fleeting impulse just to look at him and laugh at it all as if it were some kind of big joke. Sometimes when they'd get in a fight the two of them would just start laughing, as if they'd realized how silly and petty they were being at the exact same moment. This felt different. This was like dying. Her mind was racing. *I need to fix it—I need to stop it,* she thought.

Until this moment she had believed that if any man would ever do what John was doing to her now, she would just walk away. Just like that. Not even a second thought. She remembered her friend Sonja telling her how her boyfriend, Carl, of seven years, still wouldn't even talk about them getting married.

"Why don't you just leave him?" Leda said to her once on the phone.

"I don't know. I really love him, and I really love the apartment," Sonja said.

She later told John about the conversation. "Can you imagine staying with someone for an apartment? It's absurd."

But now, standing here staring at John, still himself, the one she knew, the one she loved, she understood what Sonja meant. You couldn't undo your life with someone just like that. Loving an apartment was a real thing. She couldn't just let things change. She needed to put it back together again.

"Look, John, let's just let things rest for right now with the whole thing and talk about it again in a week."

"Okay, let's do that. I'm so sorry."

He got up and put his arms around her and buried his face in her neck. *If only Sonja could see me now,* she thought.

The next few days teetered between torture and normalcy. She had said they wouldn't talk about getting engaged until the week was over, but of course that didn't happen.

"Don't you know how horrible it feels to tell someone you want to get married only to have them tell you that they don't feel the same way? You have all the power in the relationship now. Do you realize that?" she said on Monday.

"That's not true."

"Yes, it is true. I'm completely powerless in this situation. You know I love you and want to marry you, and I don't have the luxury of knowing you feel the same way."

"I'm sorry, that's not my intention."

John often apologized and said it wasn't his intention. Every time he did it infuriated her.

"Apologies don't make it better, John," she said on Wednesday. "I wish you'd stop saying sorry and just stop making me feel bad."

Throughout it all, the day-to-day rigors persisted. No matter how bad the fights got, no matter how angry or hurt she felt, at some point they just resumed things as usual. It was too exhausting to keep up such a high level of anger or sadness; she had to just let go of it and move on with the day. They would fight for two hours straight, not resolve anything, and then just clean the bedroom or make dinner. Sometimes she would try to act mad for as long as possible, but realistically it wasn't practical. There were too many hours to fill not to find temporary relief.

By the end of the week nothing had changed. John vacillated between fear and apology. Leda became more and more desperate at the prospect of their possible demise. Saturday night they decided to go out to dinner.

"I'm really sorry about this last week," John said as they ate soup.

"I don't want to talk about it." She really wanted to tell him about the screaming in her head at his millionth "I'm sorry," but she refrained.

"Don't be like that."

"I can't help it. It kills me."

"It kills me too."

"Really? How is that possible?"

"Do you think I thought I wouldn't be able to get married after all this time?"

"I don't understand you. I don't understand any of this. I don't know who you are. I feel like I'm in the Twilight Zone."

"I guess all I can say is that if you knew how it feels in my head you'd understand why I can't get married."

"*Can't get married?* You said you just needed some time."

"You know, honestly, I can't even say that right now. I'm just freaking out."

"What do you mean?"

"I don't know. I feel like my life is ending."

"Your life is ending because we'd be getting married?"

"I know that's not the case, but it still feels that way."

Leda felt like someone kept slapping her in the face over and over again. Her rage and shock and misery and disbelief and confusion and sadness and hurt and everything were hitting her over and over with each word. They were in a restaurant, though, and so she just sat there with soup in front of her, carrot ginger. A taste she would forever associate with nausea.

"What I don't think you realize, John, is that I gave up *my life* for you. *My life* is what ended. I gave up grad school, I gave up my family, I gave up my home. I did that for you. I did that to spend forever with *you*."

"I know you did, and I feel terrible about it, but that still doesn't change anything."

The moment he said it she knew he was right. No matter what he promised her or what she sacrificed, in the end it didn't matter. Whatever she labeled it in her mind, whatever she told herself the last four years of her life were, the reality was that her success was completely dependent on him. *My life is not really mine,* she thought.

"We should go. I can't just sit here and have dinner and pretend everything is fine. Where's our waiter?" she said.

They got their food boxed up and John went to go get the car. Her ankle pain had been getting worse, and it was a long walk back to where they'd parked.

She sat alone at the table waiting for him. She thought about her mom and the last time she'd seen her at Christmas. It felt very far away.

"Hey, there." An older man walked up to the table. He was in a checkered sports jacket with a brightly colored pocket square. His hair was thinning and his eyelids hung with old age. She'd seen him come in a few minutes before with a whole group of old men.

"I just want to tell you that you are beau-ti-ful," he said.

"Oh, thank you," she said.

"Do you have a boyfriend?"

"Yeah, he's getting the car."

"Of course you do. He is one lucky guy. I would do anything to have a beau-ti-ful girlfriend like yourself. My name is Marv, by the way." He put out his hand for her to shake.

"Nice to meet you. I'm Leda." Normally, she hated these kinds of come-ons from dirty old men, but tonight it felt like the greatest victory. It was as if he'd been sent to her as an angel from dirty old man heaven, a representative of the abhorrent male ego.

"What a beau-ti-ful name for a beau-ti-ful girl. Well, you take care there, Leda. And make sure that boyfriend of yours treats you right, okay?"

"I will," she said.

Marv smiled and walked over to the group of men sitting at a big round table at the back of the restaurant.

"I met a beau-ti-ful girl," she could hear him say to them.

She told John about it in the car.

"I'm an asshole," he said.

The next morning as John went out to get them coffee she called her mom. It was something she had been unable to do for fear that her mother would be disappointed in her. Moving across the country for a man's career and being left out in the cold wasn't exactly any parent's dream for their daughter, especially not her mom's. Her other fear was that her mom would come to dislike John. It was strange, but she felt oddly protective of him and of their love together. She didn't want her mom to start cursing him out, saying all sorts of unbearable things about him. It was a ridiculous fear, though. Years later she'd look back on it and say, "The one thing I regret about that horrible time is that I didn't tell my mom sooner."

"I'm so sorry, honey. What an awful thing to be dealing with," her mom said. She was calm and her voice was soothing to hear, even in a time when any kind of real comfort seemed implausible. "It's something all men go through. I really believe that."

"Really?"

"Yeah, your dad freaked out right before we got married. He told me he wanted to spend a year in India. Can you imagine Dad living in India?"

"What did you do?"

"Well, I was really upset for a while, but then I told him to just go, and of course he didn't, and the next spring we got married. Men are afraid of things women aren't. That's why they're so oppressive. They're afraid of our fearlessness."

"I don't feel fearless. I feel terrified of losing him."

"Don't be terrified. I think he'll come around, but even if somehow he didn't, you'll be fine. You can't forget that."

The talk with her mom made her feel better. When John got home they sat outside on the patio and had coffee.

"Are you okay?" he asked her.

"Not really, but . . . I don't know."

"I'm sorry about what I said last night about not wanting to get married. That's not how I feel. I was up all night thinking, and I realized that I'm just being crazy. Yes, I'm anxious about the whole thing, but it's insane for me to be acting on anxiety. And I do want to marry you. Maybe I feel nervous about doing it right now, but that's just something I need to get over. I owe that to you. You moved out here and everything. You deserve stability."

"John, even though that's all true, you still have to want this. I don't want to be pressuring you into getting engaged. It has to be something you want or it doesn't mean anything to me."

"It is what I want. I'm going to buy the ring tomorrow."

"Are you serious?"

"Yeah, I've decided." He reached over and grabbed her hand.

Leda felt a huge rush of relief. It was as if the air had been let back into her lungs. *I'll have to call my mom back,* she thought.

The next day she spent cleaning the apartment. She wanted things to be perfect for when John got home. He told her he'd surprise her with the actual engagement, so she figured he wouldn't ask her that night, but it still felt as if they had a lot to celebrate. She wanted to walk down to the market and get something special to make for dinner, but her ankles were too painful so she made spaghetti instead. Most of the day she felt happy, but occasionally she'd remember the things he had said over the past week, and there just was no way to feel good about it. Anne texted her, "How are you?" at around noon. Anne still didn't know anything, but that didn't make it any easier to know what to say. Was she happy? Was she miserable? Was there anything besides herself and the spaghetti just boiling the ever-frenzied day away, her frantic thoughts rising with the steam? "I'm pretty good," she wrote.

At around 5:45 she texted John. "Almost home?" He didn't answer, but she didn't think much of it. *He must be at the jewelry store by now.* She put on a nice dress and did her makeup. The apartment looked as clean as it ever had. She felt like a woman who had won a contest. *I'm like that sad makeup girl,* she thought. A few weeks back she'd gone on YouTube and stumbled upon a thread of makeup tutorial videos. She hadn't realized it, but apparently making a makeup tutorial video and posting it on YouTube had become a thing. Many of the videos were by preteen girls who had entirely too much money and not enough adult supervision. *How ironic that they choose to give tutorials in what they probably know the least about,* Leda thought. After clicking through a few videos, she came across a nineteen-year-old Canadian girl who had amassed a considerable following. She was a very skinny, pretty girl with overdone eyebrows. Most of the comments said things like, "You are so so gorgeous!" or "You should be a model" or "I was feeling pretty today until I saw your video. Stunning!" Almost every single one of her videos had over a million views. She even had a video devoted completely to her hair that she began by saying, "Hi, guys, I decided to do this video because I get thousands of questions about my hair nearly every week." *What must it be like to devote sixteen minutes to explaining your hair?* Leda thought. At the bottom of the page was a video titled "Victoria's Secret Runway Challenge." It opened with blurred lights and booming electronic dance music. The girl walked through an empty subway stop in red

lingerie, her skinny frame emphasizing her youth and need for nour-
ishment. Everyone was oohing and aahing over it, and after reading
down a bit Leda figured out that this had been the girl's audition for
some kind of Victoria's Secret competition open to the public.

"Did she win? She should have!" someone commented.

"No, she couldn't enter 'cause she's Canadian. Too bad you have
to be American to enter!" someone else responded.

The girl had made an entry video to a contest she couldn't even
enter. Somewhere along the line of millions of views and a video
about her hair, she'd lost perspective. Leda had tried to explain the
poignancy of it to John. She showed him a few of the girl's videos,
including the audition.

"Yeah, I mean, it's weird," he said. "But I don't really get what
you mean."

"I guess I can't explain it," she said. "Do you think she's pretty?"

He looked back at the video for a second.

"Not really," he said before turning away.

Seven o'clock rolled around and she still didn't hear anything
from him. The jewelry store was closed by now. She tried calling,
but he didn't pick up. She texted him again. "Where are you? I made
dinner. It's getting cold." She figured he must be in traffic or that
maybe things had taken longer than he expected at the store. *I'll give
it another half hour,* she thought. She watched an episode of *Everybody Loves Raymond.* Seven thirty came and went. By eight o'clock
she was worried. She called her mom.

"John hasn't come home yet and isn't answering the phone."

"I'm sure it's nothing," her mom said.

"I don't know. This isn't like him. Maybe I should call the police."

"I think it's probably a little early for that. Why don't you wait a
bit longer before really worrying."

She changed out of her dress and put on PJs. The spaghetti was
completely cold, but she didn't bother to heat it up. She took frantic
bites in between checking her phone to see if John had texted. Once
it was near ten she called her mom again.

"Mom, I'm freaking out. What if something happened to him?
What if he got in a car accident?"

"I honestly don't think that's the case. Maybe you should text him that you're going to call the police if he doesn't answer."

An hour after she texted him that she'd call the police, John finally texted. She was still on the phone with her mom when she heard the text.

"I'm fine. Don't call the police. I'm sorry," it said.

Leda read it to her mom. Her mom sighed. "I think you should go to bed. I don't know what bullshit game he's playing with you right now, but you don't need to be freaking out all night about this. He's being an asshole."

"I just can't believe he'd do this to me." She was texting him back as she was still on the phone to her mom.

"What are you doing?" she texted.

"Do you know how horrified I am?" she texted.

"How do I deserve to be going through this right now?" she texted.

"Leda, just go to bed. Do not stay up and wait for him."

"I might have moved out here for nothing. I might have given up grad school for absolutely nothing. I'm an idiot."

"You're not an idiot. Loving someone and wanting to build a life with them is what everyone wants. You're just trying to be happy."

"I feel like I'm going to throw up."

"That's why you need to go to bed."

She tried to follow her mom's advice. She brushed her teeth and washed her face. She shut off all the lights in the apartment so that he would see from the outside she'd gone to bed. Her hands were shaking so hard that when she tried to plug her phone in to charge it for the night she could hardly manage it. She lay in bed and closed her eyes. What she wanted more than anything was to just instantly fall asleep, to tell her mind to do something, to do what was best for her, and for her mind to just listen. She could hear their neighbor walking around. He was an extremely nerdy guy in his mid-forties who lived alone and masturbated loudly. Generally, John and she were repulsed by him and would complain to each other about how loud he was late at night, but tonight it was oddly comforting to hear him clanging around in his usual oblivious fashion. It was nice to know someone was there even if it really meant nothing at all.

At 2:36 a.m. she could hear John at the door. She told herself she would wait in bed. That no matter what he did or said she wouldn't respond to him, other than "I think you should sleep on the couch tonight," but as soon as she heard him coming up the steps, she shot up and ran over, her heart leaping at the thought of him actually being in front of her. *Will everything be different now that he's done this to me?*

When the door opened it was immediately apparent where John had been all night. He was drunk. He wavered back and forth in place. His eyes were completely bloodshot.

"What the hell, John?" she asked him.

"You don't know anything." His speech was slurred in an almost cliché drunken way. She'd never seen him this drunk before. He hardly ever drank and all of a sudden here was this caricature of drunkenness in front of her. It was disorienting.

"Where the fuck have you been all night?" she said. At this point she knew that there would be no getting through to him, but she still felt she should say something.

"I want to die."

"You want to die because you don't want to marry me?"

"I want to die." He walked past her into the living room and lay down on the floor. She wasn't sure what to do about it. She grabbed a burrito from the freezer and heated it in the microwave.

"Here," she said, and tried to hand it to him. "Eat this."

"No, I want to die. Fuck you."

She pushed it closer to him. "Eat this and sober up."

He took the burrito and took a big bite and spat the bite into the air. "No, fuck you."

"Whatever, I'm going to bed. You're a fucking asshole." She threw the burrito into the trash and went upstairs to the bedroom. Now she was angry, and it wasn't so hard to fall asleep.

The next morning she woke up and tiptoed downstairs. John was asleep on the floor in the same place she'd left him the night before.

The bite of burrito was next to his head; other than that the place was spotless, a sad reminder of her misguided hope from the day before. She looked at the clock over the doorway. It was nearly nine. For a second she worried John would be late for work, but then it dawned on her what day it was. The office would be closed for the next two days for fumigation. In happier times she and John had discussed spending the two days off at Lake Tahoe as a sort of mini vacation. How utterly far away that conversation seemed, so remote from reality. *To think that I actually thought that there was room for Jet Skiing in my life.* She went back upstairs and got dressed as quickly as possible. She put on her clunky arch support sneakers and headed for the door.

"Leda?" she heard John call.

She didn't answer and unlocked the door.

"Where are you going?" she could hear him say as it shut hard behind her. It was satisfactory to hear the alarm in his voice. *Nowhere, you asshole,* she thought.

She walked down around the corner to the bakery and ordered herself a hot chocolate and a muffin. The place was mostly empty. She sat by the window and checked her phone. John had texted seven texts and called four times. It was such a wonderful feeling to see her phone ablaze with his desperation. Most of the texts said things like "I'm sorry" and "I'm such a fuckup" and "Please, you have to forgive me." He also left a heartbreaking voice mail that even in her anger was difficult to listen to. It went:

"Please, Leda [sobs]. I love you so much [more sobs]. You are everything to me. Without you I'm nothing. I don't want to miss you for the rest of my life [more sobs]."

It was tempting to respond to John, but she promised herself she wouldn't. She needed a break from everything. She needed for him to know that what he was doing was wrong. She drank half her hot chocolate, finished the muffin, and headed back out on her walk. She didn't know where she was going exactly, but Noe Valley lent itself to not having anywhere to go, with all its gift stores and little boutiques. *Maybe I ended up living here just so that when this horrible, horrible time came I'd have something to do. Maybe it was all leading up to this single moment,* she thought. She went into one of the trendy little shops and looked through the knickknacks. A woman with a baby was asking about watches.

"But with the batteries, do I have to change them often? I just want something easy. Something that I don't have to worry about," she said.

Leda left and went to a clothing store.

"Can I help you?" the salesgirl asked. She was slender but pear shaped. Her hair was pinned up and she was wearing a dowdy-looking hipster dress, as was the style of the store.

"Um, no, I think I'm just looking for now, thanks," Leda said.

"Okay, well, if I can help, you let me know."

I wish to god you could help me, she thought.

She tried on a blouse and a very skimpy tank top. Neither was flattering. *I'm like a sad cow,* she thought, and left the store.

John called her eighteen more times. She tried to refrain from checking her phone as much as possible, but she would have never thought to silence it. She did want to be alone, but there was a difference between being alone and feeling alone and right now the thin separation of the two was the shoestring of her life.

She stopped in the little Eastern shop that sold mainly jewelry and decorative art. She'd bought a necklace for her mom there at Christmastime, and the woman who owned the shop recognized her.

"Oh, hello," she said with a thick accent. "I remember you." She was an older woman who had the propensity for wearing scarves as elegantly as Leda had ever seen anyone wear a scarf.

"Hi!" It was so nice to see someone she knew besides John, even just superficially.

"What can I do for you today? I always remember you. You have such good taste."

Leda hadn't planned on buying anything, but the kind lady and the warm smell of incense, combined with her extreme misery, were not conducive to passing on jewelry. She found an amber bracelet in a case by the window.

"Could I take a look at this one?" she asked the lady.

"Yes, of course." The lady walked over and unlocked the case.

"This is a very beautiful piece. It's dark amber. Everyone likes the light, but I like the dark." She put it on Leda's wrist and clasped it. "It's perfect for you with your delicate wrist."

Leda looked at the bracelet. How easy it was to assign importance to it. To say to herself, *You'll buy this bracelet and you'll be someone who is independent and strong and who wears scarves. You'll be someone who can leave him.*

"I love it. How much is it?"

"It's one twenty-five."

"I'll take it."

It was nearing noon and she was getting hungry. The thought of sitting alone and eating lunch was depressing, even with her new bracelet. She went into the little used/new bookstore to buy a book to help pass the time during lunch. She was hoping to buy *Stag's Leap;* reading a bunch of sad poems about a divorce seemed like exactly what she needed.

"Do you have Sharon Olds's new book?" she asked the hipster at the register. She'd seen him there before and never cared for him. He was always making pretentious remarks and touching his beard an unreasonable amount.

"Umm, you know, actually we don't." He was visibly embarrassed that they didn't. "I'll make a note of it, though, 'cause we should."

"Okay, well, thanks anyway."

"Yeah, sorry," he said, touching his beard. He looked as if he wanted to say something else but didn't.

In the end she decided to buy *Goodbye, Columbus.* One of her professors had once told her that her writing reminded him of Philip Roth's. She'd been meaning to read his work for a while, and now seemed like the most opportune time to indulge in the idea that her writing was like his.

She paid for the book and headed across the street to La Boulange. She didn't much care for the food there, but everywhere else was a place she and John went together, and she didn't want to deal with it.

There was an empty seat by the window. She sat down with her grilled cheese and Philip Roth. It felt for a second like she had things together in a weird way. Her whole little world barricaded down at the counter. *The first time I saw Brenda she asked me to hold her glasses,* she read. *This doesn't sound like my writing at all,* she thought.

The girl to her right was eating a smelly soup and the old man to her left was reading a newspaper. Her sandwich was too rich. It had Brie on it, which up until this moment she hadn't realized was a completely unacceptable cheese for a grilled cheese sandwich. She glanced out the window and without meaning to look at anything at all, she saw him. There was no way to miss him; it was like a screaming red bolt in the hazy gray mix of strangers. He was crossing the street. His hair was a mess and he looked like he'd been crying. She watched him enter the little shop she'd only just left. Seconds later he was back out again. Then into the shop next door. He was looking for her.

Her first inclination was to get up and call out to him like she would on any day.

I'm over here. Let's have a smelly soup together, she'd say.

But it wasn't any day. He walked up the street in and out of a few more shops before disappearing. She leaned forward in her seat to see if she could still see him, but he was gone.

She spent another twenty minutes or so picking at her sandwich and trying to read before getting up and heading back out. Her intention had been to spend the whole day away from him, but it was only early afternoon and there was already so little left to do.

In the end, though, it wasn't boredom that sent her home. It was her ankles. They started aching from all the walking she'd been doing. She sat down on a bench for a little while, but it was no use. She was too close to home to call a cab or take a bus. She'd have to ask John to pick her up.

When he came and got her, she knew he wouldn't be saying anything about not wanting to get married. She knew he'd apologize for last night and probably cry. And he did all those things. He hugged her tight and cried and cried and made all kinds of promises to her about never hurting her again. He said, "I love you so much" and "I can't lose you, ever." The rest of the night she iced her ankles and watched *Big*. Of course she'd seen it many times, but it was great to watch it with John that night. To shut off their minds and laugh at something as familiar and remote as Tom Hanks in 1988 eating baby corn like it was corn on the cob.

The next two weeks John was the sweetest he'd ever been. He told her how much he loved her all the time and brought her cute little thoughtful gifts each day. It was nice at first. They had been fighting for so long that it was great to have a respite from all the worry and sadness, but at a certain point she realized something that she'd never thought was possible: she had started to hate him. He'd come home from work and be funny and sweet and himself the way she always knew him, and she realized she just didn't care about it anymore. *I hate you,* she'd think as he'd spread peanut butter on a slice of bread. The things he'd said about not wanting to get married had damaged them. His getting drunk and coming home and falling over and spitting burrito into the air had damaged them. Here she'd been trying so desperately to hold on to what they had, and to make things work, and to keep everything together, but without realizing it, she'd already started to move on. There would be no way to stay even if she wanted to. And that's when she knew what had to be done.

As far as she was concerned, it was inevitable that John would go back to saying he didn't want to get married. She knew that nothing had really changed. She knew that all she had to do was wait and before long he'd say something about Colorado or not getting to do the things he wanted or some other miserable bullshit thing that would rip into her and make her feel like death. It was only a matter of time.

And of course she was right. Monday morning she woke up to a text that said, "I'm still really not ready to get married even though I do really love you." It was simple and to the point. Another girl might have thought it was thoughtful and fair. Another girl might have said to herself that she should give it more time and not push him, but Leda knew she wasn't that girl. She got up from bed and took a quick shower. She threw on a tank top and a fresh pair of underwear and with easy, fast motions she started packing up a suitcase. At first she was shaking a bit, but after a while it felt cathartic. She moved faster and faster. Folding shirts. Rolling up pants. She knew she couldn't easily take everything back to Boston with her, but she figured filling two big suitcases would be enough for now. She looked at her bookshelf and pulled off a Miranda July book she'd just started and an Amy Tan book she'd been meaning to read. She didn't take the Noam Chomsky. After a while her ankles started hurting so she put on her big, clunky support sneakers, and there she was in underwear and support sneakers filling her fragile little life into bags. *How easily it all just fits in,* she thought. After packing up she had a late lunch and watched TV. She didn't bother to get dressed. John got home fairly early, but even so she was ready for him. When she heard the sound of the car pulling up, she went to the bedroom and sat on the bed beside her suitcases. John walked in and called out for her. She hadn't texted him back all day so she knew he'd be worried.

"I'm in here," she said.

He came into the bedroom and looked at the suitcases. "Leda, what's going on?" he said. "I'm so sor—"

"Look, John, let me explain something to you. I can't be in a relationship with someone who doesn't want to marry me. Every time you say the stuff you do, it makes me hate you. I want to stay with you. I love you, and I wish I could stay, but I just can't stay with someone who says stuff like that to me. If you say one more thing about not wanting to marry me, or not being ready, whatever it is that doesn't equal you and me getting engaged, I will get on the next plane home and you will never hear from me again. I can't do this. Even if I want to, I can't, and I won't."

"I understand," he said, and nodded solemnly.

"I hope you do because I mean it. I mean it more than anything I've ever meant in my entire life."

❧

A MONTH LATER THEY WERE ENGAGED. SHE WAS HAPPY ABOUT IT, BUT it took a long time for him to earn back her trust. He apologized constantly and told her all the time how happy he was with the engagement and what an idiot he'd been, freaking out like that. She never really looked back on that time in their relationship with anything but anger, but as far as the ring was concerned she loved it. It was something she'd picked out. In her mind it represented everything she would and wouldn't do for their love. It was hers in a way that was strong and striking and so completely her own.

"You picked it out?" Anne said. "Wouldn't you rather it have been a surprise?"

"Not all surprises are good," she said. "And besides, I know what I want."

Six months later they were moving back to Boston. Her ankles finally healed once they were home. It was the hills after all.

PART 4

———— ❧ ————

CHAPTER 33

Wedding

SHE AND JOHN SETTLED INTO A TWO-BEDROOM APARTMENT IN HARvard Square. He'd found a job at a local start-up. She began doing some after-school tutoring and started the process to reapply for grad school. They'd both agreed that they wanted the wedding to be fairly soon after the engagement. John felt especially strongly.

"I just feel so terrible about the engagement," he'd say. "I really just want to be married."

Leda began planning for an early spring wedding. For the most part she was stumped by the interest so many women had in wedding planning. How could one manage to fawn over napkins? Where was the joy in embossed lettering?

And even worse was the hatefully competitive nature many women seemed to adopt for the eight months of their lives when *chiffon* would become a common word in their lexicon. For entertainment purposes she frequented an online forum called Weddingbee, where women would come to subtly rip each other apart using acronyms and smiley face emoticons.

"Does anyone's FI watch porn? I found a bunch of porn on my FI's computer and it's really disturbing me," one woman asked.

"Nope. FI thinks it's gross ☺" was one response.

"My SO does watch porn but only porn with women that look like me ☺? It used to bother me but now I just feel pretty proud that he's still so turned on by me ☺" another woman wrote.

There were tons of threads about engagement rings, including one where a woman complained that her SO only gave her a .5 carat ring, saying how she'd really been hoping for something bigger. A bunch of women responded and went crazy that anyone would dare insinuate that there was a diamond size (particularly their own) that could be considered small.

"I have a .2 carat ring and it's super big! A .5 is HUGE. I love my ring ☺," one woman commented. Leda imagined that this woman had seen this post and had had a pretty miserable day walking around with her .2 carat diamond ring. *Maybe she didn't even wear it all day. Maybe she took it off and put it away just to stop staring at the reminder that her husband is a failure and her life is a sham,* Leda thought. *Why, ladies? Why, why so crazy?*

On one post a woman had asked whether size matters, and the amount of women who willingly stepped forward to needlessly defend their husband's tiny penis was astounding.

"My husband has a smaller penis, but I don't care. It works great for me because I'm small myself ☺."

"My SO is VERY below average, but I love it!"

"I've always been super tight so FI is just perfect for me. Big penises hurt. I'm perfectly happy, no complaints at all ☺."

Does being married mean you have to pretend that every facet of your life is endlessly enjoyable, including your husband's small penis? Why can't these women say, "My husband has a small penis, but that doesn't change my self-worth. Sure, I wish he had a bigger penis, but I still matter. You may have a husband with a bigger penis, and this is something I wish I had, but it doesn't take away from all the amazing things in my own life."

At around the time of reading the penis post, Leda had decided that she and John should have a smaller wedding. Part of the decision was most probably related to their engagement going so horribly wrong, but realistically she never would have wanted a big wedding. It felt strange to perform this intimate ritual in front of other people.

"It's like everyone is watching us have sex or something," she'd remarked to John. "All along we've had these milestones in our relationship that have been private, and now all of a sudden the most important one my estranged aunt is going to be witness to?"

The funny thing about being engaged was that she'd expected most of her girlfriends to be happy and excited for her, but it actually wasn't like that at all. Many of them were still single and had little to no interest in discussing wedding plans. Leda tried to be sensitive to it, but it was disheartening. Anne was the worst. She didn't even want to answer the phone after the engagement.

"I have to organize my garage," she texted. "I'll call in an hour, but I'll only have fifteen minutes to talk because I really need to go through my Easter decorations."

After that their texting sort of dropped off. Leda wasn't sure who to ask to be her maid of honor.

"I've come to the realization that I hate all of my friends," she told John.

"What about Elle?"

"She's worse than Anne! I hear from her once every, like, three months."

"Then just don't have a maid of honor."

"But I have to."

"Why?"

"It's a thing you have to do."

"Who cares?"

"Everyone."

"But you just said you hate everyone."

"Yeah, but I still care what they think."

"Why?"

"I don't know."

She asked Anne to be her maid of honor.

Despite all her misgivings, and her disinterest in color-coordinated table settings, Leda did really want a wedding. She too could get caught up in it. Dress shopping proved to be one of the best things ever, and the months leading up to the wedding she'd keep a picture of herself in her dress open on her computer just to admire how linear she looked.

John was also excited and each week brought her home a new bridal magazine. It was sweet and helped ease the still-lingering tension between them.

"It's the happiest day of your life," she'd read in an article about losing arm fat for your wedding day, and she thought, *Is it the happiest* day? *Maybe my happiest day is a day I'd hardly remember where I just felt like I was okay and that everything would work out. Maybe my happiest day was the only day I didn't worry about arm fat.*

The other big concern was money. Spending an ungodly amount of money on a party for people, many of whom she didn't care about, or even like, really, for that matter, couldn't have felt more wasteful. At one point she had a mini panic attack over little glass swans she'd ordered to have placed on the tables next to the candles.

"Would you like to have glass swans placed beside the candles?" the lady who handled the tables asked.

"I guess so . . . yeah, that sounds nice, actually," Leda said.

Two weeks later she received a bill for $325. She called her mom crying.

"Can you return them?" her mom asked.

"Apparently I can't. I can't believe this," she said between sobs.

"Relax, honey, I'll pay for them. It's not that big of a deal. Besides, I'm sure they'll look really pretty on the table. Don't you think?"

"I guess so," she said between more sobs.

The night before the wedding she and John stayed together at the hotel. She had refused to spend the night away from him, as was custom.

"It seems fucked-up," she said when her mom suggested it. "It's just as fucked-up as penis garb at bachelorette parties." (Leda had declined to have a traditional bachelorette party even though Anne had offered to throw her one. "Take me to a nice place for drinks or we're not having one. I do not want to wear a penis necklace. Saying goodbye to the prospect of more penises in my life is the best part of getting married.")

"This wedding is so stupid. We should have eloped," she said as they lay side by side in the big decorative hotel bed. They could hear the couple next door to them having sex. As nice as the hotel was, the room smelled like bathroom. *I love my dress but could the love of a dress really justify six months of dieting?* she thought.

The next morning she didn't feel any better about it. John went to a separate room to get ready. His mom showed up early and said something bitchy about the weather. Anne was frantic because Dean wasn't coming after all. The caterer called and said that there would be no mini bagels. Her dress was making her sweat and her hair didn't come out exactly as she wanted it. Her heels pinched as she walked and her parents had to prop her up so she wouldn't trip on her train. As she waited for her cue to walk down the aisle, she felt anxious and melancholy and her mind wouldn't stop racing. But then the music started and the doors opened up and John saw her and it all went away. He started crying. Tears ran down his cheeks and he mouthed the words "You're so beautiful" over and over as she walked toward him. It was the most wonderful feeling she'd ever felt before. She would never, ever forget the way he looked at her. He was a stranger she hadn't known from anyone else, and now he was a man who loved her like this, like tears streaming down his face, like "You're so beautiful" over and over.

She couldn't have known it then, but as she walked toward him she was aging. The first gray hair emerged from her scalp, small and thin right at the top of her head. A crease in her forehead from years and years of worry and wonder was silently visible. She was past the point of the march toward favorable aging; from that moment on she'd be lumpier and grayer, and the skin on her face would be looser and more and more wrinkled. She was getting old. She was twenty-six. She was more beautiful than she'd ever be. She was married. And it all felt like the happiest day of her life.

CHAPTER 34

Pregnancy

AFTER THE WEDDING LEDA FELT A SENSE OF EUPHORIA SHE HADN'T thought could be possible from the signing of a legal document. She and John were married. It was a cozy feeling. It was them against the world in a way that was damning to everyone outside of their small, satisfied couplehood. Their life seemed settled and the uproar of the engagement was no longer present or pressing. Together they were peaceful and joyful and skated around through breakfasts and shallow silences that filled Sunday evenings. Her mom would call and Leda would answer, "Hello?" but it was sweet and unburdened and triumphant. These were the greatest "hellos" of her life. *Now I know why people get married,* she thought. *Now I know that before marriage I was unhappy.* This euphoria lasted three and a half weeks. It slowly drained away from the moment it began but subsequently came to a full stop the day she received her wedding photos and unrelentingly decided that in each and every single one of them her head looked small.

"John, is my head small?"

"What does that even mean?" John said.

"It means just what you'd think it means. Do I have a small head?"

"No, Leda, Jesus."

"But look at me here." She clicked open the photo of herself standing against a lattice of grapevines. "Do you see how small my head looks? It makes my body look huge. I'm a freak."

"You're insane," John said, but she didn't believe him. In the end she found three wedding photos out of the bunch that she thought least made her head look small and had them all framed.

During this time Leda didn't think about writing much. The same momentum that had led up to the wedding was redirected toward buying a house. It was to be expected. The natural progression, as it were, or so she felt in that moment. There was a shift in the foundation of her being. Now she was working toward a level of domesticity that would be as precious as that euphoria had been. Tutoring, which had formerly acted as a pincushion between phases in her life, became her focus. She no longer had a desire to reapply to grad school. It seemed silly in the context of window treatments and finished basements. She and John were saving up for a house and she would do her part. She took on as many hours as she could and often worked through weekends right into the new week with little sense of loss. Happiness seemed so blissfully achievable that she nearly felt unburdened by her lack of drive to be a writer. She was in control of her fate. And it was here, flittering in this rigid sense of self, that she suddenly and without warning wanted a baby.

At first she hardly noticed it. There was just a mild strain that some part of herself was missing. She thought buying the house would soothe her (they'd found a three-bedroom in Belmont that was "a great location" and "just perfect"), but as they signed their mortgage papers and as she stacked mugs in her new kitchen cabinet the feeling didn't wane. She felt continuously frantic and then one day it clicked, just like deciding her head was too small in all those wedding photos, just like a blooming rose opening to face the heavens. *I want a baby,* she thought.

Never before in her life had she considered that this would be something she would want so young. She tried to talk herself out of it, to think of everything else that needed to get done, that should be done in her life before having children, but the need was so stark and burning that she almost had a hard time concentrating on anything else.

"Would you like that order for here or to go?" the lady at the sandwich shop would say.

Who cares about sandwiches? I want a baby, Leda would think to say back.

Whenever she'd see mothers in shopping malls or second cousins posting pictures of their young children on Facebook, she'd feel an irrational pang of angry jealousy. *You don't deserve a baby. I deserve a baby.* She put it aside and told herself she'd just have to hold on until her early thirties. HER EARLY THIRTIES had been a fantasied time in her mind when everything in her life would come together, and she'd be ready for all the many things that she knew she needed to be ready for at some point.

"I want to be pregnant by the time I'm twenty-four," Anne had said once.

"Why?"

"Because I want to be a young mom. I don't want to be some old lady running after little kids."

"Well, I definitely don't want kids until I'm, like, thirty-three at the earliest."

"Really?"

"Yes, I don't even want to get married before I'm thirty," Leda had said before being married at twenty-six.

In late August she came to an epiphany of sorts, a visceral clarity about her life and future, where all the momentum was leading and what it was she truly wanted. It was early afternoon, and she'd just finished tutoring and was waiting for John to pick her up. The day had been exceedingly hot. Originally she'd planned to just sit in the little nearby park to wait for him, but once standing outside, the blinding concrete walkway reflecting the humidity back at her, she knew that there was no way she'd last. She looked around. There was a café about a mile down the road, but it was too hot to even consider the walk. Across the street was a small chapel that always had its doors open.

"Welcome all," the sign out front read.

Leda had seen the chapel many times. The boy she tutored had even mentioned it once.

"Ricky goes to church," he'd said.

"Who is Ricky?"

"The boy that mom watches on Wednesday nights when his mom is at work. He's kind of my friend, only I don't really like him that much."

"Really?"

"Yeah, he goes to church across the street. He says God is always watching us."

"Does he?"

"Do you think God is always watching us?"

"I don't know."

"I think he's wrong. I think no one is watching."

Leda had only ever been to church a few times in her life, twice on Christmas Eve as just sort of a festive outing for the holiday and once for a friend's wedding. Her family wasn't religious at all. When she was very young, she told a girl at school that there was no God. The girl was so upset that she had to go home early.

"Do you think God is a woman?" Leda had asked her mom when she was seven.

"Of course God is a woman," her mom answered.

Her mom had never tried to instill any sense of atheism in her, really, but she did want her daughter to believe in what was empirically there. She wanted her to be someone who considered facts before all else, to build her life around reality. In retrospect Leda felt very grateful that her mom had instilled these kinds of values in her as a child. She felt free to believe whatever she wanted, and even now she questioned the validity of the idea that God would have a penis.

Despite her misgivings about going into the chapel, she decided there really was no other option. It was just too hot out, and she figured if they had a welcome sign out front they wouldn't hassle her if she went in and sat down.

The chapel was built from a warm-colored adobe. It was a smaller structure with big, low arches in the Spanish style. Inside it was even tinier than it looked on the outside. There were only a few wooden pews and a short aisle leading to an elaborate golden altar. In front of the altar were some candles that had yet to be lit. No one was there. Leda sat down in the last row. She wasn't sure what to do with her hands so she laid them across her lap. She closed her eyes and leaned her head back; it was so much cooler than it was outside. It was nice. She thought of her day. The boy she'd tutored. The way he'd snapped his fingers as he read *My Side of the Mountain*. She thought of summer and the impending fall. She also thought of California and how the hills just rolled on and on, vast and golden. She turned her head to the left and opened her eyes and there before her was a huge painting of Mary holding the baby Jesus. She hadn't noticed it when she'd sat down, but now, looking at it in its massive scale compared with the rest of the chapel wall, she couldn't believe she hadn't. Mary was sitting upright. Her expression was stoic and soft looking down at her baby. The baby was round and angelic; above him was a bright ray of light. His expression was stoic but not soft. He was looking straight ahead, as if he were looking right at her. It was then that she felt the same familiar pang of jealousy she had so many times before, only this time it was stronger, this time it was irrational, this time it was as startling and reassuring as walking from the burning sun to the cooling shade. It was unavoidable, it was overpowering. *She doesn't deserve a baby. I deserve a baby.*

That night she lay in bed with John and told him that she wanted to start a family. Nearly seven months later she was pregnant. She hadn't waited till her early thirties after all, but she was never sorry that she hadn't. It was a feeling so strong in her that the rest of her life just seemed like a blur of stupid pursuits and empty ambitions. Wanting a baby was as close as she'd ever come to wanting something real. It's as close as she'd ever come to God.

———◦◦◦———

CHAPTER 35

Annabelle

ANNABELLE WAS BORN TWO DAYS AFTER A BLIZZARD. SHE WAS A SMALL baby with thin, rich, dark hair. She was contemplative and judicious and only laughed if something was really funny. She was named after a character in a book that Leda had read many years before, and her hands were small and clasped closed on most occasions, and until she was born Leda hadn't known that everything in her life had always been clasped up in those little hands. She hadn't realized that it was possible to feel instantly in love, instantly high off of another person's existence. The love she had for John or her parents or even herself all seemed wistful in comparison. She held her baby, and she just didn't care about anything else. There was her baby and really that was it. Life suddenly had a purpose that was actually visible. And not only just visible, it was in her arms. The depths of happiness were suddenly infinite. It was real to be alive.

Originally Leda thought that she'd take a few months off from work and then start back up. When she was seven months pregnant, she'd gone to visit a local daycare center with the plan to secure a spot for her baby once it was three or four months old. She walked around and looked at all the bright plastic and the little table and little chairs. The classroom seemed so shiny. It seemed, at the time, that you would want to have your child in among shiny things like that. As soon as Annabelle was born she realized that wasn't what she wanted at all. She called the daycare and canceled her spot, happily losing her deposit. She told John she wasn't going back to work.

"We'll cut back on cable or sell the couch. I honestly don't care. I want to be home with her."

John agreed. Somehow they managed the finances. Leda started cutting coupons and looking for sales. John sold some stock he'd been holding on to. It wasn't easy, but it felt right. She didn't worry about when she'd start writing again either. She just didn't care. And what was more, she didn't care that she didn't care.

Leda woke up in the morning as John was getting ready for work. It was his first day back after three months' paternity leave. She looked at her phone. It was nearly 6:00 a.m. Annabelle had only just dozed off a little after 3:00. She counted out the scattered hours of sleep she'd gotten throughout the night. It was less than four. *I just want to count the hours I sleep and be able to count them on more than one hand. Just for a day. I just need a day of it and then I'll be a person again.* John was pretty good about helping out through the night, but since she was breast-feeding there was only so much he could do. Generally, even the things he could do she would prefer to do on her own. It wasn't for lack of trying, but John was just never able to do as good of a job as her on pretty much any task. Whenever he'd change Annabelle's diaper he'd always manage to get poop on something. Or if not that, he'd put the diaper on too loose, and when she would poop it would be all over her. It was amazing how incapable he could be at things that seemingly took so little effort.

"How is it that men ever survived anything?" Leda asked as John struggled to get the sheet off of the crib mattress. "And somehow we're the lesser sex," she said, leaning over and unzipping it.

She knew she wouldn't be able to fall back asleep that morning. Annabelle was still sleeping beside her, her little chest rising and falling. Leda got up carefully so as not to wake her. She wanted to kiss her, but she didn't dare.

She went down to the kitchen to make coffee; a few minutes later John joined her. He talked about something at work as he fixed himself toast.

"You talk too much in the morning."

"Do I?"

"Yes, please stop talking until I can feel my face."

Annabelle woke up about an hour after John left. Her cry was soft and fairly quiet. It always worried Leda that she might not hear her if she were in another room.

"Her cry sounds like your cry did," her mom told her. "It trails off in the same way."

"I always thought babies' cries were loud."

"Not all babies."

Leda leaned down and picked her up. "You slept in, pretty girl. Mommy wishes she could have, but Daddy is too loud. You and I need to kick Daddy out of the house."

Annabelle looked at her with big, soulful eyes and smiled slightly, but she didn't laugh because it really wasn't all that funny.

Leda changed her quickly and sat down to feed her. Breast-feeding had proven to be considerably more challenging than she could have ever imagined when Annabelle was first born, but now that both of them had gotten the hang of it she really enjoyed it. She thought it had been one of the few things she'd really mastered as a new mother. At first it took some getting used to, producing food from her breast like that, right out of her side like a cow or some kind of street cat with a row of kittens. Her body was no longer her own in the way it had been. It had become something hearty and admirable, almost a separate entity from herself. Before she'd gotten pregnant she'd worried about stretch marks she'd had along her thighs. Now that she had a baby the fact that her body was pretty much covered in them didn't really bother her.

"You can try cocoa butter if you want," her ob-gyn had said once in passing. "Some women say they have luck with it."

"For what?"

"For stretch marks."

"Who gives a fuck about stretch marks?" Leda hadn't meant to say "fuck," but she hadn't slept in two days and there was a screaming infant waiting for her at home.

Her doctor paused thoughtfully and then burst out laughing. "Well, I sure as hell don't," she said.

Now that her body had made this transition Leda very often ate gummy bears throughout the day. She still cared about being linear, but she didn't obsess like she had in the past. Her body was no longer the kind of living tableau she'd fancied it before. It had grown and birthed a child. It sustained life. It was more important than a bikini, and it damn well deserved some gummy bears.

Leda leaned back in the rocking chair and almost dozed off for a moment. Indulging in every peaceful minute of breast-feeding that she possibly could was important. It was her only dependable respite from the child crying.

When Annabelle was first born, every other mother Leda knew asked her if she was a "good baby." It seemed that there was this GOOD BABY label that all parents were after.

"Emma was a good baby. She'd sleep through the night at two weeks old."

"You could take Joshua to a restaurant and he'd never make a peep. He was a good baby."

"Paige could just sit and stare and do absolutely nothing for hours on end. She was that good of a baby."

Leda was afraid that somehow she'd have one of these bad babies who didn't sleep through the night and wouldn't go to a restaurant and wanted more than to just sit and stare. She'd hoped and prayed that she too would be blessed with a good baby who wouldn't interfere with her life any more than a demanding house cat. As soon as Annabelle was born she realized that she did not have a good baby. Annabelle had a really hard time at night. The first four weeks she woke up nearly hourly.

"Is this for real?" Leda asked John once as the two of them pored over the screaming child after changing her clean diaper for a second time.

During the day things weren't much better. She had to carry her around constantly to keep her happy. She and John would have never even considered bringing her to a restaurant.

Leda didn't know what she was doing wrong. Every day seemed like a battle with the child in finding some sense of solace. As a result she'd been worrying about John's first day back to work since her daughter's birth. How she'd handle all the crying without moral support was something she was unsure of. She looked down at Annabelle, who was still quietly nursing. Her expression was serious and busy. She closed her little palm tight.

"Why don't you nurse all day and not cry?" Leda said as she kissed her little fist.

Seven and a half minutes later Annabelle was crying. Leda walked around with her and put on music. She tried changing her and burping her again, but she wouldn't let up.

"I just put my Kierran on his side and he stops crying," her cousin once posted on Facebook. "He's the best baby!"

She texted John, "It's not even 9 a.m. and she's already been crying for twenty minutes straight, and I have no idea what she wants."

"I'll be home soon," he texted.

"You'll be home soon? You aren't going to be home for eight hours."

She put Annabelle in the swing and turned it up all the way. Annabelle paused. She seemed to be considering what was happening to her, and why all of a sudden she was rhythmically flying through the air. She started crying again. Leda sat down next to the swing. She tried to imagine what another mother might do in this kind of situation, but nothing came to mind. *I can't even imagine a mother, let alone be one.* She lay down on the floor and watched the swing rise up and fall back. Somewhere outside she could hear an ambulance. *Come and take me away,* she thought.

It occurred to her that maybe the baby was cold. It had been a cool night and the house felt chillier than normal. She got up, went back upstairs to the bedroom, and grabbed a hat out of the dresser. It was a little knit hat with ladybugs all over it. She had yet to get any use out of it, as it had been too big for Annabelle until recently.

"Here you go, princess," she said as she pulled the hat over her head.

As soon as the hat was in place Annabelle screamed harder than Leda had ever heard her scream.

"What is it?" she said, and pulled the hat back off.

The child soothed a bit, but continued on crying as she had before. Leda looked at the hat. She stretched it and pulled it on her own head. It felt itchy. She looked at the label.

"Little Wonders 100% wool," it said.

She hadn't remembered where she'd gotten it. She'd bought so much when she was pregnant; there were droves and droves of hats and onesies and cute little dresses that she hardly even had recollection of buying. Something about the label seemed familiar, though, and then it hit her. She leaned down and pulled one of the little pink socks off Annabelle's foot and looked at the label. "Little Wonders 100% wool," it said. She quickly pulled off the other one, and as if she'd just let water out of a bath, Annabelle started calming and seconds later wasn't crying at all.

"It was the fucking socks?!" she screamed in delight to Annabelle and to herself and to the imaginary mother who seconds ago she couldn't even imagine. She left Annabelle swinging peacefully and ran back to the dresser drawer. For whatever reason she'd unwittingly bought loads and loads of Little Wonders socks. Virtually all the socks the child owned were Little Wonders. She pulled out the drawer and brought it back down to the living room to sort through the sock collection. Annabelle was still in the swing, mild in her manner, looking thoughtfully up at her mom. Leda held the drawer up high and dumped the socks on the floor.

"Your nightmare has ended, my love," she said. And Annabelle laughed because it really was funny.

Leda leaned down and picked up her daughter. She pulled the child in close and smelled her sweet infant smell. In the brevity of the moment she was certain her own destiny was embedded in her baby. For the past three months she'd misunderstood her daughter's personhood, and for that she felt a fierce sense of self-loathing. And then, right there, she made a promise to herself, not in words or silent prayers, or some personal ideology, but in something greater. Something that ran from her body past each stretch mark through her breast, fed her baby and sustained life. Her daughter would be bigger and better than she had ever been. Her daughter would know a life more beautiful and more her own. She'd get what she wanted, whatever that might be. "Never ever be a good baby," Leda said, and she took a giant breath in the shared airspace between herself and her child. Little could be divided between the two of them then. It was real to be alive indeed.

———⏳———

CHAPTER 36

Other Mothers

FROM THE MINUTE LEDA GAVE BIRTH TO HER DAUGHTER, SOME KIND of unspoken race began between herself and every other mother on earth. She'd figured that having a baby would grant her an immediate support system, but it hadn't been like that at all. Motherhood seemed to provoke a crippling anxiety in the majority of women. Certainly on the surface the other mothers would commiserate about diaper rashes and colic, the cost of daycare and the dangers of plastics, but underneath it all there was always the lingering competition, a vague hatred fueled by developmental milestones.

When Annabelle was very small, most of Leda's contact with the outside world was through Facebook, and it was there that she first noticed it. Her friend Ruth from high school had a baby boy named Noah. Ruth generally posted one or two pictures of Noah a week and had been doing so since the day he was born. Leda tried to "like" all of them to be supportive of Ruth as a fellow new mom, but she found the majority of the pictures unsettling. Every single one of them had a filter and a perfectly coordinated backdrop. There were no quick candid shots and nothing was ever a little out of focus. At a certain point Leda came to the conclusion that Ruth was self-conscious of her son, that she thought he was ugly. It was bizarre and it was tragic. *Poor Noah,* Leda thought. *There won't be any baby pictures of him with his natural skin tone.*

Around the time Noah was six months old Ruth posted a picture of him with the description: "And we're mobile! What am I going to do now?? #mobilebaby." Virtually seconds after it was posted, nearly a dozen comments lit up underneath. At least seven different mothers chimed in to brag about their own children in relation to Ruth bragging about hers.

"Mobile already? My Nettie started walking at eight months and it was the worst ☺."

"Uh oh! Preston didn't walk till he was thirteen months which I was glad about just for this reason! He was such an early talker though. I prefer that! I feel for you ☺."

"Too soon!!"

At a certain point Ruth had to jump in to clarify that she hadn't meant that Noah was walking yet, but just that he'd started to crawl. "But I'm sure he'll be an early walker at this rate," she said. All the other mothers seemed to take a collective sigh of relief. The comments stopped being catty and started being overtly complimentary.

"What a smart boy! Just like his mama!"

"Can't wait to see this little guy in person!"

"You go, Noah!"

The day of his first birthday Ruth posted a video of Noah "walking" where the child screamed as he wobbled between parents. His little arms were reaching up in terror for a hand to catch him. "Taking his first steps on his first birthday!" the description read. In the months since her original #mobilebaby Ruth wasn't about to lose with her ugly baby. He would walk by age one. He would be a mobile baby and he would win, even if it meant forcing him across the lawn in tears. *Yikes,* Leda thought, and liked the video.

As Annabelle became a toddler, the competitive cattiness of the other mothers became considerably more difficult to avoid. On Wednesdays Leda would walk her down to the park to meet with a group of the local mothers and their children for a makeshift playgroup. The playgroup had originated with just two mothers, Jean and Audrey. Leda had never met either of them but frequently heard their names bantered about in conversations among the other mothers on the playground. Jean and Audrey stood for all that was right in the world of parenting. Leda heard that Jean had heroically saved a child from a bee sting and Audrey supposedly made homemade yogurt. Very often she tried to imagine what exactly these two women looked like and who they were, but she could never envision a clear image of what their faces would be. All she could think of when she thought of them was the silhouettes of two women standing side by side in high-rise jeans with their shirts tucked in tight. Sometimes one of them (Leda figured this was Jean because Jean seemed more like the type to do this from what she could gather) would be clapping and saying, "Let's go, let's go, let's go."

Beth was the only mother in the group who really knew them well. She'd been in the playgroup for seven years with all four of her children. She was the one who organized things and made sure that the snack rotation was in proper order. She was a squarish woman with a triangle haircut. She never wore makeup, and the vast majority of what she wore could best be described as expensive sportswear. Leda suspected that in her younger days she was the type of woman to don miniskirts and too much eyeliner.

Beth's son Max was a wild little boy whom Annabelle actively tried to avoid on the playground. From a very early age Annabelle seemed to take great discretion in whom she became friends with. She was liked by most of the children, but she generally only spent her time with the toddlers who were unlikely to smack her over the head with a shovel. Her best friend in the group was a little girl named Eliza, a quiet, happy two-year-old who loved to play in the sand. Annabelle and she bonded right away, which was in part due to the fact that Leda and Eliza's mother, Celia, had become fast friends. Celia was the only other mother in the group Leda truly enjoyed the company of. It was in meeting Celia that she had regained hope in the idea that she could befriend another woman over motherhood. Celia had wide hips and long, dark hair. Her laugh was deep and rich, and she was always joking. But what stood out about her was her seemingly impenetrable ego. She never appeared to be aware when other mothers were bragging about their children or trying to make her feel bad about her own, and what was more, she was happy to admit to her many insecurities and unwilling to run from all that could be perceived as flaws.

Leda took notice of this her third week at the playgroup. She'd been stuck talking to Lindy most of the morning, a woman who didn't believe in vaccinations and drank green liquid out of a jam jar. Leda had asked her once what it was she was always drinking.

"It's a mix of lentils and protein," Lindy said.

Lindy's son was kind of a strange little boy who seemed well-intentioned enough. Leda could never remember his name so she referred to him as "sweetie" if he ever came over to her.

"Balloon," he said once and pointed to the sky.

"Do you see a balloon, sweetie?" She looked up, but there was no balloon.

Lindy had been going on all morning about how her son could count to ten in English *and* Spanish. Leda listened and nodded. She doubted it was true, but simultaneously with the doubt she felt a sense of worry for Annabelle, who, at just a few months younger than whatever his name was, could not count to ten and didn't speak Spanish of any kind. She was usually unfazed by Lindy, because her son was so strange, and so it was pretty difficult to be jealous of him, but for whatever reason this morning it was making her feel sad. She'd been up late the night before trying to get the house in order and Annabelle had been cranky since she woke up. The whole day was getting to her; she suddenly felt exhausted, like her knees would buckle as they stood there talking. *What would she do if I just fell over right now? Would she give me some of her lentils?*

"I just think that if you can take advantage of their brains at this young age and teach them a foreign language then you should. I think it's doing them a disservice if you don't."

Leda watched her daughter toddling over to a plastic wobbly horse that was at the corner of the playground.

"There's just so much you can do," she heard Lindy say as Annabelle put her arms around the horse's neck. She stood there just hugging it, too small to get on by herself. Then she turned around and Leda could see that she was smiling.

Just before eleven the mothers gathered around for snack. That morning the snack rotation fell on Sundya. Leda preferred her to Lindy usually, but today she was talking about her older daughter getting into some kind of prestigious pre-K program. All the mothers buzzed around impressed, asking all sorts of questions about flash cards. Leda half listened to the advice that Sundya doled out as she served some kind of fancy cookie she'd baked. Annabelle sat in Leda's lap and tasted the snack thoughtfully. A few seconds later she shook her head and handed the gnawed-on cookie to her mom. Leda took a bite. It tasted like soap. She put it in a napkin and put the napkin in her purse.

After snack she avoided Lindy for the most part by joining a group of other mothers by the swings. For a few minutes they talked about the weather and the upcoming winter, but it wasn't long before the conversation turned into a bragging contest.

"Landon just loves his music class," said Evelyn, a woman who only ever took her son to every third playgroup, as the rest of the time he was with one of his two nannies. "He can pretty much play 'Twinkle, Twinkle, Little Star' on the recorder at this point. I keep telling Matt we just have to get him onto the piano, but you know I can't find a piano teacher willing to teach piano to a toddler, which I think is ridiculous. I mean, am I supposed to wait until he's a preschooler for everything? It's absurd."

"You could give him a toy piano. Eliza loves her little wooden one at home," Celia said.

Evelyn gave a sort of half smile. She didn't know how to respond to someone who had so very much missed the point of what she was saying: *My son is amazing and better than your child.*

Leda couldn't help but laugh a little. She looked at Celia, who happily pushed Eliza in the swing. *That's what I need to be like,* she thought.

"The only thing is then you have to listen to them pounding away all day long. My sister gave her son a drum kit for Christmas. Can you imagine that? A drum kit. We went over to her house for New Year's, and we couldn't hear each other talk 'cause he was banging away. I told her to burn it," Celia said.

Evelyn was still quiet. She looked like she was about to say something but then stopped herself.

"Just stick with the recorder is all I'm saying. Wait till he's older before you subject yourself to any real torture," Celia said.

At the end of playgroup as the mothers began to one by one leave the park, Leda went over to Celia.

"You're hilarious," she said to her. "Let's meet up sometime with the girls."

From that day on Leda and Celia were pretty much inseparable at playgroup. They'd roll their eyes whenever one of the mothers would brag about her child and confide in each other their most desperate motherhood moments.

"Eddy wasn't watching Eliza this morning, and she smeared poop all over the bathtub. I swear to god I wish I'd married someone else sometimes. Someone with more money," Celia would say.

"Aw, but you love Eddy!"

"That's what I told myself this morning as I was cleaning poop off the wall."

Their friendship and time together gave Leda confidence in herself in a way she'd never felt before. She no longer feared the judgments of the other women as she had. She'd lost that sense of despondency. It was calm and blissfully reassuring.

That was how things were for the first year at the playgroup: Leda would wake up in the mornings and John would have breakfast with her and then he'd go to work and then she'd spend a couple of hours with Annabelle and get her ready and put on her little shoes and little coat and she'd watch each season pass by and her daughter would laugh and run and she and Celia would tell each other about their days and about their worries and in between it all was so much coffee.

In late fall of the following year, Leda sat waiting for Celia and Eliza on a bench by a big oak tree. She and Celia had started getting to playgroup an hour early just to have enough time without the other mothers around to gossip properly. It was cool out, so she wrapped a sweater around her shoulders. Annabelle was playing in the leaves. She clutched a little stack of chosen specimens in her right hand. In her left hand she held a stick. Celia texted that she'd be a few minutes late, so Leda took out *The Edible Woman* and read the first few pages while she waited. She no longer read as much as she used to, so she'd formed the habit of carrying books around with her in hopes to catch a few minutes of reading in here and there. It was rare that she'd actually get to it, but it made her happy to carry the books with her. Every time she'd come upon them in her purse as she reached for her wallet she had a momentary sense of relief. A relief from what, she was never sure of.

"Hi, hi, hi," Celia said, running up with two coffees. Eliza was walking alongside, holding a big red ball. "I brought coffee as an apology for my lateness."

"Oh, please, like I care? I'm late to everything."

"I know, but I pride myself on being better than you." Celia sat down and handed her the coffee. "It's pumpkin spice, which I know you hate, but I forgot when I was ordering it."

"You cow."

"Sorryyyyyy." She blew on the coffee and motioned to Leda with a nod. "So, what are you reading?"

"*The Edible Woman*," Leda said.

Celia shrugged. "I'm not a big reader."

"I'm not much these days myself, honestly."

"What's it about?"

"Well, I've only just started it, but supposedly it's about this woman who gets engaged and can't eat and starts to feel like she's dissolving or something."

"That's really weird," Celia said.

"Well, I'm probably not explaining it right."

Celia looked uninterested. She flicked a bit of foam off her finger.

"It's really good," Leda said.

Celia nodded a bit but didn't answer.

The women sat silent for a moment. Up until now they'd only ever really talked about the kids and the other mothers. Leda felt judged and distant from Celia in a way she had not felt before. In her heart of hearts she knew that she and Celia were different people and in any other context probably would not have been friends. She knew deep down that she too was an other mother. One who believed in teaching her child another language or eating organic. She could be both but not at once. Not in this friendship and its fragile dance on the crunching leaves of fall and the smell of a pumpkin spice latte that would grow cold and be thrown away, rotting at the bottom of a park trashcan to the sounds of snack times every Wednesday. Eliza would grow up big and strong and Annabelle would too, and they would go this way and that and maybe they'd keep in touch and think of each other toddling side by side in sandboxes, but probably they would not. It was inevitable, their own lives constantly diverting from the second they were born, the sound of it silent; if they could have heard it they would have heard its speed, the churning loud engine warped in passing, like a train rolling by.

Celia didn't come to playgroup the next week. Eliza had a cold, and so Leda ended up sitting next to Lindy most of the morning.

"Jean and Audrey didn't ever do it like that," Lindy said in mid-memory of a story that had been relayed to her by Beth.

Leda had heard the story before from one of the other mothers who had also heard it from Beth, or maybe from Lindy. It was tough to say.

"What were their kids' names?" Leda asked.

"What?"

"Jean's and Audrey's."

"You know . . ." Lindy took a thoughtful pause. "You know, I really don't know. No one has ever told me. Isn't that awful?"

"It is."

And it really was.

CHAPTER 37

❦

Vacation

SOMEWHERE IN A PARENTING MAGAZINE LEDA HAD READ AN ARTICLE
about taking your toddler on vacation that included tips like "bring
bright colorful chalk" and "schedule your days out, including snacks."
At the time Leda thought this article was clever and helpful and so
creative. She'd gone so far as to clip it out and save it on her fridge,
sticking it in place with a hopeful-looking kitten magnet. There was
a time when this was the level of faith she had in the decision to take
a child under five on an airplane.

The way over, things had gone well. Annabelle was thrilled by
everything new so long as Leda and John made sure to put on an
excited two-person play over all of it.

> LEDA: Look!! Airplane!!!!! Do you see the airplane??????? We're
> going on an airplane!!!
> JOHN: Wow!!!!!!!!! Did you see the airplane, Annabelle????????
> It's gonna be so fun!!!!!!!!!!!!!
> JOHN: Look at the sidewalk moving!!!!!!!! It's like we have
> superpowers!!!!!!
> LEDA: Yay!!!!!! WHEEEEEEEEEEE!!!
> LEDA: Do you want a bagel???????
> JOHN: Bagel!!!!!!!!!!!!!

By the time they'd gotten on board Annabelle was so excited that
she easily sat through the three-hour flight, watching movies and
eating the scheduled snacks Leda had brought along.

Just before the vacation Leda had noticed a small red blemish in the middle of her forehead.

"Do you see this?" she asked John.

"What?"

"This. This!"

"The dot? I guess so."

"It's awful. I can't stop staring at it."

"It's nothing. I'm sure it'll go away."

But it didn't go away, and every single time Leda looked in the mirror it was the first thing she saw. The day they got to their vacation rental Leda felt so thrilled up until the moment she went in the bathroom and caught a glimpse of herself in the mirror; even from afar she could see the red dot staring back at her. It marked the day, as if already it was not what she meant it to be.

"Pizza?" she asked John to console herself. And they had pizza that night.

Leda picked a beach vacation, figuring that Annabelle at her young age would enjoy it the most. She'd envisioned her little family in some exotic location soaking up the sun and splashing in the waves. There would be sand and laughter and showing her daughter the limitlessness of the ocean and sky as a singular horizon.

But the very first day Annabelle threw up all over the kitchen floor.

Pizza? Leda wondered as she wiped it up. They decided to stay in for the day and watch movies. She'd cook rice and hand out saltines. Unfortunately, the TV wasn't working and the Internet was too slow to stream anything, so they ended up playing 462 rounds of Jenga to keep Annabelle from climbing the curtains out of sheer boredom.

"Tomorrow we're taking her to the beach even if it kills us all," Leda said.

The next morning Annabelle was better but John was sick.

"Do you think I could handle her on my own?" she asked him. A weary vision of herself managing a toddler in crowds of tourists passed through her mind. In it she could feel the sizzling exhaustion already searing the day away.

"I'll make myself go," John said. "It'll be madness on your own."

"No, no. Rest. We'll go get pancakes and come back and check on you. Maybe by the afternoon you'll be up for going out."

They walked to an IHOP that was a block away. Before children Leda had had a strong aversion to IHOPs and all chain restaurants in general, but now she considered them to be holy sanctuaries. These were restaurants that *got it*. There were crayons and paper place mats with mazes and puzzles to be solved. The food was so tasteless no child would turn away. And, most important of all, none of the other patrons would judge you as one of your family members climbed under the table and rolled around on the carpet. There was no more room in Leda's life to be a snob about it. *Thank you, Jesus*, is all she'd think as she ate a 1,200-calorie plate of fettuccini Alfredo while coaxing a two-year-old with unlimited breadsticks.

Annabelle raced ahead of Leda as they came upon the restaurant.

"Wait for me, honey."

"I want to push the button."

"What button?"

"In the lelevator."

"There's no elevator, Anna-B, we're going to get breakfast."

"No, there is."

Leda tried to rack her brain for whatever lelevator her daughter could possibly be thinking of. "The one in the apartment building?"

"Yeah."

"Honey, we didn't go in the elevator, we took the stairs down."

"But I really want to push the button."

"You can push it on the way back."

"No!"

"Annabelle, don't you want pancakes?"

"No!"

Leda felt what was coming. There was a certain look in her daughter's eye in times like these. It was an inconsolable anguish at anything and everything in the world. Leda had read a book about it once. It was called *The Inconsolable Anguish*. It was written by Dr. Abigail Lee, a woman with a fearless expression and a confidence about pureeing root vegetables that was rivaled by little else. In it Dr. Lee explained the importance of why it is that children tantrum.

"Without allowing your child to tantrum you are stifling your child's ego. They need to tantrum to grow into whole individuals." Leda had bought the book to try to understand why it was that on certain occasions her own daughter seemed to be the most draining individual in the history of the world, and now she knew that the reason for this was some vague concept explained to her in a 347-page book.

"Annabelle, we're going to eat pancakes and then we'll go back to the apartment and see Daddy. And then guess what?"

"What?"

Leda felt a giant sense of relief that her daughter's response wasn't "no." She needed to seize this moment by acting as if she weren't as dead inside as any other thirtysomething blue-blooded woman. "We're going to go to the beach!!!!!"

"No!!!!" her daughter shrieked. And then she started crying uncontrollably. "I want to go push the button."

"We'll push the button on the way back to get Daddy. You can push it five times if you want." *Why in the hell didn't we take that fucking elevator?*

"No!! I want to push it now."

Leda knew she had two options: threats or bribery. Normally she would have gone to the threats first. She did, after all, have a responsibility to society to raise an individual who would learn that you can't have a meltdown if you can't push an elevator button, but considering that they were on vacation, in a strange place, and that she too wanted some terrible pancakes, bribery was the best solution at hand.

"Listen, Annabelle, listen to me: if you're a good girl we'll go get you a special present after breakfast." Where they would go for this special present Leda wasn't sure, but there was something somewhere plastic and pink that would suffice at any given moment. This she could count on.

"No! I want to push the button. I want the button. The button." Annabelle sunk down to her knees and then sat on the ground. Leda felt a little sorry for her child then. She was tired and had played too much Jenga the day before. So far this trip had been puking and sleeping in a strange bed. Leda found traveling as an adult stressful enough, but as a child with so little control over what terrible pancakes she ate, it really was no wonder that she wanted to push a button.

"Do you want to go back to the apartment and push the button and come back for breakfast?"

"No! I want to push it now. The button, now. The button." Annabelle was sobbing so hard that Leda was sure passersby would think "the button" was a code word for some kind of paddle those religious people use to beat their children.

"Annabelle, stop it! There's no button here. If you want to push the button, we have to walk back to the apartment to get on the elevator and push the button."

"Nooooooooooooo." Annabelle was now lying down on the concrete in front of the IHOP. Leda looked out over the parking lot. Everything was hot and sticky. It reminded her of a scene from *Breaking Bad* in a vague way. *I wish Jesse were here,* she thought, tapping into an old celebrity crush she had in hopes of escaping the moment at hand. It worked briefly.

"Noooooo, the button, the button."

An older woman exited the restaurant. "I've been there, honey," she said as she passed by. "I've got six of them myself."

Six of them? Leda thought. *Do you hate yourself?*

"Annabelle, you need to stop it. You need to calm yourself down so that we can either eat pancakes or go back to the apartment. Sit up."

Leda pulled Annabelle into a sitting position, but the child fell back down and cried to herself. She seemed no longer to be tantruming for anyone or anything, really, but more just letting her ego develop here in this parking lot. Leda thought to call John but then had a better idea.

"Hey!" she called out at the woman who hated herself with the six children. "Can you do me an enormous favor?"

Minutes later the woman came back out of the restaurant holding a single pancake in a napkin.

"Thank you so much." Leda went to hand her a five-dollar bill.

"Oh, no, they didn't charge me," she said. "Good luck with her."

It sounded like a mean remark, but Leda knew that this woman meant to her very core to wish her luck.

"Thank you," Leda answered.

The woman nodded a solitary nod. *If she could say what she's thinking, she'd say "Godspeed,"* Leda thought.

It was less difficult than Leda had anticipated to get Annabelle to eat the pancake, and as soon as she did she calmed down and Leda convinced her to go inside to get more. By the time they sat down her daughter looked as if she'd been through some kind of childhood war. *I hope this is the last bad day of this vacation.*

But it wasn't. The next day Annabelle got burned on a candle at a gift shop. And the day after, they made it to the beach, but the water was too cold to go in. They sat on the sand and eventually left after it looked as if John was getting sunstroke. Leda tried to apply some wisdom from the article. She brought snacks with her and scheduled in naps, but the days were long and fell apart easily. Annabelle was stressed-out and cranky, and as a result at every turn they ended up buying some kind of plastic novelty gift.

"We're going to need another suitcase for all this crap we're buying," she said to John as she stood in line to purchase a stuffed unicorn that glowed in the dark.

The second-to-last night of the trip Leda had a labored dream about having sex with Jesse from *Breaking Bad.* It was an intensely divine dream where he was kind to her and said things like: "You're the hottest one I know, yo." They made love on a mattress on the floor in slanted light. She felt so alive it was hard to believe she was asleep. The next morning when she woke up the dream weighed heavily on her. It was one of the best dreams she'd ever had, certainly one of the best she'd had in recent memory, and that's why she hated it. There was an element of escapism in it all, as there had been that day at IHOP, and that bothered her on a certain level, that here on her vacation with her little family she was seeking refuge in the hands of an attractive fictional meth addict, but what upset her more was the reminder of a vague ambition she'd felt after watching the series those few years ago. She and John had watched all five seasons in the span of one week. It was a feverous time when blue meth and indulgent violence kept them up till 2:00, 3:00 a.m. every day. After they'd watched the finale Leda felt inspired. She wanted to write something like that, something so suspenseful that you could not look away, only she thought she'd like to write it about women.

"Would there be a way to write a show like that that's just as thrilling but not about men asserting their masculinity over each other? What about women?" she'd asked John.

"A woman superhero maybe?" John said.

"No, that's too mannish."

Leda wrote out a few ideas but nothing came to fruition. Soon after, she got pregnant with Annabelle and forgot all about it.

Having sex with Jesse reminded her of all of it and it made her sad, although that sadness itself she could hardly understand, really. Nevertheless, the last two days of the vacation she couldn't stop thinking about it, which was a shame because the last two days were the best days of the entire vacation. Annabelle finally got over what little bug had made her so disagreeable and the weather was perfect. They went to the beach and swam and had cookouts and picnics. The sunsets were extraordinary, and she and John had sex the last night that was exceptionally sweet. But despite it all she kept turning to the dream, looking for clarification.

The plane ride home started out fine. They tried to keep Annabelle as thrilled as was possible over flying again, but she'd moved on emotionally and wasn't quite as keen to go along with everything. *She knows it's not that great,* Leda thought as they boarded, Annabelle standing silently at her side.

After they got seated, Leda watched as an older-middle-aged woman shuffled around the plane trying to be sure her family of two teenage children, a husband, and some kind of extended relatives were all settled. She didn't look tired, really, even though given the circumstance she very well should have been. "Don't worry about me," she'd overheard the woman say at one point. "I'm fine."

During the flight things went fairly well. Annabelle slept through most of it, for which Leda was grateful. A baby a few rows down cried for almost the entire three hours and the mother, a slight-looking woman who probably looked thinner pregnant than most women look not pregnant, tried to soothe the child by carrying him up and down the aisle. Leda tried to smile at her a few times in the same solidarity that woman at IHOP had given her. It was best to continue passing that along.

When they landed the captain came on the loudspeaker to explain to the passengers the reason that they'd have to taxi for "a little bit." "A little bit" turned out to be code for two and a half hours. And it was here in these last two hours that Leda made the solemn promise to herself that when she got home she would burn that article. Annabelle didn't want to sit even though the seat belt sign was still on. The TVs were shut off for some reason, and despite the colored chalk available to her, Annabelle continued to try to get up exactly every thirty-eight seconds. The mother of the baby was also feeling the ills of being forced to sit as the child screamed bloody murder, hardly taking the time to catch a breath. Leda got so used to the sound that she could almost hum along with the baby's screams. She memorized the varying pitch and could nearly make out a melody in it all. Somewhere at the front of the plane a child was complaining about missing a soccer game, and to her right was the older mother still managing her family even as there was little managing she could do.

"We'll call the car when we get out and let them know," she said loudly enough so each scattered family member could hear.

Leda thought then again of the dream and of sleeping with Jesse. But the thought disgusted her, and with some kind of ruthless whimsy she thought of herself writing again and being a writer far away from this plane and this place. She could see herself as someone else, and the feeling she expected to feel from the thought, the relief she wanted so badly, she didn't feel at all. Instead she felt what it was, and what it was was that she wanted to want something else, but she didn't. She wanted *this*. And she knew all the mothers on the plane wanted this as well. They weren't trapped like some literary heroine who burned toast and felt sorry for herself. They were fearless and they were fierce. *We're no more trapped than men with all their anger and all their violence,* she thought. *But we're mothers and that's better.* And what did that mean about her that she didn't miss Jesse and the sex? That she didn't miss writing? That a vacation as horrible as this one was the light of her life?

And then, without worrying about the seat belt sign, Leda got up and she walked to the bathroom and she looked at herself in the mirror and that red dot was there in the middle of her forehead staring back at her, and she took her index finger and pointed at it and held it there on the dot, wishing for it to go away though she knew it wouldn't. *Who are you?* she thought. But she wasn't scared and she wasn't all that sorry. And somehow she felt free, trapped in a plane that skated along the tarmac, unable to stop enough so that she and her family might be able to get off.

———— ⌇ ————

CHAPTER 38

Walking to CVS in the Rain

Soon after they got back from the trip Leda needed to run to CVS to buy paper plates because their dishwasher had broken. *These are the kinds of things we do all the time,* she thought, loosely associating the errand with every flat tire of her life, every lightbulb that went out without warning, as every lightbulb is wont to do. It was raining, but she took the opportunity to walk anyway. CVS was one of the few places close enough to her home that she could walk to now that she lived in the suburbs. Suburban life had proved to be relaxing and deafening all at once. She feared rape so much less, and yet the solitude seemed to prescribe a constant sense of imminent rape. Certainly she didn't think this explicitly, but late at night as she was dead asleep or drifting into sleep she'd find herself all of a sudden having a sense that someone was standing beside the bed. John told her that she would often wake him in a panic, asking him if someone was there.

"Is that a man?" she'd say as she'd point to a pile of laundry.

"No, Leda. It's not."

"Are you sure? I think it's a man."

"You're dreaming. Go back to sleep," he'd say.

Leda never remembered these conversations. She'd only remember herself staring at something standing still, big and bulky, shadowed and beside her, so sure of what it was, so sure that somehow a man was there in their home, just watching her. *How can you be so sure of what the laundry is in the night?* she thought.

She stopped for a moment to tie her shoe. When she was a child, tying her shoes was one of the few things she'd taken forever to learn. It was shoe tying and bike riding that had held her up. When she'd first learned to ride a bike she was ten years old and determined not to be the only child anymore who didn't have a bike. It was a taxing secret to keep from all her friends.

"I can't ride a bike," she'd have to confess in the cafeteria or standing in gym class, or wading through an aboveground pool. The children, especially those who had invested considerable pride in their bike-riding aptitude, never ceased to take the opportunity to make their dear friend feel worse about herself.

"What?! You can't ride a bike?? I've been riding since I was four."

"I just never learned. I don't know why."

"That's so weird. I could do it since I was four!!"

"I know."

"You're weird."

"I know."

For her tenth birthday she asked her parents for a bike. Her dad helped her assemble it on the driveway after she'd opened the big box it came in. She helped turn screws and handed him handlebars and wheels one piece at a time until the mess of the bike scrambled over the driveway became a solid single thing, and she thought that she almost felt more exhilarated at its deconstruction than its construction.

It took her about forty-five minutes to learn how to ride. Pretty soon she was flying over the concrete sidewalks, no different from any other suburban kid. It surprised her how easy it was, how something that had plagued her so viciously was over and done with just like that. All those kids had made her feel so inferior for so long, and for what exactly?

And has it changed? Are we not all wishing we could ride bikes before everyone else? She thought of a girl she'd known in college who cried because she was still a virgin.

"It's not all that great," another girl said in consolation.

Leda remembered herself feeling a sense of urgency over losing her virginity too. It seemed like being a virgin was some great offense to adulthood, but then you had sex and it was like you never were a virgin. Nothing, no big deal. A life milestone you obsessed over for absolutely no reason.

Then there was Anne, who in the last few months had started to panic about being single and not finding "the one" yet. Leda felt sorry for her.

"It will happen!" she'd text. But she knew Anne didn't want to hear it coming from her. Anne wanted to get married and have kids. She didn't want her married friend with a kid to hand out any kind of courageous advice. *How cruel it all is. Fertility and online dating, the living antithesis of each other.*

Leda thought again of being on the plane and her epiphany about herself not wanting to write anymore. It made her upset so she shut her eyes tight for a moment and tried hard to think of something else, something far away, blissful. Nothing blissful came to mind, but she did remember that past September she and John had found a pigeon tipped upside down with its neck bent back. At first when she saw it she thought it was dead, but then she saw it blink at her. Its eye seemed to say something powerful and fluid and indistinguishable. Leda had watched a video online only the day before about what to do if you find a hurt bird. What had compelled her to watch it in the first place seemed virtually inextricable from this moment. It was as if something that existed in the stare between them had touched her, sent her to that video, and then on to this moment, this place, this salvation.

"Put on these gloves and turn it over," she said to John.

She was nervous to touch the bird herself. John had once rescued a dove as a young boy, a story he often recalled whenever it was appropriate. "I rescued a dove once," he'd say, and because of that she felt it was better he would be the one to move the bird. He already knew what lightness it bore; he wouldn't spook at a sudden wing flap or the complicated nature of a talon. When they put the bird upright it walked a few steps but fell back over and landed once again with its neck upside down. Things looked grim, but Leda didn't want to leave it like that. She started looking up phone numbers of bird rescues. In the meantime, people on the street passing by quickly assessed the situation and would throw their two cents in: "broken wing," "rat poison," "probably dying," they'd say. Whenever they'd come to see that she and John were planning on helping the bird they'd become oddly combative.

"If it has a broken wing they'll just put it down."

"There's nothing you can do for rat poison."

"It'll probably die either way."

Why do these people care if we help the bird? Is it really too much for them to take that someone else is kinder than they are? What they should really be saying is, "Please let it die on the street so I can feel all right about my laziness," she thought.

They found a rescue organization and drove the bird over. Leda held it on her lap in a paper box with a towel over the top.

"I think it's a girl," she said to John, and lifted the edge of the towel to be sure that the bird had enough air.

The rescue people took the pigeon and seemed to think that it would be okay. They nodded and smiled, and she and John made a donation of thirty dollars. Not enough to cover the bird's care, most likely, but they still felt good about it.

A few days later Leda called to check up on the pigeon's progress.

"I'm so sorry," the lady on the phone said. "It didn't make it."

"Oh, that's too bad." Leda tried to think of something consoling to say but nothing really worked. She finally settled on: "At least she died peacefully."

"Yes," the lady said. "Hopefully next time the outcome will be better."

Next time? Leda thought.

Making her way into CVS, Leda noticed a man standing out front with his phone. As she walked past, she vaguely hoped he'd notice her. It was rare that she'd be walking around without either John or Annabelle, and these opportunities felt like the only few she'd have left for men to give her attention. Why she wanted their attention in this useless, fleeting, completely superficial way she wasn't sure, but what she was sure about was that the older she was getting, the less men looked at her, and it bothered her more than she'd even admit to herself. *What? You pass thirty and that's it? It's over?* she'd think whenever a cute guy at a coffee shop handed her a latte with the same empty expression that he gave to anyone else. *My power is going, going, gone.* She thought momentarily of the witch from *The Wizard of Oz: I'm melting, I'm melting.*

At CVS she bought the paper plates and a bag of Skittles. The girl who rang her up smiled a lot and chatted about nothing in a fast, breathless way. For whatever reason the interaction emboldened her, and on her way out of the store she smiled at the guy who wouldn't look at her. He still didn't look at her and she thought, *Pretty soon the only men who will notice me will be the imaginary men by my bedside.* By now it had stopped raining. Birds bathed in nearby puddles and she thought maybe she'd make lasagna that night, an ambition that was meritless in the context of having a broken dishwasher. *I hope there's a heaven for that pigeon.* Her mind drifted to herself on her bike as a child, whizzing over suburban sidewalks, feeling accomplished and anticlimactic all at once. *These are the things you do,* she thought, *ride bikes, tell time, save birds, and fix dishwashers.*

On her walk home she'd pick a daisy for Annabelle, and six years later she'd make a daisy chain for Annabelle to wear in her hair; many years after that, as an old grandmother lying in bed, she'd open a book to a daisy pressed between the pages and remember her mother, who cut a fresh bouquet each spring. How unaware she was of the little pieces of her life that fit together seamlessly and without touching. It was as spectacular as anything, really, as little as it was anything at all.

CHAPTER 39

—◦&◦—

A Conversation with a Three-Year-Old About a Barbie

By the time Annabelle was three virtually everything she played with was pink. There were Barbies, and baby dolls of all kinds, castles, and dress-up clothing so sparkly that it shed glitter all over the house. Leda had tried very hard to avoid these sorts of cliché girl toys. All along she gave her other toy options. For her second birthday she gave her a truck and for Christmas a toolbox. Annabelle only ever used the truck as a way to pull Barbie's horse trailer around. The toolbox was literally never opened. Every time Annabelle said her favorite color was pink or that she wanted to be a princess, Leda told her that girls can play with whatever they want and that they don't have to be princesses and that there was nothing wrong with liking blue. Annabelle would always make the same kind of expression whenever her mother would say these things. It was as if she'd already considered everything she was saying and knew that her mother was wrong but was too polite to really get into a discussion with her about it.

"I don't want her to be one of *those girls*," Leda said to her mom.

"What girls? You loved pink too, you know, and you aren't one of those girls. Let her be. She'll grow out of it," her mom said.

Leda reluctantly agreed with her mother. She too remembered when she loved pink and owned Barbies and more My Little Ponies than was reasonable, but she wanted something better for her daughter. She didn't want her to ever question herself, or to think that prettiness was a thing. She wanted her to know she was perfect just as she was, free from the torment of "female" and whatever definition it bore.

Around Christmastime Leda took Annabelle with her to do some shopping. She had been running late this year and didn't have any gifts for her parents yet, let alone for John. Generally she avoided shopping with the little one and tried to confine her trips to weekends, when John was home, but she just no longer had that option. Annabelle was being good for the trip. Partly it was just good luck on Leda's behalf at picking a day when she'd slept through her entire nap, and part of it was bribery. She promised that if she were a good girl that they'd stop in at the toy store and pick out a toy. Annabelle was so enthralled by the prospect of this that she kept reminding her mother of her commitment.

"Mommy, I get a toy if I'm good, right?" she said.

"That's right, honey."

"And I'm being good, right?"

"Yes, you are, you're being very good."

Annabelle sat quietly as Leda raced through Target and then through Macy's.

"Do you think Daddy would like a watch for Christmas?" she asked her.

"Hmm, probably not," Annabelle said with judicious fairness.

Leda was amazed at how easy the whole trip was. It was the first time in being a mother that she could envision a future with her daughter where their relationship would grow beyond the neediness of babyhood.

"You're such a big girl," she marveled.

"I know," Annabelle said. "I can dress myself."

After she got the last few things on her list, she and Annabelle headed to the only toy store in the mall. The store was called Catch a Star and at one time had only sold educational toys and games, but over the last year or so Leda had noticed that the educational toy section had grown increasingly smaller, so much so that now it only inhabited one corner at the back of the store. The rest of the store was the typical plastic junk you could buy anywhere. It was disappointing, but it didn't stop her from shopping there; after all, there was only so much social justice one could consider with a schedule that hardly allowed time to shower.

Annabelle was so excited that she was jumping instead of walking as her mom led her into the store.

"I get to get whatever I want!" she shrieked.

Leda walked around with her, looking at baby dolls of all kinds: one that peed and one that cried and another that crawled mechanically across the floor. Then there was a purse with a puppy in it and a magic wand with glitter floating around in some kind of liquid substance on the inside. Annabelle seemed very considerate of what she wanted. This was the first time that she'd ever been allowed to wander around the store like this and choose from anything (Leda knew that this promise held budget restrictions, but the good thing about three-year-olds was most of the time the toys they wanted weren't all that extravagant). She tried to steer her to the educational toy corner, if only just for a second.

"Look at the wooden castle," she said.

"Oh, yeah!" Annabelle said, and pulled down a drawbridge.

Leda carefully took the castle off the shelf and turned it around to look for a price. Education and wood generally weren't cheap. Just as she found the price and thought, *$49.99, who are they kidding?* she heard Annabelle screech.

"Mommy! I want this!"

She turned from the castle to her daughter, who proudly stood holding a bright blond Barbie in a bikini. Where the child manifested this toy from in the few seconds she'd turned away was hard to imagine, but Annabelle was gleaming as if she'd found the prize.

"Why do you want that?" Leda asked her.

"'Cause it's Barbie."

"I know it's Barbie . . ." She took the doll in her hand. Annabelle had many Barbies at home. Originally John's older aunt had given her one for Christmas, to Leda's dismay. She'd planned on taking the doll away at some point, but Annabelle was so excited by it that it seemed like more damage would be done by taking it from her than by just letting her have it.

"Okay, one Barbie is fine, but that's it. I don't want her to get any more than that," she said to John on the car ride home from the family Christmas party, Annabelle asleep in the car seat with her Cinderella Barbie tucked under her arm. Of course she didn't just have the one Barbie. She needed a brunette one, and then she asked for the Mulan one at Target, and was her mother really going to say no in the face of Barbie multiculturalism? And after that there was Barbie's little sister who had a fluffy dog, and after that there really had to be at least one Ken (there ended up only ever being one Ken), and after that who even cared? All bets were off, but this bikini Barbie, this was something new. Generally the appeal (from what Leda was able to tell) had always been the elaborate dresses. Most of her Barbies were ready to go to some kind of ball or wedding or luau, so what the child saw in this nearly naked, freakishly proportioned figure she couldn't understand.

"I know it's Barbie, but why do you want *this* Barbie?"

"'Cause she's pretty." Annabelle answered her mother with such matter-of-factness that it was hard to disagree with the child.

"Why do you think she's pretty?"

"'Cause she just looks like she is."

"But what about the castle?" Leda was ready to spend the $49.99 at this point.

"No, I really want her."

"But look at all the fun you could have with the castle. You could open the drawbridge and put your toys inside."

Annabelle paused and turned to the castle for a second with a look of great deliberation.

"Can I get both?" she asked.

"No, honey, you can't get both today." After all, Christmas was coming, and she still needed to get that watch for John.

"Okay, then the Barbie."

Leda felt desperate. It was one of those times in motherhood when she just didn't know how to reconcile her complicated idealism into the earthly concerns of her child. She wanted to explain it all to her, to tell her about patriarchy and beauty standards and how Barbie was really an image of oppression that held women back from being president and getting paid the same amount as men did.

She knelt down by Annabelle and held the doll out so they could both look at it.

"She is pretty, Anna-B, but you know, being pretty isn't really an important thing to be. There are so many toys here that are important, and this toy is only about being pretty. It's better to be important than pretty."

Annabelle looked at her mother and back at the Barbie.

"Wouldn't you rather have something important?" Leda said.

Annabelle thought for a moment. She pinched her bottom lip with her thumb and forefinger, a habit that was endearingly her own.

In another cluttered attempt Leda added, "You know you can do anything you want when you grow up, right? You don't just have to be pretty?"

"Yeah," Annabelle said.

"So do you want to go maybe look for something else?"

Annabelle looked upset, like under the right circumstance she could have started to cry. "No, I really want it." She grabbed hold of the box as her mom started to move it away. "I just like it. 'Cause I like it for me," she said.

"But don't you want to like something important?"

"No, I just want to like what I like."

Leda's first reaction was to tell Annabelle that she couldn't have the Barbie. That there would just have to be something else in the toy store and that that was the end of it, but then she thought about what her daughter had actually said. She knew that her child did just want to like what she liked. And really, wasn't that enough? Was there anything wrong with her daughter sporting a hyper sense of femininity that was centered around princesses and ponies and bright floral bikinis? Could she really condemn the child for being herself and for just liking something? How was it fair to tell her that everything she loved wasn't important? She tried to imagine a scenario where a mother of a boy would ever try to discourage him from his hyper sense of masculinity. Where she'd lean down and tell him what made him happy was garbage. Skateboards held on a higher pedestal than dance shoes. Legos over sewing. Leda couldn't bear it. And most of all, looking down at her fiery little girl whose hair was a bit matted and whose expression was rich and thoughtful. Who woke up one morning and said, "Birds don't really sing, do they? It's not a song, really. That's just something people call it." Who didn't like Cheerios under any circumstance and who could laugh at adult jokes even when she didn't know the meanings because she could tell when something was really funny. She knew that her daughter would be whatever she wanted one day and no Barbie, even one so naked and disproportionate, could take that away from her.

"You know what? Let's get you this Barbie," Leda said. "She is very pretty. What's her name?"

"Celia!"

"Well, I'm sure Celia will be very flattered. Come on, let's go."

ᖇᐤ

THAT CHRISTMAS ANNABELLE GOT SIX NEW BARBIES AND A BARBIE Dreamhouse. The following year she'd go as a policewoman for Halloween. When questioned on her choice she'd say, "I like to tell people what they should be doing. And my favorite color is blue." Leda was happy for the change but a little sad also. Somewhere she hoped her daughter saw the everlasting strength inherent in the color pink. Somewhere she hoped she'd never forget it.

———❦———

CHAPTER 40

Lunch with Elle

LEDA HADN'T SEEN ELLE IN QUITE A FEW YEARS. THEY HADN'T KEPT IN touch all that much through text, so when Elle e-mailed her and asked if she wanted to meet up for lunch, she was surprised. From what she gathered through social media Elle had married a rich financier and had three children. She lived in New York and had a summer house on Martha's Vineyard. The last time they'd really spoken she was working at a little-known, fairly prestigious literary magazine. At around this same time, Elle met her now husband. The last text conversation between them went:

> LEDA: That's so sweet! He sounds great!
> ELLE: Yeah, he's really cute! We've been spending every day
> together.
> LEDA: That's fantastic! What's his name again?

Elle never responded.

It wasn't all that surprising that Elle would meet a rich guy and be living in New York. Her family was very well-to-do, and she was so skinny, after all. Leda had suggested they meet at a nearby diner, but Elle insisted on a fancier restaurant downtown.

"What about the kids?" Leda texted.

"Sabrina can watch them," Elle answered. "My nanny."

"At the restaurant?" she asked.

"Probably at a park. Sabrina can take care of it. She's fabulous."

In the car ride over to meet Elle, Leda tried to explain to Annabelle that she'd be with three new kids and Sabrina for the afternoon.

"But where will you be?" Annabelle said.

"I'll be at lunch with their mommy."

"But shouldn't they be with their mommy?" Annabelle said.

"Probably, my love. Probably."

They walked into the restaurant, and she saw Elle and the three children immediately.

"Elle," she said, waving.

"Is that the children?" Annabelle asked, holding tight to her mother's hand.

"Yeah, let's go say hi."

"Oh my god! Leda!" Elle got up and opened her arms for a big hug.

Elle looked as skinny as she ever had. She was wearing a poncho that looked expensive and dwarfed her tiny frame. Her face was as pretty as Leda remembered it, although she'd aged considerably. No longer could she pass for nineteen, as she had so often complained about in her twenties.

"People always card me!" she'd say, holding a drink and looking chic, everyone marveling at her youth, saying things like, "Well, it's no wonder! You have such a good figure, like a sixteen-year-old!" or "Your thighs are like my arms!"

There was no doubt now that Elle was not a teenager. Her face looked tired and gaunt. She had wrinkles around her eyes. She looked older than the thirty-some-odd years that she actually was.

"This must be your daughter!" Elle said.

"Yes, this is Annabelle."

"Hi, Annabelle! These are my three, Brooklyn, Declan, and Rowan." Sabrina stood holding Rowan, waiting expectantly for either orders or an introduction.

"Hi, everybody," Leda said. "And you must be Sabrina?" She offered her hand out to the woman.

"Oh yes, so sorry. This is Sabrina. Sabrina, Leda. And Annabelle."

"Hi," Sabrina said, nodding in a passively dutiful way that was uncomfortable to be around. *How does she have this person in her life and just tell her what to do as if she were nothing more than a capable houseplant? As if she weren't just another woman, just like herself, trying to make this all work?* Leda thought.

After a few seconds of chitchat with the children, Elle sent them all off on their way.

Leda hugged Annabelle tightly. "You'll have fun," she said, but she was more hopeful than sure in saying it.

Once the children were out the door the women sat down at the table together.

"Ugh, I'm so happy to have some free time away from them!" Elle said. "I love them, but please, I need time for myself."

"Yeah," Leda said, but she was missing Annabelle already.

"Have you ever been here before?"

"Yes, John and I came here for our anniversary last year."

"Oh, that's nice. How is John?"

"He's great. Working hard as ever."

"I haven't seen him in ages. By the way, they have a great kale salad here. Are you into kale?"

"Not really, but I've heard it's very healthy, isn't it?"

"I've been doing nothing but kale juices in the morning for the last two weeks. It's kind of like a cleanse but a bit more substantive. I'll e-mail you the routine. It goes, kale, kale, kale, squash, kale, banana, repeat."

"And these are all juices?"

"Yes, all juices. It helped me lose the baby weight from Rowan."

"I'm sure you didn't have any baby weight."

"Oh, you'd be surprised. I gained about thirty pounds with each pregnancy. My thighs were chafing when I'd wear a skirt. Can you imagine?"

Leda wanted to explain that thirty pounds wasn't a lot and that thigh gap was something that the vast majority of women never experienced, let alone during pregnancy, but instead she just nodded, silently gaining perspective on Elle and the ever-growing distance between them.

Both women ordered the kale salad, but Leda also ordered a mushroom flatbread pizza to eat alongside. She no longer starved in order to impress friends. It was one of the many privileges of maturity. Elle, on the other hand, didn't touch her salad. Leda tried to count how many bites she actually took. It was three and a half (the half being if you counted when she sucked the lemon slice from her iced tea). *Is anyone ever naturally thin?* Leda wondered. *Thin enough where their thighs are like arms?*

"I'm telling you, I just can't stand these bigger smartphones. I like small purses," Elle said.

"All my purses contain at least one plastic horse. Salesclerks must think I'm crazy when I go to pay and pull out a Clydesdale," Leda said.

"Annabelle is so precious. Are you thinking of having any more?" Elle asked.

"Probably one more. How about yourself?"

"Oh god, no. Honestly, three is more than I wanted, but my husband insisted. His mom had three and so did his grandmother. It's a thing for him. I mean, it doesn't really bother me. What's one more?"

Leda figured that Sabrina might disagree with such an affirmation.

"Well, you guys all make a beautiful family."

"I feel very blessed. Honestly, I look at my friends who work in publishing or whatever, and I just feel so sorry for them. Who really gives a shit about a promotion or publishing an article on Salon.com? Once you have kids you realize what a ridiculous fantasy that all is." Elle sat up straight. "All I can say is we did it, Led. We won."

Leda didn't agree with what Elle was saying. Even in the best of circumstances it would be impossible to agree with someone who was so blind to their own privilege, but she wasn't about to argue. She thought about choices and her own choices and then about the inside of Annabelle's room and its tiny desk and chair.

"I miss smoking," Elle said. "I wish I had a cigarette."

"Do you miss writing at all?" Leda asked. She thought of the story about the woman who sold combs.

"Not at all," Elle said, and without even a moment of reflection, as if unequivocally it was true, "Come on, let's go have coffee."

They walked to Starbucks a few blocks away. Elle's shoes were very loud on the pavement.

"The thing is that it's impossible to keep up with the trends when you have work done on your kitchen. Our counters were granite when we bought the house—embarrassing. I know. We switched to marble, but now I'm thinking of going to bamboo parquet."

"Bamboo parquet?"

"Oh, it's very sustainable. My worry, though, is that it doesn't really go with the aesthetic of the rest of the house, which is more French colonial than modern. In retrospect that was a mistake as well."

Leda listened to Elle talk about decorating. She heard her voice click on words like *backsplash* and *fabric swatch*. At a certain point as they walked along she noticed a trail of blood spots on the sidewalk. She wondered what had happened and why someone would be dripping blood like this down the street. *Nosebleed*, she thought. *Fight*, she thought. *Dog with a ripped paw pad*, she thought. She didn't say anything to Elle. *You can't just talk about blood spots like that. You can't say, "Look, a trail of blood spots. Isn't that disconcerting? Someone's insides just dotting the pavement."* The trail of spots stopped seemingly without cause, and that was it.

Elle ordered a soy macchiato with two shots and Leda ordered tea. They sat by the window and Elle bragged about something Declan could do.

"But you know, Brooklyn read at five, so it doesn't really surprise me."

"They're so smart," Leda said.

About a half hour later Sabrina met them with the children. She looked tired and capable all at once as she directed them back to their mothers. *I wonder what her dreams are*, Leda thought. *I wonder who it is she is trying to be.*

On the car ride home she asked Annabelle about her day.

"So what did you think of Brooklyn, Declan, and Rowan? Did you like them?" she asked.

Annabelle took a second to consider it.

"No," she said.

"Why not?"

"They're weird." She paused thoughtfully again. "They're weird and they're mean."

CHAPTER 41

—◦❀◦—

Baby Number 2

LEDA BECAME PREGNANT AGAIN, AND SHE WAS HAPPY. IT WAS EASIER to be pregnant the second time around. She no longer feared she would be unable to handle all the late nights or that she'd never master swaddling. It was nearly wintertime. She was excited about Christmas and being pregnant for Christmas. She already bought an ornament to hang on the tree celebrating her new baby. It hadn't snowed yet, but the air felt like it could at any minute. Most mornings she'd push Annabelle on a swing in the backyard and work on teaching her how to pump. They'd have lazy afternoons together reading books and making crafts. John got home from work and they'd eat dinner.

"Let me tell you a story of when I was a little girl," she'd say as she tucked her daughter into bed. The days were quiet and lovely.

The night before it happened she'd had a strange feeling. John didn't come home from work until very late. She'd tried calling him, but his phone was dead. Ever since the time he'd acted out so terribly during their engagement she'd get nervous if he'd be late and she couldn't get ahold of him. She told herself that she was over the whole thing, but in times like these she knew she wasn't. *I'll go to my parents'. I'll just take Annabelle and go,* she thought. It was nearly eleven by the time he got home. He'd gotten a flat tire and had left his phone charger at work.

"You should have asked someone to borrow their phone. I was a nervous wreck."

"I'm sorry. I didn't think of it," he said.

As she went to bed she felt a strange unease. It was like a dizzy feeling of a half-formed memory. Once when she was a child standing in the lunch line waiting for pizza she had this same sensation. She was holding her tray up and then a lunch lady motioned for the tray, and she put the tray up on the counter and then there was a piece of pizza on her tray, and she had this same uneasy feeling of a half-formed memory. It was as indescribable then as it was now.

"I have this weird feeling," she said to John.

"What?"

"I don't even know how to describe it. It's like something has already happened, but I don't know what."

"I don't get what you mean."

"I don't either."

"You're probably just tired."

"Maybe that's it."

But as she lay in bed she knew she wasn't all that tired.

The next morning was simple and calm. Annabelle ate breakfast. They went outside and played in the yard. At around eleven they ran an errand at the post office. That's when she first noticed some cramping.

"It probably won't get there until Thursday," the man at the post office said.

"That's fine." Leda tried to think of Thursday and whether it was fine, but her stomach was bothering her too much to really care.

She gave Annabelle an early lunch and put her down for a nap just before one. Her stomach grew progressively worse, but she thought it was probably just the Chinese takeout she'd had the night before. It wasn't uncommon for her to get sick on greasy food. She took a rest on her bed and tried to sleep but couldn't really. She watched some TV for a while longer, but soon she felt like she would be sick. She got up and went to the bathroom, and when she pulled down her underwear it was all blood.

"Oh my god," she said. She looked at the toilet. There was already a good amount of blood there too. *No, no, no, no, please,* she thought. She tried to think of another situation that would yield this amount of blood, but she couldn't think of anything.

She cleaned herself up and went to the bedroom and called John. He didn't answer so she went to text him.

"Call me. It's an emergency," she typed. She was going to write, "I think I may have lost the baby," but she couldn't bring herself to do it.

She called her doctor and got her answering service.

"Hi, this is Dr. Wilson's answering service; what is the nature of your emergency?" the woman said on the other end of the phone.

"Hi, yes, I think I may be having a miscarriage," she said, the word sounding brittle as she said it, her own voice like a chamber echoing back to her.

She held her phone as she waited to hear back from the doctor. *Please call me quickly,* she thought. *Please tell me this is normal. Tell me every woman bleeds.* She sat in the decorative chair in the hall by the bathroom. No one ever sat there, but it felt like the only place to sit during such a time. How lonely and dark her house felt. The days were getting shorter. By afternoon the sun was already going down. She held her stomach and said a prayer. She always prayed in these kinds of times, but she never knew exactly to whom. A few minutes later she could hear Annabelle stirring. She checked the time. It had been nearly two hours since she'd put her down. She knew that she was waking up, and what a cruel reality it was to know that in the midst of losing one child she'd have to mother another one.

Annabelle walked into the hall clumsily and sleepy-eyed.

"Hi, baby," Leda said. "Did you have a nice nap?"

She knew that Annabelle would want to be held and carried downstairs to the kitchen for her afternoon snack. It had been their routine nearly every day since she was born. She'd always had a hard time waking up and wanted to cuddle before being able to face the day.

"Yeah," Annabelle said, reaching up as Leda had anticipated.

"Listen, baby, Mommy can't hold you right now. Mommy's tummy hurts. You need to be a big girl and walk with Mommy to get your snack. We can cuddle later but not right now. Can you do that for Mommy?"

Annabelle considered this for a second and nodded complacently. Leda had expected more resistance, as in the past any other time that she'd tried to skip the cuddling routine the little girl had put up a monstrous fight. She was grateful and saddened by how seemingly aware her daughter was. *Maybe she can sense my devastation. Maybe I'm damaging her too.*

Hand in hand, Leda carefully walked Annabelle down the stairs to the kitchen. It was so hard not to double over in pain. It was so hard not to cry and to scream.

She sat her at the table in her booster seat and gave her some Goldfish. Annabelle ate them in silence.

Dr. Wilson called back and advised her to come in.

"I have my daughter right now."

"Isn't there anyone you can ask to watch her as an emergency?"

"No." Leda knew her mom would do it, but she didn't want to ask her. She just wanted to be sure that she'd lost the baby before she scared her mom over it. Now that she was a mother, she understood how powerfully devastating the role of a parent could be, and she wanted to spare her mom that pain if she could.

"I'll just bring her along. I'm sure my husband will meet me at your office and he can watch her."

After hanging up the phone she frantically began getting things in gear to head to the doctor. She filled a plastic sandwich bag with Goldfish and a sippy cup with juice.

"Annabelle, we need to go to the doctor for Mommy's tummy, so we'll finish our snack in the car, okay?"

"Okay," Annabelle said.

It was hard to know what exactly to pack for her doctor's visit. She felt as though much could be dependent on her bringing the right things along. Would Annabelle need something to do in the waiting room? She brought a coloring book and crayons. Should she bring a change of clothes in case she bled through the pad? It seemed unlikely, but it was possible. What if it rained? Two days later she'd unpack the umbrella and crayons, and it would be the only evidence of an irrationality that would never be felt or understood again.

John called on the drive over. He sounded terrified.

"What emergency? Are you okay?"

"I can't talk much because I'm in the car with the little one." She looked in her rearview mirror at Annabelle, who was quietly munching on Goldfish. "I'm B-L-E-E-D-I-N-G. Meet me at Dr. Wilson's office."

"Oh my god. What do you think it means? Does it mean we lost the baby?" he said.

"Please, John, stop. I don't want to get upset right now. Just meet me at the doctor's."

When Dr. Wilson told her it was a miscarriage, it wasn't a surprise. It was something she'd known the second she saw the blood. So many times in her life she would know things all along and tell herself that it wasn't that thing or those things to spare herself the pain.

When she got out to the waiting room, she shook her head at John and started to cry. She wished she'd called her mother.

Suffering the loss of a miscarriage was a type of mourning that was unlike anything else. It felt like mourning the loss of a child in a certain way, but she knew that it couldn't possibly be quite as painful as that. The thought of losing Annabelle seemed like a pain that she would not be able to survive, and so she would not allow herself to really mourn as if it were a child, even though most of the time that is what it felt like. Sometimes she'd try to think of what her baby would have looked like, but she never could imagine it in any real way. Sometimes there was a boy and sometimes a little girl just like Annabelle. Then there would be a bassinet by her bedside again. The toddling sound of baby toys that rolled in place or rattled out like coins in an empty can. But everything was clouded and distant. Like a memory that you weren't sure of or the prospect of something wonderful that you know isn't true. Very often she'd have dreams that she was still pregnant. She'd wake up and have to pee and she'd naturally reach down and touch her stomach and then she'd remember. How many mornings did she look in the mirror and see herself half asleep, waking up to the pain of remembering? John tried to be supportive, but she knew that to him the baby hadn't been real in the way it had been to her. She was the one giving it air and food and water. She got sick for it and bled at its death. John was sad, but he could not suffer like that.

The burden of motherhood was never felt more greatly than the year after she lost her baby. *To be a mother is to bleed and to tell other women that you are okay when really part of you is dead.* So too did she have to be there for Annabelle and read her bedtime stories about girls who were strong and who tamed dragons and won wars. *Women don't need to tame dragons,* she'd thought one night. *Dragons are meaningless. They are for men.*

John encouraged her about having another child, saying that things would be okay.

"Whenever you're ready we can try to have another baby. I know we'll feel happy again," he'd say.

She rarely answered this with more than a nod, but she appreciated the thought.

She went to counseling at one point when she felt that maybe she'd just become too depressed to handle it on her own.

"Sometimes we blame ourselves for things that really aren't our fault," the counselor said. She was an older lady who sat in a floral chair. The session cost three hundred dollars. Leda imagined she must own a yacht or at least a very nice summer house.

In time she started to feel better. She had mourned and had healed enough to feel like herself again. Every winter, though, as the leaves started to fall off the trees and the air felt like it could snow any minute, she'd feel a sense of sadness that was as real and fresh as it had been that day. She'd sit in the hall and listen to music, and on occasion when people were talking about happiness and limitless potential, she'd know the truth and wouldn't say a word. She never did try to have any other children. John didn't push for it. He knew better. And they were happy. As happy as anyone could be despite the sadness of it all.

CHAPTER 42

Annabelle Starts School

AT A CERTAIN POINT LEDA PREFERRED TO APPLY MAKEUP USING THE mirror from her bronzer compact, which was covered in a thin layer of powder and gave her reflection a generous, warm filter. It hid the lines on her face that had solemnly begun to appear and would allow for momentary escape from her neuroses about aging.

"Oh for god's sake," her mother said, "if I hear you complain about wrinkles I'll open a vein. Get some face cream and forget about it. You young people never stop with obsessing about being young."

"But look, I have lines here, and look here." She leaned up close to her mom to show her a line going from her nose to her mouth.

"You've always had that."

"No, I haven't. I'm really getting wrinkly."

"Wrinkly in the brain. Or maybe you don't have enough wrinkles in your brain and that's the problem," her mom said.

At about the same time that Leda switched from regular mirrors to powdered mirrors Annabelle started kindergarten. She was very excited about it and carried a My Little Pony lunch box around the house the weeks leading up to the start. On her first day Leda packed her more food than would be necessary to survive a weekend in the wilderness. When Annabelle got home Leda discovered that she only ate the cookies.

"You only ate the cookies, Anna-B."

"I ate some of the sandwich."

The sandwich was pulled apart and the peanut butter had been licked off.

"You have to eat more than cookies and peanut butter, honey. Weren't you hungry all day?"

"No, we had snack."

"Well, I'm not going to pack cookies anymore if you don't eat your actual lunch too, okay?"

"Okay, I will."

The next day the cookies were eaten and three bites of sandwich.

During those first few months of kindergarten very often Leda found herself in total awe of her daughter. In five short years she'd turned from an infant unable to hold her head up to a little girl who kept a sticker collection and could count off jumping jacks. *Her knees are just like a grown-up's knees,* she thought, seeing her daughter standing on a kitchen chair one morning.

John took Annabelle to school whenever he didn't have to be in early for work. He was a really good dad, and this was something Leda admired greatly about him. He seemed to genuinely enjoy the company of his child, which was disappointingly unusual for many men. Whenever Leda would see John tenderly hand his daughter a cup of juice or lean down to scoop her up, she felt a pang of love so intense. With little notice, the love between her and John had changed over the years. Bits and pieces of what it had been fell away and new surfaces emerged that heartily sustained them. Their love was marching forward, evolving, becoming bigger. Love now was the brisk partnership of facilitating the healthy and happy life of their child. The two of them could silently maneuver together and get their daughter dressed and fed in mere minutes. If you'd told Leda then that John was not in fact part of her body, she may not have believed you.

"Do you think she'll be okay?" he asked her as they watched Annabelle walk, wobbly and resolved, through the school yard her very first day.

"I think she will," Leda said. "She's strong."

"She's stronger than I am," John said, and Leda knew just how much he meant it.

She hadn't realized it the first few months of the school year, but many of the stay-at-home mothers spent their time walking around the elementary school during the day. She'd come to pick Annabelle up early one day for a doctor's appointment when she bumped into Helen, a thin, young-looking woman with graying hair and a six-month-old baby she carried in a sling at all times.

"Oh, hi, Helen. Are you picking up early too?" Leda asked.

"Oh, no, I stay," Helen said, rocking back and forth as she stroked her baby's head.

"You stay?"

"Yes, I usually just hang out at the school until the day is out. I'm a stay-at-home mom so I can do that."

"Oh, I didn't know. Is that something people do?" Leda tried not to sound shocked or judgmental, but Helen didn't seem to be aware of how peculiar the whole scenario was; she just swayed back and forth holding her sling baby.

"Yes, myself, Patrice, Lisa, Sara, and usually Kelly all stay. You should stay with us sometime!"

"What is it you do, though? I mean for all those hours?"

"We walk around and talk and usually visit the office and see if we can be of any help with any upcoming school functions or anything like that. Honestly, the hours just fly by. I feel like I've just dropped Lucy off, and then it's time to pick her up again. I mean, if you think about it what do you do at home without her all day?"

Leda tried to think of a good answer to this, but, really, Helen was right. There wasn't all that much to do at home with Annabelle gone. Most days she found herself counting down the hours until it was time to go back to pick her up. Luckily, the school day wasn't all that long, or she might have started feeling similar to how she'd felt in California. *Maybe if I were a better housewife I'd clean things and organize and keep a home like Martha Stewart or that lady I once went to the house of who made homemade wreaths, but I am not these women at all,* she thought. Before she'd made it to Annabelle's classroom she'd resolved to go back to work.

After some consideration, Leda decided not to go back to tutoring because the hours were afternoons and weekends. She wanted to be home as much as she had been. Her friend Katrina told her of a local publishing house looking for a receptionist.

"The pay is abysmal and the work is tedious, but hey, at least it's working in publishing, right? I'll e-mail Liz and get you an interview. She's a good friend of mine."

Leda didn't even come in for an in-person interview. Liz was so happy to be getting someone who wasn't just out of college that she hired her over the phone. "I want you to start as soon as possible, if that's okay?"

"Sure, I could do Monday?"

"You can't come in tomorrow? The girl I had quit without giving me any notice at all. She had some kind of issue with her boyfriend or something. She left me high and dry and I'm really swamped."

"Oh, that's terrible. Yes, I could come in tomorrow."

Her first day was slower than she'd anticipated. The work was mostly answering e-mails and doing little odd jobs around the office. Liz was tall and disheveled in a professional kind of way. When she talked on the phone she'd say, "Well, who's to say?" and "I just can't deal with that." Leda kept to herself mostly. She couldn't help but feel sorry for herself on occasion as she'd print something out or make copies of something else. At lunch she ate a salad and thought about the woman she'd been in college. It was hard to imagine her now. When she got home she cried to John, and he told her to quit the job.

"Why are you doing it if it's making you miserable?"

"It's only been one day, John. Don't you think I should give it a chance?" She felt that this is what John should have been saying to her instead of telling her to quit.

The next few weeks, things got a bit better in the office. Leda settled into a routine, and it was nice to get out of the house. Being a stay-at-home mom had for the most part been a considerably thankless job, but being in the office had so many little rewards throughout the day that she always felt like she was accomplishing something.

"Thanks, Leda," Liz would say.

Or a client would email: "That's perfect, thanks!"

One Friday a delivery man said, "You make my day," when Leda took a package from him and offered him some candy from her desk. It was nice to be appreciated, and then at 2:45 she was out the door and could go pick up Annabelle and settle into the job she really loved.

Annabelle started her second year of school and Leda was invited to a party that Helen was throwing. "It's back to school for us mommies too!" the invitation said. It was all women and they drank mimosas and talked about summer camps and after-school activities. A smartly dressed woman named Janette talked with Leda for a long time about an article they'd both read in *The New York Times* that morning. She was funny and bright. Leda didn't recognize her from the playground at drop-offs in the morning.

"You know, I don't remember you from last year at all. Are you new to the school?" she asked.

"Oh, no. I just don't drop off. My nanny, Eloise, does. I have to be at work early. I'm a lawyer," Janette said.

"Oh, okay. I think I remember seeing Eloise." She tried to think of who Eloise might be, but it wasn't coming to her.

"What is it you do?" Janette asked.

For a second Leda hesitated. She was used to the judgmental stares of working moms when she'd explain that she stayed at home. There was always an apologetic effect to the way they'd nod as she talked about giving up her own ambitions to prepare afternoon snacks and listen to a six-year-old explain how many planets were in the solar system. But then she stopped herself.

"I work as an administrative assistant in a publishing house," she said.

"Oh, wow." Janette seemed impressed. "That must be interesting work."

"Yeah, I like it. The hours are flexible so I get to be home with Annabelle a lot."

"Wow, it sounds like you have it all."

Leda nodded. For a moment she couldn't help but believe it to be true.

That night as she got ready for bed she told John about the party and about all the other women. She told him about Annabelle and her first day of first grade.

"It was a good day," she said, washing the makeup off her face. As she stood up from leaning over the sink she caught a glimpse of her reflection in the bathroom mirror. Her face was dripping wet. She could see no lines and no wrinkles. It was just her young face staring back at her, brilliant and elegant and ready to face the next day.

"I look just like my mother," she said.

———❧———

CHAPTER 43

Dee Dee

DEE DEE WORKED AT THE DESK BESIDE LEDA IN THE OFFICE. HER OFFI-
cial title was human resources coordinator, but in reality her job
seemed to consist of little more than what Leda's did as a receptionist. She was a heavy, middle-aged woman with curly blond hair.
Her lipstick was always either a shade too light or a shade too dark.
For the first few months of working alongside her, Leda liked her
well enough. They'd exchange small talk and Dee Dee would always
politely inquire about how Annabelle was doing.

"How's she liking school?" she'd say, or "Did you do anything fun
with the family this weekend?"

Dee Dee wasn't married herself, and as far as Leda could tell she
didn't have any children. She did have a beagle named Ronald, whom
she talked about incessantly. It was because of Ronald that Leda had
her first inclination about who Dee Dee really was. Ronald came to
the office one afternoon for a much-hyped visit to meet Leda and
Ren, the new mailroom guy. They both gathered around Ronald as
he sweetly waddled from person to person to say hello. Dee Dee
talked proudly about how he could catch bits of hot dog but only
liked the kosher brands.

"He knows what the good stuff is," she said.

After chatting for a while and everyone getting the chance to pat
Ronald, Dee Dee suggested they all go for coffee.

"Ronald loves Starbucks," she said.

"Do they let him come in?" Leda asked.

"They do when I put his vest on." She leaned down and maneuvered Ronald into a little red vest that said "Service Dog" in stitching along his bulging side.

"Is he a service dog?" Leda asked, still wildly willing to believe in the goodness of her lipsticked coworker.

"Oh goodness no, but no one ever questions it. I made him the vest myself."

"Smart," Ren said.

Leda didn't say anything, but she declined the trip to Starbucks as politely as possible. From then on she tried her best to keep her distance from Dee Dee and got less amusement from Dee Dee's stories of Ronald's escapades.

A month after the Ronald meeting, the office started to stink. At first Leda only noticed it occasionally as she'd get a whiff of the smell sitting at her desk. It was a stale smell, like an old sack lunch or like a person who hadn't showered for a really long time. She bought an air freshener for her desk and tried to leave the window open as often as the weather permitted, but the smell grew stronger. For a short while she thought maybe it was Ren. He was kind of a strange guy, and very often he was all sweaty from running around the office. But after the two of them took the elevator alone together on a few separate occasions, she decided that it wasn't him and that the smell was localized somewhere near her desk. She asked Dee Dee about it.

"I don't smell anything," Dee Dee said. "But as far as I'm concerned it smells horrible here all the time."

She asked Charmaine, the other receptionist, who worked across the hall.

"I thought it was just me!" Charmaine said. "I've been smelling it for a month now. I've been burning candles, but it's not helping at all. It makes me nauseous."

The smell was so bad one morning that Leda left work early and took a sick day.

"It sounds ridiculous, but I'm seriously considering quitting. I can't take it. It's like torture," she said to John one night at dinner.

"Why don't you mention it to human resources?"

"I did. That's Dee Dee. As far as I know she's the only one who works human resources."

"There must be someone above her. Maybe just tell Liz about it."

"I think I'll look crazy."

"It's less crazy than just quitting over it."

"That's true."

Before she had a chance to tell Liz, Liz called her into her office to address the issue.

"Leda, I don't know if you've noticed, but the office stinks. Would you please send an e-mail and ask all the employees to clean out their desks?"

Leda was never so excited to write an e-mail. She pored over the words and looked up *stink* in the thesaurus. In the end she settled on:

> Hi everybody,
>   Recently there have been quite a few complaints regarding an odor in our office. If everyone could kindly do their part and clean up their work areas it would be greatly appreciated. Thanks so much!

A week passed after the e-mail had been sent and still there was no change. Eventually the smell stopped getting worse and started to blend into the other expected, stale smells of the office. Leda created a routine to keep from being too bothered. She had three different air fresheners on her desk, and each morning she'd light a candle and put on a strong-smelling lip balm. It kept the stench to an inconsistent wafting, which was, at the very least, tolerable. Charmaine quit, and Leda was convinced it was related to the odor.

"Are you feeling better about the smell?" Dee Dee said a few months later.

"I guess I've gotten used to it," Leda said.

"That's the trick to this job. You just have to get used to the worst parts of it."

"Well, I like most of the job. It's just that smell that was driving me crazy."

"Oh, believe me, I understand. I once broke up with a man for farting."

"Did you really?"

"It was my ex-fiancé. He had a lot of problems and was going through some kind of a breakdown about his career and whether he was really ready to get married and whatnot. I dealt with it for a very long time. We were together for over twelve years in total, which is a very long time to just be engaged. I was always understanding and I would go with him to all his therapy sessions and wait in the waiting room for him. He'd tell me to leave him, and then he'd cry, and I'd just sort of nod and go along with it and calm him and soothe him. And then one day we were lying in bed—I was up watching Joan Rivers, and he was asleep in bed next to me, and all of a sudden I smelled his fart, and I just lost it. I realized I couldn't spend one more second dealing with him, so I pushed him out of bed and I told him that I thought he should move out because I was tired of smelling his farts. Those were my exact words, 'I'm tired of smelling your farts,' and the next day he moved out. It was the best decision I ever made. Like I said, he had a lot of problems."

Leda looked very hard at Dee Dee. Dee Dee was chewing a potato chip. Her lipstick was too light. Her hair was particularly tightly curled. At the exact same moment, Leda came to the conclusion that Dee Dee was a very independent woman and that she permed her hair. It was like everything about this person suddenly made sense.

"Did you ever marry?" Leda asked with complete abandon. She focused her stare on a blond ringlet pressed tight against Dee Dee's temple.

"Oh, heavens no. I don't think I have enough patience for men, or for children, for that matter. I'm happy with my Ronald."

"I admire that about you, Dee Dee. You're a very strong woman."

"I'm not sure it's strength. I think it's more just not having the patience. I like to go home and watch my shows. I can't be bothered."

"And your hair is always so put-together," Leda said.

"Oh, well, aren't you a doll!" Dee Dee fluffed her curls carefully. "I just got it done today so it probably looks especially good."

"It really does," Leda said. *It's really not good, but it is put-together. And that's something,* she thought.

Two years later Dee Dee retired. They had a small party for her, and she cried and thanked everyone. Leda gave her a houseplant. It seemed appropriate. Not too many months later she ran into Charmaine on the street. She hardly recognized her at first. She was looking like a woman, no longer the young girl who bantered about the office. Her smile was the same warm smile that Leda remembered from their handful of conversations. It felt nice to talk to her. It was as if they were old friends when really they hardly knew each other. But a common memory could do that. They'd shared the experience of that place and those times, and so really between the two of them it felt as if there was a lot.

"I was engaged last year, but it didn't work out," Charmaine said, rolling her eyes. "It's whatever."

"I'm sure you'll meet someone amazing," Leda said, and she believed it to be true.

"I'm not worried about it. Right now I just want to enjoy my life."

"Smart," Leda said.

"Oh, hey, you heard what happened to Dee Dee, right?"

"You mean her retiring?"

"She didn't really retire. I only know this from Rita. She was the one who found her."

"Found her?"

"Yeah, they found her snorting cocaine in the bathroom."

"Are you serious?"

"I kid you not. They forced her to retire. They told her either she retire or they'd have to fire her and report her to the police. I always knew she was a weirdo, but still, to think of her snorting cocaine is just the most ridiculous thought ever."

"I can't believe it."

"I know. Oh, and guess what they found when they cleaned out her desk?"

"What?"

"A bunch of old sandwiches. Like totally and completely rotten sandwiches for years and years that hadn't been cleaned out. That's what that awful smell was."

"It was Dee Dee!"

"Yeah, it was Dee Dee. You know, I quit over that smell."

"I figured you might have."

"I'm not mad about it, though. It was the best decision I ever made."

They talked a few minutes longer and promised to keep in touch, a notion neither of them really expected to uphold. Leda walked home in a daze, thinking of the office and of Dee Dee and of the sandwiches. *I wonder what ever happened to Ronald. He was a nice dog.*

CHAPTER 44

Period

"When a woman has pms, that's when she's most honest. it isn't a bad thing like everyone says. Women get mean 'cause they should be mean." Leda had said this a few times, although the exact occasions she couldn't remember. She believed it to be true, but in the days leading up to her period she'd usually feel so depressed that anything as concrete as this didn't seem viable. What was honest? What was mean? She didn't know and didn't care. What she cared about was the end of the world that was ticking in her mind, the obnoxious existence of her husband, and every little misgiving throughout the day. Normally during this time she'd swear at people in traffic and unapologetically eat ice cream. She'd say things like "If men had cramps, they'd sell Vicodin over the counter," or "Let's go out for ice cream." This was not a time to go bathing suit shopping. She knew this with every fiber of her being.

"You never go swimming," Annabelle said as she sat at the dining room table eating a Kit Kat bar.

"What do you mean? I love to swim."

"No you don't. When we go to the beach you just sit on a beach chair and read. You don't like wearing a bathing suit 'cause you think you look bad."

Leda hadn't given any thought to it, but just as her daughter said it she realized it was true. She'd not gone swimming for years. They'd taken Annabelle to the beach continuously as a toddler, but Leda gained a little weight one winter, and after being unable to pull up her floral one-piece from the year before, she decided to put on a sundress and keep out of the water. She ordered a bathing suit off of Amazon at one point a couple of summers later but was woefully disappointed by it. After that she never went swimming again. When exactly she had expressed to her daughter her feelings about her love handles and the soft mess that was the back of her thighs she couldn't be sure, but hearing her little girl say it out loud made her feel loathsomely transparent.

"I wear bathing suits," she feebly protested.

"No, you don't."

"Yes, and we're going to the beach this weekend, and I'm going to swim."

That night Leda had John stay home with Annabelle so that she could go shopping for a bathing suit. In her mind she associated it with righting a wrong that she'd done; ending a perpetuation of misery in her family line, one she refused to pass along to her daughter. She remembered her mom never wearing shorts because she believed she had ugly knees. Another time, her mom had cried when she hadn't been able to fit into a gown for a benefit she was attending. Leda was little at the time, but she could vividly remember sitting beside her mom on the bed and trying to comfort her. What she said or even felt was less memorable than what she saw: her mom huddled in an evening gown that wouldn't zip up, crying and wiping her eyes. Leda had worked to protect her daughter from these kinds of images of herself, and yet without meaning to, she'd given her daughter: herself huddled in a sundress reading under an umbrella in the burning heat.

When Leda got to the mall, a man was furiously parallel parking in one of the few parallel parking spots in the lot. Surely this late on a Tuesday there were plenty of non–parallel parking spots. But nevertheless he moved the car back with ease and speed in one swooping motion. *How can a man get so much validation from parallel parking? Who are you all?* she thought as she saw him get out and check to be sure the car was between the lines.

There wasn't a good place to shop for a bathing suit for women who were neither nineteen nor ninety. Everything either was made of a set of strings tied together or had a small tent sewed around it. And so this in-between Leda subsisted in of avoiding sexiness and sexlessness led her to the swimsuit section of Lord & Taylor. She went over to a rack of one-pieces and started wading through the mess. *What size could I even possibly be?* She pulled off whatever largest size she could that wouldn't make her feel bad about herself. At one time in her life she'd been a size 6. What a wonderful number that was. It was light and airy. It tapped beach balls and drank sexy-sounding cocktails while jogging. Never has a woman felt sorry to casually banter about the fact that she is a size 6—unless of course she's a model, and then it's shameful and wrong, or she's incredibly thin and all her thin friends who are 0's or 00's might judge her about a slice of pizza she publicly enjoyed that one time—actually, there were many scenarios in which a woman could be upset about being a size 6. Leda's size 6 period was short-lived in the scheme of her life, and she sadly and reluctantly buoyed in a size 8/10 period for many years after that. Being a size 8/10 is only contextually enjoyable. After having been a 6, 8 was mortifying, but once she slipped into the size 10 category (and, let's not kid ourselves, the occasional 12), the size 8 seemed about the equivalent of Kate Moss on a heroin binge. Leda remembered herself literally dancing in a dressing room as she was able to squeeze into a size 8 pair of jeans that were incredibly unflattering but were manageably zipped up. *I'm like Jesus,* she thought as she took them off and folded them up to be left aside, as there was no way to physically walk around in them. Nowadays Leda was rarely if ever able to fit into an 8 (although god knows that's the size she would have said she was if she were in the imaginary lineup of women's judgments where one has to publicly declare one's weight, clothing size, and blow job abilities: "145, size 8, and head goddess"). Now she was usually a solid 12/14 with the occasional 16 in the mix. None of these numbers were sexy or celebratory in any way. She hid them from herself, and the world, as she walked around in her daily life living and doing so many extraordinary things. She was alive and beautiful and thriving and hating herself every minute of it.

"Looking for something special?" a sales associate with an excited face said.

"Oh, no, just looking."

"Are you sure?"

"No, I'm good for now, thanks."

"Okay, well, my name is Karen; let me know if you need anything."

Leave me alone, Karen. I'll kill you, so help me god, she thought. Unfortunately, only minutes later Leda realized that she did in fact need help and Karen was the only person around.

"Could I try these on?"

"Of course! Right this way. What's your name?"

"Leda."

"Lisa?"

"Leda."

"Lisa?"

"Yes."

Karen unlocked a fitting room and began arranging all of the swimsuits in a tight fanned-out pattern on a hanging rack.

"There you go, Lisa. And if you need a different size or style or anything just let me know."

"Thanks so much!" *I hope you die now.*

Leda locked the fitting room door and started to sort through the array of torture before her. She took off her pants and then top, all the while bracing herself for how naked she'd have to be in fluorescent lighting in mere seconds. *Cellulite isn't fatal,* she told herself while managing with all her physical might not to catch a glimpse of her reflection in the mirror as she transitioned from clothed to sausaged in waterproof spandex.

The first one she tried on was simple and black and had a special system built in for squeezing intestines together to give the appearance that your body was mostly made up of spine and eternal youth.

"Oh my god," she said out loud as she looked at her reflection. She couldn't help but laugh. Her thighs looked wide and ripply, her stomach, despite its squished intestines, still showed visibly through the suit, her belly button proudly outlined like some kind of federal lobbyist for the U.S. obesity epidemic.

She started to pull off the suit when she heard Karen wildly knocking on the door. "Lisa? How's it going in there, Lisa?"

"Fine, thanks."

"Let me know if you need anything."

"Okay, will do." *For the love of god, Karen, leave me the hell alone.*

The next suit was dotted and patterned. *Broken television set,* she thought, and took it off.

Then was one with frills on the front. *Obese bird.*

One that was ruched and eggplant. *Obese folded eggplant.*

"Lisa, how are the sizes working for you?"

"Fine." *I'll kill you, Karen. I kill you right now, so help me god.*

Leda tried on three more, each one worse than the last. Slowly and violently her self-worth began to dissipate with each suit. Who she was when she'd walked in, fully clothed and preciously alive, was no longer. Now she was sacks of fat under flowers and pleats. She was absolutely nothing else, not someone's mother or a person who'd once written a poem that had made her friend cry, or the breathing living moving soul as human as the day was long. *How is it that John wants to have sex with me ever?* she thought. She started to pull off a hot pink plunging-neckline suit but halfway through couldn't find the strength to continue, so she sat down on the little wall bench that was covered in discarded, inside-out suits. Slouched and half naked, she looked at her reflection. Her thighs were overhanging the bench, and her stomach was stuck out. Somewhere she'd once heard a woman describe the determinant of being fat as your stomach sticking out farther than your breasts. She had no memory of this woman or in what context she'd said it, but even so she felt strongly that her stomach, even when it was at its absolute worst, should not stick out farther than her breasts. Looking at herself in the mirror now, she tried to determine if her stomach fell beyond her nipple line, but she knew even if it didn't it didn't matter. She was disgusting, fat, worthless. *How dare you even live.* And without meaning to, she began to cry—not just cry, but sob, long, low, soulful tears. She pinched her arm fat and focused in on stretch marks that peeked out the edge of the bathing suit. *You gross cunt.*

"Lisa? Lisa? Is everything okay in there, Lisa?"

"I'm fine!" She didn't really shout the response, but even so her tone was audibly inappropriate.

"Oh, okay, just let me know if you need me," Karen said.

"Okay, thanks!"

Motivated by her pure hatred for Karen and little else, Leda willed herself to stop crying, stand up, and try on yet another bathing suit. This one had straps over the back and in some complicated criss-cross pattern. She stepped in and got one arm through and pushed her other arm through what she thought was the opening, only to realize it wasn't the opening at all but one of the straps. She tried to pull her arm free but couldn't get it, so she tried to unhook the other arm to start again, only to pull the other arm through one of the crisscross straps as well. *Son of a bitch.* She tried to get both arms free at once, but they were both pressed so tightly against her body that she couldn't. She pulled and squirmed and slowly started to panic. Now her reflection looked like a woman tied into a bathing suit, her skin bright red from the straps digging in and her face sorrowful and exhausted. *Well, I guess this is just my life now, living like this in this suit.* After a few more failed attempts Leda knew what had to be done. There was no other option.

"Karen," she called out. "Karen! I need help."

"Lisa?"

"Yes, it's Lisa. I'm stuck in a bathing suit. Can you unlock the door and help me?"

"Of course, Lisa. Hang on!"

Moments later Karen had freed Leda from her strap nightmare. Leda got dressed as quickly as was possible. She didn't want to leave the store empty-handed, though, to explain to her daughter why she yet again was unable to conquer her saddlebags and love handles, so she grabbed that first black swimsuit, paid for it, and nearly ran to her car.

On the way home she turned the radio up loud. She promised herself all kinds of things about eating salad and going for walks in the evening. *Maybe I'll try yoga,* she thought, a vague ambition she turned to in times of fat-related crisis. She envisioned a more linear self walking through the rest of her life. Her daughter by her side as she lifted weights and juiced. The image as it was bothered her, though. She didn't want her daughter by her side like that. She didn't want that at all. She felt like crying, and she felt like screaming. Her whole life and the fat pinching and hating her stomach. Dieting at twelve years old. Skipping cake at her own birthday party and not wearing bathing suits, summer after summer sitting on a beach in the blistering heat. Until this moment she thought that hating her body was vanity, and that it wasn't important, and was a silly girl thing, something she blamed herself over and felt ashamed of, but now she felt that to hate her body, *to hate her body,* was not a small thing at all. Her body was what kept her breathing, and living and beating on through each day. It was hers more so than all else in the world. To hate it wasn't vanity. And it wasn't a silly girl thing. It was sick, and it was devastating. *Will it never end?* she thought. *Will I be an old lady, my feet pushed under a couch to hold me down so I can do sit-ups?* And she knew that the answer was yes. And so she started to feel that she might vomit. She pulled the car over to the side of the road and leaned out; the cool night air hit her hard, but it wasn't refreshing. She retched, but she didn't throw up. Minutes later she'd have to get herself together. Minutes later she knew she'd be driving home.

When she got to her block she didn't want to pull up to the house. She didn't want to see her Annabelle. She didn't want to face her smallness and faith and the still-wild potential of her youth, so she drove around for nearly an hour. Around and around her block, until she was sure that when she went inside her daughter would be asleep.

When she did finally go home, she didn't tell John about the bathing suits or crying in the fitting room or the car ride home. She knew he wouldn't understand. He'd pretend to and say she was beautiful, and in a way that meant something, but in many ways it did not. She took a shower and brushed her teeth and on her way to her bedroom she checked in on Annabelle, who was so covered by her comforter that Leda could hardly make out her shape in the darkness, but even so she stood there and stared at her for a lot longer than usual.

The next day Leda got her period. They didn't make it to the beach that weekend, nor the next, and her swimsuit was left folded, creased, forgotten and never forgotten, like the feeling of watching your mother crying in an evening gown or the ever-present cycle of the moon. Like life and fatness and trying to find the free will to survive it all.

CHAPTER 45

School Play

ANNABELLE WAS IN HER FIRST SCHOOL PLAY. IT WAS AN ORIGINAL PRO-duction about a forest full of animals who must work together to survive the winter. Annabelle's role was small, as were all the roles, to ensure that every child received at least one line. Leda had stayed up late the night before finishing her costume, which was meant to be, as the directions explained: "An abstract idea of a woodland creature. We want our animals to all look different but be indistinguishable as to what animal they actually are."

"Can I be a raccoon?" Annabelle said after her mom read the directions aloud.

"No, sweetie, but you can be an abstract of a raccoon."

"What does that mean?"

"I have no idea."

In the end it meant a bushy gray tail of fake fur, a headband of brown cat ears, and face makeup that looked enough like a raccoon but not too much like a raccoon.

John came home from work early so that they could all drive to the school together and be sure to get a good seat up front.

"We'll be too early. No one will be there yet," Annabelle said, but Leda didn't care. She was excited for this in a way that was irrational in any other context apart from believing that her child was the greatest human who ever existed and that everything she did was revelatory and eternally impressive.

"I want to be sure we have good enough seats so I can get a video of your line," Leda said.

They got their seats up front, and Annabelle headed off with her teacher and the other two kids whose parents were clearly just as overzealous.

John and she waited and chatted a bit about work and about what to do over the weekend. Leda felt nervous with anticipation, though she had no worry of whether her daughter would be stellar as an abstract woodland creature. She thought back to the few times she'd been in school plays herself. It was always a lot of fun, and there was a certain thrill in performance that was rarely rivaled in life. She felt in a sense the same way now as she had those times and wondered if Annabelle was feeling the same way too. The thought of it coupled with the nervousness sent a chill up her back, and she shook in her seat a bit and smiled.

I'm happy, she thought.

The crowd started to fill up the "auditorium" (school gym with a stage at the end of it and rows of folding chairs), and Leda thought she ought to run to the bathroom quickly before the show started.

"I'll be right back," she said to John. "Don't let anyone take my seat."

On her way back from the bathroom a man in a suit, presumably a father also on his way to the auditorium, walked alongside her. She smiled politely when he glanced over at her, and although they were going to the same place, and had acknowledged each other's presence, it was important to keep a socially acceptable distance, so Leda kept pace so as to not be too close or too in time to his step. When they got to the "auditorium," the door was closed and a teacher's aide was standing to guard it.

"Sorry, would you guys mind going around back? Some of the students enter the show from here, and we want to keep the doors closed until their cues."

Leda and the man looked over at each other briefly before agreeing and heading off in the direction that they were meant to go.

"I didn't know this show was so fancy," the man said, and Leda laughed politely and nodded.

"Around back" turned out to mean that they'd actually have to exit the building and reenter at a door at the rear of the gym. They pushed open the door to the vestibule, but when they got to the exit door it was locked.

The man pushed hard first, and even tried to pull despite the fact that the door was clearly meant to be pushed.

"That's funny," he said.

Leda tried a few times herself but couldn't get it open. They shrugged and turned around, but as they went to open the door back to the school hallway it wouldn't open.

"It's locked," Leda said.

"What the heck?" the man said.

They pushed and pulled and tried over and over to get it open, but it wasn't opening.

Just then Leda could see the lights flickering in the hallway.

"The play is starting," she said, utterly devastated all at once.

They banged on the door a few times, but no one was nearby.

"Do you have a phone?" Leda asked him. "Mine is back in my purse with my husband."

"I do, but it's not charged, I'm afraid."

Leda's disdain for the man, which formerly had been little more than the general disdain she felt for most people, suddenly spiked. *Who carries an uncharged phone around?* But she knew John was hardly any better with his own phone (although, caught up in the moment, she wasn't likely to admit it to herself).

They banged on the glass for a while longer before just standing awkwardly together, not knowing what to do. Leda kept thinking of Annabelle in her insane outfit and how unbearable it would be if she'd miss her line.

"Well, my wife is going to be pretty angry with me over this one. I was meant to get here earlier, but I was running late."

"Tell her that it wouldn't have helped to get here early. I was one of the first people in the gym and here we are."

"Yeah," the man scoffed to himself. "My name is Charlie, by the way." He stretched his hand out.

"Leda." She shook it.

"You have a child in the play, I'm presuming?"

"Yes, a daughter, Annabelle."

"I have a son, Liam. I hate to say it, but I really don't know what he is in this play."

"He isn't anything. They're abstract woodland creatures. No one is anything."

"Oh, that's a bit sad. Isn't it?"

"Yeah."

"What will they tell their kids one day about it?"

"They'll probably have to explain that they went to one of the best public school systems in the country, so this is what happens."

"I thought we'd avoid this if we didn't put them in private school."

"Ha, yeah. I guess we failed as parents again."

Charlie nodded and leaned up against the door. Both of them likely would have preferred to sit on the floor, but neither of them pushed for it. There was a certain decorum about standing that needed upholding in this situation. It was needless, yes, but without it there'd be no separation between people and abstract woodland creatures.

They could hear the sounds of the children singing a song. It was even more devastating than the lights flashing.

"If I miss this I don't know what I'll do," Leda said. "Maybe my husband will record it on his phone."

Charlie nodded, but he didn't seem to understand.

"It just means so much to me to see this. Annabelle will be so upset if I miss it."

Charlie shrugged. "Kids are resilient. I'm sure down the line she'd never remember if you were there or not."

Leda wasn't sure if Charlie was trying to be comforting or dismissive, but the thought that this wouldn't matter to her child disturbed her. The feeling of anticipation that she'd felt along with her daughter as she'd waited for the play to start made her feel a sense of purpose so lovely and rich, and for Charlie here to denigrate it all with his flippant remarks, it only further solidified the horror of the moment at hand.

She thought back to high school, where all one hoped for was the chance to be caught in some vestibule with the boy you'd had a crush on. She'd been in love with a boy named Sam, who was sweet and bookish and popular beyond hope. Over and over she'd imagined situations where they'd be forced to spend time together and that time ending up in making out.

"What? We're stuck here in this locker with our bodies pressed up against each other? Well, might as well start kissing" was the general way the fantasy played out. And here she was with Charlie, living the high school dream, and it was hell on earth. *How much bullshit everything you want is,* she thought.

"Don't you think Liam will be sad you missed him?"

"His mom is there, so I doubt it. Kids don't really care what it is their dads do. It's their mom's being there that matters, I think."

Leda was done talking to Charlie after that. It was an impractical stand to take, though, and seconds later they were talking again.

"What is it you do?" he asked her.

"I'm a writer," Leda said.

She couldn't believe she'd said it. She had no certainty where it came from. And it sure as anything wasn't planned, but she could feel her heart beating away in her chest as she said it.

"Oh, what is it that you write?"

"Everything," she snapped back.

Just then she saw John in the school hallway.

"There's my husband!" She banged hard on the glass and John ran over and let them out.

"We got locked in," Leda said. The two of them jogged back down toward the gym, leaving Charlie bumbling his way behind. They entered through the once-again open side door, and there was Annabelle in all her abstract glory standing in center stage. Leda was far back in the crowd, but she could see her daughter fully because she wasn't seated.

"Here in the woods all of us fight through winter. But a successful winter is not one you merely survive, it is one in which you thrive."

I heard her line! Leda thought, and she couldn't help but feel every bit of wonderful. It was revelatory, it was eternal, it was everything she could have ever wanted.

CHAPTER 46

───❧───

A Call from Elle

IT WASN'T LATE AT NIGHT WHEN LEDA GOT THE CALL. ELEVEN THIRTY really isn't late. But it felt late to see "Elle" blazed across her phone. It could have easily been three a.m., given the context of their friendship, which had rarely been a phone-call friendship, let alone one late like this. She figured that maybe it was a pocket dial or some other such mistake, but even so she answered. John was trying to fall asleep beside her and she was up with a book. The light on her nightstand was the only beacon in the room besides, now, her phone.

"Hello."

"Scott is cheating on me." Leda could hear Elle's voice shaking.

"What?!" It was all so surreal, Elle's voice, what she was saying. Leda looked around her bedroom quickly to orient herself. She touched the corner of her book, sharp, familiar, paper present in her hand.

"He's having an affair."

"Oh my god."

"I'm freaking out, Leda. How could he do this to me?"

Leda really didn't know Scott. In fact, until this moment she'd entirely forgotten his name was Scott. Elle didn't have her relationship status up on Facebook, and apart from two family pictures she'd posted, there was little evidence Scott existed in her life at all, at least to Leda, who knew Elle these days exclusively through selfie smiles and the longing melancholy of food pics.

"I don't know what to do. I just found out," Elle said.

"Are you sure it's true?"

"Yes, I am."

"Oh my god, Elle. I'm so sorry."

"I am in total shock. I didn't think Scott could do this. I wouldn't have believed it if you told me. I swear to god I wouldn't."

From the two pictures Leda had seen of Scott, he looked too handsome for real life, like every leading man in a Lifetime movie or Bradley Cooper. He seemed like someone who wasn't born out of a vagina but rather just sprang up fully grown from a snowdrift in Aspen, already wearing Patagonia as he smiled and said things like: "We're headed to Cabo for the weekend" or "We're going wine tasting in Napa."

"How did you find out?"

"I went through his phone. I don't usually snoop, I'm not that kind of wife, but he left it out, and I just had this weird feeling that I should look at it."

Leda wondered what "kind of wife" Elle thought would do something like that. She imagined a woman who was pushy and nosy wearing some kind of apron and looking the very opposite of chic as she folded sheets and angrily fluffed pillows. Someone who would yell at a man to straighten up and fly right. Someone who just didn't give a damn about the mirage of trust foisted upon love. *Maybe it's actually those kinds of women who are actually secure with themselves,* Leda thought. *Maybe they're the ones we should all be.*

"I found all these text messages of him being like, 'I'll meet you at seven,' and '*She's* home.' Can you believe that I'm the *she*? That one really killed me."

"That's awful."

"Yeah, and then there were all these sexual ones, so there's no way he can tell me it's anything but an affair." Elle paused. "Her name is Chelsea. What kind of a *slut* name is that?" Elle hung on the word *slut* for so long it was like she was spelling it. The *s*, the *l*, the *t* all rang out over the phone as if semen were just pumping through her veins.

"I am so sorry," Leda said.

"She has fake tits too. He always told me he liked small breasts, but that was clearly a lie, 'cause she has Big. Fake. Tits."

"How do you know this?"

"I found her on Instagram. She has like twenty-three thousand followers. Can you believe that? It's probably the number of dicks she's sucked. Here, I'm sending you a link to her account."

Leda clicked the link and looked through the pictures. The woman was stunning in a slutty kind of way. Her tits were definitely fake, as Elle had said. They were round and alienating like all fake breasts were, existentially existing on a plane higher than anyone could reach, certainly higher than either Leda or Elle ever could. Among the pictures there were thousands of selfies. There was Chelsea in a bikini, Chelsea standing near a cactus, Chelsea wearing overalls with no shirt on, Chelsea eating some kind of sexually suggestive fruit. Scrolling through them, it was hard not to feel that her friend was in trouble. It seemed that this round-breasted woman buoyed far above the currency that was paper Elle. On the surface it would be assumed that Elle would be favorable in her husband's esteem, given the time, and the love, and the children, but staring at this perky, perfect, slutilicious figure it was clear that Elle was falling, Elle was flailing, Elle was likely worth less.

"She's ugly," Leda lied.

"You think so?"

"Yeah, she's gross and so trashy. Don't even think about it for a second."

"You really think so?"

"Yes, she's a total whore."

"I think her lips are fake too."

"I'm sure they are. They're, like, way too big."

"I bet she doesn't even look like this in real life."

"There's no way. I guarantee every single picture is Photoshopped."

"You think so?"

"Yeah, definitely."

Leda knew that at this moment in her life all Elle felt was a repudiation of everything she ever was funneled through these filtered Instagram pictures. To confirm to her that she was prettier than this woman who was having sex with *her* husband, touching him, lying beside him, filling a space that only she was meant to fill, was all Leda had to offer as a friend right now. The monumental confirmation of everything despicable and desperate that had ruined so much of both their lives was Elle's only beacon. *How cruel, how sick* were thoughts that Leda wouldn't think but certainly should have.

"I don't know what to do," Elle said.

"What did he say when you confronted him?"

"I haven't yet. It's not that easy with Scott. We don't have the kind of relationship where I can just start crying to him about this."

"What do you mean?"

"He and I, we just don't have the kind of relationship where we share everything. It's complicated, but I just can't imagine myself sitting there and telling him this. Saying her name and talking about her big fake tits and the whole thing. I cannot even imagine it."

"But you have to tell him," Leda said.

Elle was silent for a moment and then said something jumbled that Leda couldn't quite make out. She had a vision of her friend squatting in some corner with a cell phone pushed to her face. *Where is she right now? A closet in her big, fancy house while he sleeps and she sits desperately next to purses?*

"I like my life, though, Leda. He's made a fool of me, but I do like my life." Elle paused. "Do you think he goes down on her? He'd never go down on me our whole relationship. I asked him once, and he said it wasn't his thing, but he said the same thing about big breasts, so who knows."

"I'm sure he doesn't."

"I would die if he does. I would absolutely die. I've felt bad about this forever. You know, I've been with him so long now that I don't even remember what it feels like to be without him. And what am I going to have to say, I'm divorced? *Divorced.*" Elle's voice clicked heavily on the word. "That just isn't me. It's not who I am." Elle paused again. "Do you think he's told her he loves her? Do you think he loves me?"

"Of course he loves you!"

"You know how many blow jobs I've given him with absolutely nothing in return?"

Why are men so complacent about getting head and not giving it? Leda thought. *She's felt bad forever and he doesn't give a damn, because he's a man and men think their pleasure is your pleasure and your pleasure is nothing.* Leda wanted to say something about this but wasn't quite sure how to word it. "You deserve better" was the best she could do.

"And to think that I'm the '*she*' to him. I'm the '*she.*' The '*she,*' Leda. The '*she.*'"

"He's an asshole." Leda needed to tread lightly here. There was a thin line between husband/father and dirty rotten cheater that was essential to the success of this conversation.

"He *is* an asshole," Elle said, and she started to cry.

Did I push it too far with the "asshole" thing? Leda wondered.

"You know what, Leda? One of my biggest fears is that I'll die and I'll have made no difference in the world. Sure, my children will be sad, but that's it. It'll be like I never existed."

"That's crazy." Leda briefly thought back to Annabelle's tiny desk and chair. They'd long since been moved to the garage. They were upside down now, stacked, dusty.

"I don't know. Maybe it is crazy. I'm just . . . I do love him. I do. Why did this have to happen? He wasn't even acting weird, that's the part that pushes me over the edge. Everything was the same. I was just living my life, and all along he had this whole thing going on. He was living this totally separate life that has nothing to do with me or our family. I feel so humiliated. Like I was sold a lie all these years. I'm not who I think I am because he isn't who I thought he was."

Leda tried to think of something comforting to say to her dear friend. They'd grown close in these last twenty minutes. It was as if the time they'd grown apart hadn't existed at all. Trauma could do that in friendships among women. It wasn't the time to feel superior or to put your happiness out on the table, as was often the bread and butter of female friendships. No, it was the time to band together and find emotional clarity off of each other's estrogen. Leda figured that maybe the reason Elle had chosen to call her, out of all people, her friend from college whom she hadn't talked to in years, was that she didn't know Scott beyond those two pictures. He was no more to her than a fragment of Elle's life. He didn't define her in the way he surely defined her to herself. *Maybe I'm her lifeline to the lady who sold the combs,* she thought.

"Listen, Elle, you're going to be fine. You were fine before this and you're fine now. I know it doesn't feel like that this second, but it is true. Don't be scared. Be strong, be fearless. And most of all, you should be happy."

Leda and Elle talked a few more minutes after that before Elle wanted to get off the phone. She thanked Leda over and over and made promises about getting together in the near future. Leda could hear Elle's breathing stabilize and that she was no longer crying.

"I'm going to talk to him tomorrow" was the last definitive thing she said regarding the affair.

A few days later Elle changed her relationship status to "Married" and added a new picture of her and Scott on the beach together in a warm embrace. It got over a hundred likes and comments along the lines of: "You two are still the cutest couple I know" and "Perfect!" Leda wasn't all that surprised. Partly she'd sensed Elle's hesitation on the phone that night, and part of it was something she'd learned through many, many different women in her life: good women stay with bad men.

"I think it's probably a ten-to-one ratio of decent women to decent men," Anne had said not long after a bad breakup.

"Really? That seems a bit harsh," Leda said.

"Oh, yeah? Name three guys you'd date right now." Leda was already married to John at this point, but for the life of her she couldn't. She ran through a mental Rolodex of men she knew, single, not single, and so many of them were selfish or gross or unemployed. On more occasions than she'd be willing to admit she'd met a girlfriend's significant other and been wildly disappointed. Beautiful, strong, incredible women would date the most egregious of people.

At some point in her freshman year of college she'd gone dancing with a girl from her biology class named Erin in an effort to get over her ex.

"You'll be over that loser in no time," Erin said.

"Yeah, fuck him!" Leda continuously felt the need to denigrate her ex whenever she spoke to Erin, because Erin seemed to be very tried and true when it came to men. "Hey, he either steps it up or I get a new vibrator!" was Erin's personal dating mantra, and Leda was quite impressed.

They planned to go out to a sports club in downtown Boston. Leda wasn't much for clubs, but Erin had convinced her it was a great way to meet guys. After an incredibly demoralizing encounter with a guy who danced with her for 2.3 seconds, said "Let me know when it gets awkward," and then half a second later whispered "You're beautiful" and walked away, Leda became violently ill from bad Chinese takeout. She spent the majority of the night in a bathroom stall listening to women peeing and then clanking out of the bathroom over and over between stomach cramps and dry heaves. By midnight she'd managed to finally get herself in condition to head back out, where she found Erin dancing the night away with some guy wearing a bizarre T-shirt with dolphins all over it. He looked younger than he probably was and had a rat-tail down his back. When Leda tried to talk to him, he answered everything in Austin Powers quotes: "Yeah, baby!" and then "Oh, behave!" Erin laughed like it was funny, and Leda lost all respect for her tried-and-true friend. *These are the standards of a woman who told me my ex was a loser?* She took a cab home and typed out a text to her ex-boyfriend that she'd never send. "I miss you," it said. She avoided Erin after that.

It seemed to Leda women would spout ideals that were in no way reflective of the men who stood by their sides. Another friend she'd known from school, Hanna, a wickedly intelligent woman who had four degrees, including a PhD in women's studies, married a guy who regularly used the term *fat chicks* and posted all kinds of articles arguing that pay inequality was a myth. "Me and my hubby disagree about politics but we agree about snuggles," she'd posted beside a picture of them. *Snuggles?* Leda thought. *Et tu, Hanna?*

And if it weren't some conflict of ideals it was just a kind, loving, good woman matched up with a short-tempered asshole, or a cheater, or a bum. Women making excuses over and over and for what? The shallow sense of self it provided? *Is it shallow when it feels like everything?* Leda wondered.

She thought to text Elle after seeing her post. Maybe she'd frame it innocently, as "How are you?" or maybe she'd just go for it and say "You're staying???" But really she felt that she shouldn't judge her dear Elle floating and flailing in her rich relationship. Life was hard and short and happiness was complicated and dusty.

That night Leda cuddled up close to John. She felt grateful for his kindness and his warm body pressed up against her. As she drifted off to sleep, she thought about Grace, a girl she knew in middle school who gave an eighth-grade boy a blow job. It was the first blow job any of the girls had given, and the details of it circled the school three times over. "She swallowed" wafted up and down hallways as girls huddled close in disapproval and sheer awe. In the context of seventh grade the repercussions of the blow job meant many things, but mostly it meant a new tool on deck for scores of girls to feel simultaneously intimidated by and superior to Grace. With an eye roll or one giggly comment so much power could be dealt and wielded and ripped in and out of each other's hands. *How awful,* Leda thought. She then thought of Elle and her smiling face on the beach, looking as perfect as always, and she was sad and angry and exhausted by it all.

Little did she know then that the phone conversation from days before would be the last time she'd ever speak to her friend. There would be no more desperate calls or texts, no more lunches, no more contemplative reasoning between the two of them. Off into the ether their friendship would go, and that night they both slept beside men who loved them.

CHAPTER 47

Leda and Her Mom

"Do you want to take anything from the backyard?"

"What?"

"The backyard."

Leda's parents were moving to a condo. They'd sold the house, and her mom asked her to come go through all her old things to decide what of her childhood was worth saving. At first Leda didn't think much of it. She was sure that at this point in her life she'd effortlessly sort through old stuffed animals and hair accessories from 1997. Pass over boxes of dolls and school projects with ease, fearlessly donating her life away, tossing its excess into the garbage. But it wasn't like that. The moment she opened her old closet and came upon a mechanical chick that jigged across the floor circa Easter 1993, she felt an upending sense of doubt in all potentials of progress.

"How cute is this?" she said to her mom, pointing as it moved across the floor.

Her mom shrugged. "I can't believe it still works."

"Should I give it to Annabelle?"

"Will she really want it? It's kind of young for her."

"I think she will." And Leda put the chick in a box marked "Annabelle."

Within twenty minutes the box marked "Annabelle" was over-flowing.

"Leda, this is too many things. She's not going to want it all. And even if she does, your house will be overrun with all this crap."

"Well, maybe I'll put it into storage and she can save it for her children."

"Oh, please, Leda, that's crazy. Throw it away."

Leda looked over at her mom's "keep pile." It was small and elegant.

"Aren't you going to miss the house, Mom?"

"Yeah, in some ways."

"All this stuff, it makes me so sad to see you throwing it all away. I could cry. Really, I'm trying not to cry but I could."

"Don't cry for things that can't cry for you," her mom said.

"Did you just make that up?"

"No, it's a saying."

"Well, it's brilliant. But I still feel like crying."

A few hours later (after Leda spent forty-five minutes looking through her fifth-grade science fair project about ants), she and her mom went out for lunch.

"What does that say? I don't have my glasses."

"Goat cheese," Leda read.

Leda worried about her parents getting old almost every single second of every single day. If her mom told her the same story twice she'd beg her to go get tested for Alzheimer's. If her mom ever started a conversation with "Your dad . . . ," Leda would fill in the blank with violent momentum: "broke his hip," "has heart disease."

"No, Jesus, calm down," her mom would say.

To what end any of it was didn't seem to make much of a difference, and as it was she and her mom just continued along as they had always done. Leda, coming to her for all kinds of advice, admiring her, looking up so faithfully to the woman who sold her home and broke a roll over her goat cheese salad.

"So John and I got in this huge fight yesterday about the bureau. You know the one that sat unassembled in our bedroom for, like, six months?"

"What happened?"

"Well, I finally made him put it together, and of course he was a total jerk about it. He always puts me in this position of being this nagging wife and then complains when I act that way. It's like,

I wouldn't be like this if you would just do the things that you said you were going to do."

Leda thought of her husband in flashes of aggravation: the bureau never being built, her computer that still ran slow, the kitchen table he always promised to wipe down.

"Maybe you should talk to him about it when you aren't fighting. You know, tell him specific ways he could help you. I think men do better with concrete direction."

"That's what I already do."

"Yeah, but do it one thing at a time and be very praising when he does help, even something small."

"That's crazy."

"It works."

"Yeah, I don't know. I don't think things will ever change, honestly."

Leda looked down at her salad, the same goat cheese one as her mom had, and she remembered the feeling she'd felt right after Annabelle was born as she was holding her in her arms. Randomly she'd remember it, the elation. The utter and total limitlessness of the joy she'd felt. And then whatever she struggled with in that moment was instantly gone, dissolved by the memory of her happiness. "What can I say, John means well," she said, thinking of baby hands and the smell of hospital gowns.

After lunch Leda and her mom went for a walk down the bike path in the center of town. It was cool out despite the sun, but they soon warmed up as they got moving.

"So many new houses," her mom said, looking off at a construction site. "It's kind of a shame."

"Why? It's good people want to live here."

"It's just sad that it's become a town only for rich people."

"Yeah."

"I can't wait to leave," her mom said.

"Yeah, I can understand that. Although . . . I don't know what," Leda said.

They walked past all the new construction, and over the little bridge that covered a brook.

"Remember when we used to play Pooh Sticks here?" her mom said.

"Are you kidding? It was, like, the best part of my childhood."

When Leda was young she and her mom would walk to the little brook and toss sticks in on one side of the bridge. Whichever stick came out first on the other side was the winner. Her mom got the game from *Winnie-the-Pooh.* They'd read the books together, and when Annabelle was little her grandma read them to her too.

"I should have brought Annabelle along so we could have played one last game."

"One last game? We can come back anytime. We're moving, not dying."

"That's true."

The rest of the walk they talked about Elena Ferrante's novels. Her mom had just finished the first in the Neapolitan series.

"I love how all of the politics are just interwoven into the story. It's so political at times, but you'd never really think of it in those terms," she said.

"Yeah, she doesn't use it as a crutch like so many writers do. It's there but not just for the sake of deepening the novel, you know?" Leda said.

"It's masterful," her mom said.

They got back to her parents' house and started organizing the last of the boxes.

Leda took a break to use the bathroom. As she sat on the toilet peeing, she looked around the little room. *How many times I've peed in here,* she thought. She finished up and washed her hands. Before leaving she put her hand against the wall. Slowly and carefully she ran it along the tile. She watched it bump past each line of grout. *You can't take it with you.* And then she thought of her mom and how strong she was, always. She remembered the time she and her child-hood friend Caitlin were at Walgreens playing with the bouncy balls and then this scary lady came over and yelled at them and said, "Pick these up! You kids are going to cause an old person to fall." And the scary lady kicked the balls at them and she and Caitlin were crying as they put the balls back, and then her mom appeared from around the corner and she looked the scary lady in the eye and said without the slightest sense of anything but utter and total control, "Do you work here?" and the scary lady said, "No," and her mom said, "Good, then leave them alone." And the scary lady walked away, just like that.

The memory gave Leda a sense of focus. She left the bathroom and went back to her old bedroom to go through the overstuffed "Annabelle" box once again. In no time at all it too looked elegant and small.

After finishing up she came back downstairs to find her mom, but she wasn't there. The side door was opened to the porch. Leda stepped out and there was her mom at the far side of the yard. She was cutting branches off the lilac tree.

"Mom, what are you doing?" Leda said.

"I want to take them to the new house."

"The branches?"

"I'll miss it," she said.

Leda watched her mom snap off each branch and pile them neatly by her feet. How careful she was, how certainly she worked.

"Do you want to take anything from the backyard?" she asked.

And Leda said, "What?" but only to prolong the moment. She knew she'd take some branches too.

———— ❧ ————

CHAPTER 48

You and I

LEDA AND JOHN WERE NO LONGER A YOUNG MARRIED COUPLE. THEY didn't have sex more than once a week, ever. Sometimes they wouldn't have sex for weeks on end. Neither of them really complained much about it, because neither of them really minded. There was a time when Leda heard about married couples not having sex anymore and thought there was no way that she'd end up like that. She thought the women who let sex go out of their marriages were lazy or had never experienced good sex, but now she understood. Sex was something for young people. She was too tired to care about it like she had before. There were just so many other things worth doing, like sleeping. She and John talked about it after they lazily made love on their anniversary night.

"Do you think we've lost our passion?" she asked him as she lay against his chest.

"No, I think things just change."

"We still have good sex," she offered. It was true despite the lack of it.

"We're perfect," John said.

She smiled and held him tighter.

In general, Leda found herself enjoying the company of her daughter endlessly more than the company of her husband. Annabelle was ten years old, and Leda loved listening to her speak.

"Aren't these sticker books great?" Annabelle said when they were at a bookstore. She held up a little book of shiny cat stickers.

"I had so many when I was in first grade. But I never took them out of the books."

"Why not?" her mom said.

"I guess I just didn't want to ruin the book by taking one out. It already looks so perfect."

"What's so good about perfect?"

"Perfect just looks better with stickers."

Like her mother, Annabelle loved to read. She'd ask for books for every holiday or birthday. Sunday mornings she'd lie on the floor and press her bare feet up against the wall and just read and read and pass the day away. Sometimes she'd tell her mom about the books she was reading; she'd go into great detail over what she liked about this part and that. Leda adored it. Her daughter's take was so brilliantly free. She was never cynical about anything. No one had yet imparted their devastating judgments on her taste. Whatever she felt about what she was reading was her own.

"Then they eat the fudge and become invisible."

"What do they do when they're invisible?"

"They spy on people and then they see the murder, but they can't tell anyone about it because if they did they'd have to tell them about the fudge and no one would believe them."

"Shouldn't they still try, though?"

"They do in the end and then finally someone does believe them."

"That's good."

"There's another one in the series, but it's not as good. It's about magical buttons."

"Why don't you like it?"

"Too much magic."

"But isn't the book you read all about magical fudge?"

"Yes, but that's not why I liked it."

"Why did you like it?"

"Because they couldn't tell and they knew no one would believe them. It was like in real life, kind of."

"I like books like that too."

"Do you think I could have my birthday at a bookstore?"

They ended up doing a sleepover party instead. Leda did call

Barnes & Noble, but all they offered was something for little kids. Annabelle invited five of her friends to the party: There was her friend Judith from down the street, a quiet girl who was achingly polite and frequently said "thank you" even if it was unwarranted. She and Annabelle had known each other since they were toddlers, and their friendship seemed to be based on little more than proximity. Her best friend was Sasha, a girl from school who liked sports and talked loudly. Leda adored her because of her unrivaled sense of humor.

"I ate seven cupcakes and my mom told me I'd be sick, but then she was the one who threw up all over my grandma's porch from bad hot dogs," Sasha once said.

Miriam and Ally were also school friends who came over on occasion, ate snacks, and watched the Disney Channel. And lastly there was Stassi. Annabelle knew her originally through Miriam. The three girls had taken a swim class together. Leda didn't really care much for Stassi. She thought back to the time that her mom met Anne and described her as having a slutty face. Stassi was much too young to have a slutty face, but she was nonetheless not a serious girl. In a year or two Leda had no doubt that she'd be dating boys and probably smoking cigarettes.

The plan was to have the girls come over for pizza and then to watch a movie. Annabelle was so excited about her party that she'd slept hardly at all the night before.

"Now I'll be too tired to stay up," she said at breakfast.

"You'll be fine. You'll be full of adrenaline and won't feel tired at all," Leda said, and leaned down to kiss her daughter's forehead. Her hair was a warm mix of John's blond hair and her own dark hair. But her eyes were dark, like Leda's.

Once the girls arrived, the house sounded jittery and awake. Leda liked having kids over. She found children to be so much more enjoyable to be in groups of than adults. The last parties she'd ever remembered actually enjoying herself at were the ones she attended as a child. There wasn't the pretension that plagued adult parties— children were excited and wanted pizza and to play games and that was it. There wasn't some self-congratulatory reason to attend a party as a child. No promotion to brag about. No engagement ring to show off. And certainly no child ever tried to get anything out of the other partygoers; there was no effort to climb a social rank or to meet a new partner. It was pressureless in a way adulthood couldn't be.

John was gone for the weekend on a business trip. When they were planning the party, there was some concern over John missing it, but the party was already a few days past Annabelle's real birthday.

"You sure you'll be able to handle it?" John said to her.

Leda found the question amusing. She tried to envision in what capacity John would have ever been helpful in the planning of and/or the execution of an eleven-year-old's sleepover party.

"I think I can handle it," she said.

The girls made their way into the living room and started to debate what they should do first.

"Twister," Leda heard muffled in the mix of voices. She came in the room with a bowl of chips and another of pretzels.

"What do you girls want on your pizza? I was just going to get cheese, if that's okay with everyone?"

All the girls nodded except for Judith, who raised her hand. Leda was always surprised by the child's reserve, given how much time she spent at the house.

"Cheese isn't good for you, honey?"

"I just got diagnosed with celiac so I can't have pizza, but if they have steak, or something like that, I can have that."

"Let me check on that." Leda went into the kitchen and pored over the pizza restaurant's menu. There wasn't any steak. The only thing that she could find that was gluten-free was the lobster tail appetizer. Why the pizza place served lobster tails she could not understand.

"Judith?" she called.

Judith hurriedly came into the kitchen. The child was obedient, that was for certain. Leda had met her mother, Charlotte, on a few occasions. She was a stern woman with a short, peppy haircut. She never once dropped Judith off late, and if Leda was ever a few minutes late picking Annabelle up, Charlotte would purse her lips into a small, exacting smile and say, "It's no problem at all." But Leda knew it was a problem. She knew it was a problem *very* all.

"Do you like lobster tails, by any chance?" she asked her.

"Umm, I don't know if I've ever had lobster tails . . ." Judith looked troubled. "I can try them."

"No, that's not good enough." Leda thought that Charlotte might be a mother who would force-feed lobster tails to a child out of propriety, but she was not. She scoured website after website before finally finding a pizza place that had gluten-free pizza options. She ordered two big cheese pizzas for the girls and one small gluten-free pizza for Judith. Judith was so happy that she actually looked relaxed as she ate, something Leda had never seen the child be.

The girls all sat around the kitchen table. Annabelle joked about Mr. Yunni, a teacher all of them hated. Leda was amazed by her daughter's ability to be so in command of the group. She knew when to joke and when to hang back. It was obvious that each of the girls admired her, even Stassi. She wished she'd been like that growing up. She remembered herself as a child who had wanted in a way her daughter never seemed to. *Maybe she gets that from John,* she thought, but she didn't think John was really like that either. She thought of her own mother. *Maybe it's from my mom.*

"I'm so sick of school," Stassi said as she picked at a slice of pizza. She and Miriam had both blotted the oil off their slices with a paper towel before eating. Leda was sorry to see them at eleven years old already worried about pizza grease, but it wasn't her place to say anything.

"At least we have spring break soon," Miriam said. "Well, kind of soon, anyway."

"Are you guys all going to camp this year? We should all go to the same camp!" Stassi said. She seemed very sure of herself as she spoke, as if she'd already made the arrangements for the six of them.

"I'm going," said Miriam.

"I'm going too," said Sasha.

"Me too," said Judith.

"I'm not," said Annabelle. "I never go to camp."

"Why not?" said Stassi. "Camp is the absolute most fun. It's where I learned to make friendship bracelets."

"I just never wanted to go," Annabelle said. "It's just never seemed like it was something for me."

"We usually go on trips in the summers," Leda added. "What camp do you usually go to, Stassi?"

"Camp Susserton. It's in upstate New York where my mom grew up. She went there as a kid. She says the bunks look the same still."

Leda had never met Stassi's mom, but she imagined her to have a sports car and a synthetically white smile.

"That's nice. How long do you go for?"

"Eight weeks."

"What about you, Sasha? I thought you were home in the summers usually," Leda asked.

"I go to day camp," Sasha said as she took another slice.

"You know what? I think the worst part about school is just the fact that you have to be around so many people you don't like," Miriam said contemplatively. "I hate Brian Russell and I have to see him pretty much every day until I turn eighteen."

"Ugh, I know," said Stassi. "I hate Ellen Howard. She's so gross."

"Who is Ellen Howard?" Sasha said.

"You know Ellen, the one with the short hair who always wears headbands," Stassi said.

"Her voice is so annoying," said Miriam.

"Oh my god, I know," said Stassi.

"I went to kindergarten with her," Judith added.

"I had Brownies with her," Annabelle said. "She always brought the worst snacks."

Leda only vaguely remembered this short-haired, headbanded nightmare from the few days she spent leading the Brownie troop. Annabelle quit after only one year and hadn't really made many friends during her time there. The other mothers involved in Brownies were far too serious about crafting for Leda to have kept in touch. *Was she the little girl whose mother called me about balloons at 7:00 a.m. that time?* Leda wondered.

"Did you know she cried during gym once 'cause she didn't win at kickball? She's always crying," Stassi said.

"She cried a lot in kindergarten too," Judith added.

"She cries at recess all the time. One time I asked her if she was okay and she screamed at me and was like, 'Of course I'm not okay!' and I was like, 'Okay . . . ,'" Annabelle said.

"Oh my god, wait," Sasha said. "Is she the girl who wears that crazy coat that goes to, like, to the ground?"

"Yes!" all the girls apart from Ally (who was chewing and smiling but not adding anything to the conversation) said in near unison.

There's nothing like hating another girl that will bond a group of girls together, Leda thought. She considered if maybe she should step in and say something, but it seemed like an exercise in futility.

"What about Brian Russell?" she asked. "Why do you hate him?" Talking about a boy they hated seemed like a healthier direction to lead the conversation.

After dinner the girls settled into the living room to watch a movie. They'd discussed for a long time what they would watch. Stassi immediately suggested that they watch a horror film, but Leda stepped in and said no scary movies allowed. She knew Annabelle hated them, and besides that, watching horror films at sleepovers was one of the rituals of childhood she remembered dreading. There was always one kid who wanted to, usually someone like Stassi, and the rest of the kids would go along with it out of fear of ending up the next point of discussion after Ellen Howard. Plus, she wasn't about to allow a bunch of eleven-year-olds to watch a PG-13 movie at her house. She could just imagine what Charlotte would say when she found out. Probably something along the lines of "We don't allow Judith to watch that kind of thing at our house," or "Judith came home and said 'shit box.' Where on earth did she learn the term 'shit box' from?" In the end the girls settled on watching *Finding Nemo*.

"I love Dory," Stassi said.

As the girls watched the movie Leda sat in the kitchen and put together the goodie bags. She wasn't sure what should go in goodie bags for eleven-year-olds. As far as she was concerned they were too young for any kind of makeup or lotions or the kinds of gifts you might give to a group of older girls, but at the same time they were too old for the kinds of silly plastic knickknacks one would usually put together for a birthday party. She settled on ChapStick, stickers, erasers, and some candy in a pretty little purse for each of them. After putting together the goodie bags, she sat for a while at the kitchen table. She'd needed to clean up and do a few other things around the house, but she felt too tired for any of it. From the other room she could hear the girls talking and laughing, but she couldn't make out much of what they were saying. The movie was loud and muffled any conversation they were having. She took a deep breath and got up.

A few hours later the girls came back in the kitchen for cake and presents. Annabelle graciously received each gift.

"Oh, I love it!" she'd say, or "I've wanted one of these forever."

Leda took as many pictures as she could of the whole thing. She assumed that the girls would tire of her snapping shot after shot. She herself had distinct memories of begging her mother to stop with the pictures on her birthdays growing up, but the girls loved posing. In fact, all of them had their phones out and were taking just as many pictures, if not more, themselves. The scene was something unrecognizable as anything she ever associated with birthday parties and childhood. These children were documenting everything. Stassi held her phone over her and Annabelle's heads and stuck out her tongue. After looking at the photo for a second she said, "That one's going on Instagram."

The girls goofed around in the kitchen for a while longer before deciding it was time to get into pajamas and head to bed. The six of them moved together collectively up the stairs as one indistinguishable mass of prepubescent fervor.

"I'll be down here if you guys need anything. I'll check on you before going to bed."

"Thanks, Mom," Annabelle called out of the indistinguishable mass.

Leda watched a marathon of *Law & Order*, which made her feel very old, but there wasn't anything else worth watching. After a few hours she went upstairs and checked on the girls.

They were all gathered around eating candy and whispering in low, hurried voices.

"I don't like him, though," she heard one of them say.

"Hey, guys, I'm going to go to bed, but you can come and get me at any time if you need anything at all."

"Okay," they answered collectively.

"Don't stay up too late."

"We won't."

Leda lay down in bed. On days when John was away for business she often enjoyed just how much space she had to stretch out, but tonight it just felt very empty. She thought about the last time they'd slept together. It had to have been a couple of weeks at this point. She couldn't quite remember when exactly. After they'd had sex she had worried about it, how they'd just done it in missionary again and how that's all they had done the last few times they'd had sex. *Shouldn't we be doing it from behind more? Doesn't he care that we hardly ever do it from behind?* she had fretted. She didn't say anything to John about it, but she shrugged her shoulders when he asked if she was okay. He fell asleep before the issue could be resolved. Now, lying there alone in her big, empty bed, the whole thing seemed foolish. Outside she could hear the rain start. Its loud consistency was calming and she went to sleep.

"Mom." She woke up to Annabelle standing beside the bed.

"Mom," Annabelle said again.

"What time is it?" she said.

"Two a.m."

"Why are you awake?" For a second Leda had forgotten all about the sleepover.

"We're trying to pull an all-nighter."

"Are you okay?"

"Yeah, I'm just not having a lot of fun."

"Why not?" She sat up and turned on the bedside lamp. "What's wrong, baby?"

"I'm just bored of the other girls. All they want to do is talk about boys and I'm sick of it."

"Well, that's what girls usually do at sleepovers, but I understand that it can get tedious."

"I like talking too, but I just feel like I'm not like them."

"You aren't."

"But who am I like?"

"No one is like them, Anna-B. No one is really like that. People just act a certain way at parties and that's what they're doing."

"Why?"

"I don't really know. To feel like they belong? You have nice friends. They're just trying to do what they think they should do at a sleepover. Half of them are probably bored of talking about boys too."

"Yeah." Annabelle lay down beside her mom and rested her head on her shoulder. "Can't I just stay here with you the rest of the night?"

"I think if you did that you'd probably feel worse."

"But you're more fun than they are."

"I know." Leda smiled. "But you'll only look back on tonight and think of it as a good time. You had fun earlier, right?"

"Yeah."

"It's just late. I hope you guys sleep at least a little while, and in the morning you'll feel better."

"I don't know." Annabelle snuggled up closer. "I really don't want to."

"I'll tell you what, you do this and tomorrow morning, after they leave, we'll go get a big breakfast together, just the two of us, and go for ice cream afterward, how about that?"

Annabelle considered it for a moment and then nodded. "All right. Thanks, Mom."

"You'll be happier in the morning, honey. I promise."

Annabelle hugged her and left the room quietly. Leda listened to the girls' whispers and giggles. The rain had stopped and she could hear them talking back and forth a bit. She fell back asleep after feeling sure that she'd done the right thing in encouraging her daughter to go back to the party.

She woke up intermittently for most of the night after that. A few times she got up and checked on the girls. They had fallen asleep, as she had suspected they would. In the early morning, just as the sun came up, she fell into a labored sleep full of strange dreams about the party. In one of them she was walking through the house and calling for the girls but no one was answering.

"I'm here," she heard Annabelle call from the bathroom. She ran up the stairs and into the bathroom to find Stassi lying naked in a blood-filled tub. Her blond hair was still done up perfectly; her head was all that wasn't submerged by the pink-hued water.

"I got my period," Stassi said. "I'm not dying. And I'm not scared."

The next morning the girls gathered around in their PJs and ate bagels (Judith had eggs). Annabelle hardly touched hers, and Leda knew it was because she was saving her appetite for the promised breakfast ahead. How different they all acted now that the nighttime glow of the party had worn off. They were tired and disheveled. Each of them looked younger and more childish.

"I'm tired," Sasha said.

"Me too," said Judith.

Stassi just nodded. Her hair still did look nice.

One by one, each of the girls was picked up by her mother. Judith was the first to go, as was expected. Stassi and Miriam left together. Sasha left soon after. Ally was the last to go. She hugged Annabelle at the door and said, "I don't go to camp either. We should hang out this summer."

Once the house was finally empty, Leda cleaned up a bit and got ready to head out with Annabelle.

"That was fun," Annabelle said. "But I'm kinda glad it's over."

"That's how everything good in life feels," Leda said. She grabbed her wallet and keys and then her phone before heading out the door. As she walked to the car she noticed that John had texted her.

"I miss you," it said.

And all she felt was happy.

CHAPTER 49

Writing Group

SHE MISSED WRITING. SHE FELT IT ALL AT ONCE ONE DAY AS SHE WAS making a sandwich. *I miss writing,* she thought as she coolly spread mayonnaise across a piece of bread. For so long she had told herself that she didn't really miss it. Didn't have time, was already happy. But the outburst from the vestibule a few years earlier often came to her mind, and when she'd think of it her heart would race. Most of the time she could look past it and not wonder why she'd said she was a writer when clearly she was not. *Tired, stressed, trapped,* she could think, but then one day she felt something else, and it was so fully and undeniably the feeling of wanting that she couldn't simply excuse it all away.

When Annabelle was very little Leda had told her that she had wanted to be a writer once.

"You know, Mommy used to write," she said to her daughter, who was busy drawing a picture with a scented marker. It felt like a confession, even though clearly a two-year-old child was incapable of grasping the meaning of it all. As silly as it was, she felt nervous in the silence between them. Annabelle didn't even look up as she answered. "Yes," she said, as matter-of-factly as possible, as if she'd been well aware all along exactly who her mother was. From then on Leda would mention it from time to time, and Annabelle grew up accepting it as any other part of family history: a grandparent who fought in a war, the story of her father's favorite childhood Christmas. It could not be uncoiled from where it was or where it began; it was just always there, thumping away a pattern or a footprint that could scarcely be contextualized in Annabelle's life: Mom used to write.

Once Leda came to the realization of wanting to write again she wasn't sure how to go about it. So much had changed in her life since the last time she'd written that she couldn't imagine what sitting down and really putting pen to paper would feel like. It had been such a part of her, but now the parts of her that were there seemed scattered in very important directions: just the week before, she'd been at a PTA meeting, and later that night she made chicken marsala. Occasionally she would think of ideas for stories or books. Descriptive phrases or sentences would pop into her head, like "Inside the house were perfectly matched sets of furniture, not unlike dollhouse furniture."

One day by happenstance she came across an ad for a writing group. It was tacked on the corkboard at the little market near her house. It read:

Creative Writing Workshops open to public. Come join Nancy Albright as she helps us discover our most creative selves! Sessions are held Wednesdays at the VFW Center 6–9. June 1st–July 15th. $300 per six-week session. A little more about Nancy: Nancy is a great lover of books! She's spent the last thirty years as an educator/novelist/poet and painter! Her work can be read every week on her blog nancyalbrightwrites.com. Nothing makes Nancy happier than helping blossoming writers find their wings. Come fly with us!

Leda cringed reading the ad. It was desperate and pathetic. It was everything that validated giving up on her dream, and yet she ripped off a tab and called the very next day. She figured that, as horrible as it probably would be, at least there wasn't any pressure on her part to impress. She would get back into writing without feeling stupid about how long it had been and how rusty she was and how for no real reason she had just stopped.

Nancy called her back almost immediately. Her voice was as whimsical as it sounded in the ad.

"Now, what is it you'd like to get out of joining the group?" she asked.

"I'm really just looking to get back into it. I studied writing as an undergrad and had the intention of going to grad school but just got . . ." Leda looked for the right words to explain what had happened and why she hadn't gone to grad school, but there were no words that were quite right, no words that she knew of, anyway. "I got busy with other things and have been working and raising my daughter, so yeah, I'd really just like to get back into it."

"That's great!" Nancy said. "I love when people join the group who have some experience. Most of the time I only get people who have never written anything before in their lives, which I welcome, of course, but it's also nice to have some people in the mix who have written before."

"Oh, well, it's been a real long time. I'm sure whatever I bring in will be a complete mess."

"Don't worry about that at all. Just write freely."

It was nice to hear Nancy's encouragement. *Maybe she's less crazy than the poster made her seem,* Leda thought.

"Anyway, a little bit about me: I've been an educator, a poet, a writer, and a painter for the last thirty years. I like to help people really blossom into who they want to be as a writer. Blossoming is the essence of life I feel," Nancy said.

Or maybe not.

"The sessions are three hundred, and I take cash or check. Would you like to join us next week?"

"Yes, I would," she heard herself say, her voice sounding daft and frightened. "I would," she reiterated, trying to sound more sure, for her own sake.

It wasn't clear what a person should wear to a writing group at the VFW center. Certainly you wouldn't want to dress up, this was obvious, but what the appropriate attire was she could not decide. She looked in her closet. All her clothes lined up hanging or folded in messy, somewhat regulated piles. *I wear too much plum,* she thought. She tried to remember what she usually dressed like in college whenever she'd have a workshop. She dug through a pile at the far corner of her closet where she kept clothes that no longer fit, in the vague hope of one day becoming a supermodel and being able to wear the jeans she wore at eighteen. Squished at the bottom of the pile was an old cotton top she used to wear in her college days. It looked a bit worn and the color was somewhat faded, but it still maintained its shape. She wondered if she ought to try it on, but she couldn't imagine seeing herself like that, no doubt lumped up in all the wrong places, a far cry from the linear, young woman of a bygone reflection, so she didn't dare. Instead she tossed it back into the pile and threw on one of her most reliable shirts. It was loose-fitting and comfortable. It was the best thing that could be worn, given the circumstance.

In the end it turned out that all her fretting over attire was completely unnecessary. There were only a handful of people in the room in clothing that wasn't stained or ripped or just generally deranged-looking. Her worries about lumps were also misguided, as she was most probably the thinnest woman in the room.

Nancy was the heaviest of all the women. Her hair was gray and she wore it in a long braid that went down to her waist. She had on a top that could only be described as a sweatshirt crossed with a sweater. On it was an appliquéd starfish.

"Please, everyone, take a seat. Please take a seat," she called out to the room. Most people were already seated, so her imploration seemed needless and overbearing in the confines of the very small VFW center room. Nonetheless, people took notice and the few left standing were sure to sit.

"Welcome, everyone. I am so happy to be starting a new session with this group. I'm Nancy Albright. Please call me Nancy," Nancy said. "First things first, I'd like to go around the room and learn everyone's name and hear why you've joined this group. We'll start to my left."

To Nancy's left was a man in a Hawaiian shirt with long blond hair. He looked considerably tan and his hands were too small for the rest of his body.

"My name is Roger. I'm here because I've had ideas for many books, and I just need to get them out of me."

"We all have books in us, don't we, Roger?" Nancy said. She smiled in a way that was both kind and unsettling.

"Definitely. I have so many characters that are always telling me their stories, and I feel like I owe it to them to try and tell their stories for them, so that's why I'm here."

Why am I here? Leda thought.

"Well, I'm sure we'll be hearing from all of them!" Nancy said.

"Yes, you most certainly will," Roger said.

"Great to meet you," Nancy said. She was clearly ready to move on from Roger. "And next we have . . ." She pointed to a very large woman with a neck tattoo to the left of him.

"I'm Cindy. I'm here because I'm interested in writing romance novels. I love reading them, so I figured I'd give a shot at writing them."

"Romance novels are great fun," Nancy said with the same kind, unsettling smile. "Great to meet you, Cindy."

"Hi, my name is Greg, and I'm very much into sci-fi. I guess you could say I'm kind of a connoisseur. I've written a lot of graphic novels, and I'd really like to write an actual novel. I'm kind of a buff on the genre."

"Who's your favorite sci-fi writer?" Nancy asked.

Leda heard Greg answer, but she didn't listen to the words he was saying. She looked around the room as he spoke. The other people seemed to be paying close attention. They seemed to feel connected in a way she could not. A few of them nodded along. It was as alienated as she'd ever felt.

"Hi, I'm Amber. I'm here because I've always felt that I could write a novel. I've tried reading a lot of different books, but I've always felt that I could do a better job."

Don't ever speak again, Amber. Just never, ever speak. She thought back to Pinched Bralette and sexless Nick. Somewhere they were doing something probably less sad and desperate than herself right now. *I bet Pinched Bralette owns some kind of start-up or something*, she thought.

By the time they made it around to her, Leda had planned on saying: "Hi, I'm Leda. I got my BFA in creative writing, but I've been busy raising my daughter and haven't had time to write as much as

I'd like, so I'm here trying to get back into it." When it was her turn she said: "Hi, I'm Leda. I got my BFA in creative writing, but I've been busy raising my daughter and haven't had time to write as much as I'd like, so I'm here trying to get back into it," but it didn't sound as good out loud. She didn't sound that different to herself from Amber or Greg. She had been a student at college studying writing, and now she was here grasping at a dream along with people who were also grasping. The VFW center was the place, and she was no longer the young woman who had everything ahead of her. Now the things that were there weren't really there at all.

At the end of the session Nancy divided the class up into groups to rotate who would be handing their stories out first, second, and last. She picked Leda for the first group and winked at her as she said her name. Leda figured it was due to her experience. She was sorry she couldn't go last. She was sorry she hadn't just said she liked sci-fi.

"Please e-mail your story to everyone on the list by Monday night, and everyone be ready with notes for Wednesday. Great first session! And remember, you can only blossom when you breathe. Be gentle with yourselves. See you next week."

That night she sat down and tried to write. She opened the window by the desk, because she'd often found that she wrote best when she was just a little bit cold. She typed out a few words. Then a couple of sentences, but nothing was coming to her. After an hour she went to bed. *I'll try again on the weekend when I'm less tired,* she told herself as she lay in bed, worried and overwhelmed by it all.

She was no more successful over the weekend. She'd start writing a story but quickly would delete it. Everything she wanted to say or thought of was muddled. *How was I ever capable of doing this?* She tried drinking tea as she wrote or eating Hershey's Kisses, but neither thing helped.

"Why don't you write about working with that crazy lady you used to work with?" Annabelle offered.

"I thought of that," Leda said as she typed the word *watermelon* and then deleted it.

On Sunday John spent the day with Annabelle so that Leda would have more time to write, but alone in the house she found herself wandering around and finding little spots that needed cleaning and organizing. The hall closet was a wreck; the kitchen counters needed a really good scrubbing. She couldn't keep herself still enough to sit down. By the time Annabelle and John got home the house was spotless, but she hadn't written a word. Before bed she told herself she'd wake up early and bang something out. *I work well under pressure,* she thought, although even in thinking it she couldn't really convince herself it was true.

Monday morning she woke up at 4:30 a.m. It was pitch-black out still, and she felt the senseless lull of early morning, but despite it she managed to sit herself at her desk and try to write.

"The woman woke up before dawn," she wrote. "There wasn't any coffee in the house so she sent her husband out," she wrote. "Her husband, who used to beat her," she wrote.

She deleted it all, went through her saved files, came across the orca story she'd written in California, sent it out to everyone, and went back to bed. *At least I sent something,* she thought.

She was even more wary walking into the VFW center that Wednesday. It had been so long since she'd last shared anything she'd ever written and she couldn't exactly say she was all that proud of the story. In her last workshop, a girl named Kalani told her her work was "more style than substance." At the time it hadn't really bothered her all that much, as it was her last semester of college, and by then she had gotten used to that kind of oppressiveness of workshopping. Now, though, as she waited on the group, weirdo Greg and idiot Amber, the memory of Kalani was nauseating. *Don't worry about what they say. They don't know what they're talking about,* she told herself, all the while her heart beating high in her throat.

"All right, everyone, please, let's all take our seats," Nancy said in the same overbearing tone. She glanced over at Leda and smiled her kind, unsettling smile.

"First of all, thank all you writers this week, I was deeply impressed with all of you. Let us begin our workshop with Leda. Please pull out her story and your notes."

"Yikes," Leda said. She'd meant not to say anything, but she couldn't help herself. "This makes me nervous."

Nancy, who generally told everyone that everything was wonderful and great and that they shouldn't worry about anything and that they should just blossom, didn't say anything in response. She only widened her smile, the effect of which was even more unsettling.

"Who would like to start?" she asked the group.

"I would," Greg said.

Oh god, Leda thought.

Greg moved forward in his chair. He wore a tight-fitting sweatshirt and had grown a faint, unsightly mustache since the last session. He held up the story in his right hand, positioning it awkwardly. Leda felt him thinking of how he should say whatever it was he was going to say. She felt his thoughts like ripples and awkward hands and mustaches and starfish appliqués. If she could have screamed then, if somehow she could have just screamed, she would have.

"This was," Greg began, "by far and away the best story I've personally read in years."

"Yes, I totally agree with that," Cindy interjected.

"I do too. I was floored reading it," Amber said. "I was floored."

"Yeah, yeah," Roger added. "Me too. I wondered all along as I read it where the author came up with something so beautiful and painful and beautiful."

"Wow," Leda said. She knew she wasn't supposed to talk, but she couldn't help herself. "Really, you feel that way?"

"Leda," Nancy said. "This is such incredible work. Do you know that?"

Leda tried very hard to nod politely and to say something that wouldn't sound conceited, but she couldn't think of anything to say and she couldn't bring herself to nod. Instead she just started to cry. She cried and cried as the people in the room one by one told her that they loved her story. They went over sentences and words that had been her own, and they said why they loved each of them and what was so vivid and precious about it all. The tears streamed down her face and she knew how silly she must have looked, but she didn't care. She didn't care at all.

At the end of the session, as everyone got up and got their things together, Nancy came over and gave her a big hug. "Great work," she said. "I truly think you're blossoming. Oh, and remember, be gentle with yourself." She winked.

Leda never went back to the writing group. She wasn't sure why. Maybe it was because she was embarrassed. Maybe it was because she wanted so badly to hang on to that moment and how it felt, and any other experience in that room with those people would ruin that, or maybe it was just because she really didn't need to. Whatever the case, she sent her orca story out to *The New Yorker*. She knew it wouldn't get accepted, but she did it anyway.

CHAPTER 50

Horace

AT SOME POINT OVER THE WINTER A CAT MOVED INTO THEIR BACK-
yard. Annabelle noticed him first.

"He's an orange tabby with white under his chin," she said. "I
think he's feral."

That night they left food out for him and a basket with blankets.
When they checked in the morning the food was gone. Leda called
a few shelters in the area to see if anyone had been missing a cat, but
no one had reported an orange tabby with white under his chin.

"Can't we take him into the house?" Annabelle asked.

"He might not be able to be a house cat," Leda said. "Some feral
cats are just too feral to be around people."

Leda didn't see the cat until nearly two weeks later. He was slink-
ing casually along the fence line. She opened the sliding door and
called out to him.

"Hey, kitty-cat."

The cat looked back, stared at her for a moment, and then took
off and jumped up and over the fence. There was no other sighting
of him for nearly a month after this.

She and John attended a show at a small music hall in western
Massachusetts. It was a band John had liked for a few years. He'd
play them for her on occasion, and she liked them as well, although
she could never remember their name. It was something like Father
Paul Radiator, but it wasn't quite that. They played folky, alternative
music. She liked the first song on the album and a few of the ones in
the middle, but the second-to-last she'd always skip.

They were late to the show and walked in after the first song had already started. The hall was standing room only, and most of the people were gathered up front or hanging out against the walls. They waded through the pack to get as close to the stage as possible. It was loud and booming. She could feel the music in her rib cage, a feeling she so intimately associated with youth. There wasn't room for John to stand beside her in the little empty patch they staked out, so he stood right behind her and put his arm around her waist as they joined the crowd's general sway.

The lead singer of the band was a skinny man with long, dark hair and a slight beard. She'd never seen a picture of him before, and she was surprised at how attractive he was.

"We'll be playing a lot off the new album you guys haven't heard yet," he said to the crowd. "Here's hoping you like it."

The crowd cheered in response. He slinked back and changed guitars. His shoulders squared as he played; he leaned his head back and swung it in time with the music. From where she was she could see his collarbone. John let go of her waist and started to clap along with the song.

"I think I'd lay you down. I think I'd lay you do-o-o-own."

Leda thought this man must lay a lot of women down, but he seemed to be singing about just one and so she couldn't help but think maybe this woman was her. She smiled up at him and wished he would look at her. He put his guitar down and jumped around onstage. His music wasn't the type of music that crowds would normally be dancing so hard to, but he led them into it. He reached into the audience and grabbed a cell phone from someone who'd been recording the show. Holding it at arm's length, he sang into it. He was sexy with the same abandonment that was specific to music. *So often this is what we all want to be,* she thought. She felt like she did when she would dance around her room in her underwear, and she felt like she did when she was fucking.

By the next song, she was in love. He was on his knees singing a sad ballad. The microphone pressed tightly against his lips. "But I don't understand why," he sang. She thought maybe she should have married a man like him instead of someone like John. John was a good man, but how different she would be if she were with a man who sang on his knees and didn't know why. She looked to her left. There was an average-looking, bearded guy standing beside her. He'd been there the whole time, but only now did she notice him. *Or maybe I should have married him,* she thought. *Who would I be if I were his wife?*

After a few more songs she left to use the bathroom. She could still hear the music as she peed. "Ronda S. is a fuck," someone had written in Sharpie on the bathroom stall. She wondered if they'd meant to write something more but had been interrupted on "fuck." *Can you be a "fuck"?* she wondered. She left the stall and went to wash her hands. A girl in a colorful skirt was standing by the mirror wiping mascara off her face. She'd clearly been crying. Leda thought of saying something like, "Whoever he is, he's not worth it." But she didn't. Maybe he was worth it. Who was she to say?

She went back to the hall. It felt lovely to be back into the music away from the bathroom and the crying girl. Now the sound was clear and she could see her lover once more and the way he moved and swayed and seemed so skinny and so sexy that she wanted to break him into pieces and to just inhale him. She danced hard to the next few songs and tried to catch his gaze so she could smile at him. John wrapped his arm around her a few times during the slow songs. It felt nice and didn't detract from being with her new lover. *Why not us all?* she thought vaguely. The young bearded guy eventually moved deeper into the crowd, and she could no longer keep track of him. The band played her three favorite songs and the one that she always skipped. She could feel her feet aching and she was getting very sweaty, but it was so wonderful.

"This next song," he said, "is about something really important to me."

Me? Leda thought.

"The environment."

Everyone cheered. The environment was something everyone at this concert loved very much.

The song started slow. She had heard it before on the album but had never paid all that much attention to it. Now she took the time to really listen to the lyrics.

"Do you have any idea how much oil it takes to make this record?"

She liked the message, of course, but the lyrics were kind of indulgent and preachy. *That's something I'd have to talk to him about.* She imagined herself out to dinner with him, tentatively broaching the subject. The next song started, and she listened closely to the lyrics again. This one wasn't about the environment, but it was still kind of preachy. His dancing seemed pretty self-indulgent too. He really wanted to be a rock star. She could envision how irritating this would be. He'd always talk about this big thing he was doing and that big thing he was doing, as she'd be just trying to enjoy a bowl of cereal and get through the day. And where was the bearded man through all of this? Nowhere to be found. It was a relief to be going home with John after all.

"Did you like the show?" he asked her as they walked back to the car.

"I loved it," she said. "He was great."

"Yeah, he's quite the showman, isn't he?"

"And he's handsome," she said. "Hey, is calling someone a 'fuck' a thing?"

By the time they had gotten home it started snowing. Annabelle was already in bed. The dark house and the softly falling snow left an almost indistinguishable menace.

"It feels too quiet," she said.

They went straight to bed, and John fell asleep nearly immediately. She stayed up and read a bit until the house felt familiar enough to fall asleep. She turned out the light and lay on her side. Just as her thoughts began to disjoin in the pleasant purgatory between awake and sleep, she heard a loud noise coming from the backyard.

"John," she said, "did you hear that?"

"Hmm," John said, and he rolled over to his other side.

She got up and walked to the hall window that faced toward their yard. Everything was covered in snow already. She looked at the tree and then the shed and then the little slide that they'd left up even though Annabelle had outgrown it. Somewhere out there was a rake that they should have moved before the snow; somewhere out there was a sundial. *My backyard,* she thought. Then the loud noise, like a scraping, started up again. It was still just the snow, as pristine and unmoved as before, but the sound was definitely coming from the yard, this she could tell. She turned on the hall light and headed downstairs. Without even bothering with a coat, she slipped on a pair of slippers and slid open the sliding glass door that led to the yard.

It was silent again. It smelled cold and new like only freshly fallen snow could. She wrapped her robe around herself tightly and breathed in deep. Alone in the night and cold, she only thought about darkness and warmth and her feet growing damp. The elm trees that lined the right side of the yard dropped snow off their branches. For a moment she considered clearing the lone birch tree, which often lost limbs in the winter, but it was too cold to leave the little stoop. She stood for a little while longer listening for the sound, but it was silent so she started back for the house, and as she turned to leave, there he was: the bright orange cat staring out at her from the snow not six feet away.

"Hi," she said in a low, startled voice. The cat blinked back patiently and then looked up at the falling snow.

"What are you doing here, little cat?"

He looked back at her and blinked again. She expected him to dash off in a moment, but he did not. He seemed like the kind of person who would have stood in that snow beside her all night, just blinking at her and the snowflakes. He was as part of the calm as the night itself, and she thought, *What if I'd married someone like him? Would I not have felt so much more patient with myself?*

It wasn't hard to convince the cat to come inside, a few cans of tuna and some gentle coaxing. Annabelle woke up and helped her mom with the kind of quiet enthusiasm that only a child can yield at the prospect of a new pet. Before long he was in the house and eating tuna, and not much longer after that he was on the couch purring and rubbing against the cushions. By the next morning he was on Leda's lap like he'd always been there, her patient husband who would stand in snow with her. They named him Horace.

·—✑·—

CHAPTER 51

Crying at Commercials

WHEN ANNABELLE WAS VERY LITTLE SHE ASKED HER MOM WHY SHE'D always cry during sad commercials.

"Are you crying?" she'd say whenever a sad movie scene would pass or they would be in the car and a sad song would start.

"No," Leda would respond, but of course she always was.

"Why do you always cry at sad things?" Annabelle asked her.

"I don't know. I guess sad things remind me of sad things that I've felt," she said.

"But it's not real," Annabelle said.

Leda remembered feeling similarly when she was a child watching her own mother grow emotional over things that weren't real. She had the distinct memory of walking in on her mom watching *Casablanca* with tears running down her cheeks. At the time she was terrified at seeing her mother like that. She seemed fragile in a way she didn't think her mother should be.

Annabelle's freshman year of high school had been rough. Sasha moved away. She hadn't been friends with Judith in years. She had a small group of girls whom she'd hang around with, but whenever Leda would press her on what the girls were like or if Annabelle wanted them to come over sometime, she would always shrug and say the same thing: "They're not really my friends, Mom."

Leda didn't worry about it that much. Her daughter was thriving at school. Soon enough she'd be in college, and there she would make tons of friends who were interesting and good and who didn't worry so much about the frivolities of eyeliner and designer lip balms.

"You're going to love college," she said to her all the time. To which Annabelle would always respond, "Isn't that just something people feel because high school is so terrible?"

"I don't think so." Leda thought about herself being in high school and how miserable she was, and for a second she was certain her daughter was right.

Annabelle had taken to walking home from school, so it was unusual when she texted her mom and asked to be picked up. Leda was happy to go get her. Picking up her daughter from school was one of the consistently wonderful parts of motherhood. There was the anticipation of seeing her child, and then the wonderful feeling of seeing her child, and then the whole ride home when she'd get to hear everything about her child's day. In her mind she would reconstruct all the events as her daughter explained them to her.

"I painted a picture of a zebra and Mrs. Granger hung it up on the wall."

There was the painting and the wall and Mrs. Granger and the zebra.

"I played foursquare with Leah at recess."

There was Leah and the ball and the swarm of other children in the blur of recess.

"Everyone loved my science fair project."

There was the gym and all the projects and the little paper moon that Annabelle had stayed up late to finish.

It was all so vivid in her unyielding concept of her daughter as the most vibrant and stunning person alive.

Pulling up to the high school, Leda saw Annabelle almost immediately. Most of the other kids had already left and she was leaning against the building, looking at her phone. Leda beeped the horn slightly to get her attention. Annabelle looked up and Leda waved vigorously, a programmed response that was probably no longer as necessary as it had been when Annabelle was younger. Annabelle nodded and walked over slowly, continuing to eye her phone.

"Hey, baby, how was your day?" Leda asked her as she sat down in the car.

"Hi. It was fine."

"I was worried that maybe you were sick, since you wanted to be picked up. Are you feeling okay?"

"Yeah, I'm just tired."

"You've been staying up way too late with homework. I hate how much homework they always give you. It's like, what is the point of living if all you're doing is going to school and then coming home and studying like a maniac till midnight? You're a kid, you should be happy and doing kid things."

"I don't feel like a kid," Annabelle said. She was turned with her face toward the window. Her hair had darkened over the years, but it was still highlighted with bright streaks of blond. Leda couldn't believe how stunning she was sometimes. Sometimes she thought it wasn't fair that any woman should be that beautiful.

"Well, you wouldn't, would you? They push kids to grow up so fast that it screws them all up and then you have forty-year-olds who ride skateboards around."

"Where are there forty-year-olds on skateboards?"

"San Francisco."

"You think everything happens in San Francisco."

"That's 'cause it does. Maybe you'll live in California one day."

"I don't think so."

"You never know. I didn't think I ever would."

"But you hated California."

"I know, but you might like it. I'm sure they'd like you out there. They like you everywhere."

Annabelle shook her head and sunk deeper into the seat and started picking at her nails. "What are you talking about? Nobody likes me."

"Oh, stop, everybody likes you."

"You're my mom so you have to think that, but it's actually not true."

"Annabelle, you're the most likeable person I know. I wish I were as likeable as you are. Everywhere you go people respond to you."

"You're crazy," she said, closing her eyes.

"It's the truth, honey."

"No, it's not."

"Really, it is. You've got a gift."

"I don't have a gift."

"You have so many gifts. I know you're going to be an incredibly successful person. I've known it since you were born."

"Mom, please."

"Not everyone is as lucky as you are. People like you. You're smart. You're beautiful. You really have it all."

"None of that's true."

"It's all true, really. People would do anything to be you."

"Mom, stop!" Annabelle sat up straight in her seat and turned to her mother. "Don't you realize that I *hate* myself?"

Leda looked at her and didn't answer. She saw in her daughter's eyes a poison. She felt frightened for a moment.

"Don't you know how much I *hate* myself? I wake up in the morning, and I look at myself in the mirror, and I hate everything."

"No, you don't."

"Yes, I do. I hate *everything*."

"Don't say that."

Annabelle leaned in close to her mom. "I hate my thighs. I hate my stomach. I hate my face. I hate the way I talk and the stupid things I say and all the dumb things I like. I just hate it. I *hate myself.* Do you not see that? Do you not see how much I just hate who it is that I am? Do you not see that?"

Leda didn't know what to say. She felt breathless and dizzy. Where was that little girl who was so confident and so judicial and only ever laughed when something was truly funny? Who'd once walked an entire jetty by herself, leaping from big rock to big rock unafraid, emboldened by only herself? She did not look back until she had gotten to the end; she was so sure she'd reach the end. That was gone. Somewhere she'd become fragile.

"None of it's true. None of it's true at all," Leda said.

Annabelle sat back in her seat. Leda tried to tell her daughter everything that was good about her, but she knew she wasn't listening at all. She knew that no matter what she said, that flash of poison was still there. Seething, writhing, boiling away her insides. Leda wrote much of it off as Annabelle's being an angsty teenager, because if she'd had to think of what was really happening to her child, her girl, that there was an irreconcilable shift in the foundation of who her daughter was, it's unlikely she'd have been able to keep living her little life such as she had been. It's unlikely she'd have been able to be happy.

∽

A MONTH BEFORE THE START OF ANNABELLE'S SOPHOMORE YEAR THEY watched *Dumbo* together one Saturday afternoon as they ate left-over pizza. When the scene came on where Dumbo visits his jailed mother and the lullaby plays, Leda immediately started crying. It couldn't be helped. It was so sad and so dear. It made her think of so many things as tragic and as hopeless and as beautiful. She glanced over at Annabelle and saw that she too was crying. Long tears were running down her cheeks, and she wiped them away but didn't try to hide them. How sorry Leda felt that her daughter would also cry at things that weren't real. How sorry she was that it couldn't be helped.

CHAPTER 52

─────◆─────

The End of Forever

BEFORE SHE EVEN WOKE UP SHE KNEW. THE PREVIOUS NIGHT HER DAD called and told her that her mom had fainted. She listened to his voice, the very deep register of it. The same voice she heard her whole childhood broken away in branches about eating all your breakfast and shoveling snow.

"But she's okay. She's asleep now. I can wake her up if you want to talk to her," he said.

"No, let her sleep. I'll call in the morning," Leda said.

But that night she had a restless dream about lactating.

"I don't have a baby. I don't have a baby," she'd said over and over, and when she woke up she knew her mom had died. Seconds later her dad called her. It was an aneurism. He said it in the same boom-ing voice, but he was crying so hard that she didn't think she'd ever heard him say anything about breakfast or the snow.

When she was six years old Leda asked her mom, "Do you wish I was still a baby?"

"I like you at every age. I loved when you were a baby, but I love you now just the same," her mom said.

"Do you wish you were still a kid?" Leda asked her.

"No, I liked being a kid, but I wouldn't want to be one anymore. I've already been a kid."

"I think if I were a grown-up I'd wish I were a kid," Leda said.

"I don't think you will. You never miss things like that once they're gone."

Her whole life Leda found that advice to be true, that you never missed the times that were gone enough to go back to them, but when she lost her mom she no longer felt that way. She wished so much to go back to it all.

"How could you do something so stupid?!" her mom once screamed at her. *If only I could hear that again,* she'd think. *If only I could hear it again forever.*

When she told Annabelle about her grandmother dying, Annabelle cried and said something muffled in her tears.

John cried too. He said, "But I just talked to her."

Leda was sick to her stomach all that day. She felt that she should call her mom and ask her what to do, how to stop being such a wreck. Her mom would have known exactly how to not be a wreck in the situation.

How strange it is that these flowers are still here and my mom is not, she thought, looking at a vase of drying tulips.

She watched the episode of *Sex and the City* where Miranda's mom passes away on repeat that whole week afterward. It made her laugh and it made her cry. She did it when John and Annabelle weren't around. She didn't want them to see her like that.

She sat by her bookshelf and took out the copy of *Anna Karenina* that her mom had given her for her sixteenth birthday. "Dear Leda, may this beautiful book guide you into womanhood," her mom had inscribed on the first page. For a moment she held the Noam Chomsky book in her hand and flipped through it. It smelled so good. She put it back on the shelf.

At first she'd been scared to see her mother's body; it wasn't the way that she wanted to remember her. She wanted to remember her the way she was the last time she saw her: standing in the doorway and waving goodbye after they'd stopped by for dinner. It was something her mom always did. When Leda first met John, anytime she'd leave his apartment he'd only wave goodbye for a second before shutting the door. After a while she asked him if he could stand and wait until he could no longer see her before going inside. She hadn't realized it at the time, but she was trying to build a family with him that was the same as the one she had. Finding a man was a way to let go of her mother. If she'd thought about it earlier, maybe she would have understood all those desperate years in her twenties when she would have done anything not to be alone. It was all for naught, though. John would wave goodbye many, many times, but it was not her mother. In the end she did agree to see her mom's body, and she was glad that she had. It didn't replace her final memory of her. It wasn't her; it was just her body, her sacred vessel through life. Leda leaned down and kissed her forehead. She said a silent prayer about seeing her again and tried to think of something to say about love, but all she could think was, *I love you, Mom. I love you. I love you.*

Her mom had taught her how to pack a suitcase, and when Annabelle was born she taught her how to swaddle a baby.

"Don't ever let a man talk to you like that," she'd said.

Leda didn't know what love really was until her daughter was born, and she did not know what pain really was until her mother died. She wished somehow she might be in a cave for the rest of her life with just her mother and daughter beside her, scribbling on cave walls. First they'd draw a horse. Then a handprint. Years later people would think men did the drawings. They would not know there were no men.

Leda read a short story in *The New Yorker* about a woman whose mom died suddenly in a car wreck. It had a lot of visual imagery to illustrate the pain of losing a parent. An empty shoe. A woman breaking a teakettle. *Don't they know that there is no thing that is that sad? Nothing looks like this feels. Not a million teakettles. Not a thousand empty shoes.* She only read the story because she read a review of the story that praised it as "so honest it is almost a sin." She read it in hopes that she might feel better after reading it, but it did not make her feel better at all. After that she was sorry she'd ever tried to publish a story in *The New Yorker.* She was glad they rejected her, that no one had called her work sinful and true.

When she came home from her mom's funeral, she lay down on her bed. The house was empty.

"Mom," she said.

"Mom," she called.

"Mom! Mom! Mom! Mom! Mom!" she called and called as loud as she could through sobs and her voice breaking. "Mom! Mom! Mom! Mom! Mom! Mom!"

John came home, and she stopped screaming.

The rest of her life was like this. Of course she couldn't scream like this in public. No one would feel sorry for you and the sadness you carried around. This she knew. This was what you learned as a child when you'd cry on the floor of a public place and your mother would lean in and tell you to act normally. Now that her mom was gone she had to tell herself that she could not scream and cry in public, but she would not stop searching. She would search for her mom forever everywhere she would go. Life could be so unreal and so vivid all at once you'd think it was a dream. You'd think it was all an etching on a wall. One you couldn't remember carving. One that lasts forever, even when there are no more words to describe what you see.

⎯⎯◦⌢◦⎯⎯

CHAPTER 53

Waiting for a Table

THE HOSTESS WAS VERY YOUNG AND VERY PRETTY. HER HAIR WAS blond and silky, and she had the kind of enviable linear appeal of someone who regularly ate kale. The first time Leda noticed her she didn't think much of her, other than that she was young and maybe a bit silly, given her fashion and makeup choices. As the restaurant became the chosen establishment that she and Annabelle frequented whenever Annabelle came for a visit, Leda grew to strongly dislike the woman. She noticed that she had a tendency to wink at all male patrons, no matter what the situation.

"Right this way." *Wink.*

"Jones for two." *Wink.*

"The bathroom is just down the hall to your right." *Wink.*

She'd often only address the man when there was a family or a couple, and on one occasion Leda happened to catch a glimpse of her phone as she discreetly typed out a text that read:

"No U R ☺."

Leda no longer had the patience for these kinds of women, those who blatantly used beauty as currency and seemed oblivious to the dangerously transient nature of such a life philosophy. *Wait till your face falls. We'll see who's winking then.*

As her largely unwarranted animosity grew, she loathed having even the most superficial encounters with the girl. She even suggested to Annabelle that they start going somewhere else, but Annabelle refused, as she very much loved the restaurant's thyme roasted potatoes.

"Mom, please, I'm not going to give up the potatoes because of that dumb girl."

"Fine, then you make sure you get there first so I don't have to deal with putting our name down."

As usual Annabelle was late, and Leda had to put their name down.

"Hi," the hostess said, vapidly cocking her head in anticipation of a response.

"Hi, yes, I was wondering how long the wait is for a table for two?"

"Let me just take a look here." She leaned over her list of names and pushed a blond strand of hair behind her ear, revealing a lobe with a great many piercings. Leda wondered what the girl's mother felt about the flesh that she'd probably worked tirelessly to protect now with a dozen different holes poked through it.

"It'll be forty-five minutes to an hour."

"Oh . . . okay. Well, I guess I'll put my name down."

"What's the name?"

This she couldn't understand. Surely the girl recognized her at this point. She was in the restaurant on a nearly weekly basis. The vast majority of the waitstaff knew her by name.

"Leda," she said.

"How do you spell that?"

"L-E-D-A."

"Okay, great. If you want to have a seat over there and just wait, I'll call you as soon as your table is ready." She cocked her head again with the same vapid anticipation.

"Okay, thanks," Leda said.

She sat on the little bench beside the door. The air moved in and made her cold. *I should have brought a sweater. I wish I had my orange sweater still.* She thought of a bright, knit sweater she'd forgotten on the subway when she was still in college. She'd ordered it on impulse, and when it arrived she'd expected it not to fit as nicely as it did. It was one of those rare times in life where one's hopes were so far exceeded that momentarily one could forget all the endless tragedy and boredom of every day. She had the vivid memory of her reflection wearing it, the big collar coming up to her chin, the warm color bringing out all the brightness in her features. *I was so beautiful,* she thought. The very next day she'd forgotten it on the train. She called her mom, crying about it, and her mom sweetly offered to buy her another, but it was sold out. *Maybe someone found it and wore it and the sweater had a life totally separate from me where it went a great many places and did a great many things,* she considered, through the memory of her vibrant collared reflection. *Surely no one ever looked as good as I did in it, though.* Now that she was getting older it was easy to look back and remember herself as beautiful. *Why did I never enjoy it? Why did I not for a single day enjoy it?*

Moments later Annabelle came in, and Leda felt instantly happy. No matter how old her child was, she still felt the same kind of frenzied love for her every time she saw her; if anything, now that she was grown, and no longer living at home, it made these encounters more frenzied than ever. There were no more snacks to prepare for her. No more lazy days on the couch.

"Hi, Mom." Annabelle leaned down and hugged her. "Is there a wait?"

"Hi, baby. Yeah, forty-five minutes to an hour."

"Jeez, that's a long wait. This place is getting so popular," Annabelle said, sitting down on the bench beside her.

"I know. I like your coat. Is it new?"

"Yeah, Robert bought it for me."

"Oh really? He has nice taste."

"Well, I picked it out. It was for our anniversary. I mean, I didn't ask for it for our anniversary, he just remembered me trying it on and liking it from the week before, so he surprised me with it."

"That's nice."

Annabelle shrugged. "It is, but it's not all that romantic. It's been two years. I would have really liked some jewelry or something sentimental. I know he bought it thinking, 'Oh good, she likes the coat so I don't have to try.'"

"You don't know that. He might have just thought it would make you happy."

"Trust me." Annabelle took out a little compact from her purse and reapplied her lipstick. "You don't know Robert. He hates giving gifts."

"What did you get him?"

"A watch with the name of our favorite song engraved on the back of it. I had it special ordered."

"That's really thoughtful. I can see why you're pissed about the whole thing."

"It's like this every time. I've honestly thought about breaking up with him over it. I mean not for *real* real, but, sort of. I know that sounds so superficial."

"It's not superficial at all. I mean, you're giving him really nice gifts. Why can't he put as much thought into what he gives you as you do for him?"

"Yeah, but I'm a girl."

"So what?"

"It's easier for me."

"How the hell is it easier for you? I hate the whole idea that men shouldn't be held to the same standard as women. You know Rita from work, right?"

"Yeah."

"Well, she's divorced and just recently started seeing this guy, and he baked her a cake for her birthday. She was so excited that he was actually capable of baking her a cake that she took a picture of it and showed it to everyone at the office. 'Rick baked me a cake. Can you believe it? Rick baked me a cake.' All the other women were so impressed. It was ridiculous. Can you imagine ever being excited if a good girlfriend baked you a cake?"

"No."

"No, of course not. If Rita baked him a cake and was walking around bragging about it we'd all think she was crazy."

"Yeah, I guess that's true."

"You should expect that he treat you exactly like you treat him."

"I know, but it is just presents. I mean, is that really all that important?"

"Yes, it is. There are a lifetime of Christmases and birthdays and anniversaries ahead of you. What? Are you going to be miserable through all of that?"

Annabelle was quiet. She shrugged again. "How long has it been? I'm starving."

"I'm not sure. Let me go ask."

Leda got up and walked over to the hostess, who was pulling a loose thread off of the hem of her dress.

"Hi, again," Leda said. "Do you know how much longer the wait will be for us?"

"What's the name?"

"Leda."

"Can you spell that?"

You have got to be fucking kidding me. "It's L-E-D-A."

"Oh, right. Okay, it's looking like it'll be about forty-five minutes to an hour."

"Forty-five minutes to an hour?"

"Yeah, it's a busy night." The hostess pursed her lips.

"But that's what you said when I first put my name down. We've already been here waiting."

"Sorry, it's just a really busy night."

"So will we definitely be seated in an hour?"

"Probably."

"Only probably?"

"Do you have a reservation?"

"No, I don't have a reservation. If I had a reservation, I wouldn't be on the list."

"Right, let me take one more look." She leaned over her list and scrolled her finger down it. "I think you might be in after forty-five minutes. Do you want to stay on the list?"

"Well, we've already been waiting, so yes."

Leda went and sat back down by Annabelle. "If we aren't sitting in an hour I'm going to speak to her manager. This is crazy."

"Mom, who cares? I'm sure we'll get to eat at some point."

"Yeah, but I'm not waiting here all night."

"I wish you would just relax."

"You can wait all night. I want to eat dinner at a reasonable hour." The older Leda got, the less patience she had for the incompetence of everyday life. It started soon after she gave birth; there was a time when, like Annabelle, she too would have happily waited all night for potatoes, but then she pushed a human out of her vagina, and now she wanted potatoes when she wanted potatoes.

Annabelle shook her head as she quickly typed out a text message. "Who is that?"

"It's Robert. He's always crazy on Fridays."

"Why?"

"It's just his job. It's a lot of pressure. You know how he is."

"Yeah."

Leda liked Robert fine, but what she didn't like was how Annabelle was around him. She met him for the first time a few months after they'd started to date. Annabelle had dated a few men before Robert, but nothing was nearly this serious. She was always very casual about her feelings toward dating.

"I'd really like to get my career going before I worry about some guy sitting in my house," she'd say. Leda encouraged her on this front. She thought that waiting as long as possible was the way to go. She thought her daughter was too smart to waste her energies on a man, and she was proud she'd taught her to be that way.

Robert was meant to come over to their house for dinner. The week leading up to the meeting, Annabelle was a nervous wreck. Leda had never seen her like that. Every time she called she'd talk in a fast, jittery voice. She talked for twenty minutes straight about a new skin regimen she'd been trying before finally saying: "Please, just let's try to make a good impression."

"Why wouldn't we?"

"I don't know . . . I just want everything to be perfect."

"Perfect for what?"

"I don't know."

Robert was shorter than Leda imagined him to be. He had a round face and his hairline was receding. He wasn't bad-looking, really, but she thought he and Annabelle made a funny-looking couple. She was so much taller and so very pretty.

"Hi, I'm Robert," he said, reaching out to her for a handshake.

"Hi, Robert! So great to meet you finally! Please come in!"

Annabelle stood beside him with a wide smile. Leda had never seen her daughter with such a smile. It was disconcerting.

They sat in the living room, eating cheese and crackers and drinking wine. Robert talked about his job and asked questions about how long they'd owned the house.

"We've been here . . . Jeez, it's been forever," John said. "I don't even want to count the years."

The conversation was stilted at best. Annabelle was keeping quiet, mostly. She poured Robert a glass of wine at one point.

"Robert grew up in Connecticut, just outside of New York City," she finally added.

"Is that so?" Leda asked. She was talking to her daughter, but of course Robert answered.

At dinner things loosened up a bit, and the conversation came easier. Robert joked a lot and complimented the food. Leda asked him all sorts of questions, but she kept looking to Annabelle, who sat with her arm pressed up to his. She continued to smile and not say much. When it was time for dessert she refused a slice of her favorite cake.

"Do you not feel well, honey?" Leda asked her.

"No, I'm fine," Annabelle answered, still smiling.

That night as she and John lay in bed together, they talked about it.

"What did you think of Robert?" she said.

"He seems like a nice enough kid. Very eager to please."

"And what about Annabelle? Didn't she seem different to you?"

"No, not really."

"She hardly said two words. We were talking about the election at one point, and she hardly had anything to say. It's not like her."

"Maybe she just wanted to keep things light, since we were just meeting him."

"But that's exactly what I mean; I don't like her keeping things light for some guy."

Leda asked Annabelle about it, but Annabelle denied being any different around him, so she let the subject go but continued to be worried about it whenever they'd all get together. Robert still talked more. Annabelle still poured him wine.

"It seems like there are mostly old people in here now," Annabelle said, looking around the restaurant.

"Hey, I take offense at that."

"Stop it, Mom. You're not old."

"No, but I am getting fat. I need to go on a diet."

"That's crazy. You look great. I'm the one who needs to go on a diet. I need to lose weight for bikini season. Robert wants to go on a trip to the Bahamas."

"That sounds nice!"

"I kind of wish he'd save his money for an engagement ring."

"Do you want to marry him?"

Annabelle shrugged and looked away. "I don't know."

"If you don't know, then why would you want him to buy an engagement ring?"

"I don't know. I guess it's been two years and that just seems like the next step. I'm getting older. I want kids."

"You have plenty of time for that."

"It's hard working in the field I'm in. I don't have a lot of time to meet people."

"That is not a good reason to marry someone. Don't do something you don't want just because you think it's something you should do."

"But, the thing is, it is what I want."

Leda wanted to tell her daughter more, but she wasn't sure what there was to say, so she just said: "Give yourself time."

Annabelle nodded and took a deep breath. She looked the same then as she had at six years old, putting together a beaded bracelet at the dining room table.

"How much longer do you think this wait will be?"

"I don't know, but I'm sick of it." She got up and walked over to the hostess.

"Hi, how much longer is the wait for Leda?"

"Let me check," the hostess said, and looked down at her list.

Leda looked at her simple face and bright blond hair and over-pierced ear, and all she wanted was to tell her how much she hated everything about her.

"It'll be about forty-five minutes."

"You have got to be kidding. We've already been here an hour."

"I'm so sorry. I can check about the bar if you like? It might be a shorter wait to sit there if you're okay with it."

"Fine, check. I'm definitely not waiting forty-five minutes. I can tell you that."

"Okay, just one minute." The hostess turned and walked off.

Leda returned to Annabelle. "Forty-five minutes."

"Are you serious?! That's insane."

"I'm going to complain about the hostess, I swear it's her fault," Leda said.

"Maybe it's 'cause she's new."

"New? Isn't this the girl we see every week?"

"Jessica? The one you hate?"

"Yeah."

"No, this isn't Jessica. This is some girl I've never seen before."

"Are you sure?"

"Definitely."

Leda looked around the restaurant, as if Jessica would suddenly materialize and clarify her confusion.

"Well, I've been really rude to her all night because I thought she was Jessica."

"Mom, she looks nothing like Jessica."

"They look the same to me."

"That's crazy." Annabelle shook her head and went back to texting Robert.

"Do you want to leave and go get pizza?" Leda asked.

"I'm totally fine with that."

"Okay, let me just go tell the girl."

She walked back up to the empty podium and waited for the hostess's return. *Poor thing,* she thought. *She doesn't deserve all this anger. It's Jessica who does.* As soon as the girl was back within eye-shot, Leda smiled wildly at her in hopes that she would forgive her for the rest of the night.

"The bar is going to be forty-five minutes as well. I'm so sorry. Can I get you something to drink?"

"That's okay!" She moved her hands enthusiastically to emphasize how okay it was. "We're going to actually go and grab pizza, so you can take us off the list, but really it's okay."

"Oh, okay. Are you sure?"

"Yeah, I just haven't eaten much all day, and I'm starving and I know you guys are very busy. You guys really do have the best potatoes in town."

"Oh, thanks." The hostess nodded with a confused earnestness, and Leda immediately regretted the potato comment.

"Anyway, we'll definitely be back!"

"Okay, well, have a good night!"

"Thank you. Oh, and I just wanted to say, you're doing an amazing job. I know it's a busy night and you are just doing an amazing job."

"Oh, thank you so much." The hostess cocked her head in entitled acceptance of the compliment.

Leda imagined that this girl received many a compliment for the very little that she did in life. *That will change when your face falls,* she thought, but she still felt good about the exchange.

⎯⎯⎯✑⎯⎯⎯

CHAPTER 54

The Last Innate Truth

JOHN AGED CONSIDERABLY FASTER THAN LEDA DID. IT WASN'T SO MUCH his body, or even his hair, which hardly had any gray at all even as he waded into his late sixties (she had to start dyeing hers at thirty-five). The real aging happened in the ever-growing distance between them in their life together. John retired. He spent his mornings doing crossword puzzles and drinking coffee in the old chair by the window. Then he'd watch TV in the bedroom for a few hours. Then generally he'd take a nap. Then he'd wake and watch a little more TV. Sometimes he'd come in the dining room and work on a miniature ship model he'd started, or he'd go to the kitchen for a snack. After that he'd eat supper, watch a little more TV, and then head to bed at around nine. At first Leda didn't realize how routine his day had become. She herself worked a few years after he retired, because she simply couldn't bear the idea of being home all the time with so little purpose. When she finally did retire, she expected that the two of them would spend their days going on little day trips or trying the new restaurant in town, but John had no interest in any of it, really. On a rare occasion she would get him to leave the house on Saturday for brunch, but that was about it. He'd carved out a life and a routine for himself that was so vastly different from what she wanted for herself. Without her realizing it, he'd become old.

At around this time Leda and Anne rekindled their friendship. They spent dinners together and afternoons at the park. Anne's husband, Bill, was the same as John. He too rarely wanted to do much and was happy napping and eating and aging. The women bonded over it, but it was more than that. They relied on each other now for something they'd formerly received from men or their daughters, who were now all grown and busy with their own men. It was companionship, and closeness, and the forward propulsion of life. Between them was a vitality that kept pumping. There was no other name for it, really, but love. One summer they took a vacation together and as Anne said, "What color do you like?" holding up a mug, Leda had a stressing sense and she walked up to Anne and hugged her and Anne hugged her back. Neither of them needed to explain to the other why.

But as it was, only so much time could be taken up by friendship, so Leda found herself idling in her own life. Searching for something to do. She joined a pottery class. She read a lot. One afternoon she asked John if he wanted to go to the Rodin exhibit at the MFA. He said he was too tired.

"But it's the last day," she said.

John said he'd take a nap and think about it, but as she watched him walk up the stairs, cookies in one hand, the other hand on the railing, she knew he wouldn't go. She asked Anne and checked to see if Annabelle was around.

"On the boat all day with Robert," Annabelle texted. Followed by: "☹."

Leda got dressed in her best blouse and put on her darker lipstick. She threw on her new coat and went to the museum alone.

She parked in the parking garage and locked her car and stood in line to buy her single ticket.

"Would you consider a membership to the museum?" the man asked her, and she thought, *Yes, I would.* But she didn't buy it because she knew she wouldn't use it.

She made her way over to the exhibit and walked around, standing up close to this statue and that. There were couples and young families all around her. A group of schoolchildren noisily moved from one room to the next. Momentarily the room was empty, and she walked around the marble floors, listening to her echoed footsteps as she walked up to *The Kiss.* And as she stood beside the statue, her own reflection shimmered and warped in the glass case that protected art from humanity, she had an epiphany so brief and so painful and so exhilaratingly true: *The fundamental condition of womanhood is loneliness.* As quickly as she realized it, she allowed it to pass over her. It was too late to do anything about it now.

She went home, and she and John watched an old movie together. She told him about the museum, and he listened and nodded and took part in the distant way that he could, never reaching, never touching, never hearing the marble or feeling *The Kiss*.

This was the final innate truth of womanhood. It persisted from age twelve to her death.

———❧———

CHAPTER 55

Gardening

IT WAS A SMALL AMBITION, REALLY, BUT LEDA WANTED TO GARDEN. There was something romantic about it, beautiful and everlasting. She envisioned herself walking among rows and rows of roses, holding watering cans, preening bushes. If ever she built up an idea in her mind, this was it.

At the start of spring she went to a bookstore to buy a book for beginning gardeners. She came to find out that an entire section of the bookstore was devoted to nothing but gardening, plants, and flowers. There were encyclopedias and how-to guides, stunning picture books, and stacks of books with references in the title she couldn't begin to understand. *Holy hell,* she thought. A little girl sat with her back pressed up against the bookshelf just to the right of all the gardening books. She was reading some kind of psychology book that was much too mature for her. Leda couldn't help but admire the child's ambition. *Good for her. She'll be someone when she grows up,* she thought.

After a while she gave up and walked over to the cashier, a fairly good-looking man in his thirties who sat on a stool reading Thomas Pynchon. She thought of Annabelle and wondered if she and this man would get along.

"Mom, really? Reading Thomas Pynchon as he's working in a bookstore? Making some big show so that everyone can see that he's, like, so smart and so literate," she could hear her say.

"Well, at least he reads," she would respond.

Annabelle and Robert had decided to "take a break," as he put it. After seven years of dating, he needed "some space before making serious choices." Leda hated him for it. The minute Annabelle called her and asked what she thought, her voice shaking as she said, "He says this will be good for us," she told her to dump him.

"Don't you think that's a little harsh, Mom?"

"You will never forgive him for this. Tell him to shit or get off the pot. Tell him he'll never find anyone prettier, smarter, or better. Tell him to go fuck himself." She heard herself rattle off these sentences with the kind of venom that all children delicately try to avoid inciting in their parents, but she couldn't help it. Her daughter deserved better.

"Listen, honey, don't waste another seven years of your life."

"So the last seven years were a waste?"

"Yes."

"Thanks a lot, Mom."

"Well, I'm sorry, but it's true. You want to get married and have a family, right? That's what *you* want? For *your* life, right?"

"Yes."

"Then don't waste another minute on this nonsense. Not another minute."

Annabelle decided to give the break a chance. It had been six months. Every time Leda talked to her on the phone, it sounded like she'd just been crying. She wished she could do something, make her daughter date someone nice who was taller, so that she could see how great life could be.

"How are things with Robert?" she'd ask on occasion, and Annabelle either would say things were "good" or she'd start crying and tell her about some horrible text message.

"I asked him how his Saturday was going, and he said, 'Great! Out with friends!' Just like that. What does he expect me to say to that? 'Oh, have an awesome time! I'm at home crying.' I hate him."

"He's an asshole," Leda would say, but that was it. Anything more and she knew it would just cause a fight. She had to hope for the best and believe in the possibility of her daughter snapping out of it, waking up, being as direct in her relationship as she was in her career. But there was little else she could do. She couldn't save her. She couldn't bring her Thomas Pynchon like she wanted.

"Can I help you?" the young man said, putting aside his book.

"Yes, I'm trying to find a good book for gardening. Something that's helpful for a beginner."

"Oh, okay, well, let's take a look."

He got up and walked ahead of her at a sure, steady pace. She had to work to keep up with him. Behind him, she could see the slenderness of his frame. He looked almost frail. For a brief second she thought what it might be like to push him into the books.

He got to the gardening section and immediately crouched down to get a better look. He ran his finger along the spines and mumbled off titles. If Leda had been younger she may have assumed that he knew what he was doing, but as soon as she saw him crouch down at such a reckless speed, she knew he knew nothing about gardening books.

"I thought we had a book . . . ," he started, and then trailed off without looking up. For a while longer he just silently sat crouched. *Is there a way for me to rescue him from this ridiculous display?* she wondered, but she could not think of one, and so they just stayed there by the gardening books, waiting for something to change between the two of them to free them both from the circumstance.

"You know, I'd say your best bet may be to ask a florist," he finally said.

"That's probably a good idea," she said, although she was fairly certain he didn't mean a florist, exactly, but rather a horticulturist.

Thomas Pynchon jumped up as quickly as he'd crouched down and nodded one steady nod at Leda before walking swiftly away. He returned to his stool and resumed reading the same as before, if not just a bit red-faced. She said "thank you" as she left, although she didn't mean it.

There was a nursery down the block, so she figured she'd like to stop in and see what they had. The bookstore had been so depressing. She wanted to look at flowers and feel happy and excited at the potential of her soon-to-be-garden.

Even though it was only a short walk away, she decided to drive. Her knee had been bothering her lately, and it never seemed worth it to push herself.

"Won't your knee hurt when you garden?" John had asked her.

"No, it only hurts when I'm walking."

"Oh, I figured all that kneeling in the dirt would bother it."

"No," she said, but after he said it she did start to worry.

"You should get your knee replaced," Annabelle had told her.

Leda shook her head. "No way."

"Why not, Mom? You're being crazy."

"When you get to be my age, you'll understand that surgery isn't the answer for everything."

Annabelle shrugged. "All I know is I would not be going around in pain."

"That's definitely something a young person would think."

The nursery was smaller and older. As far as Leda could remember, it had been there since she was a child. It was called Betty's Garden. People in the neighborhood referred to it as "Betty's."

"Just go to Betty's," they'd say whenever anyone inquired about needing azaleas or a nice hanging plant.

She parked by the rows of Radio Flyer wagons. As she got out of her car, she hesitated as to whether she should take one or not. She hadn't intended to buy anything, but there seemed no reason that she should miss out on the opportunity to pull one of the darling red wagons behind her. The one she took was the least rusty of the bunch. It wobbled a bit on a wonky wheel, but she figured that it was a good match for her and her knee.

As she entered the nursery an older woman wearing an apron and stacking gardenias called out to her. "Let me know if you need anything."

"Thanks. Will do," Leda responded.

She walked among the many beds of flowers. It was so beautiful and peaceful, the bright earthy smell of soil, the sound gentle sway of petals in the breeze. *I could live here,* she thought. She didn't know the first thing about which flowers to pick, although she remembered somewhere someone had said that roses were difficult to grow.

She also remembered that her mom had grown pansies in the front garden of their home. Seeing their happy little faces, she suddenly was consumed by memories of her mother gardening and planting, her standing beside her mom holding flowers and helping to dig a neat little row of holes.

"What is this?" she'd asked.

"It's called a trowel," her mom said.

She'd forgotten all about the pansies, even though, really, they'd been a marker of springtime for so many blissful years. *What else don't I know of?* she wondered, and thought of the sound of scraping soil off of the walkway, and the disturbing beauty of root systems. *We really don't know what goes on underneath. And here it is and it looks so strange dangling in my hand, holding together this flower.*

She took a few containers of pansies and placed them in neat little rows in her wagon, as if she were already planting them, and walked up to the lady, who was now stacking snapdragons.

"Hi, are pansies hard to grow? I'm planning on starting a garden and I'd like to start with something manageable."

"Oh, no, pansies are a great flower to start with. And so pretty! Can I ring you up?"

"Oh, great, thank you. Yes, please."

Leda followed behind the woman, who gave all sorts of gardening tips on pansies as they walked over to the register.

"And if you have any trouble, just stop on by. I'm always happy to help."

"Thanks, that's very nice of you."

They continued to chat about the weather and then about all the many local stores that had gone out of business over the last few years. They both agreed it was a shame.

"Well, I'm glad I can at least count on you guys always being here."

"It'll be seventy-two years come the end of March."

"That's incredible. Are you related to Betty, by any chance?"

"Me? No, there is no Betty, actually."

"There isn't?"

"No, the man who founded it named it after his dog."

"Oh, how funny. I always thought there was a Betty."

"Well"—the lady stacked the pansies back into the wagon—"there was, but she didn't have a garden."

They talked for a little while longer before Leda turned to leave. She looked back at Betty's Garden, and the place looked smaller and sadder than it ever had before. She hoped the next time she came in the lady wouldn't be around, although she wasn't sure why she felt this way.

When she got home, she put her pansies out on the back stoop with the intention of planting them the next day. But the next day it rained hard, and so the garden had to wait. The day after, she was getting lunch with Annabelle and didn't have time, and the day after that was John's birthday. By the time she got around to her pansies they'd already died.

"You can't just leave them in those containers," John said.

"Well, why didn't you tell me that when I first bought them, John?"

She didn't have tolerance for the things men thought they knew about everything anymore. She certainly had very little tolerance for John.

Spring meandered on, and she didn't get around to gardening like she hoped. She kept planning on weekend after weekend, but something always came up. Her energy was limited and fall was fast approaching. On occasion she'd go out into the yard and start clearing areas of brush, but she'd tire quickly or her knee would hurt. With little else to go off of, she'd always promise herself tomorrow.

There was a moment so delicately placed at this time in her life. It was so fateful and so still: She was sitting at her kitchen table. To her left was a pile of unopened mail and to her right was the mug of coffee she'd made for herself. The mug had penguins on it that had faded due to many trips through the dishwasher. She thought about her garden and the summer coming to a close. It already wasn't reasonable to plant anything. There already wasn't hope. She thought of Elle, who she'd found out only recently had divorced her husband. She wasn't sure of any other details, whether it was related to the affair or whatnot. All she knew was that Elle was living in an apartment now rather than the giant house she'd shared with him. She still had a nice car, and based on some of the pictures she posted, it seemed as if the apartment wasn't too bad either. But there was a quiet desperation in Elle now that her marriage was over. She'd constantly post pictures of cocktails and memes with snappy sayings like, "Today is yesterday's tomorrow!" At one point she asked friends if anyone knew a good lawyer. Despite it all Leda was sure that, even now, even at their age, Elle was a woman who would bounce back. She would find her footing and she would be okay and probably meet another millionaire. There was hope for her, and Leda was happy that her old friend had found the strength to move on. Leda heard a rasping against her kitchen window. It was the birch tree that had overgrown and was invading their home. A tree expert had come out and told them they needed to trim back the branches, but she hadn't been able to bring herself to do it yet. The tree had grown up beside their home, and it seemed wrong to cut it back, as if it didn't have the right to thrive. She thought again of her garden and its endless possibility that had seemed so within reach when she'd first come to the decision to plant it. *I didn't even dig one hole,* she thought. And then in this moment with Elle and her divorce, the fading penguins, and the rasping birch, she considered something so bold it was almost sublime. In this moment of her life she was in complete control of her most conscious and immediate destiny. She got up and made a phone call to Betty's Garden.

"Hello, Betty's Garden." It sounded like the same lady as before, but she didn't care.

"Hi, I'm just wondering if you know of a landscaping service in the area that you'd recommend?"

Three days later Leda and John had the most spectacular garden that either of them had ever seen. It had been very expensive, and it wasn't the same as planting it themselves, but it was beautiful beyond belief. There were rows and rows of roses, beds of every varying pansy, and tulips as far as their yard stretched. They set two lawn chairs in the middle of it all and sat outside soaking in the sun for hours. They breathed in the rich smell of reincarnated springtime and the inescapable feeling of accomplishment. By the next year it would be mostly gone. Few of the flowers grew back, and they didn't bother calling anyone out to maintain it. When she and John became too old they'd sell the house and move to a condo, and at the condo there wouldn't be a yard at all. Leda would remember it as such: turned soil, and opened blossoms, a birch tree that would never be trimmed.

─◦◦◦─

CHAPTER 56

Never Reading Noam Chomsky

ON THE LAST DAY OF HER LIFE LEDA FELT A SURGE OF ENERGY THAT was greater than any she'd ever felt before. She'd been too ill for days to get out of bed, and even though she still couldn't get out of bed, she felt that she might be able to soon, and that was enough to make her happy. On the last day of her life she was happy.

John had died a few years before. He'd had some health issues that left him bedridden for quite some time. In the end he died peacefully in his sleep, something she would forever be grateful for. She'd moved in with Annabelle and her husband, Philip, and their two children, a daughter, Nina, and a son, Michael. It was a quiet and pleasant life. She spent most of her time in her room watching TV or playing with the grandchildren, but she missed John terribly. She'd often dream of him, and when she woke she expected him to be beside her. She expected to smell his skin and hear the sound of him breathing.

"Are you going to work?" she remembered sleepily asking him so many times as he woke early in the morning. She fixated on this memory of him in the darkness, kissing her goodbye. Sometimes she felt as though maybe this wasn't a real memory at all, but simply something she wanted so strongly to have happened that she'd envisioned it to be real. She celebrated his birthday each year, and on their anniversary she'd sing "Dónde Está la Playa" to herself, although she couldn't easily remember many of the words.

Quite suddenly she started having some heart trouble, and the last two weeks had been spent in the hospital. She knew she was dying and she thought Annabelle did too, but between the two of them nothing was said.

Annabelle and the children came and visited her that morning, and Philip was planning on stopping by with Annabelle later that night. She liked Philip and thought he was the right kind of man to be with her daughter. He was easygoing and kind. He let Annabelle lead, and work, and when she cried that she didn't see the children enough, he told her the kind of lies any good man does when a working mother is sad over everything she's missing.

"Mom, tell them to leave the window open," Annabelle said as she cranked the hospital window a few inches ajar. "It's good for you to get fresh air."

"I'm fine, honey. You worry too much."

"Grandma, this is an Asian elephant. They can live sometimes almost as long as people," Nina said, pointing to a picture in a book she was holding. Each visit she brought a new book to show and explain in detail. Michael mostly just jumped around the room and made the kind of loud noises that could be expected of a six-year-old. On occasion he'd climb up on the bed and say: "Hi, Grandma." It was so lovely.

Sometimes she looked at Annabelle and thought she looked too skinny, and sometimes she looked at Annabelle and saw her looking older and older. She was no longer a young woman in the way she had been for so long. Sometimes she saw herself in her daughter and sometimes she saw the fierce elegance of her mother. She thought that Annabelle was something greater than both of them, and this made her proud.

The last six months of her life Leda was unable to read. Her eyesight was failing her, and she tired quickly. Annabelle would read to her on occasion, but between the children and work she didn't have all that much time. That morning she read her an old *New York Times* article about being able to fall in love with anybody. The article proposed that so long as you read each other a long list of questions and stared into each other's eyes, you would be able to fall in love.

"This is something women want to believe," Leda said as Annabelle finished reading.

The children and Annabelle stayed for lunch and they all shared a pizza. After that Annabelle told her mom she'd stop back again tonight with Phillip.

"Bye, Mom. Please make sure they leave the window open for you. I want you to have fresh air." And she looked back at her mother and waved.

The nurse came in soon after that, and Leda told her that she was feeling much better and thought she'd be going home soon. As she said it she thought, *Maybe I'm not dying at all yet.* The nurse was positive and cheerful in her response. She was the kind of exuberant woman Leda had tried to avoid most of her life, and here she was, the last woman she would ever see.

A few hours after the nurse left, Leda felt suddenly very tired. She thought that maybe she should lie still, and then she thought of herself and the way it felt to sing in a shower and how good and free she was then, like there was lightning all over her body and the whole world was taking notice of the electricity. Then she thought of herself as little fragments drifting into the universe in tiny little pieces, and then she thought of each little fragment as separate and singular to herself, and she could not tell if she were only the fragments or if she were ever anything bigger than that. She closed her eyes and the hospital ceiling was the last thing she saw. The last thing she heard was the sound of her own heartbeat, improbably consistent, uniquely her own. She counted the beats, *one two three four five six seven eight nine ten* . . . But then there were no more numbers or words. There was just her heart. The sound of her heart to herself, a sound she'd heard so many times, a sound she barely ever listened to. And then there was nothing at all.

When she died, she died alone.

Epilogue

IT TOOK ANNABELLE QUITE A WHILE TO GO THROUGH HER MOTHER'S things. She hadn't expected to feel so completely devastated by her mother's passing. Certainly she knew she would be in deep grief, but she had not anticipated the utter and absolute devastation it caused her, like everything in her life was no longer real, like she was no longer who she thought she should be. For a brief time she considered quitting her job and staying home with the children, although she knew that wouldn't solve anything. Nina was also having a tough time. She'd ask her mom when she would be happy again, and she wasn't eating very well. Michael was too young to know what was happening, really, and for that she felt both grateful and sad. On the one hand, he was being spared the pain; on the other, she knew he wouldn't remember his grandmother much, and that really bothered her. He was the youngest person to know and love her and, as such, was the one with the greatest potential for her memory to be carried on with the longest. Perhaps Nina would pass the memories to her children, and so maybe that counted. All of this mattered to her a great deal. She was fixated on the idea of her mother somehow becoming immortal. She told Nina stories about her every single day, but then she feared that what she was telling her daughter might distort her natural memories and so she stopped.

Philip told Annabelle to take her time with going through her mother's things, so each day she did a little bit until it became too painful. Once her father had passed away, they sold the condo, and so most of her mom's things had already been donated or thrown away. What remained was whatever she'd brought along with her, and so Annabelle took great consideration of the fact that what was left were all things that her mother had already deemed important enough to hang on to. Clothing was easy enough to give away, and there were knickknacks that could easily be stored. But her mother had been a great lover of books, and so most of the room was bookshelves upon bookshelves filled to the brim. Annabelle didn't want to give away too many of them, and so she took care in deciding which should stay and which could go. All the classics would be given to Nina and Michael. There were all her Toni Morrisons and Margaret Atwoods, and so of course those would stay. By her bedside was a pile of books that as far as she could tell her mother had wanted to get to reading. One was dog-eared on page 67, a sure marker that her mom had started it but was unable to finish it as her eyesight worsened. On the bottom of the pile was the Noam Chomsky. Annabelle held it in her hand and flipped through it. She brought it up to her face and took a deep breath of the old paper. She didn't know of her mother's intentions to read Noam Chomsky. She did not know that she never had. She tossed the aged book in the donate pile and continued going through the room. Just like that.

Two days later, as she was nearing the end of her cleanup, she came across a notebook with a short story her mom had written. She'd read quite a bit of her mom's work before, but this was a story she'd never seen. It was titled "The End of an Era." It was funny and smart, beautiful and sad. Annabelle thought it was very much the best thing she'd ever read of her mother's. She wished so badly she could tell her that she loved it, and that she thought it said so very much. She'd keep the story, and when Nina and Michael were old enough she'd read it to them and Nina would remember her grandmother, and she'd wonder what the line *she was so alive she almost wasn't at all* meant. She'd wonder about it, and she'd go over it and over it again and again in her mind as she saw and did so many things, and little by little time would pass and she would live her life like every woman, beautiful, irreverent, oppressively real.

ACKNOWLEDGMENTS

I'd like to thank the following people: my family—my mom for making me love books, and my dad for giving me his sense of humor. My husband, Jake, who listened to me read every single one of these chapters at their earliest stages. Without his encouragement and support and love this book could not have happened. Amelia Atlas for her passion and hard work to find this book the most perfect home. Her vision has been spot-on from the get-go. I'd also like to thank everyone at Knopf for their phenomenal work and support, especially Jennifer Kurdyla for her keen eye and for helping make my book as beautiful as possible, and Margaux Weisman for her contagious enthusiasm and dedication. Thank you to Steve Yarbrough, who worked with me many years ago when this book was just a vision. Marti Leimbach for her encouragement and consistent wisdom. Gail Mooney and Dona Cady for being fantastic mentors and friends. Every dear woman in my life whose love and heartbreak was the inspiration for this book. And finally, I'd like to give a special thanks to Mr. David Lambert, my fourth-grade teacher. He told me I was a good writer and it changed my life.

A NOTE ABOUT THE AUTHOR

Jana Casale has a BFA in fiction from Emerson College and an MSt in creative writing from Oxford. Originally from Lexington, Massachusetts, she currently resides in San Francisco with her husband. The Girl Who Never Read Noam Chomsky *is her first novel.*

A NOTE ON THE TYPE

This book was set in Monotype Dante, a typeface designed by Giovanni Mardersteig (1892–1977). Although modeled on the Aldine type used for Pietro Cardinal Bembo's treatise De Aetna in 1495, Dante is a thoroughly modern interpretation of the venerable face.

Composed by North Market Street Graphics,
Lancaster, Pennsylvania

Printed and bound by Berryville Graphics,
Berryville, Virginia

Designed by Betty Lew